CHANCE OF
Snow

CHANCE OF *Snow*

S. G. McAfee

ARPress
45 Dan Road Suite 36
Canton MA 02021

Hotline: 1(800) 220-7660
Fax: 1(855) 752-6001

Ordering Information:
Quantity sales. Special discounts are available on quantity purchases by corporations, associations, and others. For details, contact the publisher at the address above.

Printed in the United States of America.

ISBN-13:   Paperback   979-8-89389-013-6
            eBook   979-8-89389-014-3

Library of Congress Control Number: 2024907395

To Sis,
I looked up the word "friend"
Your picture was there – next to mine

Contents

Introduction

Rock and roll dances through the seventies joined by the Hustle and Disco. Right now, "Life's Been Good" incites a sing along with Joe Walsh at Papa's where a meeting of minds, however small, is being conducted at the tables beside the jukebox. And right now, the group is just thirsty customers on another crowded, crowded, crowded Friday night. No one's the wiser, but Leora and her best friend Sydney will be calling them prayer meetings and not because the people sitting at the table pray. Quite the opposite. Discord sits at the table across from corruption, which goes hand in hand with the likes of blackmail, extortion, racketeering, money laundering, shakedowns, the M-word, yes, all teetering on a foundation of distrust and greed. A tidy well-oiled partnership now with more cracks and crevices than an English muffin.

The one keeping the civility in check at the table is Mayor Evely. The quiet one is Ralph Jackson, a lawyer, a newcomer, getting his feet wet, and unimportant under the circumstances. Oh, the one with the rug on his head resembling a dead animal is Carl Yarborrough; councilman and business owner, whose wife, well, ex-wife, was running Stephen Lister, Esq., the brains. He handled everything: drawing up deeds for fictitious corporations and fake properties, forgeries, money laundering – keeping very tidy books, very tidy. Not anymore. He dropped dead.

Now all that seems to be well-oiled are Hector and Jammer, the greasy, dumb-looking gophers Leora and Sydney call Heckle n' Jeckle sitting on either side of Shaun Griffonetti. Griff has his hands in more shit than a proctologist trying to disembowel New York's underworld; planting evidence, ratting them out, setting them up, yeah, setting up his family! His family, mind you! He migrated to Pennsylvania implanting himself up the line a ways with a little newspaper stand. Yeah, right. It's a front for his numbers racket. Who don't know that? Come on, do you see a turnip truck?

Then about two years ago, he made a wrong turn on his way to the sulkies down Brandywine Racetrack, ending up here in Delaware County, pleased with the area and deciding to set up shop. Where else but Media! Across the street from the courthouse of all places! Right next door to a lawyer, yep, Stephen Lister. Mr. Opportunity knocked, and Lister answered, joining into a partnership. So Griff has a little newsstand up the line, has a little newsstand down here with, up and 'til Lister checked out, a very lucrative business now in the crapper.

Griff glares at each of them. Discontent apparent on their faces. Lister was the one who spread hush money around, not him. That's over. Done. They can moan and groan 'til the cows come home. His problem is bigger. Way bigger. Where is everything: the money, the ledger, the evidence? Griff doesn't have any of it. Neither do the Feds. Not yet, or heads would be rolling around the courthouse floor if you get my drift. So who's lying? Who's sitting on everything? If Griff is to believe all of them are in the dark, then it's time for him to explore new avenues and stop wasting time following everybody. It's time to dig up Lister's life. Backtrack. He downs his scotch and water, watching the barmaid, detaching himself from the conversation. It doesn't matter what they say. He still isn't giving them anything. He has free reign. What are they going to do, have him arrested? If he goes down, they go down. He refuses his gopher's offer to run for a refill, taking the initiative upon himself, walking through the crowd for a third time.

Leora opens a cooler, bending over to reach down inside for a bottle of bubbly, but not before spotting the pain in the ass out of the corner of her eye. If she has to listen to his raunchy mouth one more time, she swears she is going to punch him in his face. He stares, gawking as if she were lunch.

She serves his drink with indifference. He grabs her wrist for the third time, shoving a fifty dollar bill in her hand for the third time, with his phone number written on it again, no doubt. *Are you kiddin' me?* Her skin is creepy-crawly. She wants a shower. She holds this one the same as the other two between her fingers a third time, nodding a third time, not looking at him a third time, thankful for the throng of thirsty patrons.

Come to Papa's

"*L*ast call!"

The words . . . gone . . . swallowed by old time rock and roll. The standing-room-only crowd oozes between bar stools with hands full of six-packs, quarts, empty bottles, empty glasses, drained pitchers, and money.

"There must be a full moon," Leora hollers, leaning toward Eva as they stand at the middle of the bar drawing draft beer. "They're comin' out of the woodwork."

Eva nods, glancing up and down at the crowd along the wall where four ten-by-ten mirrors capture the opposite side of the room. Tip toes boost Eva's short stature, enabling her to also scan the reflected side. First the entrance and then down the wall toward the other end of the room; walk-in box, tables, jukebox, pinball . . . and people . . . people, people, people.

"Bacardi and Coke, White Zinfandel straight up, and a Peach Schnapps."

"Gimme a bottle of Bud and two shots of Jack Daniels."

"Tequila sunrise . . . two of 'em, and a glass of ice."

"Three white Russians."

"Two wine spritzers on the rocks. Port."

"Man! It's only quarter of—come on—last call? Are you shittin' me? Back me up two."

"Three Harvey Wall Bangers."

"Two slow, comfortable screws and three sea breezes."

An older woman with dark red lipstick and stiff black hair squeezes between two guys. "A black Russian, an old fashion, and two Gordon's and tonic with a twist," she orders throwing a ten on the bar. "Keep the change."

Friday night at Papa's is almost over—history. The two barmaids working their way around over sixty feet of bar, serve what seemed to be an endless array of drinks to an endlessly thirsty lot. Papa's gives new meaning to the old adage "Variety is the spice of life." Five different drafts fill glasses, pitchers, and chilled mugs; not to mention the assortment of bottled bubbly and chilled wine in coolers sandwiched between the center tap and stainless steel triple sinks with ice bins at either end. Speed racks, surround each sink, holding a multitude of liquors for the heartier palate, completing Papa's variety. On the other side of the slightly kidney-shaped structure, an opening under the bar toward the center was used to service tables. But that idea was abandoned years ago. If you're thirsty, you belly up to the bar. So with no waitress, the aperture was an exit to locking the front door, clearing tables or speedy access to break up fights over a pool game at the front of the tavern instead of the main opening at the far end. Black lights illuminate glass display shelves; one on either side of the opening. Unopened bottles of liquor fill the four shelves to the left of the opening and unopened bottles of wine fill the other.

Two registers sit as sentinels built into the lacquered bar, at the front and beside the support column just past the wine. Looking at the rear of the tavern, a granite counter sits centered in front of a large stone charcoal pit. On the right, the wall ends at the men's room, directly across from the ladies' room sitting behind the charcoal pit. A shuffleboard machine occupies the last of the right wall, fitting neatly up against the outside of the men's room. Over on the left, the room expands three feet or so past the jukebox where a trash can sits under a wall-mounted payphone with an ashtray and its directory hanging on a chain facing the rear of the building. The far left wall completes the room, running from the telephone all the way to the rear entrance. A storage room wall curves from behind the pit, its door facing the long empty wall as it runs parallel with the latter half of it to the glass doors, creating a hallway complete with slight echoes.

R-r-ring! R-r-ring!

"Papa's," Leora covers her other ear. "Joey!"

"Six Miller nips . . . three shots of Bailey's Irish Cream."

"Three Captain Morgan's and Coke."

"Two iced teas and Corona with lime."

"Two Alabama slammers."

"Sloe gin fizz and a melon ball."

"Margarita straight up. Where's the salt?"

R-r-ring! R-r-ring!

"Papa's," Eva points the phone at Mouse and continues her rounds.

"Two Calvert and cokes."

"Tangeray on the rocks."

"Three mugs of Budweiser."

"Three cans of Coors light."

R-r-ring! R-r-ring! "Papa's . . . Fox!"

Papa's is on the way home—well, the general direction of home in the west end of the city of Chester on the Delaware River. From Philadelphia down to the First State, a lot of thirsty workers stop here, their favorite watering hole; industrial workers from Sun Oil, Sinclair, Vertol, Viscose, the railroad, Baldt Anchor, Scott Paper, Philadelphia Airport, Westinghouse, Sealy Mattress, Congoleum, Witco, and Sun Ship.

Bordering the state of Delaware along the river is the tiny borough of Marcus Hook which not only has refinery workers, but is also known as one of the busiest ports on the east coast, with merchant marines and longshore men unloading black gold (oil) from the Texas Gulf and freighters from foreign countries. Yes, there are a lot of jobs between Philly and the Diamond State, which boasts its own hardworking thirsty populace from its racetrack, auto-maker, steel mill, and mall.

Leora grabs empty glasses and mugs; two at a time, scrubbing them on the double brushes in the first sink, dip in the second full of blue disinfectant water, then rinsing in the third before the drain. She gropes through the sudsy water for soaking shot glasses and then dunk, dunk, drain!

In the meantime, Eva is halfway in the cooler trying to retrieve cold beer mugs.

Leora grasps three mugs from the drain on her way to Eva. "E," she yells, tapping the older buxom brunette's hand, "it's empty."

It is really busy. They have to wash glasses to give last call. Eva emerges from the cooler, too fast. She immediately becomes lightheaded. With her dark eyes crossing and laughing out loud, Eva nods, shutting one eye to see Leora patting the three mugs. They savor the interruption then rejoin the throng.

R-r-ring! R-r-ring! "Papa's . . . Bopper!"

"Two Dewar's on the rocks, side of water."

"Three shots of Gallianno . . . pitcher of Michelob."

"Four cans of Pabst Blue Ribbon."

"Two Cutty and water on the rocks."

Leora signals toward the front of the bar, catching the attention of a good-looking young buck with an abundance of dark brown hair that tumbles to hazel eyes. Smiling, he answers her hitchhiker gesture with a wrap-it-up gesture. She nods her approval with three mugs of beer in each hand. He downs the half bottle of beer, pockets his money from the bar, and walks to the front of the barroom past the pool table to turn off the window lights. Around the lattice room divider, camouflaging one of four support columns in the huge two-story building, he walks left toward the front doors, flicking switches for outside lights, including the sign light. Three bar hoppers scurry past him in the darkened foyer for the last drink of the night as he dead bolts the glass double doors, following the late comers through the inside door. After closing the curtains, he heads to the back of the tavern past the glass walk-in box, the scatter of tables and chairs, pinball machine, jukebox; all the while maneuvering his way through the maze of people.

It's not like he has to do it. Crow is in fact, a customer. And he has a job: second shift at one of the refineries. Second shift doesn't leave much time for partying, but it all depends on how you look at it. It doesn't leave much time for trouble either. No, just enough to throw down a few cold ones and hang out, shoot some pool, bullshit.

The jukebox cranks out "Philadelphia Freedom".

Crow steps inside the glass door of the walk-in instead of wheeling the hand truck around the side through the large metal delivery door. He grabs cases of long necks, nips, ponies, and cans, stacking them outside on the dolly. Whistling toward the bar, he holds up a couple of fingers, tapping each case. After several nods and matching fingers from Leora, he climbs back into the walk-in, piling the needed cases inside the door.

Besides, Crow was helping Mr. Mac the clean-up man who lives with his wife, Janie, within walking distance. Monday through Friday nights in the wee hours of the mornin', you find Bill "Mr. Mac" McIlroy with a push broom, dustpan, and brush. He sweeps the floor, cleans the bathrooms, piles cases of empty beer bottles and trash cans along the left wall at the back entrance, and sometimes loads the coolers behind the bar. No set hours, some nights were dirtier than others, like tonight, as long as he finishes before day shift rears its ugly head, which is never before nine. So any time after three in the morning, the main use for McIlroy's back door key is tappin' on the front window. It is a good trade-off. Crow becomes a second set of hands for the retired seaman and feels privileged tapping Mr. Mac's wealth of knowledge from engines to woodwork and listening to occasional yarns of far-away places. Yeah, he likes Mr. Mac. And he likes the old broads (a dig). They're like big sisters (another dig), especially Leora.

He had met Leora roughly eight years ago in the West End Village; one of four housing projects in Chester. As a single working parent, Leora had moved into the low-income-development-row home in front of Crow Sheppard's row house. Two years earlier, Carrie Sheppard had ripped Andrew III and his younger siblings from a tree fort by a stream trickling past their rented five bedroom rancher on three acres of woods to the public housing dwelling. Widowed and struggling to raise six children, Carrie depended on Andy, who felt helpless watching his mother break her ass. Crow, a nickname bestowed upon him by his late father, longed for the past; a tent drenched in moonlight, a canopy of stars, the chorus of crickets, the twinkle of fireflies, a serenading stream, the smell of honeysuckle, fishing and his dad. Dad . . . how he missed him! But life goes on. Get out of the way or get trampled. The taste of life is bitter and hard to swallow; really hard for a not quite thirteen-year-old. Shattered by the loss of his dad and overwhelmed with responsibilities, Andy acted out, angry at home and aggressive in class, finally dropping out of school at seventeen. Life was not fair. But with help from his only sister, Molly, the second oldest, and notes his mom left on the refrigerator, life became doable.

Pregnant and married at nineteen, divorced at twenty, Leora struggled, too. Then at twenty-five, Leora tasted life. Her world crashed around her with the loss of her five-year-old son.

Mrs. Scott Kershaw lived in a one-bedroom unit perpendicular to that of Leora's. The elderly white-haired woman's family visited her daily, bringing homemade dinners and baked goods. Standing on tiptoes to unlatch the back door, Tink became a regular visitor of Gertrude's, welcomed company for the blind widow. He would call to Miss Trudy, touching her hand to reassure her of his presence. That one dreadful day a different presence: taunting, mocking behind her, now in front of her. But Tink had touched her hand. Or did he? Why didn't he answer her? She heard movement on the stairs, the closet door, primal grunts, someone with bad breath inches from her face . . . the back door slamming shut. The petit woman opened her front door and screamed. Mrs. Kershaw had been robbed. Counted among the missing items were a cameo necklace, her late husband's gold initial cuff links and her heart-shaped diamond engagement ring, long since too large for her frail fingers. The abandoned little league with its overgrown field adjoining the back of the project yielded nothing. Not until after the officers' arrival did Crow and the neighbors realize Miss Trudy wasn't delusional. Tink 'was'there, smothered under Gertrude's late husband's raccoon coat and blankets dumped from the closet shelf by the rummaging thief.

Salvatore Papariello was beside himself. Feeling overwhelmingly helpless and useless, Papa, donated a thousand dollars to start a fund swelling to over six figures within a matter of weeks. Some of the proceeds were used in renovating the abandoned field, complete with uniforms, scoreboard, equipment, dug outs, a playground, and a snack stand with a percentage going toward the upkeep.

And so it was Son Shine Park became a reality dedicated to the memory of a little boy with sunshine hair and sky blue eyes.

For five long months, while "Lea-Lea" Leora, struggled to return to living again, the old world Italian held her job. Life was not the same. Neither was Leora. No longer able to qualify for public housing, she moved in with her best friend, Sydney, sharing her two-bedroom apartment above the bar. And then six months ago, Papa purchased property along Trainer Creek, offering it as a rental to the girls. But Leora was so captivated with the three-story stone house and its wraparound porch she begged and begged Papa to let her buy it (haunting him actually) until a month later he sold it to her.

The jukebox pauses. '"Free Bird" begins accompanied by whistles, cheers, and flicking Bics.

"Last call!"

Ice cubes tinkle in glasses drained and then sat on the bar. Customers tap empty bottles and wave money.

"Back me up."

"Two Bud nips".

R-r-ring! R-r-ring! "Papa's. Jasper!"

"Give me a blow job," says a guy with a wide grin as he leans into conversation with a brown-eyed brunette joined by a giggly blonde. "Make it two and a mug of Coors Light."

"Pitcher of Bud Light and a slippery nipple."

"A pink squirrel, a grasshopper, and a pink lady."

"Straight up or on the rocks?"

"Rocks."

R-r-ring! R-r-ring! "Papa's. Just a sec—" Eva gestures to Leora at the front of the bar. She walks back to the wall phone hanging on the support column by the register, and grabs the receiver laying in the beer well.

"Hello, we're busy right now. We're mobbed . . . no . . . I don't want to . . . what?" Leora looks at the phone with distaste. "What? I'm busy . . . not really. We're closin' . . . what the hell? I gotta go . . . Yeah right . . . good . . . Who cares . . . Who the hell you talkin' to? I don't have time for this . . . Bullshit! I don't give a damn . . . I'm closin' . . . Kiss my ass. . ." Leora hangs up and returns to the thirsty, cheering patrons.

"Four boiler makers with Southern Comfort."

"Two sea breezes and three bottles of Michelob."

"Shot of Kamikaze." He counts a show of hands. "Make it a pitcher of 'em."

R-r-ring! R-r-ring! "Papa's. No he left . . . 'bout an hour ago." Click.

A guy peels a skinny girl off of him. Her long nose, long neck, long red hair, and her long skinny arms reminds Leora of a mosquito. "Bottle of Bud and two fuzzy navels."

"Hey, give me two more. Give 'em to her. I got it."

"Three screw drivers."

"Two Rollin' Rocks."

"Two Christian Brothers."

R-r-ring! R-r-ring! "Papa's . . . no, haven't seen him all night." Click.

The girls continue to work the bar, trashing used straws, exchanging empty bottles for full ones, chucking ponies, replacing wet coasters, emptying ashtrays, saving the long necks, chucking the nips, and dumping used ice cubes into over flowing drain funnels to wash glasses for their last refill of the night. Six-packs and quarts were bagged (No, you can't drink it at the bar) and paid for. *Diehards. It's paid for, and they're gonna drink it one way or another.* Hell, some patrons, the regulars, had gone to a different establishment for the sound of a live band then staggered back home to Papa's. Others had been there practically all evening, acquiring pyramids—shot glass pyramids.

By the end of the night, they flip their shot glasses over for straight shots, usually bottom shelf—quick and painless. It beats the hell out of three or four opened bottles of beer getting warm and flat. Or just goin' to waste, you know, back on the drain. No, they use them or give them away to buddies. Yeah, their buddies—this guy on the right or, hey, that girl across the bar. All transactions are to be completed by 2 a.m. It's the law in Pennsylvania, not Leora Anne Wells's law (L.A.W.), including all drinks on the bar. You start last call ten of two, sometimes twenty of, depending on the size of the crowd. But it doesn't seem to matter. It's always way after 2 a.m. when the girls escape from behind the bar. Then it's clean-up time. Ashtrays to wash, beers to stock, registers to close, tables to clear, glasses and shot glasses to be cleaned, the bar to wipe down . . .

Air guitars join Lynyrd Skynyrd.

"Take out for a six-pack and give me change for cigarettes."

"Two Chablis with ice and a JB and water."

"Quarters. Dollar's worth."

"Two bloody Mary's and two sex on the beach."

R-r-ring! R-r-ring! "Papa's. Pockets!"

"Three boxcars, with two sides of seltzer and a side of Coke."

"A Granddad and Coke and two bottles of Bud."

"Give me two rock 'n' rye and a mug of Miller."

R-r-ring! R-r-ring! "Papa's." Eva points the phone at Leora, who dismisses it with a wave of her hand.

"No beer, two blackberry schnapps."

"A pitcher of Michelob and three ginger brandy."

"Bottle of Heineken and two blueberry."

"Give me a Catawba Pink on ice . . . Oh hell, make it two."

"Two creamsicles."

"Three peppermints. Give one to her," Thin Man says, handing an empty shot glass to Leora and pointing across the bar.

"Three jelly beans."

"Two Absolut and tomato."

"Two Harvey Bristol Creams. Chilled.

R-r-ring! R-r-ring! "Papa's." Eva nods to Leora. She rolls her eyes and turns her head.

"Seven and seven with a twist."

"No, it's not for kamikazes—it's for beer." Eva yells grabbing the shot glass, "Beer! You dip shit!"

"Two Windsor and gingers."

"A vodka and grapefruit. Give me a fruit loop."

"No, you get a draft beer. Not a shot, not a bottle—a glass of beer."

"Give me a Miller draft. Can I buy a shot?"

Leora nods.

"Give me a shot of Jack Daniels."

"I'll take a Kessler."

"Two Amaretto and orange juice."

R-r-ring! R-r-ring! "Papa's." Again Eva nods to her coworker.

Leora takes a deep breath grabbing the phone and stretching the twenty feet of cord to get out of Eva's way. She maneuvers it around her manager, walking toward the support column again.

"I'm not here!" she enunciates, slamming the receiver onto the wall phone.

And the multitude sings "American Pie".

"A bottle of Miller and two snake bites."

"Give me a rock n' rye."

"No, you can't take the shot glasses home."

"No, you can't bring 'em back tomorrow – It is tomorrow!"

"He bought you a beer. A beer! Not a six pack."

"Two Jim Beams and a seven."

"Two Micks and an Anisette.

Leora and Eva glance at each other with an instinctive look. After almost four years, they work well together: full-figured Eva, piercing dark eyes, brutal honesty, quick-tempered, sure of herself; and Leora, also with a quality of honesty, raw, younger, faster, taller, free-spirited, both from the village. In fact, they became friends while Eva was on a mission selling candy bars for her daughter, going door to door. The top seller in the school would receive a one-of-a-kind Timex wristwatch of his or her choice. As far as Eva was concerned, it was in the bag. She pounded the pavement, sold to relatives and sat a box at all times by the beer taps. Many a customer had a candy bar with or without nuts, sitting next to their alcoholic beverage.

Leora had answered a knock on her door that Friday afternoon. She was running late for work as a cashier. Instantly, she remembered Eva from junior high school two years her senior. Eva got 'in trouble' and shortly after Easter vacation that school year, the teenager dropped out, giving birth to her son in December. They reminisced of days ago, of classmates and teachers. Leora bought a candy bar and offered her services for the cause, taking a box of twenty-four to her minimum wage job, agreeing to bring the proceeds and the remainder of the candy to Eva's place of employment. Leora sold them all, taking the money to Papa's. She had a good time and an eventful one for the very next afternoon, Eva introduced her to Papa. Boda-boom bada-bing. Papa's niece Sophia, was more than happy to share her hours, genuflecting and blessing herself. Although she loved her uncle, she had a life, too. She was not a barkeep by trade. She had skills, secretarial skills. But family is family. Family comes first. Her Uncle Sal had cleaned house or rather bar and was in dire need of people without a sticky-fingers affliction. It had been five months. If she could do it, Leora could. Eva had pull. Sophia pushed. Leora became a barmaid. Sophia was overjoyed, giving up Friday nights and elated at giving her Monday nights and Wednesday nights too, leaving Sophia with Tuesday and Thursday nights, Friday day work and a life! The same with Leora. Instead of working six hours a day, six days a week, it was now three nights a week and a life, not to mention practically tripling her take home pay!

Eva drains bottles and pitchers, sinking used shot glasses in hot, sudsy water and dumping funnels of ice and used fruit (lemons and limes) into the trashcans. She hits the remote, sending the TV into blackness, snatching a bar rag to clean tables on her way to double-check the back lock, turn off the pinball, shuffleboard, and air conditioner. Pool table and jukebox were last—always last.

Leora continues to work the bar; stacking empty ashtrays, bagging six-packs and quarts, separating the long necks, brown in one box, clear in another, sinking more shot glasses, putting three opened bottles of beer in the ice for Crow. The demand dwindles. The crowd trickles out the door. She gathers tips, shoving them into the large stainless-steel shaker on the shelf under the register.

"Last game on the pool table!"

Eva returns behind the bar after piling full ashtrays, pitchers, glasses, mugs, and bottles from the tables onto the already packed area of bar. She washes glasses, returns clean mugs to chill in the cooler, drains long necks in an empty sink, rinses the bar rag, crams more tips into the shaker, and wipes down empty sections of the bar. Leora stuffs ice into two tall chaser glasses, pouring vodka and Coke for Eva and VO and water for herself. She slips onto a bar stool and sits for the first time since 6 p.m. Crow steers the hand truck stacked with beer onto the wooden slats behind the bar and starts loading the depleted coolers. Eva grabs the tip shaker, turns the jukebox down, the house lights up, then drops on a stool beside Leora.

R-r-ring! R-r-ring! Crow hands Leora the phone. A key tapes the front window.

The Empire Club

It is close to 3 a.m. as Leora engages the clutch, easing the mint-green, two-door '64 into a parking space, then turns the key, cutting the music and the Chevy's engine. She takes a deep breath, chewing the hell out of her gum. Did she want to go in? *No? Yes? Maybe? No.* She yawns, rooting through her pocketbook for her Crown Royal pouch full of tips. She counts out twenty ones then pulls the drawstring tight, wrapping the twisted cord around the jingling purple sack then shoves it back in her bag. Leaning to her right, she straightens her left leg to cram the Georges into her left pocket.

"Its show time," Leora mumbles out loud. She opens the visor mirror for a quick check. Pulling out hair clips, she shakes her head, freeing her long, layered hairstyle to cascade in natural curls more pronounced in the unusually warm November weather. The striking brunette pulls a black pick from the inside zipper pocket then changes her mind and roots for her velvet cognac color lipstick.

"The car matches your eyes, Doll," she says sarcastically to blue-eyed Leora in the mirror. "Yeah, right. Do these look like green eyes? That colorblind ass wipe."

She really didn't want to go in the after-hours club. He, is not what she wanted to do. She just wanted to go home and go to sleep. Tomorrow, rather today is Saturday . . . off 'til Monday. They were so busy tonight, as busy as last Friday night when the likes of Shaun Griffonetti first showed up. Shadowed by Hector and Jammer, his two goons, or "Heckle n' Jeckle" if you ask Leora, the thirty-eight-year-old main line bookie worked his way to Leora's end of the bar with his self-centered, egotistical attitude in overdrive, breaking C notes for the jukebox and buying drinks for anyone who listened to his unimportant ramblings. And as the evening wore on, his personality wore off.

"If you come around here and sit on my lap, we'll talk about the first thing that pops up." He had said sneering and pointed to empty glasses for Leora to fill amidst the snickers.

"Them jeans look good on you, Doll," Shaun remarked, undressing her with his eyes. "Know what else would look good on you?" The pudgy man answered his own question, "Me."

Easy on the eyes Leora is, but it is all that's easy about her. The girl was not for sale, and she was not impressed. She had ignored the lewd compliments and propositions with more snickers from his growing free drink club. *Your sister!*

"Hey, Puppy," Leora called. Crow acknowledged the pet name she had given him. He walked around the pool table toward the mirrored-wall where instigator Leor was leaning in front of his drink on the bar directly across from Griff.

Crow leaned forward. "You are bad," he whispered swallowing a laugh.

"Ya wanna see him turn into a dick?" she whispered to her ex-neighbor, shifting her weight from one side to the other, arching her back. Glancing in the mirror behind Crow, she watched the smug, yes, male appendage practically drool in his scotch and water with a fixed stare on the now over-tight jeans as she tried to slip a finger in the back pocket. Crow down right laughed out loud and ignored the leering from across the bar.

"Can you get me more ice?" Leora spoke aloud to her cohort.

"Sure, Doll-l-l," Crow drawled turning his head away almost laughing out loud again. He walked the length of the bar toward the rear of the building, talking to Goo Goo at the end, then across the back to the ice machine in the storage room. Goo Goo lifted his glass to Leora with his laughing eyes and broad smile. A few years older than Griff, funny likable Giuliano "Goo Goo" Giangiordano was also in the "business" only locally with a preferably lower profile. Not at all like Griff: arrogant, greedy, obnoxious, aggressive, taking what he wants when he wants – and that's just scratching the surface. Underneath he is cold, calculating, deadly, and set on Leora. He had tipped her a fifty dollar bill three times writing his phone number on each one.

"Wanna hear a joke?" Leora asked a scowling Griff while wiping the bar in front of him and placing a fresh glass of ice on a new coaster. Drunken Griff gazed at two Leoras with a stupefied look, trying to grin and focus at the same time. With one eye opened, he nodded to one Leora. His two goons Hector and Jammer leaned in.

"What did the elephant say to the naked man?" Leora asked not waiting for a response, "How do you breathe through that thing?"

The answer traveled in little groups, raising giggles and shrieks from the ladies.

Shaun Alfonso Griffonetti rose from the bar stool with an expression as if he had a mouth full of vinegar. Heckle n' Jeckle, one on either side, steadied him as he swayed back and forth like a cattail in a summer breeze.

"Well, he wasn't talkin' to me!" the hotheaded drunk stammered, trying to pull his gray knit pants up over his "spare tire."

"Oh, look! You have a dickie do!" Leora yelled over the music. "You're belly sticks out farther than your dickie do!" she quipped.

The inebriated bookie hadn't really heard Leora's insult. All he heard was the word dick, then cheers and laughter. With a self-satisfied smirk, spewing obscenities and grabbing his crotch, he swayed backward into Heckle n' Jeckle, who lead him to the door for a quiet departure.

"Your sister!" the twenty-eight-year-old says aloud spraying Chantilly on her wrists. *It was bad enough he called bore assin' me Monday night at work, then Wednesday night at work, but then last night a white Lincoln Continental just like his follows us home, then we had to take the phone off the hook. Whatever, I'm out.* She drops the cologne into her handbag, replaying tonight's phone conversation in her mind.

"Come on, Doll, meet me at the Empire Club."

"We were really busy tonight."

"Come on, Doll . . . We'll have a couple a drinks, shoot the shit."

"It's too crowded on the weekends."

"Then I'll come to your place." Leora cringed.

"Nah, I don't date the clientele."

"What clientele? I was in there one time," he muttered, trying not to sound drunk or agitated.

"I'm beat, besides we go-a lo-o-cl . . ." She yawned.

"What date, just drinks. I wanna talk to ya. I got a little somethin' for ya, you know, to make up for last Friday. That was all a miss-standing-under," he slurred.

Bopper put Leora in a gentle headlock, kissing her on top of her hair before laying a ten dollar bill on the bar for three six packs in his other hand. Thanks, girl, later."

"We got a lot a cleanin' up to do," Leora repeated without yawning.

Griff really was drunk, and he really was agitated.

"Get your puppy to do it. He won't mind. He does anything for you. Arf-arf."

He was gettin' iffy with the wrong person.

"Yes, he does," Leora purred. "Puppy!" she called to Crow speaking into the phone, "Stay and finish up with Eva. I gotta go." Crow grinned, shaking his head as he handed the ten spot for Bopper's beer to Eva. Leora held the phone out toward Crow nodding for him to say something. "You are a bitch," he mouthed as she held the phone out farther toward him, nodding harder.

"What, again tonight, Doll-l-l?" Crow asked loudly. "You need to go to bed, I mean to sleep. Look at those bags under your eyes." Eva took the phone.

"Hello . . . Hel-l-o-o," Eva sang.

"Hello!" Griff barked.

"Hellew . . ."

"Who's this? Hey, hello, Doll? Doll! Hey!" Griff spouted obscenities.

"Hello . . . Hello! Who? Leora? Just a sec, she's sayin' good . . ."

"Put her on the damn phone! You dumb bitch!"

Eva banged the receiver several times on the bar. "Hello, who? Leora Law? Wait a minute, hey, Dol-l-l, it's for you-u-u!"

"Hey! Is that . . . Hey! Doll! Come on! Hello?"

"Pay attention. Hold on, she's sayin' goodnight to a cust —YO! Get your tongue outta her throat!" All three banged heads, trying to listen to his trench mouth.

"Do you kiss your mother with that mouth?" Eva interjected as all three struggled to stifle laughter. Raunchy Griff spewed a few more vulgarities before he slammed the receiver down.

"You broads are not right." Crow laughed. "He's pissed off."

"Better than bein' pissed on," Leora quipped.

Yeah, he definitely needed an attitude adjustment, and then he needed to be kicked to the curb. She had done her best dodging him all week. This guy wasn't giving up. He was having a hard time wrapping his inflated head around rejection. Not a problem. Leora was in a deflationary mood. She had been headed home then thought better of it. A crowd is exactly what she needed. She did not like him or trust him. What part of no did this creep not get? She was not, is not, and will not be interested.

His teeth are as yellow as an ear of corn. His breath smells almost as bad as his B.O. He must think personal hygiene is a butler. And his hair, eww! It's time for an oil change. I swear I saw hair comin' out of the crack of his ass, and that was before he bent over. Hit that? Not in this lifetime. I wouldn't hit that with an indentured servant!

Draining her beverage, she opens the door, dumps the ice, chucking the empty glass on the passenger seat. She closes the visor mirror and grabs her club ID and keys. She exits the car, patting her bra to check the three fifty dollar bills, before stuffing her pocketbook under the seat. Heading for the club, she slips her keys in her right front pocket spitting out the chewing gum when arms surround her from behind.

"Were you busy tonight?" a voice asks. The familiar smell of Jade East brings a smile to Leora.

"I'm not gonna tell you." She replies as he kisses her cheek. "And where've you been hidin'?" She turns and gives Tom Dayton a hug.

A regular at Papa's, Tom is a divorced father of a twenty-one-year-old daughter in college, and a manager of one of his brother-in-law's businesses, an auto parts store open seven days a week. Tom and Leora are friends, good friends. He had taken her son's death hard. He pulls out his wallet and flips Tink's kindergarten picture over. Printed on the back by Tink is: to Gus. He is feeling no pain. Tom had told Tink his name was Gus. He had said it in passing just in case he came over for a little foo-foo a boyfriend would be looking for a guy named Gus instead of a guy named Tom. The name stuck. Tink called him Gus and Tom never corrected him. She slips an arm through his as a playful breeze tosses Tom's salt and pepper hair. His steel-blue eyes soften as he closes the wallet, tucking it back in his rear pocket.

"What did you do, shit the bed?" Leora asks. Tom is out of place at the club.

"No, I'm on vacation. Salvatore invited me down his beach house for a couple days. I'm takin' car parts, you know, break shoes, points, plugs, oil," he explains, unwrapping Leora's arm. "A little fishin'." He casts a make-believe line. "Then who knows? Look for a mermaid, a little foo-foo, a run to the casinos. And to wrap up my vacation, I got two tickets for 'Marvelous' Marvin Hagler versus Willie 'The Worm' Monroe fight next weekend. I'm takin' Andy. We'll leave bright and early Saturday morning."

"You're kiddin' me! Crow will like that!"

"They're from my brother-in-law. Oh, and as of"—Tom checks his watch – "yesterday, my brother-in-law made me a partner in the auto parts store."

Leora screams, jumping up and down, hugging and kissing him . . . couldn't happen to a nicer guy. "That's great, congratulations!" she squeals.

"I was talkin' to Goo Goo about it. He's down there."

"Hey, Goo Goo was askin' me if I ever heard this Griff guy mention him. I told 'im no and asked him if he wanted me to pump him and Goo Goo said no, let it go."

"Damn straight let it go! Your boy's into blackmail, assault, theft, arson, even murder. He's originally from New York. A while back, I'd say fifteen years or so, his father died along with the Four Families' tolerance of him. He's been down this way maybe four or five years mostly out on the main line, inching his way down. He's off the wall. His little front selling newspapers and cigarettes in Media was right next door to Stephen Lister's office, one of the best lawyers in Delaware County. They're from different sides of the track, but they were cut from the same cloth. Goo Goo's got his hands full."

Leora mumbles, "Lister, Lister. I don't remember the name."

"Sure ya do. Every time you turned around, Lister was in the paper shaking hands with a new "not guilty"politician friend."

Leora thinks, shaking her head with a puzzling look on her face.

"The newspaper nicknamed him Loop Hole, No-soul Loop Hole."

"Oh-h-h . . . Loop Hole, I know that name. Didn't he squash the case against that district judge, and the county solicitor?" Leora's eyes widen. "And Mayor Evely?"

"Yeah, that's him. They're all connected. He had somethin' on everybody."

"What's he gonna do? Get Griff? Uh-huh! Uh-huh!"

"No, Lister was found dead back in April, slumped over the steering wheel of the Mayor's BMW just as the Feds were getting ready to indict all of them on racketeering, money laundering, blackmail, extortion, payoffs, numbers, and so on. Griff threw the New York fellas in it, saying they whacked Lister! And the Feds let it be known too. Sure they know it was a heart attack. He was just trying to stir things up to get the attention off of himself and his illegal activities. They looked at Alice too, Lister's girlfriend. Good-lookin' blonde. Smart. She said her jealous ex did it. She was married to Carl, one of the mayor's buddies, and was runnin' one of the mayor's other buddies. It turned out to be Lister, *and*, he was Alice's divorce lawyer too. What a mess. After he died, she unloaded their joint properties, including the office next door to Shaun. It's now a Chinese takeout. I bet he loves that, although I think he'll sell more newspapers." He chuckles. "Everybody knows he doesn't sell enough of anything to pay the rent. Everybody! But there's no proof. No matches on the signatures, no paper trail. No money trail and I'm talkin' truck loads. You can't trace cash. He must be sittin' on a ton of it. He's in the club at the far end of the second bar actin' like an asshole as usual."

"Well, I always say there's no sense in being an asshole if ya can't act like one."

"Goo Goo's at the first bar with Shout, Jocko, and Chicarella," Tom states. "Don't take any wooden nickels."

"I'm not takin' anything from him," Leora says, showing Tom the fifty dollar bills. She slips them back into place. "Not even tips. I can't stand 'im. He's hauntin' the shit outta me. Every time I turn around he's there starrin' at me! He sucks, big time! I'm out."

Tom is solemn. "You be careful, girl." He kisses her hand and starts for his car.

"Have a good time," she calls. "Congratulations, Gus." He turns and blows her a kiss.

Leora dances down the red carpet-covered steps in time with the live band's version of "Bitch." *How appropriate.* Bear, sitting at the podium on the landing, winks at Leora while engaged in conversation with a couple of men in sharkskin suits. Blade and Coma, two of the club's bouncers, smile, waiting their turn for a hug before backing up to let her go by. When she does, Bear reaches out and gently pulls her over for his hug. She kisses the husky man's cheek as he whispers, "He's had three coffees at the second bar. These guys are undercover." Two couples pay the cover charge to Bear and descend into the club.

"Have you met Miss Law?" the manager introduces Leora to the unfamiliar suits. They nod, checking her packaging.

"Haven't seen you in a few weeks," Bear leans in for Leora's ears only, "He's trouble. He spends a lot of money, but he's trouble. Are you with him?" Leora shakes her head no, with a smile for the two suits. "There's always a problem when he's around. The boys (bouncers) here got your back. Chooch is here." Leora gives him a quick peck on the cheek, giggling like a school girl at this naughty man's suggestions; an act for the ogling audience. Leora slips into the smoke-filled room. The club is crowded but not overly packed. She hears her name coming from the kitchen on her left and waves to Pearl, kitchen manager, and a couple of the waitresses. As her eyes begin to adjust, she peers through the darkness, scanning the first bar, then the middle of the massive room with the stage against the back wall, the dance floor in front of it then a scatter of tables and chairs aligned with the end of the bars to allow for a walkway to maneuver through the maize of structures and people. As her eyes focus, she spots Griff to her right at the second bar, puffing on a cigarette and checking his watch. Behind her along the back wall are a pay phone, ladies' room, a wall bar (half an oval) then a little boys' room on the other side. She stands facing the room again spying Sydney sitting at the first bar across from the tables.

"Yo, Chooch!" Sydney yells, waving her hands in the air. Leora reaches her just as the band finishes their set, taking a twenty-minute break. Sydney orders a VO and water from Tony, one of three bartenders at the first bar. She hands it to Leora as a guy offers his stool to the brunette. She declines, standing with her back to the second bar, raising her glass in return to a wave from Goo Goo down the end of the bar toward the stage. Mickey, the lead singer, places his white Stetson on her as he retrieves non-alcoholic beverages for the other Churn band members. Snare does a little drumroll and salutes Leora with a drumstick when she glances at the stage. The apprehension Leora had felt with Bear and the two unknowns dissolves in her drink.

Two men sitting across the bar watch the two curly-headed friends deep in conversation. Finally the balding gentleman with a beer belly waves to get their attention. "Excuse me," he yells over the jukebox, "me and my buddy here got a bet. Are you two sisters?"

Before Sydney could open her mouth Leora answers, "Yes, she's the oldest."

His crew cut buddy slaps him on his arm. "I told ya!" he says holding his hand out for a twenty spot.

"Wait, wait. She's taller, and you're hair's darker," Beer Belly states.

"Different mothers," Leora explains demurely, not blinking an eye.

"Pay up," Crew Cut says. Beer Belly hands him a twenty, and Crew Cut orders drinks for the "sisters."

"Very good," Sydney says out of the side of her mouth to Leora, ordering two shots of Galianno.

Leora covers her mouth by rubbing her nose. "They don't have to know we have different fathers, too."

"Cheers!" they say in unison as they throw down the top shelf syrupy liqueur and lift the empty glasses to Crew Cut. Leora licks her fingers before laying five ones in the well. Tony winks, pouring two more Galianno shots for the girls pointing to Goo Goo. They throw down the shots, lifting the empty glasses to him.

"Well, I'm gonna mingle," Leora announces, grabbing her drink. "Later."

Sydney flicks ashes off her cigarette. "Yo, Sis, ya want me to walk by in about twenty minutes?"

Leora takes a drag and hands it back to her. "Nah-uh, Chooch. I'm not gonna be that long. It's all over but the shoutin'. This guy sucks big time. Enjoy the show." Leora walks straight across the empty dance floor in front of the stage to the second bar where Griff sits, facing away from the stage between Hector and Jammer. Jammer taps Griff on the arm, leaving his stool for the brunette. Griff turns with a smile, pointing to the stool and orders a drink for her. Leora downs the rest of her drink, standing, and leans over the bar stool, placing the glass of ice cubes on the bar. Griff smiling, hands her the fresh one, taking a glimpse at the "girls" (cleavage) in a lilac short-sleeved v-neck. Leora takes the drink, stirring it, licking the swizzle stick, continuing to stand beside the stool. She is not at work. She is at her playground with her rules. Griff, still smiling, points to the stool again. Leora licks the swizzle stick again. Heckle and Jeckle slip jukebox money to a couple broads in Griff's ever popular free drink club.

The bookie pats the stool. The barmaid puts the swizzle in her mouth and slowly pulls it out. "Come on. Sit down," Griff says finally looking at Leora. She gives him a blank stare. "Come on . . . come on. Sit down, will ya? Sit down . . . please." Leora lifts her right leg over the stool and sits facing Griff, straddling his leg resting on her stool rung. He leans over to kiss her. Leora turns away then offers her cheek. He is pissed. She sees. And she doesn't care. He sees.

"I'm takin' a trip to the Poconos," Griff begins. Leora stirs her beverage and takes a taste . . . straight VO. She asks Nino for a half glass of water. Dumping VO and ice into the glass, she stirs it, tastes it then turns to Griff.

"Have a good time."

"Ah, it's business, Doll. I might invest in the Oak Hills Country Club. I'm gonna check it out. Figure we could leave about four this afternoon and come back Tuesday some time."

Leora looks at him quizzically. *Is he for real?*

Hector comes over, holding a consultation with Griff. Nino places a drink in front of Leora and points to Matt at the end of the bar one of her dancin' partners. She waves, placing her hands together and nodding a gracious thank you. Griff shoots daggers at Matt, raising four fingers at Hector, who then takes a walk.

"I'm not goin'."

"What da ya mean?" Griff directs his daggers at Leora. "What are ya goin' with him?" he retorts, nodding his head in Matt's direction.

Leora ignores the second question. "I don't know the first thing about you."

"Yeah, well, it'll be like a date. We can get to know each other on the ride up. I ain't no clientele. You don't work here." The girl pours more VO into her ice water. She doesn't dare look at him for fear of spitting in his face. She really doesn't like him. The VO starts kicking in. Mickey comes over to retrieve his Stetson for the next set. He thanks her and kisses her hand. Griff smolders. Leora takes a deep breath to center herself then takes a big gulp of VO and water.

"I am not going," she repeats slowly. "Some of us have to work for a living." *There.*

Shaun lays two C notes on the bar smiling at the "girls."

Leora's blood boils. She silently counts to ten, sliding off the bar stool. She throws five ones in the well before taking her drink.

"Sit down," Griff growls.

"For what? Stay, heel?' Leora's voice grows louder as anger dances in her eyes.

"I said sit down!" he demands, grabbing her arm.

Leora breaks his grasp. "Don't get kicked in the balls," Leora hisses. "Before ya get kicked to the curb."

Griff's face contorts with anger. "Sit down!" he says through clenched teeth. "Before I put your ass on that damn stool!"

Leora's eyes narrow. "You're right," she spits with a lewd smile tugging the corners of her mouth. "You ain't no clientele," she states, pulling the fifties from their hiding place. Griff watches her ever so slowly lay the phone number bills one by one on top of the two C notes. "You ain't no clientele," she repeats looking in Griff's eyes, "and you never will be." She shows Griff the back of her head.

Griff is livid.

"Hey, look! Look! You son-of-a-bitch! What's this? WHAT'S THIS?" Leora yells, turning to leave. "This is me walkin' away from your sorry ass!"

"You skanky bitch! Don't you walk away from me!" Griff yells. Leora starts across the dance floor toward Sydney. Griff kicks the stool over and goes after her. Heckle n' Jeckle grab him before Blade and Coma latch on to him. "I was gonna give you this, you trashy bitch!" Griff yells dangling a set of keys. "A brand new car out there in the parkin' lot!" Leora doesn't miss a step and does not acknowledge him. "I'm gonna give it to the first whore I see!" Griff screams, his face flushed.

"Good! Don't forget to go with her!" Leora yells over her shoulder.

"I'll fix your ass!" Griff snarls.

"It ain't broke!" Leora shouts, spinning around, walking backward, "It's supposed to have a crack in it. Oh, that's right, you never saw it." The veins in Griff's neck bulge as he tries to get away from Hector, cussing

LaHeada (Loretta), swinging at Jammer, pointing at Matt, and shouting obscenities at Easy Louisie and Faye the Lay. He no sooner begins to get a grip when Churn opens their set with an instrumental medley of "I Fought the Law and the Law Won." Griff goes ballistic trying to get on stage. Tackled by Blade, he works free only to run face first into the edge of the stage floor. A gash appears between his eyebrows, swelling like a third eye. In a stupor and blinking blood, Heckle n' Jeckle help the human cattail make a quiet departure from yet another establishment.

"Good show, Momma," Sydney says, handing her best friend a beverage. "And you said you couldn't dance."

"So you recognized the stomp," Leora answers her partner in crime.

I'm In!

Saturday is quiet except for some mouthy bluejays in the old oak tree outside Leora's second floor bedroom in the front of the house. The tree towers above the pitched roof of the gracious building, filtering the sunlight and keeping the air cool. On this side, the southwest side, the afternoon sun will reach the first floor, warming only the dining room unprotected by the wraparound porch shielding the den under Leora's bedroom. A variety of plants thrive near and on windowsills in their designated family room where closed windows allow no access to the heated air. Two younger, rather large maples shield the rest of the home while a cluster of trees including mulberry, oak, locust, birch, and willow drench the back of the property in shade as it dips to the creek. On the third floor, a powerful attic exhaust fan, with a temperature control setting, sends warm, stale air out a louvered opening, replacing it with cooler air pulled through shaded windows opened three inches or less throughout the dwelling, creating a constant breeze.

The jays continue their ruckus as Leora rolls over on her back, stretches, and yawns. She blinks at the clock radio, closing one eye to see the time. *1:05. No. 10:55.*

"What is your problem?" Leora asks, walking to the pair of windows in the front of the bedroom. The jays carry on high, with raised topknots, flitting from branch to branch in a frenzied display. Leora peers through the glass panes in the direction the birds are looking and sees her orange and white short-haired kitten batting acorns and chasing dried leaves on the porch roof.

"Wheezer," Leora calls pulling the pale green sheers around the hanging philodendron basket before lifting the window. As soon as he hears his name, the ten-month-old tabby flops on the roof. "What are you doing up here? Are you learnin' to fly?" She removes the screen and Wheezer gives one last glance to the delicious birds, scolding safely from the tree. He jumps through the window, half-wheezing, half-purring, and loving Leora's hands making it almost impossible to replace the screen. "You better love me. If you had to hunt, you'd starve to death." She lifts him off the sill and cradles him in her arms. He lays content, half-purring, half-wheezing, eyes closed as if understanding every word while he loves her hand. "Listen, if you're gonna sneak up on somethin' hold your breath."

Leora lays him on the bed and walks through the bedroom doorway, her lavender nightgown billowing as she follows the carved oval railing on the right, passing Sydney's atrium bedroom on her way to the bathroom where the rail makes a 180-degree turn to join the open staircase, descending to the foyer on the first floor. A mirror image of the wooden banister to the left, past Leora's room, curves to a floral print curtain, across from the bathroom, dancing with the light breeze while trying to conceal a stairwell climbing to the third floor. The old handrail joins the open stairway on the opposite side to the floor below. The hallway, leading toward the back half of the stone house, passes two more bedroom doors, staggered one on each side of it before ending at a homemade linen closet not quite as wide as the door hiding it.

Leora closes the bathroom door just as Wheezer arrives. He sticks a paw under it, playfully batting the air before amusing himself at the top of the stairs. The young cat flops when Leora calls his name on her way to Sydney's room. He tumbles down three or four of the oak steps before recovering and scooting around the banister on the hardwood floor ahead of Leora. He leaps onto the bed, wheezing loudly and loving Sydney's hand. Lying on her stomach, her blue eyes cross when she opens them to Wheezer, who loves her nose and chin. She covers her head and shoves her hands under the pillow.

"Not now, Tiger. Your sister," Sydney mutters. "Go get those jays."

"Wheezer," Leora calls from the doorway. He flops on Sydney.

Sydney laughs, uncovering her head and sitting up. "What was that about?" she asks, referring to the jays.

"Oh, Wheeze was on the porch roof," Leora starts. She sits on the bed and rubs Wheezer's head and neck. "They told him to jump, and he told them he doesn't listen to bird brains. It was gonna get ugly."

They both laugh as Leora lies at the bottom of the bed, hugging Wheezer. Sydney leans over and grabs her dungaree pocketbook from under the bed. She fishes out a 35mm film container and a pack of TOP rolling papers throwing them down on the bed. "Here, twist one," Sydney calls on her way to the bathroom. "I'll be right back." Wheezer chases after her, swatting at her black nightgown, racing her to the bathroom. Unable to stop on the slippery surface, he slides past the bathroom and returns too late to enter. He reaches under the door and again bats the air with mouth agape and wheezing.

Leora reaches under the bed and retrieves a shoebox lid. She dumps some of the weed in the lid, rubbing it between her fingers and thumb to break up buds and loosen the seeds. She glances around the bedroom at the fake tiger-skin rug under her feet, the leopard drapes, black satin sheets (Sydney calls them her panther sheets) and leopard comforter. "Definitely a cat lover," she tells the giant stuffed lion on the cedar chest at the foot of the bed. With the cardboard flap on the pack of papers, she scrapes the pot into a pile at one end of the lid. Lifting the lid on an angle, Leora scoops up the smoke and sprinkles it in the top of the lid. Sticks, seeds, and larger pieces slide down to the bottom. She continues the cleaning process, scooping and sprinkling, until all that's left is fluffy grass. She lays the lid down, removes a paper, folds it in half and lifts the lid again, scooping the fluffy remains onto the cardboard flap. Leaning over the lid, she empties the flap, filling the full length of the folded rice paper. Leora makes both ends of the folded paper the same height, then slides the sticky side taller as she starts in the middle and rolls, pushing toward the ends. She licks the sticky edge and rolls it together, twisting the ends. She scrapes the unused portion to the corner of the lid, empties it back into the canister, grabs a blue Bic off the pack of cigarettes on the nightstand and lights the joint.

Sydney appears with a mug of instant coffee for Leora and a cup of hot tea for herself. "I gave Tiger some dry cat food. Um-m-m, I smell skunk." She closes her eyes, taking a big whiff, walks toward the bed, and trips right over the fake tiger head almost spilling the hot liquid in her best friend's lap.

"A-h-h-h-h!" Leora yells, rolling to the other side of the bed, choking on a hit.

In a split second with a forward momentum in full throttle, Sydney double steps, spins, sticks her butt out, and ends up barely sitting on the edge of the bed. A few drops of hot tea spill on the comforter. "Coffee?" she asks, blinking with a cheese grin.

"Instant replay!" Leora laughs, getting out of the other side of the bed and walking around the cedar chest to Sydney. She exchanges the bone for the coffee. Sydney takes a long drag. "Where are your glasses?" They both look toward the nightstand. Leora picks them up and hands them to Sydney, who in turn gives her the J.

"They don't have anything to do with it," Sydney explains. "It's them." She points to her size nine feet. "And these, see?" She sticks her hand in front of her face, hiding behind it. "When God asked me if I wanted 'em big, I said, 'Yeah—twice.'"

Leora blows an ash off the front of Sydney's nightgown, inhales, and hands the joint back. "They're not that big," she disagrees holding her breath.

The leggy redhead puts on her John Lennon's, takes a big toke, and looks down at her chest. "I know," she exhales the words with smoke. "They're little, but they're cute." She passes the skunk weed to Leora.

"No, no, I mean your hands," Leora says seriously. She takes a long hit and holds the doobie for Sydney to toke. Swirls of smoke escape as Leora hits it again; offering it to Sydney, who takes another long drag. "I don't think your hands are th-a-at big," she states, placing the roach in the ashtray.

"Yo, Sis," Sydney calls. Leora turns around to her best friend, who's holding both of her hands up in front of her face. "Peek-a-boo," she says, leaning her head over and looking around her hands. Leora cracks up. "Come on, Sis," Sydney continues. "My ring size is bigger than your shoe size. Hey, you can wear my gloves on your feet!"

Leora looses it. "What kind of reasoning is that, Sis?" she asks, crawling on the bed with tears rollin' down her cheeks.

"No, no, think about it," Sydney reasons. "I wear an eight ring. You have seven feet. Never mind. My gloves are too big for your feet."

"Quit it! Stop!" Leora laughs. "Seven feet. I don't want to wear your gloves."

"I know. They're too big."

Leora holds her stomach, shaking her head.

"When God asked me a third time if I wanted 'em big—"

"No, come on, stop," Leora begs.

"I didn't want to seem greedy, so I said no."

"No to Mae West's?"

"I didn't know anything about boobs. I was a baby. I thought he meant my ears."

"Your ears aren't big."

"Compared to what, my feet? Yo, Sis, I could walk on water. And at least my glasses have somethin' to hold them up. But me in a strapless gown with suspenders is not a pretty sight."

Leora roars. "We both wear ten jeans," Leora says to her five-foot, seven-inch comrade. Her cheeks are so sore from laughing she forms the letter O with her mouth, trying to relax the muscles.

"That's another thing," Sydney questions, sitting Indian-style on the bed. "I'm two inches taller than you. How come you're built like a brick shit house, and I'm built like the outhouse?"

They glance at each other and say in unison, "Different mothers!" as they laugh their asses off.

Leora sits up with her back to Sydney. Her stomach muscles hurt, and her cheeks hurt. She can't look at Sister Syd for fear of laughing hysterically again. Leora turns around with her hands in front of her face, doing her best to suppress the laughter.

"Hey, where'd you go, Sis? What . . . are ya hidin'?"

The laughter starts again. Leora puts her hands down to scooch off the bed.

"Oh, there ya are."

She walks to the doorway, holding her ears and shaking her head.

"Tits, shits. All I know is if my tits were ears I'd be deaf."

R-r-ring! The girls stare at the white princess phone. R-r-ring! R-r-ring! Leora gives Sydney her gag-a-maggot gesture by pretending to stick her finger down her throat, and starts for her room. She walks right into Wheezer, lying in wait for attack outside the doorway. He runs in front of her, taking several steps on his hind legs then tap-tap on her legs (Tag! You're it) and scoots into her room, disappearing under her bed. She sits her coffee on the vanity, tossing her nightgown on the bed before straightening the rainforest comforter. She pulls on a pair of cutoffs and a yellow tank top, then to the window to close the sheers. She weaves them between the window and the healthy philodendron. A white Lincoln Continental rides by.

"Yo, Sis!" Sydney yells, "Pick up the phone."

"Okay!" Leora yells back, grabbing the white and bronze French phone and pulling it to the bed. The anaconda phone cord is no match for "Attack Wheezer" as he springs from under the bed, striking with a series of bats, rolls, flips, kicks, and the fatal bite. Leora stamps her foot, sending her hero back to his hideout as she lifts the receiver.

Sydney is laughing hysterically. "You are ornery."

Goo Goo chuckles. "What, Blaze? A hundred dollars to suck your toes. He's a foot freak. I said don't ya just love the way her legs go all the way up and make an ass out of themselves? Hell no, he wants to suck your toes. He likes them red toenails."

"Hey, for a hundred dollars he can suck mine, too," Leora says laughing. "What's happ'nin'?"

"My toes," Sydney answers. "And devil dogs."

"What . . . cupcakes?"

"No, a girl's little patch of mink . . . right, Goo?"

"A girl's, say what? Ahh, hey! I like that better, a patch of mink. Yeah, like the girl at the club in them white stretch pants."

"I don't think I remember her," Leora ponders. "I really wasn't lookin' at any girls."

"What color was her hair?" Sydney asks.

"I don't know," Goo Goo answers. "I wasn't lookin' at her hair."

"He was lookin' at her devil dog," Leora says with a long southern drawl.

Leora and Sydney laugh.

"Ah-h-h, the girl standin' at the table across from where you were sittin', Blaze."

"There was a hen party standin' there. Let me think white pants, white pants . . ."

"Yo, Sis, the one with no rhythm," Leora offers. "She was standin' in front of the guy in the powder blue suit sittin' at the table."

"Oh . . ." Sydney searches her mind. "Oh, I know, you mean Scary Mary."

They all laugh.

"Yeah, she was talkin', he kept noddin', but he wasn't listenin'," Goo Goo says.

"He was mesmerized by her devil dog," Leora adds still with the drawl.

"Yeah, well, later on, Irish, he probably hypnotized her with his cobra," Goo Goo answers, snickering.

"Come on, Goo, his pants were tight, but I didn't even see a hint of garter snake, let alone a cobra. I think it was more like Willie the Worm. White pants said give me nine inches and hurt me. So he screwed her three times and punched her in her face."

Goo Goo roars. "You girls are somethin'."

"She had sandals on. Her toenails were pink."

"Hey, Blaze, I thought you didn't look at girls."

"That's fashion, Goo—toenails, hair, fingernails, etcetera."

"See, Goo? So the toe guy is fashionable," Leora adds.

"Yeah," Sydney agrees. "What's his name, Goo?"

"Sullivan. Barry Sullivan. I almost went to jail 'cause of him."

"What? He sucked your toes?" questions Leora.

"Hell no! No, no, he worked for me. You know, answerin' my phones. The cops broke my door down and arrested him. I wasn't there."

"Na-uh, arrested for toe-suckin'?" Sydney deduces.

"Heh heh, he used to call people and say he wanted to lick their toes, suck their toes— whatever. It was a Monday. Ahhh, I went to do payouts, grab some coffee, and got back around noon. I saw all these cop cars. I had the cash, owe sheets, ledger, pay out list—everything on me. It was a busy weekend. When I drove around the corner and saw all those flashin' lights, I almost shit my pants. I thought they were after me. I left everything in the car and walked over to the apartment. I said, 'What the hell's goin' on?' The dumb son-of-bitch. Harassment by communication. That's federal for Christ sake! On my business phone, my numbers phone talkin' about lickin' toes, wackin' his carrot!"

The girls lose it.

"Hey, hey," Goo Goo calls. "Wait, listen, listen . . ."

The girls laugh uproariously. Sydney coughs and chokes on a mouthful of tea.

"Hey, hey," Goo Goo repeats laughing. "Hey, look at the bright side. He'll never be arrested for rape."

Leora making Os again, "No . . . stop! I thought his aftershave smelled funny."

Sydney laughs, coughing, "No, that was Absorbine Jr.—his mouthwash!"

All three get the laughing jags. Leora chokes on her coffee, her eyes watering now breathing through an open mouth.

"Ahhh, you believe it? The cops traced 'em back to my damn phone. My work phone!"

"Ah ha ha! That's too funny!" Sydney says, wiping her eyes, "Oh, my God."

"No, shit," Leora talks with giggles trickling in her voice.

"He asked for your number, Blaze." Goo Goo is blowing smoke.

Sydney knows it. "You can give it to him, Goo."

"Ew-w-w, ew-w-w," Leora starts laughing while trying to form Os again.

"What . . . for real? Na-ah, what am I missin'?"

The girls laugh.

"It's disconnected," Sydney confesses.

"What do ya . . . hey, ya need some money, Blaze?" Goo Goo questions.

"Oh, no. Thanks, Goo."

"Come on, Blaze. How's Sullivan suppose to call ya?"

"Your sister." Sydney smiles. "Take a message."

Goo Goo snickers. "No, I'm serious, you guys. You need somethin'?"

"Nah, Goo," Sydney starts. "Vertol owes me six weeks unemployment. It should be comin' any day now."

"You still didn't get that, Blaze? How long can you collect?"

"If everything goes well, hopefully about a year."

"She's comin' back to bartendin', Goo, fill-ins for now, but we're gonna work on Papa for Saturdays permanently."

"I'll come see ya, Blaze. There's no business on Saturdays. Well, it's date night."

"Oh, please, Marcie sucks. If she's a bartender, I'll kiss your ass in Speare's window." Leora changes the subject. "Sydney's livin' here. Most of her furniture's here. All of her clothes are here. In fact, Crow and a couple young bucks said they would help us move the rest of her stuff later on today."

"Oh, then Marcie is gonna rent the apartment."

"Oh, I don't think Papa's rentin' it out. He's actually usin' it for storage. Gina, his youngest, brought a ton of shit back from college."

"Take ah you time. I'm in ah no hurry," Leora speaks in a deep voice.

"Yeah, that was . . . wow! Sis, that was four months ago, like July," Sydney concludes. "Time sure flies when you're havin' fun."

"We're slower than molasses in January goin' uphill."

"Better late than never," Goo Goo adds.

"You go, Goo Goo, with your little ditty," Sydney commends him.

"Whadaya mean little? What cha call it, Blaze?"

"No, Goo, the saying . . . the little ditty," Leora explains, suppressing laughter.

"See, Goo, you are ornery," Sydney says. "I think you should call Angie."

"I sent Angie to the beach. She rounded up three or four of her girlfriends. They're in Atlantic City. They're gonna go see Tony Bennett and Kenny Rogers . . . which brings me to my first question."

"You need arm candy? No wait . . . wait, I know, a sleep over," Leora teases.

"No way, Sis," Sydney chimes. "Angie'll tear us a new ass. Did she take your new Cadillac?"

Goo Goo chuckles, shaking his head. "You girls. Nah, one of her friends drove down. What the hell? I paid for the rooms."

"So what's the question, Goo?" Leora asks.

"What are you girls doin' tonight?"

"Well, we're gonna meet Crow and his buddies later this afternoon," Sydney explains. "We have to call 'em first."

"Yeah, then we have to pay 'em . . . Six packs and cheese steaks."

"I mean later on," Goo Goo continues.

"Oh, I don't know," Leora says, sighing, "I was gonna wash my hair. How 'bout you, Sis?"

"I was gonna do my toenails purple."

Goo Goo laughs. "I wanna pick you up around ten, ten-thirty tonight and bring you back tomorrow morning. There's five hundred in it for each of you."

"Who we gotta kill?" Sydney questions.

"Nobody," Goo Goo answers with sincerity. "Just pack a small suitcase."

"Road trip!" Sydney squeals. "Yo, Sis . . . . . . Sis?"

"Hey, Irish."

Sydney whistles.

"Sorry, about that. Wheezer attacked my philodendron. He jumped up and ripped a hunk off it. What were you sayin'?"

"Just say, 'Yes, Momma,'" Sydney says, stretching the curly receiver cord, the telephone cord and her arm to Leora's doorway waving a joint.

"Yes, Momma," Leora repeats also stretching for her half of the hits. "I heard you're gonna pick us up tonight and bring us back tomorrow and . . ."

"Five hundred each," Sydney states.

"Oh, wow! Who we gotta kill?"

"Great minds think alike," Sydney says laughing. "We have to pack a little suitcase, right, Goo?"

"Yeah, but it's not a road trip, which brings me to my second question."

"Let it rip." Sydney takes a hit and holds her breath.

"Can you stay in a hotel room until morning with no phone, even if it rings?"

"No phone?" Leora takes a hit and exhales. "How do we contact you?"

"We have adjoining rooms. Just knock. Lock your side. I'll be there all night."

"Yeah." Sydney takes a hit, looks at Leora and crosses her eyes.

Leora turns her back trying like hell to suppress laughter. "Okay, suitcase, no phone, five big ones, and you're next door." She takes a toke.

"Oh, yeah, I almost forgot. There's room service." Goo Goo sweetens the pot.

"Arm candy," Leora exhales. "I'm in."

Sidney blows smoke rings. "Me, ta."

Legs Galore

Crow's '62 pickup squeaks and groans as he cuts the engine, pulling into the driveway where four humongous spruce trees on the right seclude the regal structure and most of the property. The atrium protrudes between the side of the stone front porch and the dining room, its picture window dwarfing the already small kitchen window. An enclosed patio shades the length of the back of the house where Leora is unhooking the flimsy spring on the wooden screen door.

"Awww, poor baby," Leora shouts to Crow and his brother Pete. She shades her eyes, walking to the candy-apple red truck to inspect the contents. "Holy shit!" she comments.

The stock 283 Chevy didn't just look filled but upon closer inspection, it is packed like a sardine can. "You owe me big time," Crow says, patting the truck lovingly.

"Hey! Hey!" Leora interjects, gently caressing the scarecrow mural on the driver's door, "Sister Syd owes you big time not me! What is all this?"

"I don't know. She pointed and we loaded. Hey, guess who came out of the bar and watched from his car, Doll?"

Leora rolls her eyes. "Did he get in a white Lincoln?"

"Yep, what'd you do hit 'im last night, Lefty?"

"Noooo!"

"He had sunglasses on, but you could see the stitches. He looks like he has one long eyebrow," Crow laughs. "Goes clear across his forehead. That's funny as hell! One time when we came down with a load, he was standin' in front of his car with one of those guys that were in the bar with him last week. He had his sunglasses off. His eyes are black. Betcha he was lookin' for you, or tryin' to."

Stocky, smart-ass Pete taunts her by jogging past her, bobbing and weaving, sparing like a boxer, the spitting image of his big brother. Leora rolls her tongue inside her mouth, nodding and smirking at her nineteen-year-old teaser. He grins walking backward to unlatch the tailgate of the truck, keeping an eye on Lefty. Leora takes a step toward her tormentor. "Where's Sis?" she asks, stalking her smiling, cocky prey.

"She's gettin' sandwiches at Two Js and then swingin' by the Beer Cellar," Crow explains. "She should be here any minute. I'm starvin'." Crow cracks up again, grinning at Leora and shrugging his shoulders. "He looked like a raccoon."

"Yo, Chooch," Sydney calls with her entourage on their way through the house to the patio. Joey, Chris, and Greg sit packed boxes, six-packs, cheese steaks, and potato chips on top of chairs, counter, and kitchen table before following Sydney outside.

"Hi, Hoe!" Leora calls. "What's happ'nin'?"

"Hey, Momma. What da ya think? I did good, huh?"

"And then some . . . Wow, a book case, oh, a coffee table . . . it's gorgeous. What's that under the blanket? Yes, a roll top desk. What's that, another desk? Oh, it's like an executive desk. Shit, Sis, you did real-l-l good!"

"Papa was in the bar when I called ordering the sandwiches. He's up from the beach, but he's goin' back down. He said he'll call ya. All of this stuff originally came from this house when he bought it," Sydney explains. "He said we couldn't have timed it better. He had people emptyin' a big movin' van. It's so big it would have taken up the whole parking lot in front so they had to park in the back, unload it, bring everything through the bar to the front, and take it up the stairs. You should see the apartment. It looks like a furniture store. You can't move up there!"

"This is like Christmas!" Leora says, peeking under sheets and blankets at a bed frame, stereo, filing cabinet, and smoke stand. "Wow! A console color TV. I'm impressed!"

"There's a portable one in my trunk and who knows what else. Papa kept sayin' take it, take it. The movers even helped. They had to get stuff outta there to make room for the stuff they were bringin' in. He's paintin' and puttin' in new carpet down there. They helped fill Crow's truck then started stuffin' my car: the trunk, back seat, passenger seat. I drew the line at the roof. Nah, nothin' on the roof."

The smell of cheese steaks becomes overwhelming. Sydney whistles to gain the attention of the quartet of helpers walking toward the kitchen. "Yo! Yoohoo! Don't go empty-handed. Grab somethin' out of the truck."

"Yeah," Leora agrees. "We'll just put everything in the family room and empty Syd's Thunderbird then eat." We'll hold our breath walkin' through the kitchen."

Greg, the Italian Stallion of the bunch, hops up on the tailgate to begin the distribution of furniture. "I'm so hungry I could eat a horse."

"I don't know why," Chris answers. "Ya ate four boneless chickens and a half a pig at my house. Not to mention toast."

Friends since childhood, the trio grew up blocks from each other in Lennox Park, Highland Gardens, Buckman Village, and then later included Crow in McCafferty Village.

"He's a growin' boy," Joey counters, grabbing two desk chairs. "What's your mom say, Greg? She'd rather pay your rent someplace than feed ya."

"Yeah, he's growin' all right," Chris says smirking. "He's growin' sideways."

"It's just more for Angie to love," Greg announces to his comrades.

"Hey, Syd," Crow yells, "I hope you have two sandwiches for Greg 'cause he ain't gettin' mine." Greg grins, sitting smaller pieces of furniture on the tailgate and helping Joey sit the larger ones on the ground.

Leora was busy folding the array of bedding, or was she? Waiting until Pete's hands were full, Leora sneaks up behind her curly-hair victim.

"Ya got it?" she whispers, tugging Pete's ponytail playfully. Pete is had. He nods, smiling.

"Gooood," Leora purrs, giving him a wedgie. "Don't drop it," she says innocently, leaning forward and batting her eyes. Pete sits the headboard against the truck, unzips his jeans, and adjusts his underwear.

With the truck empty, Joey helps the girls clear the boxes from the kitchen to the den, hooking the console to the outside antenna, and setting up the stereo while the group grabs the portable TV and most of the boxes from the T-bird. Soon the kitchen was abuzz with popping beer tabs, ripping paper, and ice cracking in freshly poured homemade tea and ingestion. The light conversations of cars, girlfriends, and fishing turns, to inquiries of the night before; with the girls purposely omitting Griff's vindictive behavior and explaining him away, more or less, as an implosion of self-destructive stupidity. But Crow knew better, actually they all knew better, about how Leora was. Maybe not Pete, being younger than the rest of them, but Leora had been like a mentor, a big sister, when Crow was younger and so angry with life. Her home in the village had been an escape for a troubled teen and his buddies, a refuge instead of the streets; a world away even though it was only sixty feet. And she kept it real, no matter how painful the truth. She lies rather awful. So does Sydney for that matter. She also keeps it real like her best friend; not lying, just not telling all the truth. Crow has long since outgrown the cover-ups and half-truths. He can read between the lines, and so he takes a bite of sandwich leaning forward chewing and gawking at Leora with a wide-eyed stare; just as Leora would do when Tink would finish her ice tea, eat her candy, or hide her car keys to stop her from going to work and leaving him. She would tell her little one she could see his truth in his eyes . . . always.

"Where's my cupcake?"

"I don't know, Mommy."

"Did you finish my tea?"

"No, Mommy."

"Where are my keys?"

"I don't know, Mommy."

"Well, come 'ere, look in my eyes and say, 'Mommy, I don't know where they are,'" she would say to him. He would look at his mom with his eyes wide then blink, or he would look at his mom, eyes wide, look down, giggle, and nod, shrugging his shoulders or talk fast and wide-eyed, his voice full of laughter. And always she would leave him with hugs and a kiss to last until together again.

Leora stands looking wide-eyed back at Crow then winks. She walks out back, standing on tiptoes then jumps, tapping underneath the green canvass awning to flip the turned-up skirt back down. She walks over to the back of the truck, folding the pile of covers just as the phone rings.

"Yo, Sis!" Sydney hollers, stretching the kitchen phone cord through the archway onto the screened patio. "Goo says about nine-thirty instead of ten-thirty. Ah'ight?"

"Sure if you're cool with it, I'm in," Leora answers, spotting the forgotten Mickey Mouse blanket. She lifts the worn printed fabric to her face, closing her eyes, and inhaling its presence. She opens her tear-filled eyes to the Indian summer sun, outlining puffy clouds in fire white on its descent into a pastel sunset of orange, pinks, and purples—and she remembers, oh, how she remembers, precious and treasured snapshots of time, tumbling from her guarded heart rendering her helpless to stop the cascade that once was reality. She has no choice as the autumn flavors of dried leaves, honeysuckle, earthworms, and empires stir the longing within her. She succumbs, with sweet surrender, blinking tears as she remembers laughter and giggles, wonder and silliness, smiles and hugs.

A squirrel scurrying to a nearby maple scatters her memories into reality. Blinking tears, she spies Inspector Wheezer smelling the truck tires. "Wheezer," she calls. He flops then jumps into the empty bed of the truck for further inspection. "You comin', Wheeze?" Leora asks walking to the patio with the folded covers.

Crow stands on the patio. "Did ya get everything?" He pretends not to notice her red nose. Diamond cuts on the small gold Celtic cross given to Crow by his father glistens in the sunlight as he holds the screen door ajar for her. She nods, handing him the pile turning to refasten the screen door spring.

"I can tighten that for you," Crow offers.

"Oh no," Leora answers, sniffling, "I need it just the way it is. Wheezer pulls it open near the bottom and slips in to sleep when nobody's home." She points at the protruding closet to the right of the back door. Its left sliding door is slightly ajar.

Crow peeks in then slides the right side open, exposing a narrow-paneled closet with a familiar red flannel shirt still in the cardboard box sitting atop a milk crate.

"Neat," Crow says closing it.

"What's neat?" Greg asks, peering between Chris and Joey. Pete belches, leaning on Joey's shoulder.

"Cat bedroom," Pete answers, slightly slurring the words. Chris, Joey, and Greg look back and forth at each other and then at Pete. "Right?" Pete questions.

The trio glances at each other again grinning. Pete is high and full. "Hey, you guys look like the Three Stooges."

"They are the Three Stooges," Sydney answers, crossing her arms and leaning in the kitchen doorway. With her best English accent, Sydney adds, "I'm Mary Poppins, and you're Batman, Love."

Pete tilts his head back to focus his eyes on tall, lanky Sister Syd, and smiles like a Cheshire cat. "Well, where's your umbrella?"

"Parked out front," Sydney teases.

"Yeah, next to my broom," Leora takes the lead. "Where are your tights?"

"Under my pants," Pete says, bucking his eyes at Sydney. "Wanna see?"

Crow pushes Pete's baseball cap down over his face and starts to shove the covers in the closet.

"Oh, no, no, no!" Leora says, "They go upstairs." She slides the door shut. "That's for seasonal stuff," she says, sliding the left side open again, exposing leggings, coats, and scarves hanging above boots, gloves, garden tools, and a spider . . . a big, big spider! A huge, brownish, wooly-lookin' thing on the back wall just above the clutter.

Leora screams, backing up. Pete smashes it with his size twelve, leaving a gaping hole in the paneling and drywall, the spider stuck to the bottom of his sneaker. In the blink of an eye, Pete takes two hops on his other foot, while ripping the buggy sneaker off and running out the screen door. Leora and Sydney dodge the sneaker on their way out. A couple of the guys duck. Everyone is laughing.

"Oh. My. God!" Sydney speaks in between pants. She bends over, leaning on her knees. "He was big enough to ride!"

"His relatives are gonna come kick your ass!" Leora says as a chill runs down her spine causing shivers. "Ewww!"

"Bullshit! He ate all of them!" Pete even shivers. "He's probably after the cheese steaks."

"You're lucky he didn't grab your foot and throw you're ass!" Sydney shivers, watching Crow wipe the sneaker in the grass then chucking it to Pete. "Ewww! That's gross!"

"He'd a probably climbed your leg if you missed him," Leora added, contorting her face in disgust.

"Who . . . miss? Pete the Feet?" Chris asks, patting Pete on his back. "No way, your boy could walk on water."

"Yo, Crow!" Chris calls from the house. "Jennie's on the phone."

Crow trots through the screened-in patio for the kitchen phone and returns.

"Look at you. Aren't you just so brave?" Leora digs.

"What brave?" Crow asks innocently. "Hey, you screamed, everybody ran. I thought you saw a rat. I came out to get Killer Wheezer. Scared of a little spider."

"Little my ass, he was takin' names," Leora calls after him. "Your sister!"

Frogs and crickets singing earth's lullaby harmonize with the creek as Pete walks toward the edge. Wheezer follows, rubbing his friend's legs, purring, and of course wheezing. He had belonged to Pete first. Pete had found the tiny, frightened tabby across the street from McCafferty Village where his brother and friends rent one of four garages. The orange and white furball quickly became a fixture with the diversified group, especially Pete, carrying the mascot draped around his neck. Content and wheezing, "Killer" sat in on conversations of carpentry, refrigeration, electricity, and of course, cars. When he tired of small talk, Killer would go to his cat bedroom, climbing staggered empty metal drums to a cardboard box with a red flannel shirt. And he could come and go as he pleased through a broken pane in the rear of the garage. The feline really liked his home and became accustomed to the familiar smells of exhaust, gas and pizza. But Killer was a cat's cat. He had rules. He didn't do noise or water and would disappear at the first oompas from engines or splashes from the bucket brigade. And then one day, the young male started adding his own masculine scent to the menagerie of odors. Yes, this was his territory too, damn it; his domain, and he marked it. Thus becoming, Wheezer, when he went to live with the girls in the apartment. They had him neutered and tried turning him into a house cat equipped with kitty litter. He hated it. But unconfined here at the edge of the creek with the smell of the water, the mud, wet leaves, sweet pea, honeysuckle—this is the hot set-up. Now this is a menagerie of odors. This is a domain. This is Wheezer's domain.

Pete bends down to pick up his friend. Wheezer jumps onto his back and curls around Pete's neck purring and smelling Pete's hair.

"Welcome to Wheezerville," Leora calls to the pair silhouetted against the evening sky.

"He remembers," Pete gushes walking to her. "He got big. Look how far down his feet hang."

"Let's go Cat Man," Greg calls from the back of the pickup. "That was a great idea to move everything first 'cause I sure don't feel like it now." He does a long burp.

"Damn!" Chris says.

Crow starts for the truck

"Yo! You forgot the beer!" Sydney yells from the house. Crow makes a U-turn.

"Oh, shit! Crow, grab my tool box!" Joey hollers from the truck.

Leora walks to the patio. "Take the portable TV too for your garage."

"Cool," Crow says.

The phone rings. "Yo, Sis, it's Papa."

"And don't forget the rest of the sandwiches," Leora tells Crow, following him to the house. "We already have our two for tomorrow."

"Yeah, right," Crow answers. "I can always carry 'em in my teeth."

Sydney hands Leora the phone.

"Hi, Papa." She sits at the kitchen table.

"I got 'em, I got 'em," Sydney says, placing the steak sandwiches in the bag with the half case of beer.

Crow grabs the toolbox and portable television in the den. Sister Syd places the bag with the steaks and beer on the TV stand and carries them to the truck, following Crow. Leora mouths the words "thank you" and throws Crow a kiss.

By the time Sydney says her good-byes to the young bucks, Leora had fed Wheezer, showered, dressed, packed an over night bag, and was sitting on her bed twisting some doobies.

"You fed Tiger, right?" Sydney stood at the doorway in her robe with a towel wrapped around her wet head.

"Doobie doobie doooo," Leora sings to "Strangers in the Night." "Yes, I did."

"He went out. I put food in his bowl on the patio for later. Boy, Pete is a piss."

"He certainly is," Leora answers with a smile, "He's ornery."

"He was so impressed, Wheeze remembered him."

"How 'bout the size of that spider, Sis? If Pete missed, you coulda bitch-slapped it into tomorrow."

Sydney pulls her robe tight and shivers. "I don't care how big my hands are. I ain't slappin' nothin' unless it's on my skin or your skin, Sis. That son-of-a-bitch could outrun us. He had eight legs!"

Leora cracks up and hands Sydney a one-hitter and a lighter.

The redhead depletes the tiny container and exhales. "You know, a white Lincoln drove by while I was out there," Sydney tells her best friend. Leora gathers everything off the bed, grabs her overnight bag, turns off the light with her elbow, and follows Sydney to her bedroom. She puts everything on Sydney's bed, drops the bag on the floor, and makes herself comfortable while Sydney dresses.

Leora sits with furrowed brow. "Well, so much for the Poconos," she says aloud.

"I don't think he had any intention of going to the Poconos."

"That's what I said to Papa earlier. I wouldn't go across the street with the scumbag, let alone go for a ride. Papa thinks this guy has an agenda, and it has to do with me."

"What do you mean, Sis? You mean like he's warped? Obsessed?"

"I don't know. I said to Papa, 'An agenda with me? I'm no Chrissy Snow.'"

"Well, he's definitely no Jack Tripper! More like a Jack Ass."

"Papa said this whacko wanted to rent the apartment."

"Nah-uh! The one I rented? You're shittin' me!"

"I wish. He wanted to go look at it, and Papa said it wasn't for rent. Griff was sorta adamant. He had like eight hundred in cash and said he would pay three months in advance. Oh, but he could wait until the young ladies moved out."

"What is up with that wad?" Sydney hollers from the bathroom. She throws the towel in the hamper and collects her deodorant, toothpaste, and toothbrush.

"I don't know. Papa said maybe he's tryin' to keep a low profile away from the heat up on the main line. He doesn't want him in his bar, but there's no reason to flag him. And he doesn't want me to get upset 'cause at least in the bar we know where he is. I think there's more to it than that.

Anyway, Papa's goin' away 'til Thursday or Friday, probably Friday because he bought an apartment complex one block from the ocean and three blocks away from his beach house property. He has to take care of some paperwork. That's where all the furniture came from, six apartments. Papa says you keep ah you friends close and you keep ah you enemies closer."

"Gee, Sis, if he gets any closer, he'll be stuck up your ass!"

Laughter fades to silence. Both sit deep in thought.

"So are you the "Get"or what?"

"I hope not. The only thing he's gonna "get"is tired—tired of the word no."

"Not if he's a degenerate, or obsessed!" Sydney closes her sock drawer with her hip as she shoves her makeup bag into her pocketbook. She throws the socks in her overnight bag, zips it, and sits on the bed.

"Maybe its Goo Goo," Leora reasons.

"What? You think Goo Goo is the Get? Hoe, no. You think Griff tipped you all that money, haunted you with phone calls, and wanted to take you to the Poconos because he's into guys?" Sydney lights one of the joints.

"No, Hoe," Leora replies laughing. "Not Goo Goo himself. I mean maybe this wombat wants to get Goo Goo's territory. Maybe he's tryin' to get ta him through us."

"You have a mouse in your pocket? Us? Your sister! You mean you?"

"No, no, Sis, think about it. As of last night, it's us. As of 'young ladies', it's us. As of you out back . . ."

"It's us." Sydney thinks a minute. "Maybe that's why Goo wants to talk to us."

"Maybe not. We can't say anything unless Goo Goo brings it up, right? I mean what if Goo Goo doesn't know anything? What if this loser is just that, a loser?"

"But what if it is Goo Goo he's after. Shouldn't we say something?"

"See, those two words again: what if. What if he's just a freakin' pervert?"

A black Cadillac pulls up and honks. The girls gather their belongings and head downstairs, turning the night light on in the front window. The door locks behind them.

Your Sister

. . . .

"Call the cops!" someone in the migrating crowd hollers. Leora is already from behind the bar when the argument escalates into physical contact just as one guy charges head first at the other, sending them into the rack of pool sticks hanging on the side wall. The wooden cues clatter to the floor as the inebriated pair waltz along the front end of the building, knocking over the little table in the corner. Eva turns the lights up and the jukebox down, producing subtle moans interrupted by the sound of shattering glass as bottles and mugs from the table impact the floor. *Ahhh, another Friday night.*

"You're a fuckin' moron!" the first guy yells, restrained at one end of the table.

"You're a asshole!" the second guy yells back, restrained at the other end.

"You're done," Leora yells, catching a damp bar rag from Eva. Crow heads for the storage room to retrieve the dust pan, bucket, and mop.

"WHAT?" the first guy grunts, shrugging his shoulders at Leora. "WHAT? He touched the ball! First he says he was up, his quarters were next, but he wasn't. Then the son-of-a-bitch miss cues, and he moved the fuckin' ball!"

"Watch your mouth!" Leora says dryly. Eva opens the register and takes two quarters, handing them to Leora. She in turn hands them to the intoxicated man.

"What the fuck is this?"

"I said watch your mouth!" Leora says slowly in monotone, almost through clenched teeth.

46

"We were playin' for a dollar."

Leora breathes deep and hands him a dollar from her back pocket.

"It's over," she states.

"No. I'm gonna kick his ass," he says, pointing at the second guy.

"You're gonna kiss my ass, right here," the second guy yells, grabbing his crotch.

"Take it outside," Leora says as someone takes the bar rag and goes to give Crow a helping hand.

"After I finish the game," the first guy answers defiantly.

Leora walks in front of him, crossing her arms and making eye contact.

"I said . . . it's over. Ya got your dollar. You're done." She turns around with her hands on her hips, confronting the second guy who stands unsteadily, pulling paper bills from his pocket. Blinking, he slowly tries counting them unaware of his own involvement in the drama as he stumbles out of the way of the clean-up crew. Leora shakes her head, breathing deep, and starts placing the pool sticks back in the rack. The owner of the next set of quarters proceeds to feed the table.

"Hey, get the hell away from there. I got the table. It's my shot."

Leora cringes. *You drunk bastard!* She spins around, taking a deep breath, rolling her eyes. The pool cue makes a sharp slapping noise when she drops it to the floor and stomps to the table.

First guy stands, facing her direction, trying to focus his eyes to glare at her and bracing for a confrontation. Leora leans over the table, flailing her arms, shoving all the balls in all the pockets and turning off the light hanging above.

"You don't have any balls. The table is closed."

"No balls, take it outside girls!" booms a voice from a familiar paunchy patron, James "Fat Cat" Senkowsky to be exact. Smiling at Eva, he raises his empty seven and seven glass, holding up two fingers. One thing was for sure, the customers at Papa's love their billiards and do not take kindly to prohibited use of the past time, especially because of unknown drunks. And calling the police was the last resort. As long as no one is robbed, there is no gun and no blood is drawn; the tavern community patrols itself. Too many phone calls to the boys in blue can result in fines or being labeled a nuisance bar subject to closure. A girl could lose her job for not defusing situations, like now. To leave the table open is only asking for trouble.

Besides, you don't argue with a drunk. And nine times out of ten, flagged and with no audience, the drunkards will meander out the door.

Smiling at Fat Cat, Eva dims the lights and turns the jukebox up before making his drinks. Ahhhh … music to sooth the savage beasts. The sparse crowd relaxes, migrating to the bar away from the darkened area. The neon lights in the windows across the top of the front wall cast a soft glow on the two unknowns oblivious to each other, staggering to the front door. Eva places upside down shot glasses in front of Crow and his helpers. Leora slips through the aperture and resumes her role as mixologist. *God, it's only nine-thirty. This is gonna be a fun night.*

"I thought the full moon was last weekend," Eva says. They stand against the draught beer, eyeing the clientele.

"Yeah, that brings out the asswipes, but stupidity is every weekend," Leora answers wistfully. They turn and face the mirrored wall while the velvety voice of Barry White fills the room.

Eva tiptoes to peek in the mirrors then glances toward the far end of the bar. Goo Goo, in his usual seat at the end of the mirrored wall, nods, smiles, and rolls his eyes, shaking his head. Doc is beating Goo's ear. Eva chuckles to herself. Goo raises his empty glass. Eva waits on him, giving him a fresh glass of ice and drinks around for Chicarella, Shout, Jocko, and Doc. Leora serves a few people then stands at the taps again. Eva joins Leora scanning the mirrors. Eva chuckles again a little louder, trying to check her French twist in the mirror.

"What's up?" Leora presses the dark-eyed beauty.

"Stupidity," Eva answers with eyes wide and grinning. Fidget and Pockets stand in front of the taps, nodding toward the darkened table. Fidget lays his hand flat on the bar with a five dollar bill peeking out from under it. Leora glances at Fidget's hand. With a puzzling expression, she looks at Fidget, shakes her head, and holds up ten fingers then resumes her conversation.

"Stupidity runs a muck," Leora agrees with her coworker. She knows Eva is talking about Doc. Middle age, clean cut, studious looking with his Clark Kent glasses Doc. On-again off-again, Dick Doc. First he's married, then he's not. Then he's separated, then he's not. It's fine with Eva. She doesn't want Doc, only his money. He thinks she's a kept woman—his, and so full of himself, he doesn't realize Eva lets him think that.

"He went back with Trudy again last weekend," the buxom brunette says smiling at Goo and his group. Goo looks like a deer caught in a car's headlights. Eva smirks at him. "I didn't hear from Doc all week until earlier this afternoon."

"And was he sorry . . . again?"

Eva nods her head up and down, looking forlorn with an exaggerated pout.

"And did he get back into your good graces?" Eva nods again, still looking forlorn, still the exaggerated pout. "And did he let slip a secret accidentally on purpose?" Leora questions with her curiosity now perked.

Eva laughs out loud. "Does a bear shit in the woods? The only way Motor Mouth keeps a secret is if he doesn't know it. He said Goo is holdin'." Leora laughs, almost choking on a sip of orange juice. "But listen, last Thursday, Doc told me he was takin' me to see Kenny Rogers on Saturday down Atlantic City. He went back with Trudy on Friday and took her. I was hot. Willie was here Saturday night when I strolled in, and he invited me to go gamblin'. He said we'd split whatever we won. I hit five hundred dollars at the Golden Nugget on the slot machine. He won six hundred on blackjack. Doc just handed me seventy-five dollars for my car payment."

Leora snickers. She thinks back to Saturday night eatin', drinkin', and talkin' with Chicarella and a relaxed Goo Goo in the hotel room. Afterward the girls didn't see them again 'til Sunday morning when they piled into Shout's car to go home. Goo told story after story. One in particular of lending cash to Eva for her new—or shall we say newer—car being paid back in monthly installments and how Dick Doc is on the payroll. Goo pays Doc. Doc gives money to Eva, and Eva gives it to Goo for a car payment.

"It's my money! What the hell? I'm payin' myself," Goo Goo confessed. They all laughed.

The light goes on at the pool table. "Yo!" Leora yells. Pockets points to a ten spot resting on the bar behind the taps. Leora makes a face, shaking her head. She holds up ten fingers and points to her wrist. Fidget comes over for the ten dollar bill. Leora mouths the words ten o'clock. He nods and relays the message to Pockets. She waits on a few more drinkers. The table light goes out. She stands, watching from the taps while cantankerous

Eva waits on her younger admirer, Willie, her gambling buddy, sitting at Eva's end across from the seasoned quartet. And sitting a few stools away from Willie is Harry, also younger, also an admirer.

Leora giggles. *She's gonna have Doc talkin' to himself. Oh, that's too funny.*

"Ya smell good, Baby," Willie says, bucking his eyes at Eva.

"I taste good, too," Eva adds, leaning forward.

"I see that," Harry chimes in. Practically everyone laughs at Eva's end of the bar except deflated Doc. He downs his drink to get Eva away from the young bucks. She caters to the foursome then struts slow and deliberate to Leora, boom ditty, boom ditty. Both sides of the bar watch. The younger barmaid looks toward the pool table, faking a cough to hide her laughter.

"Dick Doc just gave us another twenty for our tips," Eva tells the Irish lass.

"I'm in! No wonder Goo Goo looks like he saw a ghost."

"The way Doc tells it, there's more where that came from," Eva states. "Goo did real good last weekend."

"Good! Nobody picked the right numbers. Job security." Leora concludes.

"Oh, I don't know about that, but last weekend somebody stole Goo's Cadillac."

Leora thought back to Sunday morning piling into Shout's Oldsmobile. "The new black Caddy? Whoa!"

"Yeah, telephone, telegraph, tell-a-Doc. He says Goo and Chicarella booked a red eye to Vegas and rooms at the airport hotel with a couple of bimbos Saturday night. Somehow Goo's car went missing. Goo acted all upset and canceled the trip. He's up for an Academy Award." They giggle, leaning into each other. "He only put seven hundred dollars down. He didn't even make his first payment yet. The insurance company is payin' eighteen thousand. The airline was very apologetic giving him four comp tickets for whenever."

Leora does a wolf whistle. "Oh, my God! Are you shittin' me? Now what's he drivin'?"

"His old blue one, old, what's it two years old?"

"And paid for!" The girls laugh. "At this rate, you're gonna end up with the whole eighteen."

"Not me, well, not this week end anyway. Doc says he'll call me when I'm done work. Yeah, right. I'm out. He shoulda called me last weekend. My kids are gone 'til Sunday night. I'm not sittin' home starin' at the phone or babysittin' him and his ego. That's Trudy's job." She musters up her best rendition of Peppy Le Pew's accent, "Zee love nest, how you say, is close-ed."

"I think Sydney's love nest is close-ed for good. It won't hurt my feelings. We got the phone bill today, forty-two dollars!"

"You're kiddin' me!"

"Would I lie to you? I ran to get gas and Sydney called the phone company. But it's in my name so they wouldn't even talk to her. When I came back, I called 'em. I was hot to trot. I was on hold forever. I told her I didn't even know half these numbers. She got her supervisor on the line. We found out the calls weren't made from the telephone at the house. They were made from a payphone and billed to the house phone. Are you kiddin' me? Rob the Verb made phone calls and charged 'em to my number. The piece of shit. Syd called one of the numbers. It was the ex-girlfriend; the paycheck. Sis freaked!"

"Able Mabel?" Eva offers.

Leora gives Fidget a thumbs-up. "Yepper, and Sis has been puttin' him off for weeks. She's not into 'im. Bad vibes. It seems he's always got his hand out and his pants down."

"He don't make her feel warm and fuzzy?"

"He probably would for about fifteen minutes."

Eva laughs, bagging a takeout as Leora continues.

"What? I'm serious. The night after he first introduced himself at a gas pump he showed up on our doorstep. When was that four weeks ago? He was there all of twenty minutes. He wanted bod-da-boom, bod-da-bing. Yeah, rabbits are warm and fuzzy."

"Doesn't he work at some club?"

"He says he works weekends at the Chateau Club as a bouncer."

"Oh, yeah, I remember. Goo Goo mentioned it before. That's a hike."

"Yeah, well, he's been all over her like a cheap suit tryin' in her car in the parkin' lot, in his car in the parkin' lot, in her car in front of the house, in his car in front of the house, in the house, every room except mine. He's been hangin' around all this week. Think he'd get the hint? Hell no! You might think he's up for Boyfriend of the Year. Every time I turn around I'm lookin' at him with his Michelob and pup tent! I said, 'Yo, Sis, bod-da-boom, bod-da-bing and get him the hell out of here! I'm done, too!"

R-r-ring! R-r-ring! R-r-ring! Leora hustles to the phone maneuvering around; Eva doubled over with laughter. "Hello, Papa's . . . sure. Breeze!"

Leora is in a mood and can't shake it. *Anxiety, agitation, aggravation; D—all the above, whatever.* She breathes deep. *And that's just the As.* Eva draws a pitcher of beer. Leora sits glasses on coasters for three patrons. She takes the money, rings up the pitcher sale, and reaches around Eva, laying the change on the bar.

Eva finishes drawing the pitcher and sits it on the bar, turning to Leora. "Ya know, it doesn't matter if they're six foot tall with broad shoulders," Eva holds up her hands and measures the air, "Or five-foot-five and this big." Eva holds up her pinky. "Give 'em enough rope, and they hang themselves every time."

"Stupidity runs a muck. I guess I wasn't suppose to look at the phone bill, but I'm not just another pretty face. Sydney's comin' in, but first she's gonna go get the money. I told her to be careful. She is pissed. Hey, we were the bimbos Saturday night."

Eva looks wide-eyed at Leora. Smiling, she signals 'wait a sec' and caters to several customers. She walks back to the taps, waiting, watching Leora, and cocking her head in Leora's direction, anticipating some juicy gossip.

"Sydney and I," Leora says, walking back to the taps, "Had an adjoining room with Goo and Chick. They came over for room service. We could eat and drink, but we weren't allowed to answer the phone. It only rang twice anyway. Goo answered it. He was trashed. He talked about business bein' down and whispered he was talkin' to the Verb, we have Goo callin' him that," Leora laughs. "Goo said somethin' about Mable stoppin' by his place with homemade chili. That's the Verb's favorite dish. And why would she take it to Goo's place if he wasn't there?"

"Cause," they both make quotation marks in the air, "Robbie was there!" They say in unison.

"I don't think Goo remembers talkin' about it," Leora says, leaning toward Eva. "But Sis was all over it because Rob"—Leora contorts her face with disgust—"told her he was bouncin' that night. Lie! Lie! Lie!

Well, that took the cake. That was last weekend. And the phone bill is the icing. Besides, he walks all over the house, looks in boxes, moves stuff around. Shit! He moved this one box five times, countin' today. It must be his favorite. He kept puttin' it on the kitchen counter. I stuck it out back. It sounds like stuff from a desk drawer. We don't even know what's in all the boxes. I don't like him. All he does is bullshit! He'll talk for an hour and say absolutely nothing or give ya a song or dance. He blows smoke. It gets on my nerves. I want to tell him to walk into this!" She puts her arm out and slaps the air back and forth furiously. "Sydney did three loads of his laundry today. Hey, listen up, you get one phone call when you get arrested, so I might have to leave early to go bail her out. If not later then later, later. We're torchin' his clothes."

"You know, Goo Goo told me he met Rob in the mall parkin' lot about two months ago when Shout's Oldsmobile wouldn't start. They were gonna have it towed. Rob just happened to be drivin' by. He said he could fix it and drove 'em to Joe's Junk Yard. When they came back, he fixed it right there on the spot. He got into Goo Goo's good graces. He's a gopher and a cheap handyman for Angie's apartment building, too. Occasionally he lives with his parents out toward the Chateau, so they say. He ain't got a pot to piss in or a window to throw it out of."

The girls stand side by side drawing drafts, glancing up and down the bar. "A gopher infected with stupidity, who knew," Leora concludes. "He might be a handyman, but he's definitely not a right hand man. Hell, he's not a left hand man. Hell, he's not even a man. Don't get me started."

"Well, I guess that's what you do in Goo Goo's line of work," Eva comments. "Surround yourself with all brawn and no brains or jerks so full of themselves they can't see past their noses. Not smart enough to rip ya off but smart enough to talk and chew gum. Speakin' of Doc," – She snickers – "I knew Goo Goo wouldn't step out on Angie. I didn't say that to Doc. I just let him rattle on with his diarrhea of the mouth. He thinks every man is as egotistical as he is. Goo knows you don't shit where you eat."

"Yeah, and you never let your right hand know what your left hand is doin'."

"And Angie owns the damn building anyway. She'd throw him out on his ass."

"And that's why it's Goo Goo's business, not Doc's."

"Yeah, 'cause he'd give it away . . . to a woman."

"Yeah, you!" Leora shrieks.

The girls laugh. Crow waves good night to the ladies. He will be ready, willing, and able when Tom comes bright and early tomorrow morning.

"So, I guess Rob stays with Goo."

"I guess he hovers there when he's down around here or not tryin' to populate the area. But he really was Sydney's little tag-along this week. She took full advantage of it too. She got work done on her T-Bird. He bought her points, plugs, changed her oil, new brakes all the way around. Oh, yeah, the 'Bird is purrin'. She gave him a six-pack, pizza, ten bucks for gas, and a promise." Leora raises her eyebrows up and down, smirking. "And then he said he needed a hundred dollars to get his car fixed. Sis pulled the dumb blonde routine and said she didn't have it, but she'd ask me and he said, 'Oh, no, no, no, that's okay, never mind.' Yeah, shit in one hand and wish in the other and see which one gets filled first!"

"The honeymoon is over!" Eva flashes her pearly whites.

The ladies glance up and down the bar. "Yeah, Zee love nest is close-ed." And it's a miracle. He drove away in his Charger just fine! Fix this!" Leora smacks the air with flurries again.

"Yeah, he's got sponge-ability," Eva agrees.

"There were a few numbers on the phone bill. I guess he was linin' 'em up. I don't know. All I do know is I hope he doesn't come to the house anymore. I'm so sick of hearin', I'll help you carry that upstairs, I'll help you move that out of the den, let me get that, I'll help, I'll do, I got it, what the hell? Get this! And the wanderin' through the house at night, insomnia this! I'd rather watch paint dry than talk to his sorry ass. He hangs his hat where he drops his pants, and Mabel puts up with it. There's no way she's an ex. She snaps her fingers when she finds out he strays."

"Yeah, like this." Eva rubs her fingers together the sign for money. "Rob says," Eva speaks in a sultry voice, "Snap it right over here, Momma!"

"Thank you, thank you very much," Leora adds, impersonating the King. She glances around the bar. The crowd was not quite large enough yet to keep two barmaids frenzied. They turn to glance at the front door opening. Griff and Heckle n' Jeckle stroll toward the rear of the building, sitting at the table next to the jukebox along the wall. The girls turn back around and watch through the mirrors. Leora shakes her head. She cleans up where Crow was sitting, loosens ice in the ice bin, and just generally tries to look busy. Thank God it is Friday and Eva's here. She does not want to wait on them. She waited on them Monday night and Wednesday night. On those nights, they sat at the bar, cordial and polite. Jammer left and came back, left and came back, like a yoyo. Leora really doesn't like them. At first glance the other night, Griff's swollen forehead did look like a third eye with stitches resembling eyelashes. She had almost laughed in his face. If she was drinking, she probably would have poked him in it. They acted like customers. She acted like a lady, well, she acted professional. It was fine with Leora as long as he leaves her alone. She hears Hector order a round of drinks for the trio. The crowd multiplies and soon Friday night is in full swing. The jukebox, once sporadic, now plays non stop.

Gabe yells above the Doobie Brothers, "Give me a VO and water on the rocks." He leaves a tip and blows her a kiss, heading for the pool table.

"A Godfather and two mugs of Miller."

"Rollin' Rock and two snake bites."

A man in a three-piece gray suit leans on the bar. "Do you know how to make a Rob Roy?" Nodding, Leora wipes the bar in front of him and empties the ashtray. "Okay. No, never mind. Do you really? Okay, we'll see." *See this.* "I'll have a Rob Roy chilled straight up, a margarita with an extra slice of lemon and a bottle of Michelob. Can you remember that? Do you want me to repeat it?"

Leora breathes deep. She did not like his condescending voice. "Do you prefer a glass or chilled mug with the Michelob?" she enunciates.

"Oh, yes, yes, a glass will be fine. Thank you."

Thank this. What a pain in the ass drinks. She gathers the strainer, salt, napkins, small stainless steel shaker; buries the stemmed glass and a rocks glass in the ice; and slips a tall chaser glass on the bottle of beer. *Ya look like a Rob Roy.*

"My name is Derrick. What's yours?" Mr. Better-Than-Thou-Attitude asks. She lays two lemon slices on a napkin calculating a total.

"Five seventy-five," she says aloud, looking into menacing brown eyes, "Leora."

No school-girl look, no apprehension, no innocence. *Head game this, Derrick the Derelict.* His intimidating look wanes into her deliberate stare.

He diverts his eyes, clears his throat, and slowly gropes his back pocket for his wallet, trying to salvage a morsel of control. Leora rolls her eyes, moving over to wait on some regular customers lining up next to him.

"What am I, flagged?" Sal asks grinning. "Give me a bottle of Bud."

"Busy, huh?" Bopper waves a ten. "Pitcher of Bud, three glasses."

"You know what I want, Sugar," Stick says. "Oh, and change for cigarettes."

By the time Leora finishes with Stick, she collects a ten off the bar in front of Derrick. He leans toward her with his hands full. "Keep the change," he says with a piercing look. Leora does not play into it.

Keep this, you phony bastard. "Thank you," Leora says demurely, walking away, never meeting his eyes.

Eva had settled her end of the bar and slipped down to cover Leora's end while she completed the time consuming drinks. She empties bottles, ashtrays, washes mugs, glasses, and shot glasses lining the well at the sink. Taking a step backward, she leans toward her coworker at the register. "Do you know who you just waited on?"

"Your sister," Leora answers, watching Fidget bank the eight ball corner pocket.

"Mayor Evely," Eva states. Leora turns to Eva, expressionless. "I don't know who the other two guys are, I can't really see from here, but they're sittin' with Griff."

Leora gets a sinking feeling in the pit of her stomach. She takes a deep breath, bobbing back and forth around customers, and goose necks the table. Eva finishes washing mugs and glasses and sits them on the drain. Leora smacks Eva's arm to get her attention while pointing to the far end of the bar. The barmaids stare stupefied at four empty seats. Goo and company are gone. The growing crowd swallows the empty stools as Friday night kicks into high gear.

"Two rum and Cokes."

"A Godmother, an iced tea, two bottles of Bud."

"An iced tea," Eva repeats, "Is this for you?"

The freckle-faced redhead grins at Eva, pointing to his buddy. "It's his birthday."

"Oh, I usually want to see what the person looks like before drinking this. Happy birthday!" Eva notices wet spots on his gray T-shirt. "What's it rainin'?"

"Yeah," he says to Eva's "girls." "It just started. It's dumpin'."

Leora spies Jammer going out the front door.

"There he goes again. Don't eat the beans!" Leora yells. "Eat cheese!"

"Rice! Eat rice!" Eva chimes in.

"Don't chew the gum!" Leora yells back to Eva.

Eva laughs. "What gum?" she yells to Leora.

"That laxative gum. The one Renee's kid gave to her ninth grade homeroom."

"He don't look bulimic to me," Eva hollers.

"He don't look clean either. Did you see his nails?"

"Yeah, did you see the corners of his mouth?"

"I think he needs an oil change in his hair," Leora shouts.

"Hey, I know! Maybe he has a toilet fetish."

"Nah, I don't think water is one of his strong suits."

"Well, then he's lookin' for the kitty litter."

"Yeah, his fingernails are dirty from coverin' it up."

"Let me have two bottles of Miller, a scotch on the rocks, and a harbor light."

Lightning flashes. Thunder claps. Lights flicker plunging the room into darkness, bringing the sound of silence.

Ana Gram

Within seconds, screams and laughter fill the ominous darkness followed by flickering Bics and Zippos. Eva opens the drawer under the register. Seeing with her hands, she identifies the flashlight and turns it on. Nothing. "Are you kiddin' me?" She roots through the drawer and comes up with a baggy of tea light candles. Leora dumps it one handed with a Bic in the other, spilling twelve or so onto the bar for lighting, placing them in empty ashtrays to scatter around the bar. In the meantime, Eva opens the cabinet door under the drawer, moving Leora's pocketbook and her own, feeling for the extra ashtrays. She lights more of the candles to place on the tables. Another flash . . . Growling thunder . . .

Sounds and voices seem amplified in the stillness as if reverberating off the darkness. It is almost like eavesdropping. Fifteen minutes pass. "I wonder why the emergency lights aren't comin' on." Eva's voice carries.

R-r-ring! R-r-ring! The phone demands attention. "Papa's . . . Hi, Papa!" Leora pats Eva on the arm. "No, they didn't. We were just talkin' about that. I don't know why they're not on." She nods to Eva. "Wow, really. No, well, we did find some candles. Yes, yes, no, okay." The lights blink on. "Oh, Papa, we have lights. Everything's back o—" Lightning splits the sky, bringing blackness once again as the powerful roar of thunder rattles windows and vibrates thoraxes. The phone goes dead.

"Keep those candles lit!" Eva yells.

"Papa said we can leave when Sonny and Hank show up," Leora tells Eva. "He thinks half the city is out. I guess now, all of it is."

No TV, no music, no exhaust fan.

"Are you still open?" asks rugged Simon, his five o'clock shadow visible even in the glow from a tea light. He stares straight ahead at nothing in particular. Leora leans on the bar in front of him. His smile is soft, his eyes empty.

"Well, why wouldn't we be open?" Simon turns in Leora's direction, leaning back a bit to focus holding on to the bar. He is tripping. She gazes into his brown eyes, searching for him, placing her hand on his forearm. Her face waves like Old Glory in the flickering light. He smiles.

"Yeah," Eva adds. She also leans on the bar in front of him. "We don't need television or music to be open." Simon turns slowly in Eva's direction, leaning back a bit to focus again. Her eyes and nose melt into her mouth. He smiles.

"Hell, we don't even need electricity." Leora cups her chin in her hands, waiting for her ex-neighbor's response. He is a mechanic, a good mechanic. Older than Crow and his buddies, around Leora's age, Simon had mentored the young car buffs. But that was a life time ago. Now he rents a room at the Star Hotel just over the bridge into Marcus Hook doing auto repair by word of mouth and lawn care. He tries to play along, speaking slowly in his unmistakable husky voice. His movements are sloth-like, turning back in Leora's general direction, talking to the air.

"But you can't ring up drinks without electricity."

"Oh, but, we, can." With her left hand, Eva taps a few of the keys on the register, mimicking a sale. Then with her right hand, she opens the opposite side of the machine, reaches in and pushes the release lever. Ding! The drawer pops open.

"Wow!" Simon turns slowly to the sound next to him. "How'd you do that?"

"Batteries, it works on batteries," Leora continues the ruse, trying to sound believable. "Uh, four of 'em."

In slow motion, Simon tries to tighten the rubber band in his dark brown hair. No success. He grins at the air in front of him. He can't focus on anything now. The girls know he's twisted. Simon is safe. He leans against the bar, closing his eyes, and taking a deep breath. He opens one eye in Leora's direction. "Oh, four, huh?"

"If it wasn't for the batteries, everything would be free." Eva follows suit.

"Free, huh?" Simon plays along, turning slowly to Eva with his one eye open. He closes it then opens both of his eyes. He stands up straight, holding on to the bar for balance, trying to focus and closes them. Leaning toward Eva, he pops one eye open again. "Free! I'll have a bottle of Bud!" He slurs his words slowly, turning his head left then right, smiling, trying to see something, somebody. He blinks, opening both eyes wide. The soft glow from the candle was not a hindrance. Flood lights wouldn't help.

"Oh, we can't give it to you for free." Eva leans on the bar in front of him.

"Awww, no." Leora taps his arm and leans in front of him, too, shaking her head. "It's simple, you didn't say Simon says!"

Simon blinks, mouth open, then stares blankly. He shrugs his shoulders, sighs, and smiles a warm smile, an honest smile. He digs in his pockets for money. A tatoo on each arm peeks from under his green short-sleeved shirt, exposing Marco-1968 in a banner under an eagle with wings spread and Bobby-1969 on a ribbon wrapped around praying hands. Simon's own tour of duty in Vietnam lasted a little over a year. He came home with a presidential citation, a Tet Offensive campaign ribbon, a Vietnam combat ribbon, post-traumatic stress, and drug addiction. He lost his brother Bobby in Nam and Lucas, his best friend, died in his arms there in Nam. His marriage fell apart, he lost job after job and himself. Leora sits a tall glass of ice water in front of him. Leaning sideways, he slides onto an empty stool. He smiles.

No shuffleboard, no pinball, no pool table. Some customers depart to the black world outside. The rest sit or stand in groups around the little candle bonfires in the immense room. Their conversations hang in the still air, mingling with cigarette smoke taxed to dissipate into the darkness above.

"It's gettin' stuffy in here," Eva says, grabbing a paper bag and fanning herself.

"Yeah, I think I smell armpits," Leora agrees. She ducks under the bar and drags one of the chairs from the tables to the darkened foyer.

"What the hell are ya doin'?" Fidget asks, perplexed, appearing from shadows in the front of the room.

"I'm proppin' the door open."

"Oh, I thought you were gonna try and check out the emergency lights. You still wouldn't be tall enough." Fidget laughs, flashing an ornery smile. Eva, Leora, and Fidget have known each other since junior high school.

Leora mimics her girl Gilda. "That's so funny I forgot to laugh."

"Hey, if she stands on your shoulders and you stand on the chair, she still won't be tall enough," Eva yells.

Fidget laughs again. He grabs another chair to prop the outside door.

"We don't need that one," Leora tells him. "That door has a stop on the bottom." Fidget shoves the extra chair to the table then helps Leora prop her chair under the doorknob. They walk into the darkness. Leora opens the right side of the double glass doors, kicking the stop down with her foot. Water drips from the eaves as the torrential rain smacks the sidewalk and parking lot, producing a sizzling sound in the city's blackout. Leora welcomes the cooler air rushing past her. They stare at the blackness. "A lot of strangers here tonight."

"Not any more. We're on a first name basis. I'm in their pocket," Fidget answers, lighting a cigarette. He offers the orange ember to her.

She takes a drag. "Ahhh, you must be winnin'!"

"Yeah, but I'm not playin'."

"You're not playin'?"

"Nah."

"Oh, who ya backin'?"

"Nobody, they're playin' partners."

"Oh! Side bets!" Lightning moves beyond the houses and trees. Thunder whispers in the distance. The rain slows to a hissing sound on the sidewalk and parking lot. Leora takes one more drag of his cigarette. "Who's playin' partners?"

Traffic lights blink on simultaneously with arc lights outlining city blocks. Night lights in businesses along the street join in; one by one, the neon lights in the Belle Shop windows and barber shop windows up the street from the night lights inside Gino's. Across the street from Gino's, neon reds and greens and yellows and blues pierce the darkness in the small shopping center. First the library, then bakery, deli, Chinese takeout, Laundromat, Papa's, and Sun Pharmacy. Across the one-way throughway, between the shopping center and Penn Fruit florescent lights illuminate empty registers in the front of the market. Homes twinkle on. The fixture above the front door suddenly drenches the entrance way with light as power is restored to the city. Moths protected under the eaves from the downpour fly in circles at the light. Water ripples through the parking lot toward Booth Street.

"Whoa!" Fidget yells. They shield their eyes like Indian scouts scanning horizons while they adjust to the light. He blinks at Leora grinning. "How?"

Leora blinks at Fidget. "And how." Her laughter and the sound of the exhaust fan fade into "Stayin' Alive" as the tavern lights and machines declare business as usual. "Who's partners? Who you bettin' on?"

Fidget grins. "Gabe and Fat Cat. They're crushin' 'em. I'm doin' fine." He displays a wad of money halfway out of his pocket for Leora's eyes only.

They walk through the door just as Gabe comes around the lattice carrying a pool stick. "You leavin'?" he asks, smoothing his beard with his free hand.

"Hell no." Fidget flicks his cigarette out the door.

"Ah 'ight, these guys wanna leave. But Cat and I agreed to a re-rack. Nothin' was made on the break before the lights went out, you in?"

"Hell yeah."

"It's showtime!" Leora says to her old classmate. She rubs his shoulders. "Loosen up! Loosen up!" She moves over to rub Fidget's shoulders. "Oh, shit! You're not playin'." They all laugh.

"Yo, Chooch, change me to Rollin' Rock," Gabe says, pointing to a couple of upside down shot glasses, "and a roll of quarters." He hands her a ten spot.

Leora and Eva are in demand. Spider taps his empty beer bottle on the bar.

Eva stops what she's doing and stands, holding three mixed drinks in one hand and three bottles of beer in the other. "You know what ya can do with that, don't cha? You're gonna wait. You'll be the last person I wait on, ya twit!"

"I just want a drink."

"Yeah, and what do you think everybody else here wants, my autograph? Stand in line." The girls handle the patrons even the returning ones. Leora spots one of the mayor's sidekicks heading for the bar. She has seen better rugs on a mannequin. She busies herself.

"Can I have a green elevator, bottle of Miller, and a brain hemorrhage?"

"I got it!" Leora sits an empty shot glass in front of Bart and Ernie. The mayor's sidekick waits.

"Make it two," Ernie says. Leora sets up another shot glass and fetches a bottle of Miller from one cooler and the bottle of Bailey's Irish Cream from the other. She makes a screwdriver and adds the green crème de menthe. Eva handles the Mayor's sidekick. *Good.* Leora grabs the grenadine and peach schnapps from the speed rack, along with the Bailey's on the drain. She pours half a shot of peach in both shot glasses then adds the Bailey's. Heavier than the schnapps, it sinks to the bottom, resembling a pile of worms in the form of a little brain. She adds a touch of grenadine. Voila! Brain hemorrhage. Bart and Ernie down them and order two more.

Sonny and Hank come through the front door, eyeballing the table by the jukebox. "Your So Vain" begins. Leora does a sing along with Carly Simon.

"Our relief is here!" Eva meets Leora at the taps.

"Everything okay?" Hank asks the girls.

"So far," Eva answers, "Everything's back on."

Fifty plus Sonny Liotta straightens the collar of his navy blue polo then pats his salt-and-pepper hair, making sure it lays flat. "What about the emergency lights?"

Eva shrugs her shoulders, shaking her head. "They never came on."

Leora makes a drinking gesture. The managers nod. She makes two Cutty and waters with lots of ice. A jingling tool belt precedes a young buck carrying a red tool box. A green T-shirt, atop tight jeans, strains against broad shoulders and sculptured biceps.

"We need to check his license," Eva says.

"Yeah," Leora adds, "he sure doesn't look like he's twenty-one."

"Twenty-one, who cares? I want his address!" The girls giggle.

The repairman looks about at the emergency lighting, shakes hands with Hank and Sonny, following Sonny to the storage room.

"That's the mayor over there," Hank says pointing to Griff's table.

"So it is," Eva plays stupid.

"Are the other two guys bodyguards?" Leora jumps on the bandwagon.

Hank crinkles his face. "No. The one is Carl Yarborough, I think. He couldn't beat his way out of a paper bag. He's a city councilman. The other guy is . . ." Hank goosenecks. "Ralph . . . Ralph Jackson. He's a lawyer. It is" –Hank goosenecks again –"It is Yarborough, with hair."

Eva snickers. "Well, he better get another one, that one sucks!"

Now Leora laughs. "Yeah, it looks used."

"I wonder what brings them to this neck of the woods. They usually haunt the Trade Winds in Media. They've been around here three or four Saturdays now."

"Griff's probably payin' 'em to show up." Leora's statement drips with sarcasm.

Eva adds to the mix. "They stick out like sore thumbs in their suits, especially sittin' with casual, classless Griff."

"This is a neighborhood joint," Leora says. "No phony plastic people allowed."

"Is that the worst horsehair?" Fiftyish Hank Pizzarelli runs his fingers through his thick gray hair; his matching chest hair protrudes from the top of his unbuttoned brown sports shirt.

"Yeah," Leora agrees.

"He looks like he has a dead animal on his head," Eva adds.

Leora laughs. "He looks like he's bein' attacked."

"He will be when somebody tries to beat the shit out of it!" Hank takes a swig of his drink then chews on the stirrer.

"What's he suppose to be? Incognito?" Leora asks.

"Yeah, like a sore thumb!" Eva answers.

"Hmm, think he's ever been to Red Run Cove?" Leora looks at Eva wide-eyed, fluttering her eyelashes, hoping Eva remembers her and Sydney's anagrams.

Eva nods smiling. "Oh yeah. Anna Grams, I know her." She knows there are four. Now all she has to do is remember the other three. Well, one of them anyway. "I don't know, ya think?"

"What, Cove?" Hank asks.

"Do you think he's lookin' for Stooping Leo?" Leora says with a big smile showing her teeth and fluttering her lashes again.

"Well, only if he's lookin' for Theresa Kale." Eva remembers one.

Leora nods, smiling. "Or if he knows Sarah Treet!" The barmaids do a high five.

"Remember you told Goo Goo to memorize them there would be a test later, and he played along and failed?" They laugh.

Hank is totally lost and confused. "What Theresa? Sarah? Leo who? What the hell are you two talkin' about? Hey, he's the mayor."

Leora mimicks Chevy Chase, "And you're not." She offers no explanation for their confusing conversation.

Sonny joins the trio huddling at the bar. The repairman jingles, bringing in an aluminum ladder.

"That's Carl over there, isn't it?" Hank asks Sonny.

"Yeah, I stopped by the table. You think it looks bad from here, you oughta see it up close." Sonny, only slightly taller than Eva, tiptoes squinting at the table.

"And is it alive?" Leora asks, wide-eyed and nodding.

"Yeah, I went to shake Carl's hand, and it went after me." Sonny smirks, bucking his eyes back and forth at the girls.

"You better get ready. You're gonna need one pretty soon." Eva refers to his thinning crown.

"He can have some of mine," Hank offers.

"Anything but a comb over," Leora says. "Besides, bald is beautiful."

"On some people," Eva adds. "What's he tryin' to recapture his youth?"

"Probably. His old lady divorced him last year and soaked 'im." Hank drains his drink just in time for Eva to place two fresh ones on the bar for the managers. She points to Gabe. They nod, raising their drinks.

"Is she a blonde?" Leora questions the duet, thinking about her conversation with Tom Dayton.

"Yep, her name is Alice. She's a realtor. Lister was her lawyer," Sonny says, yawning. "You know about Lister, right?"

"Yep, somebody whacked 'im." Men love to correct women. Leora counts on it.

"Nooo." Sonny drains his drink. "That's what Griff wants everybody to think. You see, the mayor, Griff, Lister, and Carl, Alice's husband, were partners. Plus Alice and Carl owned businesses together too—real estate, used cars, and an auto tags business. She ran the real estate business out of Media." Sonny tastes his fresh beverage.

"That's not all she ran," Hank explains, stirring his drink.

"Yeah, yeah," Eva agrees. "That was all over the papers. But so was Carl Yarborough. He ain't no saint either." Eva leans on the bar in front of Hank. "What about Carl and Back Alley Sally? That was in the paper, too. Why don't cha mention that? You men are all alike." Leora listens intently to the heated discussion. Kansas City blares from the jukebox. Sonny shuffles his feet, bouncing up and down.

"Besides, Saint Hank, you've been with Alice! Boda-da-boom, boda-da-bing!" She glances at the table, her eyes narrowing, looking back at Hank. "And Back Alley Sally! Bod-da-boom, bod-da-bing!"

Hank stands with his mouth wide open, dumbfounded.

Eva smiles a defiant smile. Leora looks at Eva then at Hank then back at Eva then back at Hank. *Holy shit! Your turn, Mr. Horny.*

Sonny continues the conversation. "Alice's divorce hearing was in Delaware. But Ralph Jackson, Carl's lawyer, sittin' there at the table, tried to move it to Pennsylvania. The courts go by main residence, and their house was in Delaware. Carl ended up with the used cars and auto tags businesses in Media, Alice got the real estate business and the mortgage free house. And when she was awarded alimony, Carl threatened both of them right there in the courtroom."

"But he didn't kill 'im, so what's the problem?" Leora asks above Kiss.   .

"No," Hank answers, perturbed. "The problem is Griff involved New York."

"See, in the beginning of April, the Feds were gettin' ready to indict the four of 'em," Sonny explains. "When Lister was found dead, Griff yelled hit tryin' to keep the Feds at bay, you know, takin' heat away from Carl, him and the mayor's illegal activities while they regrouped someplace else. The Feds knew Lister had a heart attack but sat on it. So when Griff cried wolf they were hopin' New York disappeared him. But it didn't happen. He must really have somethin' on them big time! And Alice can make a saint swear and the devil say a prayer." Sonny cuts his eyes at Hank, then blinks back and forth at the barmaids. "So when she batted her baby blues and told them about Carl's threats, they were more than willing to jump back in it."

"And there's no love lost between Griff and Carl," Hank adds, "because Griff knew about Lister and Alice and never said anything to Carl."

"So what is the big deal? It's business as usual." Leora shrugs her shoulders.

Sonny leans on the bar. "It's a little more than that. The Feds cited probable cause and raided Carl's businesses in Media and the mayor's office, uncovering a shitload of dummy corporation papers and deeds to fake properties."

"Oh, so it's hot in Media. That's why they're hangin' around here. They left their pitchforks in the car." Eva straightens up, folding her arms in front of her.

"Salvatore said it was okay as long as there's no trouble and he stays away from you." Hank turns his head and looks straight at Leora.

"Why would Papa believe him?" Leora questions. "He'd lie if the truth fit. Just look at the table. If they're all pointin' fingers at each other, why are they sittin' there rubbin' elbows?"

"It's like keep your friends close and your enemies closer," Eva concludes, nodding affirmatively and grabbing a bar rag on her way to clean up a spilled beer.

"Well, I guess," Hank says, "if you're Ringo and your friends are George, Paul, and John."

Leora laughs so hard she starts coughing.

"What?" Eva folds the bar rag on the beer well. Leora repeats Hank's statement. Eva cracks up. "What? You named them?"

Hank shakes his head. "Tsk! Tsk! You girls don't know nothin'. That's the signatures on the fake properties and the dummy corporations that weren't signed by any of them. They got samples of their handwriting. None of them matched. And the talk is there's some kind of flaw that proves the contracts were typed on the same typewriter Lister used for his business transactions. But they can't find it. It's in the wind along with a ledger full of names, numbers, payoffs . . . everything!"

"So now it's one down, three to go. Which one's the blackmailer?" Leora looks at the table of suspects. "Imagine" plays on the jukebox. She sings along, leaning her elbows on the bar with her hands straight up and resting her chin on her right bicep.

Eva leans on the bar next to Leora and also stares at the table. "I got nothin'."

"Carl would kiss and tell. So would Jammer and Hector," Sonny offers.

"I think the mayor would destroy all of it," Hank says. "Bad for re-election."

"Well, Griff would blackmail his own mother. Or maybe they lost it. Remember the big bust last year, that whole garage full of weed. It all went missin'." Leora changes position, folding her arms on the bar. "No evidence, no charges. How convenient."

"Yeah, so then everybody's in the clear." Eva nods in agreement.

"Not necessarily." Sonny stirs his drink with his finger. "Where's the money?"

Eva looks puzzled. "Confiscated. The Feds confiscated it. It's evidence."

Leora looks puzzled. "Wait a minute. There's no money, no signatures, no nothin'. No evidence. The Feds know he wasn't whacked so they get to keep the money, and everything goes away. End of story." It makes sense to Leora.

"Come on, you think they'd all be sittin' at that table if the Feds had the money?" Hank sits his empty glass on the bar. "We're talkin' a lot of money here."

"You have to remember you can't trace cash unless it's put in a bank account. Nobody's been arrested, so somebody's got a matress full. Somebody's loaded." Sonny also finishes his drink, sitting a tingling glass of ice cubes on the bar. "How long have they been here?"

"Too long," Leora says dumping the ice in the funnel to make fresh beverages.

"Alice is in deep shit," Eva states.

Hank has no patience. "Do the math. Griff, the Mayor, Alice's ex. She's not sittin' at the table." He dismisses Eva with his hand.

Leora places drinks in front of the managers. "Hey, ya got Huey, Louie, and Dewey." Leora counts on her fingers. "They're all sittin' at the same table. They're not pointin' at each other. Why wasn't Alice invited?" Leora gawks at the table. "I know, the devil dog made 'em do it!"

"Saints preserve us!" Eva yells. The girls laugh themselves simple.

Sonny takes a big gulp of his Cutty and water. "Salvatore doesn't need this."

"Need what?" Leora glances at the table. "Are they gonna shoot each other?"

"No, no, no, everything's fine." Sonny pats Leora's arm.

"Well, somebody is in deep shit. That's probably why Griff called this stupid tea party. He's probably sittin' on all of it, and now he's tryin' to decide how to set one of 'em up, or all of 'em." Leora looks at the table, right into Griff's cold stare. Anger surges over her, swallowing her feeling of intimidation and flushing her cheeks. She scratches the side of her face with her middle finger, turning back to the conversation with the trio.

"Well, I think maybe one person has the money, one has the ledger, and one has the typewriter." Eva says, counting on her fingers. "You can destroy the ledger, but the typewriter is still out there. The only happy person is the one with all the money. Which one's smilin'?" All heads at the table seem bowed in deep discussion.

"It's a prayer meeting. Those devils! I knew it!" Eva nods in agreement, laughing again.

Sonny and Hank stand, shaking their heads. Leora leans in with a somber look on her face. "Hey, I think Griff would steal a loaf of bread, eat half, give you the other half then turn your sorry ass in." She places coasters on the bar for Tuna and Mortimer.

"Yeah," Eva says, leaning on the bar, "and that's experience talkin.'" Sister Sledge sparks a sing-along as Eva starts for her end of the bar, doing the cha-cha on the way to Bart and Ernie waving for her attention. Leora digs in the cooler for two Bud long necks.

"Yo, Chooch!"

Careless Whispers

"*Y*o, Chooch!" Sydney hollers again.

"Yo, Chooch!" Leora yells, popping the caps off the beer bottles. "I was gettin' ready to send out reinforcements." She places the bottles on the coasters. Mortimer kisses Leora's hand, pushing a ten spot to her. Tuna points to Sydney.

"Boy, did it pour! It got cold!" Sydney says, doing the Bump with Tuna.

"You missed it, Sis. We lost everything, even the emergency lights. It was pitch-black in here," Leora tells her cohabitant on her way to fill three customers' needs.

Tuna puts his arm around Sydney, noticing her bell-bottom jeans wet halfway to her knees. "Look at your feet." Sydney glances at her Dr. Scholl's. "Where's your umbrella?"

"Oh, I wasn't walkin', I was drivin'. I stepped in a small flood gettin' in the car. Ninth Street is flooded, too just before Joe's Junkyard. I had to drive through Buckman Village and down Keystone Road."

Fat Cat nods, waving to Tuna. Tuna nuzzles Sydney's hair. "You better not be walkin' in the rain. Sugar melts." He places two dimes in her hand to call him, a ritual he performs when their paths cross. He follows Mort to the pool table.

"So, what's happ'nin'?" Leora asks, bursting at the seams, sitting a Michelob in front of her and pointing to Tuna.

"Yeah, what's up?" Eva asks, joining them in the middle of the bar.

"Where's Goo Goo?" Sydney glances around. She spots Griff's table whispering back and forth gawking at her. Sydney glares at them with disdain.

"Yeah, what da ya think of that tea party?" Leora asks nodding toward the table.

"What's he readin'? Tea leaves?" Sydney asks sarcastically. She turns to Leora with a wide-eyed stare, blinking profusely.

"Now, now ladies," Sonny says smiling, interrupting Sydney's signal.

"Maybe they're lookin' in his crystal balls," Eva says. "Right, Sonny?"

"What? Oh! What you're askin' me? Tsk, tsk, tsk." Sonny bucks his eyes.

"Well, he's not readin' cards 'cause we know he's not playin' with a full deck." Concern creeps across Leora's brow as she studies her best friend's somber stare. "Yo, Sis, let me give you some 'ketchup.' That is actually a prayer meeting. You know Heckle, uh, Hector, whatever. Then there's Donald and his three nephews. The one guy droolin' is Mayor Evely, the one with the dead animal on his head is Carl Yarborough. He had an auto tags place, sold used cars and did real estate with his soon-to-be ex-wife, Alice. She ran the real estate business part in Media and ran Griff's partner in crime Lister, you know Loophole, the lawyer, they found dead in the mayor's car from a heart attack. The other guy is a lawyer, somebody Jackson. I guess they needed a new one."

"Oh, and," Eva adds, "Doc went back with Trudy again last weekend and thinks he's comin' to my place tonight. My kids are gone 'til Sunday. I'm goin' clubbin'."

"You're kiddin' me." Sydney tries sorting everything in her mind.

"Oh yeah," Leora talks above Kenny Rogers. "There's a lot of money some place, well, stashed or somebody's sittin' on it or the Feds have it, I don't know. Not like in a fake property or business, but in dollars. But not in a bank account 'cause then the Feds could confiscate it. Sonny and Hank said it's like piles of money." Leora makes an ugly confused face. "I guess they're waitin' for somebody to come right out and say, 'Hey! I got it!' Damn, I was sorta hopin' for a High Noon at midnight but it came and went. They're like long lost friends.'"

Sydney leans on the bar listening intently, mouth open trying to follow and absorb. "You're kiddin' me!"

"Would I lie to you, Sis? Oh," Leora whispers ever so softly, "we're done early tonight. I can leave any time."

"Yeah, I'll stay here a little longer, split the tips and clean up a little. I'll see you at the Empire Club." Eva grabs an empty pitcher for a refill.

"Oh, before I forget," Sonny starts.

"Right, Sonny?" Leora places her hand on Sonny's mouth. "Right? Right?"

Sonny removes her hand and kisses it. "What? What? What?"

"You and Hank are here for the duration, right?"

"Yeah, sure, sure, you girls can go any time. But before I forget, are you busy tomorrow night?" Sonny questions Sydney.

"Ya want me to be?" Sydney says smiling.

"Well, yeah, maybe." Sonny stands next to Sydney and pats her hand. "Just a couple hours, there might be a party, birthday, anniversary, I forget. But Marcie might get swamped. You know, like eight to ten or eleven, you know a couple hours or so."

"Yeah, three customers and Marcie's swamped." She clears her throat. 'I'm in."

"So what's happ'nin'?" Leora leans toward Sydney.

"Yeah, what's up?" Eva says chewing at the bit.

Sydney forces a gigantic fake smile for Sonny and takes a big swig of her Michelob, stalling until he meanders out of earshot. "He wasn't there."

"He wasn't there? What do you mean he wasn't there? What . . . you mean like you just missed 'im?"

"Na-uh, he wasn't there. The first three people I talked to never heard of him." Sydney stands with her back to the tea party. "He hangs there every now and then. He don't work there. He's never worked there. Nobody has seen him for about two months since he started workin' at Red Run Cove!"

The barmaids stand silent. Eva with confusion on her face, Leora, eyes wide, mouth wider. They look at Sydney then each other then Sydney, then each other . . .

Magic Carpet Ride breaks the silence. The men at the table stand, shaking hands. Leora works her end of the bar and Eva works hers. Sydney stands, facing the bar across from the taps, getting a glimpse of the trio through the mirrors as they leave. Griff heads for the men's room. Hector walks to the bar to refill their drinks, standing to the left of the lanky redhead grinning at her. Leora nods to Eva. Eva stands in front of Sydney.

"Hi," Sydney says demurely. She slides her denim bag on her shoulder and jams her hands into her jeans' pockets. Eva works him too. She cups her ear, leaning slightly toward the bar, pretending not to hear him. "Huh?" She takes a couple steps closer, leaning in front of Hector. "What?" She stands in front of him, leaning forward. Hector leans on the bar and talks to the "girls" as if they are speakers for ordering drinks.

"Later," Leora tells Eva, grabbing her jeans jacket, and pocketbook on her way to the open end of the bar. Watching the men's room door, she walks to the opposite side of the charcoal pit, toward the back exit, disappearing into the storage room.

Eva places an upside down shot glass in front of Sister Syd pointing to Hector. "Thank you," she purrs, reaching across in front of him with her right arm for an ashtray, thus making her lean ever so close. Emeraude surrounds him, permeating his nostrils.

"I think I'll play the jukebox," Sydney says aloud to no one in particular. Hector lifts his drinks from the bar and follows limping. He sits the drinks on the table and stands ever so close to femininity, feeding the jukebox.

"A-22," Sydney tells the aroused buyer. Hector does his best rendition of manual labor, pushing buttons for her selections. Bopper walks over and bends his six-foot-six frame, kissing Sydney on the top of her head. "Mrs. Jones," he suggests.

"C-11," Sydney says, practically cooing. Hector obliges.

Griff returns to the table by the jukebox, eyeballing Sydney. He stirs his drink. "You didn't get a glass of ice?" He yells at Hector.

"Huh?" Hector looks into Griff's stare, getting an instant reality check.

Griff grits his teeth. "I'll get it." He walks to the bar with a Hector shadow. Sydney turns her head to the left, fluffing the right side of her hair and watches. Sonny waits on Griff. Eva busies herself, tiptoeing to watch angry Griff in the mirrors. He looks up and down the bar, scanning the room then turns to Hector with a flurry of obscenities. He hustles out the front door with his glass of ice and his Hector shadow. Now it is Sydney's opportunity to disappear into the storage room, privy to the chosen few with its brooms and mops and buckets and dustpans, an ice machine, extra bottles of Jacquin's, Smirnoff's and what-not while on the other side is a locked safe, a filing cabinet, and a black princess telephone atop a mahogany desk where Leora waits in darkness. In the middle standing by the back wall are steps.

The girls forego the lights, climbing the wrought-iron spiral staircase leading to Sydney's old apartment. Leora unlocks the deadbolt on the apartment door, returning the key to the old homemade hide-a-key magnetic box. She hands it to Sydney, who offers it to the underside of the metal steps where it grabs with a click. This was Papa's apartment. Years ago when he arrived from Italy speaking very little English, he settled in Philadelphia with his wife and first child. Hardworking in this land of milk and honey, he was ready, willing and able when an opportunity of becoming a business owner presented itself. Long hours and train rides to Philly drained him. He hired help for his business while remodeling the huge areas above the bar into two apartments. Upon completion, he took the rear apartment as his home away from home, no longer commuting on a daily basis. He built the metal stairway for safety purposes, avoiding the outside world altogether where evil lurks in the darkness, waiting for its own kind of opportunity. The deadbolt shuts, sealing them in stuffy darkness. They flick their Bics, maneuvering through the cramped quarters.

"He's a liar," Leora whispers, opening the apartment door, taking a deep breath. "I don't care what he told Papa. If looks could kill, I'd be dead tonight. I don't like 'im. I don't trust 'im and if I did I still wouldn't like 'im."

"Hey, when he noticed you were gone he freaked!"

"He's gonna stay away from me? Yeah right . . . and I'm a virgin! Why doesn't he just worry about the Feds and go proposition somebody? What is his problem?"

"I don't know. All I know is I'm gettin' bad vibes." Sydney shivers with a chill.

"I hear ya." They walk through the long hallway with nothing but wall on the left, past the empty front apartment on the right then down the stairs to the glass front door. The lights from the parking lot illuminate the left wall. The girls stand against the wall on the opposite side, invisible in the darkness.

"Ya think Goo has the money? Ya think Griff has it? Leora grabs the door handle, turning to Sister Syd. "Ya think Griff is settin' Goo up? Ya think that Alice chick is bein' set up?"

"Maybe they're settin' you up." Silence reigns, and they both get wet. You could hear a pin drop, but they hear footsteps approaching the door. The girls stand, pressed against the wall, unable to breathe. Someone jiggles the locked door.

"What are ya doin'?" They recognize Hector slurring his words.

"Oh! I'm waitin' for a bus!" Griff shakes the glass door violently. "What the hell do ya think I'm doin'?" He cups his eyes and peers through the glass.

"They're not out back. Their cars are still here," Hector offers in his own defense. "They're in the bathroom."

"What, gettin' a bath? Don't mention their names, ta anybody, ya hear me, nobody? Where the hell is Jammer? What the hell is takin' him so long? Son-of-a-bitch!"

"I shoulda went with him."

"Yeah, 'cause you're useless here . . ." Their voices diminish, walking the thirty feet or so back to the barroom door.

The girls breathe deep, relaxing from their frozen positions in the corner against the wall. "What the hell is goin' on?" Leora whispers. "He's nuts!"

"Nuts ain't the word for it! He's obsessed!" They step nervously out of the shadows, looking out the glass door.

Leora sighs. "I thought he heard my heart poundin'."

"I did!" Sydney swallows hard.

"I heard your stomach growl," Leora says, rootin' for her car keys.

"Thank God that's all it was!" They laugh. "I'm glad he yells."

"We gotta get outta here! We can walk past the bar door to get to our cars down the other end, or we can take the long way around the back to get there."

"Or," Sydney whispers, "We can use Eva's car. Her vibes are nervous, too." She jingles the keys. They peer out the door and see Eva's green Pontiac backed into the parking space right in front of the pharmacy on the left.

"Oh! My God! Go, Eva! I owe her a drink!" Leora squeals. They wait a few minutes, mustering up courage then bolt for Eva's car, scrambling into the back, shadowed by the front seats blocking the parking lot lights. Their courage seems to work rather well in the shelter of darkness. Long-legged Sydney sprawls across the backseat while Leora sits on the floor behind the driver's seat. There is plenty of room what with the front seat pulled forward, compensating for Eva's short stature.

Sydney pulls the multicolored granny squares afghan from the back window, flips it down over her feet, and completely covers herself, offering some to Leora.

"How did you get so wet?" Leora whispers, sitting up a little to peek out the back passenger's side window at the tavern's doors.

"When I left the Chateau, it was dumpin'," Sydney whispers back. "I thought Mother Nature unzipped a cloud."

"What time did you get there?"

"I got there before it started rainin'. What a hike. I finally spoke to one of the barmaids and a waitress. They said, 'Oh, you mean Daffy? He told them he got a job to do one thing but was really gonna do somethin' entirely opposite. I rolled my eyes and listened. You know the standard double talk. He told them he was gonna gain trust and infiltrate an operation by setting up a chance meeting but couldn't give 'em any details. It's a Red Run Cove!" Sydney says with a deep voice.

"What? Espionage? Puh-l-e-e- a-se! What the hell's he think he is . . . a spy? Spy this! There's no way he could work for the Feds. If he is, this country's in trouble."

Sydney snickers. "I asked the two of 'em if he was Matt Helm. They giggled. He told 'em he has a wife and two kids in "Okra'oma" Sydney enunciates. "I asked 'em if he leaps tall buildings with a single bound. They giggled again and said they didn't know about that, but he did clear a table one time when somebody decked 'im." The girls muffle their laughter with the afghan. "That's why I said Red Run Cove earlier. You know, undercover scrambled is red run cove, right? I was gonna say Stooping Leo – (stoolpigeon), but it's more like Theresa Kale – (there's a leak) or Sarah Treet – (there's a rat). Anyway, I told the bimbos at the Chateau, Daffy has more bullshit than Carter got little liver pills. The parkin' lot was full of ripplin' rain from the downpour when I left there. I went home to change. We got a problem, Sis."

"What at the house? Did the creek flood?"

"No, but Ninth Street is a wash out this side of the junkyard."

"Did you see Wheezer?"

"I didn't see Tiger, but I saw a Theresa Kale and a Sarah Treet at the house."

Fifty feet away from them the bar door opens. They throw the afghan over their heads. Leora pokes her finger through the afghan, stretching the holes a bit to see who it was. Her heart is pounding again. It was only Hector. He glances around, scratching himself, yawning, stretching. He flicks his cigarette then heads inside the bar.

Leora locks all the doors and cracks the driver's side windows. "What are you sayin'? Somebody was in the house?"

"Well, not somebody, two bodies, and they had flashlights. I came home the back way up Township Line Road and turned on to Chestnut Street. The whole city was out. I went to pull up at the house, and I saw a light movin' in your bedroom and a light movin' through the downstairs. I went around the block and came back down the street. The closest vehicle to our house was a black van, so I parked behind it. It was facin' me, but it was the closest thing I could find."

"Oh, wow, Sis! Did you call the cops?"

"I was gonna go in and call after they left. So I waited. Then I saw a flashlight comin' toward me. I bent over and laid on the seat thinkin', *Please don't let 'im have a gun.* I thought I was a goner. I thought he was comin' after me. But he stood in the street and opened the side doors on the van. I held my breath. Then I heard 'im talkin'. He said, 'Come on, say something.' Talk, damn it!" She takes a deep breath. "Sis, it was Rob!"

Leora's skin crawls. She shivers. "You mean Goo Goo's Rob?"

"Yeah, Sis, Rob the Verb. The piece of shit that says he hails from Okra'oma! I thought he was talkin' to me, so I sat up just in time to watch him climb out of the side of the van. I saw his flashlight disappear through our front door. I sat there awhile. Then the rain stopped, and the lights came back on, so I decided to get the hell outta there. I drifted past the house with my lights off until I hit Ninth Street. It was flooded, so I went up Langley and turned into Buckman Village. I came down Keystone Road. Hey, he's got a van. He probably cleaned us out."

"Oh, my nerves!" Leora says. She grabs Sydney's hand. "Oh, your nerves! Let's play somethin' else. I don't wanna play this anymore. What is goin' on?"

"I got to thinkin' while I was sittin' there. Remember last week we were so full of ourselves thinkin' they were gonna try and get to Goo Goo through us?"

"Yeah, mums the word unless he mentioned it first, right?"

"Well, ya think they really are after him? Or do ya think Goo Goo is settin' us up? Ya think he has all the money and made up the story about a stolen car?"

Leora cringes. "And paid us with marked bills to get 'em off his trail and put 'em on ours? He was here earlier tonight and booked when they showed up."

"Well, they won't find mine," Sydney states. "They're restin' comf'tably in a plastic bag in the box of laundry detergent."

"Mine are in the paper towel roll. Let's get the hell outta here."

"Hey, you drive," Sydney whispers, handing the keys to her best friend. "I'll tie myself up in knots tryin' to climb up there."

Leora pushes the back of the passenger's seat forward to climb into the driver's side just as a vehicle turns into the parking lot entrance right in front of them. The girls assume their positions. They hear it stop a short distance past them, and they hear the bar door open. Leora sits up and pokes the afghan again with her fingers. She taps Sydney. Sister Syd leans on one arm and stretches the afghan with the other.

Griff and Hector walk over to the black van. Jammer slides out of the passenger side, a cattail on sea legs. "Where the hell ya been?" Griff yells, holding the door. Jammer high steps toward the bar. "Where the hell ya think you're goin'?" Jammer cannot walk and talk. He stops.

"To get a drink," Jammer answers, slurring his words facing the bar.

"That's the van!" Sydney whispers. "That's the van!"

"Well, make it to go! And you," he yells, pointing to Hector, "go get my cigarettes and my jacket."

"What kind of beer?" Jammer yells above the running engine. "Yo, Rob—"

"Michelob."

"Did you find it?" Griff asks, holding the door open.

"No," Rob yells, leaning toward the open door, "I didn't think it was broke. I couldn't find the box. She moved it or emptied it. I did two new ones in different places. They're more high tech. We don't have to get so close."

"What about the typewriter?"

"No. I didn't see it. It's in a black case with the word 'Royal'on it, right? I looked in as many places as I could. Oh yeah, I caught your boy drinkin' their VO. I put some water in the bottle. We're late because he lost the key. I found it and put it back."

"That asshole." Griff shakes his head. "I want that son-of-a-bitchin' machine! I can't believe the jackass piece of shit dropped dead!" Frustrated, Griff screams leaning toward Rob. "What about the ledger?" Rob's negative answer sets Griff off again. He punches the inside of the door then shoves it. It squeaks to its limit then snaps back, hitting him in his face. He spews an array of vulgarities, breathing through his mouth, holding his face. He pulls a wad of bills out of his pocket and peels off three or four, throwing them on the passenger seat. "Drop him off at my apartment," Griff barks, wiping his face and checking his hand for blood. "Don't give 'im the keys. Shove 'em under the passenger seat."

The girls hold each others' hands with white knuckles. They had seen enough. They had heard enough. They slide down, lying as flat as humanly possible under the afghan. Griff's jingling car keys fade. The bar door opens several more times.

"Over here, you dumb bastard!" Griff yells to Hector, trying to climb in the van following the beer. He points to the van and then at the street. "Get outta here!"

Silence reigns again. Several minutes pass before Leora finally sits up slowly, peeking through the afghan until the bar door comes into view. She scans the parking lot. All's quiet on the west end front. They uncover their heads, still holding each others' hands.

Leora climbs into the driver's seat. "Do you want to go back in the bar?"

"Hell no! I'd rather put salt in my eyes! These are some twisted-ass people! I'm not gettin' out of this car! Let's just go with plan A and get the hell outta here!"

Leora pulls straight out of the parking lot, hangs a right, and guns it. Sydney rolls the back window up and shivers. Their stomachs are in knots. She pushes the back of the passenger seat forward and turns the radio down. She cracks the front window and lights cigarettes for her and her best friend. Leora catches a green light at Booth Street and flies to Highland Avenue, making a left. Not until they make their way onto I-95 north to the Empire Club does the duet begin to relax.

Sydney tries to lighten the mood. "Hey, if Hector ever went to stupidity school, he'd be last in his class."

Leora laughs. "Or first with honors. He's sure not the brightest star in the sky."

"Bright? Let's face it, he don't even twinkle. Hey, you realize when we get to the club we have to get out of this car."

"Yeah, but first we'll stop at the Sunoco station at Twenty-Second and Edgemont? We'll use the bathroom, and I'll buy Eva some gas. That's the least we can do. Then we'll go to the club and wait in the parkin' lot 'til she gets there."

"Sounds like a plan. I'm in." Sydney takes a deep breath. "And whatever we do, we do it together."

"Yep, there's strength in numbers," Leora agrees, pulling into the gas station.

"I'll drink to that. Let's calm our nerves."

"Calm 'em, hell! I'm drownin' mine!"

They buy gas, use the bathroom, and shoot up the road, breezing through four green lights then down over the creek into Woodlyn where the street morphs into Mac Dade Boulevard with a right-turning lane for entrance into the shopping center of the same name. They ride slowly through the parking lot. "What is this? Bring your black van tonight? What the hell?" Sydney yells out the window as Leora pulls in front of the fifth one. Satisfied this also was not the van in question, the girls cruise for a parking spot, finding one right near the front.

Leora's mind wanders through the evening's chain of events. "We shoulda got a six-pack and went home." On beer, Leora is like a rattlesnake after you wake it up.

Sydney roots through her pockets and denim bag.

"Woulda, shoulda, coulda." Leora watches Sydney with a bit of perplexity. "What are ya doin', Sis?" Leora rubs her forehead.

Sydney turns to her co-conspirator. "Well, you said the word 'we'. What da ya got, a mouse in your pocket? I'm lookin' for mine."

Leora laughs. "Nah-uh, It's me, myself, and I and then with you, yourself and suds. I'm in!"

"Oh, strength in numbers, well, that's our back-up."

"What?"

"We got the big guns, you on suds! You drink, I'll point!"

Leora nods. "Ah 'ight. I'm in!"

"Yepper! That's the hot set-up! I'm in!"

"Besides, I'm gettin' a headache," Leora says, rubbing her forehead and temples.

"And she's gettin' a headache! Well, we can tie one hand behind your back! Get'em, Sis!" Sydney holds the back of her neck. "I'm gettin' one, too. Couldn't be our nerves, could it?"

"Oh, hell no! Just because on the one hand we're bein' set up by the Feds or Goo Goo or Griff or D—all the above." Leora cuts the engine, holding the top of her head. "While on the other hand, we have this obsessed bastard in need of some wall to wall counseling on the definition of the word no." She sits back and turns to Sydney. "And plus on top of all this, we're sneakin' around like we did somethin' wrong."

"Nah-uh," Sydney answers. "That couldn't possibly be it." She sighs. "I know, we're dehydrated."

Eva toots, riding by and pulls into a parking spot at the end of the row.

"Mums the word," Leora says, taking a deep breath.

Sydney nods, returning the folded afghan to the rear window. "Ready, Sis?"

"Yeah, I'm in. A bottle of beer no glass."

 Help Me, Rhonda

"*H*ey!" Eva yells, walking to the curly twosome. "What a strange night. We made like one eighty-two a piece! I thought you'd be waitin' in the club."

"Na-uh, we didn't want ya to walk down there by yourself. You know, bad vibes," Leora answers, taking the money from her coworker. "Thanks."

"I'll tell ya," Eva starts. "Ya know, Hank is such a putz. I'm tryin' to leave, and he's up the end of the bar actin' like he owns the damn place, orderin' drinks for him and some bimbo. I waited on 'im and charged 'im, too. Now he's a pissed puttz. Wow, that's the fastest I've seen him move in a long time." Eva laughs a deliberate laugh.

The live band can be heard outside the entrance to the underground club. "Ladies." A couple of hop heads shuffle to the door. "How's it goin'?" The last one lingers, watching Leora tuck three tens in with the "girls" and slip the rest of the money into her back pocket.

"It's goin.' It's good. Ah 'ight." All three give answers to the candy man; a known supplier of Christmas trees, black beauties, and Quaaludes.

"Hey, speakin' of bad vibes, I heard Griff tell Hector he wasn't goin' to jail for nobody dead or alive," Eva starts. She elbows Leora, bucking her piercing black eyes. "You think he was pissed when you left" – she points at Leora then points at Sydney – "when he found out you disappeared he went berserk! He told Hector he was gonna have 'im castrated. He was tryin' to whisper, you know, like through clenched teeth. You know how that goes. I got bits and pieces here and there, somethin' about laundry.

Come to think of it, it might have been laundering, somethin' about bugs and rats, ahh, oh, and about blackmail, back stabbers, evidence."

"I wonder who he's settin' up. You'd think Heckle 'n' Jeckle. But he can't replace them. He can't find anybody as stupid as they are. I just wish he'd stay the hell away from me." Leora closes her eyes, rubbing her temples.

"He really wanted to know where you disappeared to, but he didn't dare ask Sonny or Hank or me for that matter. You were in my car, right?"

"Oh, yeah, snug as a bug in an afghan," Sydney answers. "But we couldn't get out of the parkin' lot 'cause they kept comin' outside."

"I know!" Eva says, exchanging car keys with Sydney. "He was cussin' up a storm! He gave Jill ten bucks to check the ladies' room. He told her he'd fire Hector's sorry ass, but he's so dumb—"

The girls say in harmony, "How dumb is he?"

"He's so dumb he'd probably try to collect unemployment. And Jilly Bean the dingbat is so dumb—"

Interrupting again, the duet repeats almost in monotone, "How dumb is she?"

Eva snickers. "Well, he spent like fifteen minutes explaining about payin' cash, you know, under the table. I walked by one time, he was sayin' somethin' about Feds with magnifying glasses, another time about sittin' under a microscope, another time about tax evasion, backstabbers, ya know, the whole nine yards. She looked him right in his face and said, "Well, it doesn't matter" —Eva wrinkles her nose, mimicking Jill's nasal voice – "If he is a loyal worker, it doesn't matter who you work for, a loyal worker is a loyal worker. My brother-in-law collected when he was laid off, you work all that time you should collect. He should collect." Eva shakes her head. "Ya know how she never shuts up. Griff stood there stone-faced. I guess maybe she thinks he sits under the table and pays 'im. I don't know, whatever. He motioned to me and ordered her a drink and told me not to hand it to her but to put it where she was sittin' and get her the hell away from him. He was grittin' his teeth the whole time." She walks behind them laughing. The live band's rendition of "Atlanta Rhythm Section" escapes through the glass door Sydney is holding open for the two barmaids. "Ain't he just adorable?" Eva laughs again.

"As a tarantula." Sydney smiles, nodding to the beat of the music as the glass door clangs shut.

"Look who it is! No wonder we had all that rain tonight," Bear announces to Blade and Coma as he steps from behind the podium. Just like Tom Dayton, visits to the club for Eva were few and far between; although five years ago, the single-mother-of-two-turned-barmaid, had waited tables at the club. Part time, she became a weekend fixture, perfecting the equation of a man and his ego equals a fool and his money . . . with plenty of egos equaling plenty of fools to practice on. And at the time, there was less Bear and more hair. "How are ya, Miss Eva? Broken any hearts lately? I haven't seen you in two years?" he exaggerates, kissing her hand.

Eva captures Bear's smug grin with a piercing stare and a smirk, tugging the corners of her mouth. "It's only been about nine months." The buxom brunette tilts her head, batting her eyes going in for the kill. "As a matter of fact"—her lilting voice steadily becoming deeper and enunciated—"it was your birthday, this past February, when your wife came down the steps with a birthday cake complete with candles and saw a platinum blonde in pasties pop out of your other birthday cake. Did the hospital find all the candles?" She tilts her head to the other side; no blinking, just staring.

"How's the kids? How's the kids?" Bear ushers Eva to the top of the last flight of steps, nodding to Leora and Sydney while turning beet red. "It's great to see you, always great to see you. Have a good time." He flips his hair over the back of his collar, rushing back to the podium and busies himself; still a blush color. The trio whistles and yells, waving to Pearl in the kitchen. They wade through the crowded club to the first bar as the band Chaos finishes their set. Leora spies Griff and Hector at the far end of the second bar in his usual seat. She had never really noticed Griff as a permanent fixture at the club, partly because her presence was few and far between, and Griff's profile was low and uninteresting unlike now with his belligerent attitude and hostile behavior. Leora nudges Sydney for a heads-up. Tony points at Sydney. She leans in with a ten spot; ordering two bottles of beer and a vodka and Coke. She removes the chaser glasses from the long necks, sitting them on the ten dollar bill. She nods a thank you to Tony then gathers the liquids passing them out. The glass containers clink as they toast stupid horny men with money. They stand against the left wall near the front of the first bar, out of the high traffic area, scanning the far end; no Goo Goo. The atmosphere is totally different from last weekend. The rowdy crowd borders on obnoxious.

"What a difference a band makes," Leora states. She takes a big swig of beer. Sounds of breaking glass, cussing, and fisticuffs announce a fight further up along the wall. Bouncers Shout and Hacksaw jack two guys in wrinkled sports coats, handing them off to Coma and Blade at the steps just as another ruckus breaks out at the tables. An Asa Buchanan look-alike tips his white cowboy hat to Eva, offering his stool at the bar. Eva declines, shaking her head while making a mental picture of this man and his ego in a white suit, western tie, and cowboy boots. She meets his eyes with a warm smile, then disappears into waves of taller people who seem to wash over her then deposit her at the bar where she pulls a twenty from the girls. She signals Tony, holding up three fingers, laying the Jackson on the bar. The cowboy summons Tony, leans forward, and whispers to the black and white, pointing to Eva and tapping a C note on the bar in front of him. Tony winks at her, placing the drinks on the bar, and points to the cowboy hat. He exchanges Eva's twenty for the western wrangler's phone number twenty. She watches him take her twenty dollar bill smell it, kiss it, and slip it into his shirt pocket. She laughs out loud and nods a thank you before tucking the phone number twenty between the girls and gathering the drinks.

"Hey, girl!" Leora turns to a girl with shoulder-length mousy brown hair framing her face.

"Rhonda, right?"

"Yeah!" The young girl tries to focus her eyes, slightly swaying back and forth. "I thought that was you! You remembered!" She does the bump to Henley's "All She Wants to Do is Dance" playing on the club's jukebox. "Long time no see, since Virginia. What's new? You guys still live over top of that bar?"

"Nah. You still livin' in Bethel Township? You still work at the courthouse?"

"Yeah, yeah." Rhonda blinks then jiggles her head like a duck shaking off water, turning to her friend with overkill makeup and straight black hair pulled into two ponytails. Both of them are pretty well lit. "Dana, this is Leora, Sydney and—"

Leora nods, acknowledging the introduction. "This is my coworker, Eva."

"Boy, I haven't seen you guys in months. You don't come here much, do you?"

"Nah, not if we can help it." Leora's speaks before she thinks. She is rattled and not really in the mood for a coffee clutch. Neither is Sydney.

"We usually do midnight knockin'." Sydney changes the subject, taking a long gulp of beer.

"What is midnight knocking?" Dana asks.

Sydney swallows then burps. "Oh, excuse me. Well, if you're a day person, you go to lunch with friends. If you're a night person, you go visit after midnight and wake 'em the hell up." Sydney suppresses another burp.

"Unless you wanna broaden your horizons, here at the meat market." Eva takes a gulp of her drink then looks around. "You know, what I'm sayin'? Throw one away and come get a new one." She starts pointing out her idea of new ones. "There's one, there's one . . ."

The laughter of the five women is joined by the clinking of bottles and glasses as they toast stupid horny men again.

"So when are you gonna get Virginia again?" Rhonda jiggles with a noticeable slur, turning again to Dana the hobby horse. "She reads your palm and does your cards. Remember, I told you? She said she saw me in the emergency room. And I was. Remember, I told you? My mom had appendicitis." They wobble, leaning into each other with agreeable nods.

"I don't know," Leora answers, remembering the first encounter she and Sydney had with the fortuneteller. Virginia had predicted within a year of the reading Leora would ride in a big black car; a rose, the symbol of love; and a birth or death at 12:21 among other things. Tink's time of death was 12:21. Leora rode in a black limousine and Tink's little friend placed a rose in his casket just eleven days shy of a year. That was the first time. Since then, the girls had hosted two more readings, each one doubling in size and lasting from midday to well into the evening. Rhonda had been a friend of a friend of a friend at the last reading. "Hey, it hasn't even been a year yet," Leora interjects into the buzzing conversation.

"Yeah, when was that, December? She won't do anything until after a year," Sydney adds. "We've got a few weeks left."

"Yes." Leora agrees. She looks at Sydney. Sydney breathes deep, rubbing her temples. They didn't want to mingle. Actually they really didn't want to be there. Each drink made them more aware of their underlying problem. They glance at the steady stream of partygoers descending into the smoke-filled club. Eva wades into the stream to go answer a call from Mother Nature.

"Hey, she told me somethin' about a pearl. I was gonna have a pearl, give a pearl, save a pearl." Rhonda's voice wanes. "Oh, shit. I forget. I hope it's not the pearly gates." Rhonda blinks and jiggles her head again. "Wait, wait. She told me lucky numbers too." She snaps her fingers, thinking. "Uh-h-h, oh, oh, thirty-two, nineteen and . . . two. Yeah, two, that's right."

"She told me my lucky numbers were . . . now let me think," Sydney jumps in, grateful for a topic of conversation. She shuts her eyes, holding her forehead, "Uhhh, twenty-nine, forty-seven, and eleven."

"Wait! Hold on! Hold on! Let me get your phone number. Dana, you will be so impressed." Rhonda gropes through her pocketbook, ripping a chunk of paper from an envelope. Dana produces a pen for her friend. "Do you remember the numbers the fortuneteller told you?" Rhonda blinks and jiggles at Leora.

Leora is glad for the distraction. She does not want to give this girl her phone number. "Yeah," Leora answers, closing her eyes. "Umm, twenty-eight, ummm, twenty, ahhh, and thirty-one."

"She told me I was gonna shy away from an illegal act," Sydney continues the chat. "I did," she says, thinking about Rob the Verb. "Hey, Sis, she told you somethin' about a pearl, too. Remember? See you in a pearl, in with a pearl, a pearl around you?"

"Yeah, well, Pearl works in the kitchen. Hey, wait a minute. Remember Christmas time. We had our picture taken with Pearl, a whole gang of us. She has us hangin' up. Everybody sees us in the kitchen with Pearl.

Rhonda turns to Leora. "Oh, yeah, yeah, listen. Virginia said she saw ants. I thought she meant, you know, infestation, but my sister just had twins. So I'm a plural aunt. Get it? Two are gonna call me aunt!" She laughs out loud, snorting.

"There ya go!" Sydney says in agreement, turning her head toward Leora and crossing her eyes. She plasters a smile on her face before turning back around. "Hey, you're 'de plurable' aunt." Glasses clink for yet another toast.

"She spoke about somethin' in the dark will light up or out of the darkness somethin', somethin' will come into the light." Leora shrugs her shoulders.

"Yeah, whatever that is. It sounds sinister, do-do-do-do, do-do-do-do," Sidney hums music from "The Twilight Zone". "And she also told you somethin' about a monkey. You see a monkey, you capture a monkey, a monkey with dirty hands, a friendly monkey; a monkey's uncle, monkey around. I don't know. No zoos for us."

"Oh, and she said sometimes I look at life backwards, well, in reverse or opposite." Leora holds the top of her achy head. Rhonda gives Leora a quizzical look, then blinks and jiggles.

"She can write backwards. It's called mirror writing," Sydney explains.

"I can write backwards, everybody can write backwards." Rhonda jiggles her head, nodding to Dana, who is also nodding.

"No, no, no, no; cursive writing, long hand." Sydney sighs. "Writing backwards, not printing backwards." Sydney takes the pen and paper from Rhonda and hands it to Leora.

Leora writes Sydney then Leora backwards in cursive above the numbers.

The younger duo inspects Leora's handy work. Rhonda jiggles her head, peering at the piece of paper. "What the hell?" Dana digs in her pocketbook for her compact and holds it open, swaying back and forth. Rhonda grabs Dana's arm, holding it steady until the backward cursive words are framed in the elliptical-looking glass. "Wow!"

"Wow, that's really neat!" Dana leans in, looking under and over the piece of paper into the mirror.

Now Sydney speaks before she thinks. "Yeah, it's right up there with disposable diapers." She gawks at Leora with her lower lip protruding in a huge pout but really wanting to bite her tongue.

"We use mirrors at work." Now Leora changes the subject. "We have like four huge mirrors along the back wall. "They come in handy for patrolling the bar. We can practically see the whole room."

"Yeah, everybody in the mirror that's married wears their wedding rings on their right hands," Sydney adds.

"And they cross their hearts and hope to die with their left hands raised."

"Wow, it's like Wonderland." Rhonda and Dana nudge each other nodding, swaying and listening intently.

Leora rolls with it. "Yeah, I've seen the rabbit and the mad hatter in there, too."

". . . And the twins." Sydney rolls her head back, writhing.

Rhonda and Dana laugh. The foursome raise their drinks, toasting the twins.

"Nobody wants to leave there," Leora starts again

"Yeah, it's that damn caterpillar," Sydney continues the ruse. "Him and his smoke rings. Everybody's got a contact."

"Alice is in deep shit!" The curly hair girls say in unison, holding their heads, laughing their asses off at the double meaning for Alice.

Dana and Rhonda giggle along. "You guys are crazy." Bottles and glasses clink to Alice and Alice.

"Well, if you're ever in the vicinity, stop in. After a couple of drinks, you'll see what we're talkin' about." Leora takes a step away, trying to end the conversation. "See ya later."

"Maybe we will stop in before we get our fortunes told the next time." Rhonda sips the last of her Bacardi and Coke, making empty straw sounds.

Sydney also takes a step away, speaking over her shoulder. "And bring a pencil and paper so you can write it all down . . . later." Aqua De Silva encircles the quartet, preceding six-feet-tall Shout; with abounding muscles, chiseled jaw, and afro topping. A gold bust of Christ with a diamond crown of thorns hanging from a gold rope chain nestles in dark curly chest hairs. On his way by, he reaches for Sydney and does the bump to a couple bars of "Rock the Boat." The two younger girls practically drool in their glasses.

"She covers past, present, and future." Leora takes another step backwards, bouncing to the music. "Things that occur within a year, five years, your work, love life."

"She really is good." Rhonda says to Dana, "Remember I told you." She jiggles, turning to the escaping girls. "She told me I was gonna change jobs. I thought no way. But guess what? I did change jobs, about six weeks ago. I mean I'm still at the courthouse but now I work with the bail bondsman, a lot of traffic in there. See that man over there at the end of the bar," Rhonda squints, tiptoeing, pointing to Griff. "He's a lawyer from California. He's stayin' with his nephew Rob. I can't tell you his name because he's tryin' to be inconspicuous. And he told me to act like I don't know him if I see him on the street, which I completely understand, because he doesn't want his cover blown. But he's so nice." Rhonda blinks and jiggles. "He's always in and out of my work with the mayor and a couple of the other lawyers. In fact, he bought everybody lunch today. They didn't say anything to me, but I heard them talkin'." Rhonda blinks and jiggles again, leaning forward. "He's got an ex-girlfriend who emptied one of his bank accounts and took off. They're all tryin' to help him find her. He hired a private investigator. It's just a matter of time before he comes across her and his money. She has family in the area. They've got surveillance and everything just like in the movies." She blinks and jiggles. "Come on over, I'll introduce you." Dana and Rhonda start for the second bar.

Speechless, with eyes as big as saucers Leora gasps, snapping her head in Sydney's direction as if slapped simple. Sydney stares back in the same stupor with her mouth wide open. She could catch flies. "California, huh?" Sydney blurts the words aloud in a knee-jerk reaction to stall them as Leora stands with one hand behind her back, squeezing Sydney's hand.

"A movie star, is she a movie star from California?" Leora yells, hoping to spark an explanation.

"Oh, no, no." Rhonda begins her explanation, blinking and jiggling her way back with Dana.

Leora drains her beer, pulling a Hamilton from the "girls". "I'm thirsty. Come on, let's get a drink!" The foursome shuffles through the ever growing crowd, single file to the front of the first bar, ten feet away but seeming like fifty. Squeezing in between stools and people, Sydney hails Tony. She turns to hand a Bacardi and Coke and an Amaretto and orange juice to the unknowing canaries.

"Thank you," Dana says, exchanging her empty glass for the full one.

"Thanks. Oh, hold on a sec. Here, let me give you my number." Rhonda jots her phone number on Leora's mirror paper and exchanges it for her drink. "Come on, I wanna introduce you guys."

Chaos prepares for their next set, jumping on the stage to a rousing applause.

"Wait a minute," Leora shouts above the boisterous throng, "here comes Eva." She tiptoes, shoving the paper into her top jean pocket, flailing her arms for Eva who disappears into the crowd on her way to the hen party. Sydney taps Leora's shoulder like a woodpecker while pointing with the beer bottle in her other hand to Doc and Trudy coming down the steps. Trudy walks along the back wall, past the payphone to the ladies' room, unaware of Eva who spots Doc depositing money and making a phone call.

The petite barmaid changes course, making a bee line for Doc through the swarm of people. Sydney and Leora bolt in pursuit of their comrade while the band warms up with a "testing one, two" here and there; some percussion; some bass; and some intermittent Richter scale crowd interaction.

"Hello, hello, Eva?" Doc yells in the phone.

"Hel-l-lew!" Eva yells from behind him.

"Hello, Eva, Eva, hello. Is that you?"

Eva steps closer, tapping Doc on his shoulder. "No, this is me, that's you!"

"Go home!" Doc screams in shock, looking back and forth at the phone then at Eva; the phone, then Eva.

"Oh, I'm goin' home, you asswipe! Just as soon as I tell Trudy, her name should be tattooed on your arm not your ass!"

Momentum is stifled as Doc, still holding the phone to his ear, swings with his other arm across the front of his body, missing by a mile. He drops the phone, lunging at a defiant Eva, shoving her by her face into the ocean of bodies where her backward motion pushes one guy into another guy, who in turn is pushed into another and so on; initiating sheer bedlam with Eva sprawling on the floor at the feet of her rescuers. The girls gather a disheveled Eva and head up the stairs passing Bear, Coma, and Hacksaw on their way down to the ruckus.

"Are you all right?" Sydney asks outside as all three hustle to Eva's car.

"Yeah, yeah." She gives the girls a reassuring pat. "You believe that jackass?"

"You got your keys?" Leora asks, pulling her Bic from her pocket and holding the lighter near Eva to inspect her face. "Where'd he hit ya?"

"Oh, he didn't hit me, the jerk, but somebody stepped on my damn hand," Eva states, watching the flame as Leora moves it back and forth in front of her. "What the hell are ya doin'?"

"I don't know. I saw it in a movie," Leora answers, taking a deep breath, holding her forehead.

"That's for concussions! I'm all right."

"Nah-uh, she's half left," Sydney offers. "You okay to drive home, Momma?"

"Yeah, I'm fine." She starts the car, hits the power button to put the window down, and shuts the door. "You goin' back down the club?"

"Hell no! Right, Sis?" Leora looks at Sydney.

"Yeah right, that's enough fun for one night."

Eva throws the car in reverse, easing out of the parking space and adjusting the seat. "I gotta get gas. Hey! You got me gas?"

"Yeah, thanks for your help earlier."

"Yeah, nice afghan." Sydney knocks on the back of the car as Eva rolls out.

They climb into Sydney's car down by the after hours club door where a steady stream of rowdy patrons spill into the shopping center parking lot. "Think she's done with Dick Doc?" Sydney asks, taking a big swig of beer.

"If you mean his bullshit, yeah," Leora answers chug-a-lugging. "But if you mean done milkin' him, he better buy a cow. Did you see her pat that phone number she has tucked away? Dick Doc is about to get some serious competition from a cowboy."

"Yeah, in a white hat." Sister Syd downs the remainder of the long neck.

"And Doc only knows three things about a horse: win, place and show." Leora leaves Sydney coughing and laughing to go chuck the empty beer bottles into the round refuse basket at one of the designated light poles.

Petrichor permeates the morning air as it cools over the damp earth and fallen leaves producing fog already covering low lying areas. The best friends make their way through the east end of the city to the entrance of I-95 on Kerlin Street. "Hey, you want me to drop you off at your car or you wanna come with me?"

Leora pulls their emergency pipe from the glove compartment for the ride home. "What's up?" She lights Lucky Pierre.

"I'm goin' to a bonfire. And you're invited."

"Yo, Sis, it rained tonight. Who's havin' a bonfire?"

"Well, we are, down in front of Goo Goo's. I've got everything we need: lighter fluid, nail polish remover, pack of matches, clothes."

"Ohhh, yeah, that's right. I'm in. Besides, strength in numbers, remember? I'll get my car tomorrow—well, later today."

Sydney drives by Goo's blue Cadillac and Rob's black Charger in front of the apartment building on the right hand side. She pulls over on the opposite side of the deserted street at the top of the slight incline just past the arc light piercing the fog.

Popping the trunk, she gathers toppled clothes shoving them back in the plastic laundry basket. "Eva musta went around corners on two wheels." She states sitting it on the street to help Leora, already searching for the elusive liquids. They grope in the trunk around two boxes, holding Sydney's knickknacks and bathroom accessories yet unpacked from the apartment, finding a screwdriver here, a pair of pliers there, a wrench under this, a brown bag of fuses. "What the hell? Everything's everywhere. How big is my damn trunk anyway?" Sydney whispers, her voice full of frustration. She flicks her Bic several times, cupping the flame to protect it as she moves it around the trunk.

Leora stretches, feeling her way to the back of the trunk. Her hands identify a plastic bottle of nail polish remover and the lighter fluid resting against a hard plastic case of some sort. "What's this?" Leora whispers, now on tiptoes locating its handle pulling it to her. "When did you start bowlin'?"

Sydney flicks the lighter several more times, lowering it in front of her best friend. The glow from the lighter chases the darkness, illuminating the word 'Royal' for a split second. Sydney blinks, trying to adjust her eyes only to see the word 'Royal' every place she looks. "Oh! My! God!" She tries striking the lighter again, but the whole top of it is hot to the touch.

Leora hands taller Sydney her Bic while keeping her other hand on the captured object as if it would try to escape in the blackness. Sydney flicks the Bic, sending darkness into shadows as Leora unhooks the clasps, exposing a typewriter. They both gasp in disbelief.

"That's it! That's the typewriter, isn't it?" Sydney strains to whisper, almost hyperventilating.

"Are you shittin' me? Are we bein' set up?" Leora's tries to whisper. She refastens the clasps.

"Hey, maybe Rob has his own blackmail goin' on. Remember he told that scum bag he didn't know where it was. What did he do? Put it here to blackmail us or hide it to go after Griff?"

"Or is he gonna hide it at Goo Goo's and then tell Griff." Leora's inside are shaking as she grabs the combustible fluids in the darkness and covers the incriminating evidence with her jacket; a basically useless act, but so is crying. Sydney pushes the sought-after evidence back to its hiding place then pulls the trunk lid down, pushing it until it ever so lightly clicks. The partners in crime dump clothes on the street, squirting the nail polish remover into the laundry basket adding clothes, squirting lighter fluid, adding more clothes and squirting (like a lasagna of clothes), topping it all off with the remainder of the two containers. Sydney sprinkles all but two matches on the pile of threads. She strikes the first one and tosses it on the clothes—nothing. She strikes the last one, lighting the empty match pack then chucks that on to the flammable pile. Swoooosh!

With the T-Bird in second gear, the clutch engaged, and the ignition switch to the on position, the vehicle slowly drifts away from the curb, disappearing into the fog. The roar of a three-ninety Ford engine becomes a whisper in the distance.

Debug Detail

$\mathcal{T}$he fog had dissipated by the time the girls stirred in mid afternoon. Although it was late, they hadn't had much luck with sleep. First they had sat in the car discussing probables and most-likelys, then decided to retrieve the questionable machine from the trunk while there was still the double cover of fog and darkness. Wheezer meowed in that darkness from his usual perch on the roof, busy patrolling for the ever invading stray leaves and seemingly unfazed by the earlier storm. In two leaps—to the oak and then the ground—the young feline greeted them, loving against legs, flopping, purring, and wheezing. Still unable to sleep, they downed aspirins with their mugs of tea and coffee in the bathroom, discussing more probables and more of the most-likelys but only after they propped a kitchen chair under the front doorknob and stood an ironing board against the door jam with a cow bell dangling from it. The more they kicked around the list of players weighing facts and motives, the less productive the process of elimination became. Around they went with Rob, Griff, the mayor, Rob, Alice; even Goo Goo until . . . CRASH! Headaches vanished, adrenaline rushed, hearts skipped. Grabbing their weapons of choice, propped in the corner by the bathtub, they tiptoed to the top of the staircase with Leora in the lead holding the sponge mop as if it were a lance. Sydney followed with a can of hair spray tucked into her waist, and the broom minus the brush. Wheezer, his face full of cat eyes, looked six ways to Sunday. He crouched third step from the top, puffed like an orange dust mop following his attack on the dangerous cow bell now resting at the foot of the steps with its string still tangled on the leg of the fallen ironing board. The chair remained steadfast in its appointed position, lodged under the doorknob, denying entrance. Yawns followed sighs of relief as Inspector Wheezer was escorted to the enclosed patio, his safe haven, with replenished food and water, and the ironing board once again stood against the door jam with the cow bell dangling above the chair. Although well into the daylight hours, the exhausted girls gathered sheets, pillows, and blankets to create a slumber party at the linen closet. They concurred Rob's involvement was pivotal to say the least; working for Goo, working against Goo, working for Griff, working against Griff, maybe working for the Feds or even maybe working for hisself. Both admitted to a feeling of guilt having given him access to the house and Sydney's car. And they were in full agreement the illegal act Sydney should shy away from was indeed Rob the Verb. With feet against the thick linen closet door, sponge mop, and broom handle at respective arms' lengths, they prepared a to do list-mumbling back and forth in half slumber until succumbing to a restless sleep. *Let's see . . . find the key, check for the van, look for the planted bugs, empty that damn VO bottle, oh, yeah, good one, hide the typewriter we put behind the shower curtain, find the cook book. Find the cook book? Oh, right, Lister the chef. He cooks the books.* Leora tiptoes in bare feet through misty, overgrown bushes and weeds along the side of a brick house. Peering into the kitchen window, she sees Stephen Lister's newspaper picture standing at a sink, wearing a huge chef's hat while holding a meat cleaver in his hand. She stoops and waddles like a duck away from the window, then crouches in the tall over growth. *Yo, Sis, get the ledger! Did you find it, Sis? It's gotta be here some place. Can you hear me, Sis?* She stands up, glancing at the kitchen window. Stephen Lister's newspaper picture now stands in front of the window, holding the meat cleaver above his head. *Where are my shoes? Yo, Sis, where are you?* She searches the bramble with a bare foot and steps right on some thorny underbrush. *Owww!* She glances at the kitchen window now with a black cat on the windowsill, ears down, back arched. *Run Wheezer, run! Yo, Sis, grab the book! Run! He's comin'!* Leora tries to lift her bare foot. *Owww!* She tries again. "Owww," Leora moans out loud. Arousing from her nightmare, she props on one elbow, feeling stickers in the bottom of her foot again. She sits up half-Indian style, trying to focus her eyes, checking her foot, and pulling the bottoms of the sheets and blankets up to inspect them for stickers or something pointy or sharp or sting-ee. An orange and white playful paw reaches from under the linen closet door, batting the air. Now two playful paws appear in a flurry. "*Wheezer!*" Leora yells wide-eyed.

Sydney jumps straight up off the floor, but not before grabbing her broom handle. "Get out!" she screams in a kung-fu stance, scanning the hallway, trying to focus her eyes.

"Yo! Sis! It's Wheezer! He's in the wall! He's in the wall!" Leora runs to her bedroom, opening a window, calling her furry friend, trying to coax him out from however he got in. She removes the screen. "Kit-ty, kitty, kitty, kitty, kitty, kitty, kitty, kit-ty!" The girls race down to the kitchen, grabbing a box of dry cat food and a flashlight.

"I hope Tiger remembers his way out," Sydney says running up the steps two by two with the flashlight on in broad daylight. "When we find the hole I'll shine this in. Maybe he'll see it."

Bounding up the staircase shaking the cat food box, they find Wheezer sitting in the windowsill, primping. He cringes at all the noise and commotion coming through the bedroom doorway. Flopping at the sound of his name, he falls onto the roof then leaps back upon the sill where Sydney scoops him up, taking him to the bathroom. Leora leans as far as she can out the window, searching for a hole or any kind of entrance way. *Crow's gonna be busy when he gets back.* Slight traces of honeysuckle float on the clean, crisp breeze as Leora shields her eyes from the setting sun, scanning the street for a black van. She takes a deep breath of the sweet air before replacing the screen, then closes the window. Waiting her turn for a wake up shower, she busies herself with gathering the bedding fabrics from the hallway. Wheezer escapes when Leora opens the bathroom door. "Comin' through!" she calls to Sydney in the shower, retrieving their drinking vessels for some fresh, hot refills to begin the rest of the day ahead of them. Downstairs, she removes the phone receiver, laying it on the counter by the sink and drains the VO bottle. Throwing the empty bottle in the trash, she remembers the box Rob kept moving around—the one she stuck out in Wheezerville on the patio. Wheezer follows her out to the patio, pushing the screen door open and escaping to parts unknown. Almost soppy from the blowing rain the night before, she places a hand under the weak cardboard, carrying the rectangle gingerly into the kitchen, and places it upside down on the table. *Give it up.* The upside down box spews its contents as she lifts it. It stands with one side sagging when she drops it to the floor. She sifts through the damp pile—stapler, paper clips, stapler remover, tacks, push pins, white-out, glue, an S initial keyring, a torn piece of white stationary matted together by coffee stains, markers, highlighters, pens, pencils, scotch tape, note pads, coffee stained receipts, twist ties. *Junk, junk, and more junk. What's this? Oh, my God!* She turns the listening device over and over in her hand.

Sydney appears from upstairs. "What the hell?" She gawks at the device. The girls lock eyes. They immediately head upstairs to the bathroom, shutting the door.

"So this is why it was his favorite box." Leora chucks the device into the toilet, then sits on the edge of the bath tub.

Sydney flushes the toilet, putting the seat down and sits. "Well, if it's a set-up, why are we bein' bugged?" She pulls a doobie from behind her ear and the lighter from her jeans. She unites them, taking a long, long hit.

"I don't know. It's always somethin'. Nothin' is ever cut and dried with us, as usual." Leora takes a hit thinking. "Hey, Rob would snow his own mother. I think Griff needs a snow shovel. Ya think Rob and Griff are workin' together or suppose to be but Rob is workin' against Griff? I mean, because Griff can't see past his own arrogant ass. Then again, if the typewriter is so incriminatin' Griff wouldn't let it out of his sight, right? So if he don't have any of it, then he never did, right? Or do ya think Griff is settin' us up? Maybe Rob's just playin' along."

"Well," Sydney says with furrowed brow, "I think Griff has zilch, especially the way he was screamin' last night in the bar parkin' lot. That wasn't an act."

"Yeah, and tellin' Rhonda he's a lawyer from California. "Puh--lease! What a liar!" Leora takes a humongous hit handing it to Sydney.

"Not to mention, sneak! Ridin' past the house, slinkin' around the parkin' lot, and sendin' Rob to our house!" Now Sydney inhales.

"But wouldn't Rob remember where he stashed shit? After all, he's hidin' it from everybody and their mother—Griff, Goo Goo, the mayor, the Feds, hell even us."

"So if we're bein' bugged by Griff, it's 'because he's got muckus and we got . . . ?"

"Personality," Leora says smiling, taking another hit. "Plus a connection to Goo Goo."

"Yeah, but so does Rob."

Leora sighs, rubbing her forehead, closing her eyes. The conversation was starting to sound like the previous one with no solutions, only more questions. "Yeah, but he doesn't have a real connection, like us. Think about it, we know more about Goo Goo than even Doc does. Doc'll kiss and tell in a New York minute, and Goo Goo is well aware of that. He tells Doc what he wants Doc to know, you know, safe stuff. Hey, those bimbos Doc told Eva about last week were us. But Doc doesn't know that. Goo Goo didn't tell 'im. And Goo Goo has known Doc a long time. He's only known Rob a couple months. The guy is a gopher. He fixes shit. I can't see Goo Goo trustin' this guy with his life. And we agree if Griff had the typewriter, he wouldn't let it out of his sight and he was pissed. So he never had it, he wants it, he bugs us, and Rob plays along."

"Plays along? These guys are not playin'. They are no joke."

"And the way Hank and Sonny tell it, we're talkin' tons of money. He's gonna get us killed."

"Which begs the question, 'Who did Rob rob?' Where the hell did he get it from? Who the hell does he know? Is that why Griff thinks we have the typewriter?"

"Maybe Rob told Griff he saw it here. God, he will get us killed! Ya think there's somebody else involved in this mess?"

Party of the first to wit thereof! "Holy shit! Ya got Griff, Goo, Rob … why involve us?"

"I don't wanna play this! Let's play somethin' else!"

"Me neither!" Sydney shivers. She grabs Leora's hand, leading her to her bedroom and points to her bed pillows. A towel wrapped around the typewriter gives a fluffy appearance to the pillow case they sit inside. The girls cast nervous glances around Sydney's bedroom before going their separate ways; Leora, to get a change of clothes for her shower, and Sydney downstairs out the front door after slipping on a jacket.

After a refreshing shower, Leora feels regenerated and ready to take the bull by the horns so to speak. She heads downstairs to the kitchen where she whips up a cup of instant coffee for herself and a cup of hot tea for Sister Sleuth. Before the tea pot whistles, she peeks in canisters, drawers, and cabinets. She stands on a chair to check the top of the back door, the top of the pantry door, on top of the refrigerator, and the top of the cabinets; not to mention underneath the cabinets, kitchen table, and sink. With her curiosity satisfied, she places the hot beverages on the kitchen table, adding moo juice, and stares at the sugar bowl. Doris Day flashes across her mind in "Caprice" with a listening device in the shape of a sugar cube. She lifts the lid, peering inside the bowl and without provocation, chops any and all sugar lumps larger than a granule with the sugar spoon before dispensing a scoop in each beverage. She slips into her jacket, carrying the mugs out front where she finds Sydney sitting on the porch's shaded side wall by the driveway with her foot resting on the glider, petting a purring and wheezing Wheezer. A zephyr filters through the peppermint plants all along the side of the house and porch, bringing the dying aroma of mint to mingle with scents of honeysuckle and drying leaves, arriving on their own zephyr from the sun-drenched wraparound porch on the other side of the stone house. Sydney sips the hot tea, holding it with both hands.

"Come on. Let's go in," Sydney says to Leora.

"What? You're kiddin' me!" Leora yells. Sydney's smile says it all. "Nah-uh!"

"Yeah, I did!" Sydney answers, holding up the once elusive house key.

"High five!" They slap hands. "I'm impressed, Momma!"

"It's nothin', just followin' the clues." Sydney points to the muddy foot prints on the porch. "And this is probably where stupid lost it." She points over the porch wall where muddy impressions and trampled peppermint tattle on earlier activities of the darkness.

"Where was it hidden?"

"Here, I'll show ya." Sydney stoops at the side of the glider, reaching underneath then toward the back and pulls out a magnetic hide-a-key box, handing it to Leora.

"Wow! I'd a never found that. My arms aren't long enough."

"Yo! Sis!" Sydney holds her hand in front of her face.

"Peek a-boo to you, too!" Leora gives her a Yogi Bear reply, bucking her eyes at the jingling box.

"Here." Sydney hands the metal box to Leora. "Remember the key ring in my glove compartment with all the keys I don't have a clue about? Well, that's one of 'em."

Leora slides the container open, exposing a key. "Are you shittin' me?"

"Would I lie to you, Momma? See, the top of it looks like ours, but it doesn't even fit in the keyhole, which is a good thing 'cause if it did, they'd probably break it off in the lock tryin' to make it work."

"Yeah," Leora agrees, handing the box back to Sydney, "Way better than changin' the lock. They'd be on to us. I like it better this way. We're on to them."

"Me, ta. We gotta find the bugs. We're lookin' for two, right?" Sydney asks, placing the magnetic box back in its secret position.

"Yeah, I started the kitchen. Nothin'." Leora looks up and down the street. No black van.

"What else do we have to do? What about the VO?"

"Oh, I dumped that shit earlier."

"Great, and the 'you-know-what's' in my bedroom in the 'you-know-whatever' so all we have to do now is find the bugs, and then we'll go get somethin' to eat before I go to work."

"Sonny said about eightish, right?"

"Yepper," Sydney answers, trying their newfound house key in the front door for a perfect fit. Wheezer flits around and between them, being first through the front door. They climb the stairs in silence and scour Leora's bedroom with no luck. Their full attention turns to Sydney's bedroom—still no luck. It was going on five o'clock. Sydney's stomach growls. Frustration and aggravation follow them to the kitchen.

"I thought for sure they would be there," Leora says. "At least one of 'em."

"You don't suppose the bathroom, do you?" Sydney asks, popping her head from under the table, making a shushing gesture. The girls have to choose their words carefully.

Leora nods affirmatively to Sydney's gesture and shrugs her shoulders to her girlfriend's question. "He loves those catnip toys," Leora says aloud. "We'll find 'em."

Scanning the kitchen, Sydney gives her cohort the okay sign. "The last place I saw one was in the den. The blue one. Yeah, it was the blue one," she adds to the cover story.

"Yeah, I think it was the blue one, too," Leora says aloud, nodding each time Sydney points.

Sydney leans on the table, cupping her chin in her hands. "Hey, did you check here in the kitchen?" She stands up and points to her chair, tilting it backwards and looking under the seat. "Maybe it's under the stove."

"Yeah, maybe," Leora agrees, checking her seat. She walks to the stove, opening the drawer under the oven, and starts rattling pots and pans for a full effect.

"It is! Look there it is!" yells Sydney, holding another kitchen chair backwards with one hand and making the shushing sign with the other, then pointing to the exposed transmitting device.

The oval bug carefully duct taped to the underside of the chair was all together different from the one flushed down the toilet. Leora gasps. "You found it!" she blurts aloud. "Oh, it is the blue one!" she adds, recovering her composure.

"Now all we have to find is the red one!" Sydney shrugs, with eyes wide, throwing her hands in the air, joining in the cover conversation.

"I think the last place I saw that one was upstairs!" They nod affirmatively to each other, heading up the steps and bolting into the bathroom, shutting the door.

"Great Kugamooga! Good God!" Sydney tries to whisper looking in the mirror.

Leora's stomach is flopping. "Boy, this sucks big time! Whatever this is, we're right smack dab in the middle!"

"Hey, we gotta check bedrooms again. It has to be here someplace, them sons-of-bitches!"

Leora stands next to her best friend looking at her in the mirror. "Sis, ya think they came in here when we were sleepin'?"

Sydney's eye balls liked to pop out of her head! She was speechless for about 20 seconds. "Nah-uh. We would have smelled the arrogant one's aftershave. The other one, well, we would have just smelled him."

The sleepy sun's descent in the November sky brings elongated shadows with their blanket of darkness. The portable TV and table lamp in each bedroom are not enough light for a second search. Sydney closes her bedroom curtains before turning the ceiling light on. Leora scans the street for a black van. Then she too closes curtains and floods her bedroom with ceiling light.

After ten minutes or so, the sounds of banging drawers and doors ceases in Sydney's bedroom. Leora checks places and spaces to no avail. She feels around in the rhododendron plant and in the bottom of the macramé hanger. *This is bullshit!* She turns and sees Sydney sprawled across the foot of her bed, moving her arms back and forth straight up in the air holding two reefers and a Bic. Leora sighs. She stands over upside down Sydney emptying the redhead's hands then sits on the bed, lighting one of the doobies and slipping the other behind her ear. Taking a big hit, she coughs then falls backward on the bed opposite Sydney. She leans on her elbows. "How hard is it to see somethin' red?" Leora questions her best friend out loud.

Sydney follows Leora's lead, folding an arm over her forehead to shield her eyes from the bright ceiling light. "Well, we gotta think like a red catnip toy. If I was a red catnip toy, where would I hide?"

Leora passes the J, rolls her eyes, shrugs her shoulders, and falls back on the bed. She exhales and also places an arm across her forehead to shield her eyes from the ceiling light. She is losing patience not being able to speak freely in her own house, and she is hungry, too. "It's gettin' late. We gotta get ready and go."

"Yeah, I'm starvin'. Let's go to Hook and take a look. We'll find the toy later."

"What time? Ya remember?" Leora sits up Indian-style and pivots to face her concerned friend.

"Huh?" Sydney peeks from under her arm shielding the light with a shocked look on her face. *Oh, my God! The girl is losin' it!*

"You know, let's get it over with." Leora puts her finger to her lips shrugging nodding rapidly. *They wanna play? Let's play.*

Sydney nods. "Uh, I don't know, around six, six-thirty." The words roll off her tongue like the truth. She shrugs making an e-gads face. "What time is it?" Wheezer joins the duet, purring and wheezing. He flops by Sydney's head, batting a curl here and there. She turns toward the bright ceiling light with her eyes closed, and feels for the tabby above her. He playfully bats her hands as she lifts him above her, blocking the glaring light with the lovable feline every now and then. "What are you doin', Tiger?" He purrs and wheezes, dangling like a cat rag doll, eyes half-closed the tip of his tail wiggling.

"It's always good to be early, isn't it?" Leora continues the deception. All of a sudden, Sydney places Wheezer on the bed and jumps up walking around circling the ceiling light. *Oh, for joy, she's daft!* Sydney waves to Leora to come over as she rocks back and forth, blinking at the bright light, squinting. Leora's blinking eyes follow Sydney's arm, pointing to the light. Leora shrugs her shoulders, shaking her head. *She's hallucinatin'!*

"Well, they say the early bird catches the worm." Sydney speaks aloud, still pointing and moving over pulling Leora with her. "It would be nice to catch a whole can of 'em."

Leora finally spots the oval shadow inside the glass cover of the ceiling fixture. "Yeah, and twice on Sunday!" Leora feels downright giddy and giggly.

"Hey, remember the game ya played when ya were little?"

"What game's that?" Leora stifles laughter.

"I spy! I spy somethin' red!"

Leora slaps the element of surprise on her face. "You found it! You found the red one!" She can't stand it. She giggles.

"That's the way, uh-huh, uh-huh I like it, uh-huh, uh-huh!" Sydney sings, nodding to Leora, then giving the Italian gesture for "up yours" several times to the ceiling light. She feels light and bubbly, too. "We better get movin', uh-huh, uh-huh."

"Yeah, time is money uh-huh, uh-huh!" Leora smiles, giving the other Italian gesture for "up yours" from under her chin in a flurry of both hands to the inanimate recipient. "Last one there's a rotten egg."

"Speakin' of eggs," Sydney yells as they shuffle down the steps with jackets, pocketbooks, and Wheezer. "I was thinkin' of gettin' a salad, a big salad with blue cheese," she continues from the kitchen, placing the phone receiver back into its cradle and gathering some old newspaper.

Leora turns on the night light in the window, "Mmm, make it two!" She shuts the front door behind them, sitting Wheezer on the glider. He jumps down then over the porch wall, disappearing into the peppermint. "And two rolls with butter!"

"Maybe three. I'm so hungry I could eat a—"

"Bear!" they say in unison.

"That's so funny I forgot to laugh!" Leora mimics her girl Gilda walking to Sister Syd's car. She turns to speak to Sydney, who is still on the porch. *Now what the hell is she doin'?* She watches her wrap the welcome mat in newspaper and then position the unwrinkled object between the side wall of the porch and glider.

"They don't have a key anymore, but they don't know that," Sydney announces as they climb in the car.

"Not yet," Leora adds, lighting the other J and passing it. "Good idea, Sis." They both gawk and gooseneck for a black van. "Hey, wait a minute. Remember Daffy Rob told Uncle Donald, I mean Griff, that the ones in the house are better than the first one we threw in the toilet, which means they're probably stronger. So we won't see the van now unless we ride around two blocks, six blocks, whatever."

"And you know what else, Sis? If Griff shows up without Rob, we'll know Goo Goo's not in on it, right?" Sydney glides over the Market Street Bridge spanning the railroad.

Leora is bubbly. "Yeah, because Rob don't wanna be seen with Griff because he's stayin' with Goo Goo." Leora reasons. "If he shows up with Griff then he's in cahoots with Goo Goo and Griff is in the dark. But if Goo Goo doesn't know anything then that means if those two are seen in public together, they get killed instead of us."

"Uh-huh, uh-huh!" They sing a duet and laugh.

"Well, what if everybody that was at the table last night shows up?"

Leora looks at Sydney wide-eyed thinking. "You mean, instead of Uncle Donald and Daffy it would be Uncle Donald and his three dumb nephews?"

Sydney pulls into the back of the L-shaped parking lot. The first seven out of ten spaces behind the diner are full as well as the six on the side of the diner and the five against the fence. "They be the ones," Sydney answers, backing her car in the last space on the end by Green Street.

"Well, then I guess its duck soup for everybody!"

Food for Thought

Marcus Hook: Cornerstone of Pennsylvania, first port of call for Philadelphia. Home to Marcus Hook Diner, open twenty-four hours a day, seven days a week. The diner's peak hours—lunch, dinner, and after 2 a.m. right into breakfast—are hectic. Not to say the off-hours are slow. Off-hours only means the herd dwindles to a steady stream of hungry clientele. The diner's success is based upon the owner's expectations of dining out. The short and sweet of it: offer generous portions of delicious homemade foods, family-oriented atmosphere, clean dining areas; and they will come. Word-of-mouth puts Marcus Hook Diner on the map, international and otherwise. It shines like a new penny with stainless steel and chrome on the walls, framing the glass doors, sparkling from the tops of glass cylinder sugar dispensers, salt and pepper shakers plus napkin holders so bright and shiny they double as mirrors in a pinch. And what dining room is complete without a color scheme? Navy blue is splashed about generously; as confetti flecks in the gray Formica counters and table tops. Splashed as trim on white tier curtains accenting each window, hung more for decoration than for privacy, veiling only the bottom halves. And navy blue vinyl in booths match vinyl padding on open stools atop chrome pedestals bolted to the navy blue and gray checkerboard tile floor.

Entrance, at the S intersection of Green and Tenth Street or truckers route thirteen, is up two steps from the north or the south into a small foyer with its windowless wall occupied by a cigarette machine, wall-mounted pay telephone, and umbrella bucket. Aromas of fried chicken, roast beef, and baked macaroni and cheese welcome the famished duo. "Mmmm, smell," Leora says, inhaling. They settle on the left behind the register, opening the thin white linens for a grand view of the street and parking lot entrance. Laughter emerges from the next booth where three boisterous refinery workers in coveralls sit conversing with a forty-ish Shelley Winters look-alike in a gray pants suit with her strawberry blond hair piled in a bouffant style. The end booth—also the refinery employees—empties into the bedlam of full, satisfied patrons while waitresses, five in all, scurry about clearing tables, wiping counters, and ringing out customers.

"Hits ya right in the face, don't it?" Sydney says, breathing deep. "Yo, Momma! Got your keys?" she asks, flipping through the metal index pages of songs left to right, right to left in the gleaming miniature jukebox just like its larger counterpart. She finds a few good selections and pushes the corresponding letter and number buttons after feeding it a couple of quarters, giving it permission to channel melodies to their table.

"Yes, I do," Leora answers, pushing the high volume button. "Purple Haze" about blasts them out of their seats. All heads snap in their direction as the twosome push volume buttons—the high one, medium, the low one, the rejection button—trying to stifle the blaring music. The dark-haired fellow with deep blue eyes and a smile to get lost in, sitting next to the strawberry blonde, kneels in the booth behind Leora. She slides to her left out of the oil worker's way. He nods and winks at Sydney while bending over the booth, supporting his weight on the table with one hand and shaking the device with his other as if to dislodge a tiny record inside. Marie, their waitress, places an arm full of dirty dishes on the counter from the end booth and rushes to the dilemma, hitting a switch in the back of the malfunctioning machine, turning it off. She slips them a couple quarters as they move to the end booth where opened curtains on the side and along the back behind Sydney produce a panorama view.

"Whew! That pinned my ears back," Miss Strawberry Blonde says, blue eyes wide, smiling at Sydney.

Sydney smiles back. "Huh?" She cups her ear, pretending that she's unable to hear. Chuckles rise from the oil men. Sydney bucks her eyes, mimicking Edward G. Robinson, "Yeah . . . see . . . we stick out like sore thumbs . . . see?" She watches early evening traffic out the side window.

Leora goosenecks to enhance her view of the parking lot out the back window behind Sydney. "Yeah, I feel like I'm on TV."

Marie with Raggety Ann eyes, her light brown hair in a French twist, smiles through an overabundance of freckles, ready to take their order. "How ya doin' this mornin'? Ahh, I mean tonight, oh! You know what I mean, this evenin'." She places two ice waters on the table. "Breakfast, right?"

"I don't think so," Leora says, looking at Marie then Sydney then Marie then Sydney, "How 'bout you, Sis?"

"I don't think so," Sydney joins in the head game, looking at Marie then Leora then Marie then Leora, "How 'bout you, Sis?"

"What time is it?" Leora pretends to look around for a clock.

"What time is it?" Sydney apes her best friend. Conversation slows to a trickle as the strawberry blonde's table eavesdrops. "Hey, hey, hey, waait aaa minnnute, I know you. Don't you work night work?"

"And so it goes," Leora mimicks Rod Serling. "Doomed to repeat and repeat in "The Twilight Zone" in "The Twilight Zone"."

Marie shakes her head laughing. She's known the cantankerous girls a long time. In fact, Marie had watched Sydney Odessa Nethery and her siblings on more than one occasion back in the day. "It's me." Marie plays, too. "It's really me."

"No, no, no, this is me, that's you," Sydney answers in a squeaky voice, looking at Marie then Leora.

"No, no, no, this is me, that's you," Leora chimes in, also with a squeaky voice, looking at Sydney then Marie.

Marie tries to grab her nose in child's play. "Well, does MeMe want the usual? Scrapple, scrambled, and home fries lyonaised?"

"Nah, we're roughin' it," Sydney answers. Both of them shake their heads.

Marie gives them a furrowed brow. "Wow, I've never seen you guys eat anything other than eggs fried, scrambled, or poached."

"Well, get ready 'cause we're gonna eat 'em hard." Laughter erupts from the neighboring booth. Leora pretends to bite her tongue, crossing her eyes blinking at Sydney.

"You girls are startin' early, aren't you?" Marie bucks her eyes, grinning back and forth at the jokesters.

"Yeah, well, if your day was like our day today, then you'd say, 'Hey, okay,'" Leora answers.

"No way!" Marie says laughing. "What are you off tonight?"

"Hell, she's off every night."

"Besides that I don't work Saturdays," Leora adds to her best friend's answer. The threesome snickers and high-five each other.

"Oh, I have to tell you the specials." Marie scratches her forehead with her thumb and sighs. "Wait, wait. Let me think."

"And she talks about us," Sydney starts again. "Have you been nippin' at the cookin' sherry again?" She keeps it going.

"Nah, it's the beer," Leora adds. "She's gotten the crabs drunk again."

They laugh. "Come on now, let me think." The girls are always a pleasant distraction. "Oh, I remember. We've got a couple of 'em. Ya ready? Listen: chopped sirloin, chicken croquettes, or breaded flounder. All of them come with a roll and butter, choice of two sides, ahhh, wait a minute, wait a minute, ahhh, mashed potatoes, peas, corn, applesauce, or coleslaw, and an appetizer of soup or salad. You have a choice this evening of either New England clam chowder or split pea."

"So what time is it really?" Leora asks. "Are you here early or late?"

"I was about to ask you the same thing. No, I'm just coverin' the dinner hour for Carol. She went home sick. I'll be back on my graveyard shift later tonight. I'm gettin' ready to sneak out in about twenty minutes or so."

"Oh, that's right," Sydney says. "Lefty's on vacation. You're the manager. You HAVE to cover everything. Oh, great, lucky you."

"That's right," Leora adds. "Head jobs come with responsibilities." Talk about speaking before you think! She did it again! Leora, thankful her back was to the audience, holds her forehead blinking again with lips pursed. Sydney gives her a high five as laughter roars from the peanut gallery.

Marie even cracks up, pulling a pencil and pad from her navy blue apron. "Well, before I get to my head jobs, what can I get ya to drink?"

"No, Coke, Pepsi," Sydney mimics John Belushi.

"Oh, no Pepsi, Coke," Leora adds, her imitation glancing at Sydney. "Make it two."

"Together, right?" the thirty-something waitress asks, referring to the check. She slides the pencil between the two staples, holding the check pad together and slips them into her apron, that quick.

"Oh, wait, Speedy Gonzalez! We're ready to order," Leora tells Marie, already two steps away.

"Oh, yeah, we don't need a minute," Sydney adds. "A salad." She holds up the peace sign. "Two of 'em, right, Sis?"

"Oh, yeah, and we need two of those Bouno Brothers rolls."

"Mmm, yeah, the Kaiser ones."

"Oh, that's easy." Marie steps back, whipping out her pad and pencil. "You want the chef salad, with meat and cheese?"

"Oh, no, no, the rabbit food," Sydney looks at Leora, nodding.

"Oh yeah, just run it through the garden." Leora's stomach gurgles and growls.

"What kind of dressing?" Marie asks, writing down the order.

"Blue cheese," the girls answer together.

Marie weaves between the standing refinery workers. Deep Blue Eyes winks again at Sydney and smiles while the strawberry blonde yanks his coverall sleeve off, freeing his arm to retrieve his wallet from his pants pocket. Almost six o'clock, the end of their dinner hour, the guys place cash on the table and present food vouchers at the register. Vouchers are presented by companies to hardworking employees, pulling doubles or doing shut downs. They are honored twenty-four/seven with no expiration date; just like money, except for one little flaw. They are useless as a tip. So the fellas dig for food vouchers and cold cash for their hardworking waitresses.

Marie serves Sydney and Leora their orders placing the check upside down on the table and thanking them for their tip before departing. The girls settle into some serious grazing—hard boiled eggs, fresh cucumbers, crispy lettuce, juicy tomato wedges, chick peas, onions, radishes, croutons; all smothering in blue cheese. The girls are startled by Deep Blue Eyes tapping the side window, winking and smiling on his way back into the diner. He checks around the register, searches the floor, and scans the table. The strawberry blonde turns in his direction. So does Leora. Marie walks from back in the kitchen, standing between the two counters. She sits four orders of French fries and a bottle of ketchup on the end of the counter and pulls a set of keys from her apron tossing them to him. "You left them at the register." He gives her a salute.

"See ya later, Alice," Deep Blue Eyes says with a rugged voice, smiling through a five o'clock shadow at Sydney.

Alice the strawberry blonde stirs her coffee. "You'd forget your head if it wasn't attached." The best friends' attention shifts to the woman in gray. She turns back around, holding her coffee with two hands, propping her elbows on the table, sipping the refill of the freshly brewed beverage. Peeking over her cup, she meets stares from the partners in crime and smiles at them. The girls, seemingly in a trance, snap out of it, returning weak smiles, but smiles none the less, with Leora whipping back around, facing Sydney. Now deep in their own thoughts, they chew, staring out the window until they are startled by Marie, knocking on their window, waving good-bye.

"My brother really liked you." Alice nods at Sydney with smiling eyes.

"Your brother?" Sydney tries to sound calm and nonchalant, masking the antsy feeling in the pit of her stomach.

"Well, actually my baby brother, Luke. He thinks you're hot to trot."

Leora sits, legs propped, back against the wall, looking at Alice. "I can see the resemblance. You have the same eyes."

Alice smiles a warm smile as in walks Gregory in Levi jeans and a three quarter length black leather coat over a metallic-blue Van Heusen half sleeve. Sydney's was-band, her ex, meanders to their booth. Their paths had crossed at least a dozen times since their divorce; each time passing like two ships in the night with nary a hint of acknowledgment from Sydney, not even a glance, leaving arrogant Gregory's ego bruised and hungry. Now the conceited control freak slides into the booth next to her.

"Hello, ladies," Gregory says, folding his arms, leaning on the table. "You look good, Kitten." She did look good: patchwork jeans, tan three-quarter sleeve top, blue eyes to swim in, liquid silver and turquoise earrings, plus a cold shoulder for her ex-husband. Six feet tall Gregory Anderson; his dark brown hair cut in a mullet style with the back pulled into a tail, almond-shaped brown eyes, and a five o'clock shadow hardly noticeable, claiming Indian heritage somewhere along the line. Gregory, the longshore man, arrives in Marcus Hook Port every ninety days or so. And Gregory, the ladies' man, arrives in other ports every ninety days or so; a fact Sydney learned the hard way and did not wish to revisit, ever. Not so if Gregory had his way. So what? A man gets lonely. So what if he was married to a couple of them. He had told her before the divorce hearing she was the cream of the crop. She had told him to "Cultivate this!"

Sydney does a deliberate scooch over closer to the window. "What time is it?" she asks Leora, ignoring the ex.

"Ten 'til," Leora answers. She checks out the side window then looks at Sister Syd. "It's almost show time."

Sydney dips her last bite of buttered roll in blue cheese dressing. "Should we get popcorn?"

"Sure. Buttered," Leora answers with a smug look on her face.

"What? Are you goin' to the movies?" Self-centered Gregory cocks his head, arching one eyebrow profiling for his cornered audience, waiting for glances to fuel his humongous smug attitude.

Sydney knows the look which means its coming. She roots through her jeans bag, pretending to stare out the window but really watching Leora feeding the arrogant jackass her smug smile, saying not a word; then she too waits.

Gregory cannot stand it. He devours Leora's smiling stare. "What are you gonna go see?" He smiles back, turning to Sydney for more ego fuel, and catches his reflection in the window. He assumes his profile position again, head cocked, eyebrow arched.

"Yo, Sis, what's the name of the movie?" Leora flutters her eyelashes.

Sydney shrugs her shoulders. "I don't know." She smiles at Leora, waiting for it.

Leora smiles at Sydney. "Me neither, but it's about a man with three eyes!"

"And a dickie do," Sydney adds. The girls laugh and high-five each other.

Egotistical Gregory sees nothing funny. "I see you two are just as confusing as ever."

Marie's relief, Helen, walks to their table with pencil and pad in hand. Greg didn't really want to order anything. He had seen Sydney's car in the parking lot. He holds Helen's hand, kissing it, and orders a coffee to go, turning to see if all eyes were on him. They weren't. "Give them what they want."

"Hmmm. Order of French fries with brown gravy," Leora says, smiling at Helen. "Just one." She goosenecks the parking lot out the window behind Sydney, who in turn keeps a vigil looking out the side one. "How long are you in town for?"

"Until Monday night," he answers, assuming his profile position and turning to Sydney, flipping through the song menu and singing along with "I'm Already Gone." "So what are you really doin' tonight?"

"Washin' her hair," Leora blurts right before Sydney answers, working.

The control freak gathers his thoughts, looking back and forth at the two connivers. Leora blinks, staring at Sydney who in turn acts like Judy Miller on Sturday Nght Live. "Workin'? I thought you worked second shift during the week."

"Overtime," they answer together. He didn't have to know she was laid off.

Carl Yarborough sprawls in the booth across from Alice, back to back with Leora. The girls are there just like Shaun said they would be; but his ex?

Two of Gregory's friends signal to him from in front of the register just as Helen, the waitress with wisps of white hair at her temples, brings French fries, coffee to go, and the check. He slips her a five dollar tip, scooping both his check and the girls' dinner check from the table. He stands, holding up a wait-a-minute finger for the attention of his buddies. "I've been thinkin' about you. You're the best thing that ever happened to me. I'll call you tomorrow night." He catches his reflection one last time in the window as he walks to his comrades. Sydney shows the vain bigamist the back of her head and gives his departing reflection a thumbs-up gesture for rotate.

"Bye, thanks," Leora says demurely, remaining silent until Gregory is out of earshot. "Wait 'til he finds out your phone is shut off!" She laughs. "And you moved!"

"Yeah, well, party of the first!" Sydney exhales the words, cocking her head and blinking almost uncontrollably, "To wit thereof!"

Leora leans toward her with a puzzling look. "Huh? What's up, Sis?"

Helen gives Alice a refill after serving a coffee to Carl. He is going on and on with the same nonsense as his phone calls; Shaun apologizes but he wants his papers from the business, he wants his ledger from the business, he wants his typewriter; he'll pay for any inconvenience, blah, blah. Alice is sick of it. Something is pretty important and if she locates whatever it is before Griff does, it will be pretty expensive, too.

"I don't care what Shaun wants. People in hell want ice water." Alice speaks slowly, clenching her teeth and trying to keep her voice low to avoid drawing attention. Leora almost gasps aloud with cheeks flushed, stomach knotted. She instinctively knows better than to turn around. Sydney moves over, eclipsing Alice with Leora. She leans toward her, mouthing the word ...wig. Leora mouths the word ...Carl as Sydney reaches over and pushes the low volume button. "I'm Not in Love" now sounds like a soft instrumental.

"Well, the trail leads to you."

"And you know this how?" Alice asks as her eyes drift to the rug on his head.

"Oh, don't tell me. Let me guess, 'cause he says so. How many times do I have to tell you? I don't have anything. If I did, you all would be in jail right now, you simple son-of-a-bitch! Get a hold of yourself! There is no trail except in his depraved mind!"

Carl stirs sugar into the black liquid. "You know Robert Wakefield."

"So do you! I know Shaun, so do you!" Alice growls. "The guy fixed my car. I was broke down, Robert happened to come along and he fixed my car! I don't have Shaun's damn book, his typewriter, his papers, or whatever else he wants!" Her eyes find the top of his head again. "Sing somethin' different!"

"Well, what about the properties?"

"What, pray tell, do they have to do with it?" The realtor holds the front of her head, glaring at Carl then sits back, folding her arms in front of her. "Oh, so that's what this is about? Properties." She adds two creamers and sugar to her coffee. "You're pissed off because you couldn't touch any of 'em at the divorce hearing. We were legally separated when Stephen and I went into business together."

Carl's jaw tightens. "That loser was holdin' out on you."

Alice fidgets in her seat. "Loser?" She exhales, leaning forward with eyes wide and mouth wider. "Holdin' out?" She sits back then leans forward. "Holdin' out what?" Saucer and spoon clatter as she sits the cup down. "They were all joint properties, one in Ogden, the apartments in Media, two in Drexel Hill, one in Concord. Hell, even his three-story office in

Trainer he converted from apartments back into a three-story house on what's that street? Chestnut? They were his babies. I sold all of them; they had mortgages. I couldn't afford 'em. So what? Whatever other business dealings you, Shaun, and Derrick had with Stephen has nothin' to do with me. Tell Shaun to chew on that. Tell 'im to quit passin' the buck. Who the hell does he think he is? Who the hell do ya think you are?" Alice was livid. She wanted to tell him to go pound sand and thought better of it. She did not want to burn bridges, not yet anyway. "Oh, Shaun didn't send you, did he? He doesn't know you're here, does he?" Alice plays with his head.

Leora and Sydney mouth words back and forth to each other: the house, Rob, cars, the typewriter.

Carl studies his ex. He is all too familiar with her controlling ways. He was married to her. Well, he's in charge. He's asking the questions. He ignores hers. "Who ya meetin'?" Carl thinks he has put two and two together; the girls and his ex but he is wrong, as usual, although a mysterious meeting would be much more intriguing than Alice's quiet dinner alone. Leora and Sydney sit like statues with hearts racing.

But not only is he wrong; he is outmatched in a head game with Alice. She makes a disgusting face, shaking her head. "Well, it ain't you! It's none of your business. Who are YOU meetin?"

Carl gulps his coffee, signaling Helen for refills. "Well, what are ya doin' here?"

"What is this, twenty questions? What are you doin' here?"

He stirs his cup of Joe, sitting in silence. A few minutes pass. This time he doesn't ask a question. "Well, Shaun is just missin' some shit and wants to . . ."

Alice cuts him off. "Sounds like a personal problem to me. I take it the typewriter is included in the shit. Well, it ain't me. He oughta check his own backyard, or should I say his own trunk? Did ya happen to look in his trunk? Hell, no! You think he's the see all, be all – is all? Well, pay attention. Shaun is holdin' out on you! What do you think of that?" Alice makes a face as if her mouth were full of vinegar.

Yarborough sips his coffee. He's on to her. He's not falling for it. "No, he ain't. You're blowin' smoke. Your boy was holdin' and you know it."

Carl is trifling to Alice. She doesn't have "anything" and doesn't know where to find "anything." She does know she would like to shove her detailed sex life with "your boy" down Carl's throat, but now is not the time. No, now is time for a little dissension among the troops. And now is her chance. She takes a deep breath, pinching her bottom lip together from side to side with her thumb and finger, gathering her thoughts. "Shaun was at Stephen's office in Trainer more than I was. How 'bout that? He was there more than you or Evely. Do you know that? Hell no, you don't know that," she taunts him.

He is on to her. He is supposed to be doing the pumping, not her. "Yeah, I know that." He gloats like a twelve-year-old.

Alice lets him think he's one up, but only for a second. Then she let's it rip. "He showed up brown baggin' it all the time. How 'bout that? Do ya know what 'that' is? Well, it wasn't his lunch. It was money. Bets, payoffs, shakedowns, hush-sh-sh money." Carl looks down, stirring his coffee. Alice glares at his toupee. "Take that damn thing off your head! I don't know whether it wants to bite me or shit on me."

Silence reigns, and they both get wet. Embarrassment flushes an uneasy Carl. He gawks at Alice then quickly avoids eye contact, scanning the diner and thinking. He is fraying at the edges, losing focus on the topics of discussion: the typewriter, names, this meeting, now brown bags, and money. Confusion crosses Carl's face. He tries to regroup. "Well, you were livin' with the guy. You had access to everything."

"Yeah, livin' with him, not babysittin' 'im, and I didn't live at his office. That wasn't our love nest." Alice has him rattled. She makes a loose fist with one hand and with the other she pushes her index finger in and out of the hole. Carl unravels, slamming a fist on the table. Self-satisfaction tugs at the corners of her mouth.

She is lacking cooperation. Carl is lacking patience. Frustration creeps over his face. "Well, you were there a lot."

"Wow, nothin' gets by you," Alice says sarcastically, thinking he brings new meaning to the word 'nitwit'. "Hell, you're so bright your mother calls you son." She continues to push his buttons. "What do you need? A brick house to fall on ya? I told you Shaun was there, too. When I went there, Shaun would already be there. It was a place of business. Before I sold the place, I told him to get down there and get what he wanted. He had a key too, ya know. As far as I know, he used it. He took what he wanted."

Carl stares at Alice. *I'm in charge. Get her mad enough, she'll slip up. That's what Shaun said.* But he was never married to her. She can make a saint swear. And now she's got Carl's full attention, dancing with doubt because she is making sense. Shaun knew Stephen was sleeping with Alice and never said a word.

Shaun, Stephen, Derrick, and me were partners, right? Alice is in cahoots with these two broads, isn't she? Shaun knows everything, doesn't he? Find the typewriter and the ledger, then we're home free, aren't we? Shaun said so. Pictures swirl in his mind: the typewriter, the ledger with names and dates, money, a key, paper bags, his naked ex-wife.

"I know the good mayor sent ya, right?" Alice twists him like a pretzel. "There's no way you're here because Shaun said so. After all, Shaun and my Stevie were best friends. You're not that stupid". She ties him in a knot, hoping his head explodes.

Wide-eyed Leora mouths the words – holy shit – to her best friend.

Carl tries like hell to focus. But his mind wanders again. *Who cares if Shaun and Lister were best friends? So what if Lister and Alice were rutting all over town and Shaun knew. That's spilled milk, water under the bridge, so to speak. There are more important things, like prison, freedom, the incriminating ledger, the typewriter.* Carl swallows hard on the defensive. She's doing it again. "Derrick wants answers." He follows her lead, changing horses in midstream. "Your boy died in his car."

That's it! Alice is done! She is ready to burn some bridges. She wants to bitchslap this manipulated loser. "Derrick wants answers? About what, the typewriter? Ask Shaun! The ledger? Ask Shaun! And while he's at it, tell 'im ta ask Shaun about the safe! Like I said, he got what he wanted. How 'bout that, ya hand puppet?"

Carl's mind is spinning. *She's tryin' to play me,* he thinks. *What safe? He never mentioned a safe. Maybe 'cause he already has it. My take on what, the situation?* He sits with two fists in his lap. His eyes narrow as he stares at Alice, stretching his left arm across the top of the booth, gazing out the window to his right. She's doing it again. He's on to her. He tries to focus. *She's buyin', right? No, the two broads are buyin', no, wait! Who has the typewriter?* His mind wanders *what brown bags, what safe, Shaun had a key, money.* "Smart mouth bitch," he snarls.

Alice stares at Carl, shaking her head, pinching her bottom lip to hide her smirk. "Ya Bic."

"What the hell's that suppose ta mean?" he snorts.

"What are you writin' a book? Kiss my ass and make it a love story."

"You're crazy."

"Well, it's better than bein' disposable. That's what you are, disposable." She plants the seed. "Have ya checked your-r-r trunk lately? Out on a wild goose chase with a trunk full of evidence and money. Why, you set up you!"

"Shut the hell up, you loud mouth bitch!"

A white Lincoln slowly entering the parking lot catches Alice's attention. Leora and Sydney spot it, too. Alice leans toward the window. "Speak of the devil!" She cups her eyes on the window, blocking the glare of the diner lights. Her chance of getting a phone number for her brother disappears as Leora and Sydney book, grabbing a mint on their way out. "Now look what ya did!" Alice quips. Carl believes he interrupted an exchange between the two tables alright, but not an exchange of phone numbers. He leans toward the window, making hand binoculars. The ex-couple watches the car pull in, stopping at the end of the diner right behind Sydney and Leora's now empty booth. Carl stands, throwing money on the table. "Leavin' so soon? The party's just gettin' started. Come on, we can check everybody's trunk!" Alice taunts. Carl slips into his jacket. "I bet the mayor's with him. What da ya wanna bet? Your cut?" He walks to the door. "Oh, that's right, sorry," she calls after him sounding almost apologetic, "Well, your IOU is good!" She leans toward the window, getting a glimpse of him as he hurries past. "Hey, wait a minute," she says softly. "Ya wanna buy a bridge? Ya frickin' hand puppet."

Schminkin'

* *

Leora and Sydney book—out the door to the left, down the two steps past several newspaper dispensers, and then another left around the Green Street end of the diner, to the familiar safety and security of Sydney's car. They wind down windows in silence, inhaling hints of autumn scenting the air, rustling through the young trees lining the narrow one-way thoroughfare with cars parked like sardines on either side, parallel parking at its finest. The arc light directly across from them in front of the municipal building peeks through the agitated leaves. Loud voices coming from in front of the diner pierce the sounds of light traffic . . . angry voices . . . men's voices.

"My heart's pounding, feel," Sydney says, taking Leora's hand and placing it on her heart."

"Mine's in my throat, see?" Leora answers, opening her mouth. She turns the release latch on the glove compartment door. "How'd we get into this?"

Sydney raises her hand. "I did it." She takes a long draw on her cigarette.

"No, somebody lied on us." Leora makes a V with two fingers tapping her lips for a drag. With her other hand, she plops her denim bag on her lap. The small unzipped pocket on the inside is empty. Repositioning the bag, she digs in with both hands, fingering several empty different colored Bics before locating the elusive Marlboro flip top box minus the cellophane laying flat on the bottom. Both girls root through the glove compartment for Lucky Pierre. "She really stirred things up, didn't she?"

"What?" Sydney answers, lost in thought. "Oh, you mean Alice? Are you kiddin' me? Her ex thinks we were meetin' her. You can't make this stuff up."

"And she didn't have a clue of what he was talkin' about. She went along with it just to piss 'im off. That couldn'ta been timed more perfect." Leora pulls the cellophane pouch of stash from inside the flip top box and packs the seldom used wooden bowl in the dim light of the glove box. She places the cigarette pack into its original hiding place in the little zipper pocket before closing the glove box door. She wiggles two fingers in the top pocket of her Wrangler jacket for her Bic sandwiched in the folded piece of paper from Rhonda. "Hey, listen," she says, grabbing Sydney's arm, stopping her from starting the car. "Let's ride back through the parkin' lot." Leora fires up Pierre, taking a long draw then passes. Sydney takes the bowl and lights it with her own Bic.

"You got a deathwish?" Sydney hits the bowl again before passing it back.

"Not really. I was thinkin' maybe we should ride back through and write down license plate numbers. It seems like everybody and their mother had a black van last night, or should we just give 'em the damn typewriter?"

"I don't know. That's our leverage. What if we give it back and it's not theirs? We get killed. If it is theirs, we get killed. Besides, give it to who? Rob, Griff, the mayor, Carl?" Sydney corrects herself. "Well, Rob, Griff, the mayor anyway."

A white Edsel exits the lot followed by a red Camaro. "Yeah, you're right. It's like that he-said she-said shit adult style."

"Yeah, with guns," Sydney adds.

"And we're caught in the cross hairs."

Sydney raises her hand again. "Yeah, I did it."

"No way, Sis, you didn't hide it in your trunk."

"Well, I hope we find out who did before they remem—" Slamming car doors silence the angry voices. Sydney starts her car and whips on to Green Street with not even her running lights on. With a go ahead green traffic signal some sixty feet away, she makes a right then another right back into the small L-shaped parking lot just as the white Cadillac pulls away, disappearing around the back of the diner.

"Oh! Oh! Oh! Oh! Oh!" Leora yells, turning the radio down as if it will help her see better. Sydney holds on to the steering wheel, pulling herself forward. She slows her vehicle to almost a stand still, inching around the side of the diner. A flicked cigarette flies out of the Continental's passenger side window along with the continuing angry voices as the white luxury car sits at the exit. The girls stare at the obscure license plate wide-eyed, then squinting, blinking . . . winking.

"Can you see it?" Sydney asks, leaning forward with furrowed brow.

Leora pulls the piece of paper from her top pocket and opens the glove compartment again, this time digging for a pen. "Hoe, no!" She answers, glancing in the glove compartment then blinking at the darkened tag while feeling with her hands just as the Lincoln's headlights drench the municipal building. Now the Lincoln's brake lights join the illuminated tag. Griff slowly turns on to the narrow street. "What is it? Do you see it? One, one, one, is that it?" Leora gawks at the tag.

Sydney blinks. Leora blinks. "Seven! It's one-one-seven! What's that an eight? Eight, nine? Wait, three, nine!"

"A! It's an A! Three, nine, A, Sis!" Leora writes: **11739A** above their backward names on the ripped piece of paper with Rhonda's phone number. "Okay. One, one, seven, three, nine, A, right?"

"Yepper! One, one, seven, three, nine, A," Sydney repeats, idling at the exit. She has no plans of going anywhere near the Lincoln. She has enough trouble driving forward, let alone driving backward down a skinny one-way street crammed with parked cars and being chased by the likes of the unsavory car load to boot.

Leora slips the paper back into her top pocket. "Pennsylvania tag, right?"

"Yepper, the Liberty Bell's in the middle." The red light finally changes, giving Griff permission to make a left turn. Sydney whips out of the parking lot then makes a quick right, switching her lights on. Leora checks out the back window, making sure the losers continue north on thirteen as Sydney heads south past the refinery's massive sprawl enclosed in cyclone-fencing topped with barbwire, running the length of Green Street to the loading docks at the river, eleven blocks counting Marshall Street, and running down thirteen to Delaware with lit towers, a constant hissing, billowing smoke, eternal flame, a capillary network of pipe lines, and an odor of oil which is usually carried east, dissipating over the river toward New Jersey. Railways snake through the refinery then run parallel with the Delaware River to points north and south. On the opposite side of route thirteen, barbwire-topped fences outline the diner property and the row of Green Street homes, enclosing the refinery's tank farm also running down to Delaware. One road, Blue Ball Avenue, intersects with thirteen and provides the last chance for drivers to remain in Pennsylvania before heading into the Diamond State. Its steep bridge spans a fire access road, pipe lines and four public railways, cutting through the refinery's tank farm separated with barbwire fencing and gravel. No trees, no curbs, and no sidewalks all the way to the Ridge Road traffic light. The curb on Ridge Road joins the fencing north to Green Street and south into Delaware.

Leora stuffs the pipe. "What a mess," Sydney mumbles, her voice sounding apologetic, taking the lit bowl offered by her best friend. They relax, lost in their own thoughts. Leora turns up the radio as Led Zepplin belts out "Stairway to Heaven" on their scenic cruise up Blue Ball Avenue then left onto Chichester Avenue, a right onto Larkin Road then after the stop sign, a merge onto the Killer Con, route three twenty-two, heading back toward Chester. It was still a little too early for Sydney to show for work.

"Hey, ride by my car. I wanna check it out," Leora tells Sister Syd.

"Ya wanna ride by the house first?" Sydney asks. "It's on the way."

Leora takes a deep breath. "I'm in."

Taking the exit ramp, they make a right onto the Township Line Road and a left onto Chestnut. Nothing out of the ordinary. No black van, no flashlights, just the soft glow from the night light. Pulling into the parking lot behind Leora's car also netted zilch. They felt better, well, not really. Leora did. Sydney, on the other hand, still felt miserable.

"I was thinkin'," Leora offers to Sydney driving in silence. "Ready? Listen. Think about it, Sis. Why hasn't anybody bothered my car?"

"Because we've been ridin' together," Sydney answers, sighing.

"Huh? Yeah, but I have a trunk, too. Why ain't my trunk important? What is the common denominator?"

"Hey, I sucked at math."

"Okay, then let's make it history."

"Grant."

"Grant? Who the hell is he . . . ?" Leora's voice trails.

"I thought you were gonna ask me who's buried in Grant's tomb."

Leora snickers. "Don't blame yourself, Sis. You're kind, considerate, adorable, and understanding. We were set up, that's all. Think about it. Rob walkin' all over the house like he was Helpful Hanna. Shit, he was rootin'and waitin'." She raises her eyebrows up and down. When that didn't work Griff wanted me to go away with him. He was never interested in me. He just wanted access to the house and got tired of waitin'."

"Yeah, access to plant the bugs."

"But you had already kicked Rob to the curb, Sis. And they planted 'em anyway. Anybody coulda planted that one in the box Rob carried around like a stuffed animal, the one that got all wet? Rob could a done it or it coulda been done while I was workin' and you were at dinner with Rob. They had a key." Leora tries to shake Sydney's guilt. "Yo! Sis! Who do you think did it? Come on, pick a loser. We got a choice: Carl, Hector, Griff, Jammer, the mayor, Rob. Hell, it's an epidemic! Just look at the loser I was tied up with, well, almost tied up with. What'd that last, all of four days?"

"Oh, you mean his royal highness, Vince the Prince?"

"Yeah, he was royal alright, a royal pain in the ass."

"The guy thought women were oral subjects, I mean royal objects." Sydney laughs. She enunciates. "Royal subjects. You know what I mean. Whatever."

"Yeah, snappin' his fingers at me when he went upstairs to use the bathroom."

Sydney laughs again, snapping her fingers. "What was it you said to him?"

"If I'm not there in five minutes, start without me."

"He was so full of himself. Hell, he was worse than my ex."

Leora closes her eyes, shaking her head. "What a loser! What was it, two months ago? Three? Who needs that? See, it happens to the best of us, Sis. Think about it. Last night is really the first time the house has actually been empty since you dropped Rob the Verb. Crow went to Atlantic City, I was workin', and you were on a wild goose chase to the Chateau. Rob was just a distraction." Sydney idles at the stop sign at third and Booth. She rests her chin on her arms folded on the top of the steering wheel and sighs. "He was!" She hits the bowl and hands it to her best friend. "He was really nothing but a distraction. They had a freakin' key, Sis! He was a nice distraction though," she tries to lighten the mood, "with his washboard abs, biceps, pecker, I mean pecks . . ." Leora starts panting.

Sydney laughs and coughs, handing the extinguished bowl to Leora.

"You could bounce a quarter off everything!"

The girls laugh hysterically.

"He fixed your car and Alice's car, but first he fixed Goo Goo's, remember? You see where I'm goin' with this?"

"Ahhhh, third time's the charm?"

"Hmm, good point, Momma, but that ain't it. He didn't do anything to my car. So if Rob put it there, why would he check everybody? What's he playin' dumb? Why?"

"Maybe he's stallin'," Sydney answers, "Maybe it's the process of elimination. Maybe he didn't do it but saw who did it. Maybe he was gonna blackmail 'em. Maybe he really was gonna set us up." Sydney is disgusted. "I don't know, whatever."

"Hey, maybe Goo Goo has the money. Maybe his Caddy wasn't stolen. Good grief, I don't know either. Here we go again. I'm so confused." Leora empties ashes from the pipe out the window and chucks it back in the glove compartment.

"Hey, maybe we should give it to Alice."

"Maybe we should give it to the authorities, but who? I don't trust the cops."

"Hey, I know. We could write a note on the men room's mirror in lipstick. Help!

Being held hostage, signed, the typewriter. Nah, they'd know it was us."

Leora's mind wanders. "Orrr, we can type a note, find Griff's car at the club parkin' lot and slip it under the windshield wiper. That way it won't be limited to Papa's crowd. People from all over go to the club."

"Yeah, maybe he'll think guys from New York really are around."

"Yeah!" Leora agrees. "And leave us the hell alone."

"Yeah, sounds like a plan! I'm in!"

"Me, too!" The girls head home on a mission, backtracking up Booth Street to Ninth past Papa's. Now a black van sits in the parking space next to Leora's Chevy—a black van with a right rear whitewall tire. They glimpse Jammer and Hector standing on the passenger side of her car with the both doors open.

Oh, my God!" Sydney yells, driving erratic. "What are we doin'?" She grabs Leora's arm. "What are we doin'?"

"Drive! Drive!" The closed bakery's night lights illuminate the scene.

"Don't ya wanna get the tag number?"

"No, no, no, let's go to the house!"

"Do you believe this? You're kiddin' me! Ya think they're buggin' your car?"

"I don't know, but there's no sense in callin' the cops. They already know."

"How do ya figure? Are you clairvoyant or what? Are you sure, Momma?"

"Sure as shit. They used a Slim Jim. My car was locked."

"You're kiddin' me! This sucks big time!"

"You didn't see any broken windows, did ya?"

"Nah-uh. Wow, they're gettin' really desperate. It's gettin' *really* scary!" Miss Lead Foot practically makes an L-shaped turn onto Chestnut Street, drifting into the driveway after cutting the engine. Crickets and cicadas sing, all is right with the world as the twosome are greeted by Wheezer flopping on the porch wall and falling off. Although the black van sits next to Leora's Chevy up the road, the rattled twosome map out a plan before entering the house. They drop pocketbooks, jackets, and keys inside the front door. Leora retrieves a flashlight to check the newspaper on the porch for any telltale signs of recent activity pertaining to the new house key. Meanwhile Sydney retrieves the typewriter from her bedroom, pillowcase and all, in the dark. On her way to the kitchen, Leora collects several sheets of paper and an envelope from the den, then ever so quietly places the bugged kitchen chair out the backdoor on the enclosed patio.

"The newspaper on the porch is fine," Leora whispers.

Sydney removes the typewriter from the pillowcase and flips the fasteners. Wheezer jumps onto the kitchen chair. He can help. He watches intently with just ears and huge eyes visible above the table. Sydney removes the cover, exposing the manual printing machine. Leora slides the sheets of plain paper closer to Sydney. Wheezer helps . . . now! In a split second, he springs like a jack-in-the-box, pouncing on the paper with his front paws, then sits with just ears and huge eyes visible above the table again. The jittery girls jump, muffling screams.

"Yo, Tiger!" Sydney half whispers as Leora crumples a sheet of paper into a ball, tossing it on the floor. Wheezer disappears from sight, enthralled in his own adventure.

The girls inspect their mechanical hostage, looking in the cover and in the keys searching for a telltale flaw. "Ya think this is really it?" Leora asks.

"I don't know." Sydney's response sounds doubtful. "It doesn't look all that important to me." She glances at the clock: 7:25. "When I pick it up, you move the bottom of the case so we can sit it flat on the table."

Leora places the bottom in the lid.

"How ya wanna do this?" Sydney interlocks her hands and stretches as if cracking her knuckles then wiggles her fingers trying to lighten the mood.

"Very carefully," Leora says laughing. Neither has typewriter experience.

"Wait a sec, wait a sec." Sydney closes her eyes, thinking. "Should we put names, like Dear Griff? Nah. No names. I got it! How about, To Whom It May Concern?"

She types:

To whom it may concern: Help!

Leora folds the note in three like a business letter, but it was just too much paper for so few words. "It looks stupid!" She folds another piece of paper in threes.

"Let's see." Sydney sighs then inserts the sheet of paper rolling it down past the first crease, biting her bottom lip the whole time. "Okay, I think I'm ready," Sydney states, finally glancing at her best friend.

She types painstakingly:

TO WHOM IT MAY CONCERN: HELP!
    BEING HELD HOSTAGE!
    YOURS TRULY,
    THE TYPEWRITER

Leora stands with the note. "Yo, Sis! Yo!" She shoves her face to paper, looking up at the light looking down toward Sydney.

"Okay, huh?" Sydney plays, too. "Yo, Sis," She calls, holding her hands in front of her face. "Peek-a-boo!"

"No, no, look! Look at this!"

Sydney focuses her eyes on the back of the paper and sees tiny holes, five in all. "Oh no, Wheezer put holes in it!" She checks another sheet.

"No, no, no!" Leora answers in disbelief. She lays the holey ransom note flat on the table. The capital O of the typewriter acts as a paper punch.

Sydney holds the paper to the light, looking at the front, the back, the front, the back. "Oh, my God! You're kiddin' me!"

"Whoaaa, Momma!" Leora swallows hard.

"I think we just became the hostages!" They both sit, staring at the typewriter; Sydney as white as a ghost, Leora flushed taking deep breaths. It is one thing to think about the seriousness of the situation. It's another thing to stare at it.

"Some things people are better off not knowin'."

"Some people are better off not knowin' things."

Speaking at the same time, the girls look at each other quizzically, then gawk at the mechanical monster. Leora breaks the silence. "Is this like holdin' Tiger by the tail?"

"Yeah, and sorta wakin' up a rattlesnake and holdin' his tail, too."

"We really can't let 'em know all of this!"

"Hell no! Definitely not!" Sydney agrees. "Yo, Sis, we can put 'em all in jail now! Let's get rid of 'em ASAP."

"His arms are too long," Leora answers, referring to Griff's reach to the outside world from a prison cell. "And the Feds won't protect us. They'll leave us twistin' in the wind."

"Who else, Sis? Who? Oooh, didn't Alice say she owned this house with that Lister guy?"

"Yeah," Leora answers, "Griff's business partner, and we have his spare key."

"So maybe she really was gonna blackmail 'em or put 'em all in jail."

"Yeah, maybe she was sittin' on it, playin' dumb." Leora sucks air. "Maybe she doesn't even know Rob five-fingered it!"

"Yeah, and he worked on her car, then my car!" Sydney starts typing. Wheezer appears, bringing his captured treasure to his comrades. Leora crumples the paper into a tight ball again and tosses it. Wheezer, so excited, runs in place before momentum takes over, fueling his hot pursuit into the next room. "You still wanna do this?"

"Yeah, I mean, I guess." Leora sighs. "I don't know. I mean we don't have to, I mean we can always change our mind, but at least it'll be there in case we want to."

"We should slip the note in the van. They wouldn't find it for days, Momma."

Leora laughs. "Months, Sis. We'd probably have to call 'em and tell 'em!"

Sydney slips the folded note into the business envelope and hands it to her partner in crime.

"Wow!" Leora licks the envelope, sealing it shut, handing it back to her best friend.

"Hey, I gotta work, Sis." Sydney tries to give it back.

"Well," Leora responds, "I gotta get drunk. Just prop me in a corner until you're ready to go. Remember, strength in numbers. And let me know tomorrow if I had a good time. Besides, he might not even be there tonight. Who knows, who knew, who cares, whatever. You hang on to it, Sis, until we need it. We'll figure it out."

Sydney takes the machine back to its hiding place. Leora brings the bugged chair back into the kitchen. They gather keys, pocketbooks, jackets, and Wheezer with his newfound toy before closing the front door ever so softly with just a click from the lock. Across the street, the fading colorful field of grass cattails, Queen Anne Lace, Blue Cockle (Chicory), Toad Flax, Sweet Pea, and Daisies is blackened in the ominous darkness, adding to their emotional upheaval as the girls make their way to Papa's.

In the parking lot, the black van is nowhere to be found.

"I didn't see it at the house, did you?"

"Well, I wasn't really lookin' for it. Hang on, Sis, we're goin' around back." Not all the cars in the large back parking lot are Saturday night marketers. A few decorated cars give a hint of wedding reception revelers. The girls ride around the back of a black van and breathe a sigh of relief when they spot the telltale whitewall tire. Sydney drives back around for the tag number before entering the narrow throughway between the market and the side of the shopping center on her way to the front of businesses. She pulls into an open space facing Ninth Street. Leora retrieves her jacket from the backseat for the piece of paper in the top pocket. She repeats the numbers to Sydney, making sure they each memorized the same number before locating the pen in the glove box again and writes: **53145 – van** sideways on the piece of paper.

"We're runnin' out of room."

Sydney opens her compact to freshen her makeup in the bright lights from the Laundromat behind them. "Ready? Let's go."

After a dab of Chantilly, Leora reapplies her lipstick. She turns, squinting at her car. The nervous Nellies scan the small front parking lot: no white Cadillac, no Griff, no Rob; no Heckle 'n' Jeckle. The hustle and bustle begins to dwindle in the mini strip mall while empty parking spaces multiply. Another Saturday night is becoming history.

"Listen, if you see the mayor inside, turn off one of the neon window lights. It doesn't matter which one. Just pull the chain."

"And what are you gonna do?" Sydney points at Leora.

"I'll walk around back and get the tag number. Tom said the mayor drives a BMW."

"Whew! For a minute there, I thought you were gonna say a black van!" Sydney pulls her jacket from the backseat of the car then stands doing a three-sixty, scanning the parking lot. "And what else are ya gonna do, Momma?" They know each other like books. Sydney just has to hear Leora say the words.

Leora leans toward the open door. "Well, with help from my best-friend-in-the-whole-wide-world, I'm gonna check my car."

"Well, what if your best-friend-in-the-whole-wide-world is inside and you're outside? How is that helpin'?" Sydney leans on the open car door, peering into the vehicle at her partner in crime.

"That's okay, Sis. If anybody asks where I am, tell 'em I'll be in. I'm out back."

"Anybody?"

"Anybody, Sis. Anybody! I'm out back."

"Yo, Sis, are you sure?"

"Sure I'm sure. Does a bear shit in the woods? I'm in." Leora slides the pen into her pocket with the paper. "I'll wait for your signal."

Not knowing what will be going on and unable to be able to find out will be driving Sydney bonkers. She chucks her car keys onto the driver's seat. "Here, in case ya get lonely." Now Leora has to show her smilin' face in the bar.

Leora smiles, placing Sydney's keys in the ignition. "Ya want mine?" she teases.

"Hell no!" Sydney answers her best friend as she walks across the parking lot to the tavern. She turns around, walking backwards. "Yo! Sis! Be careful!"

Plant This!

Leora sings "Love Train" with The O'Jays as she pivots and scoots her back against the passenger door to get a good view of the front of Papa's out the rear window. She couldn't see her car from this position, but it was all well and good. Alone with her thoughts, Leora is her own worst enemy. *I wonder what they were doin' in my car.* She flicks her cigarette over her head out the window. *They planted somethin'. Oh, maybe money. Yeah right, and maybe I glow in the dark. It's gotta be drugs. Geez, it would be nice if it is good drugs. Hmmm, Acapulco Gold, or Panama Red. Yeah right, that's only pot. They wanna nail us to the wall, up against the wall fothermucker.* "Maybe its al-l-l in your mind, my dear," she imitates Boris Karloff. *Nah, I lost my mind.* She watches the traffic on Ninth Street. *It's probably tick or some other kind of junk stuff.* She pulls her denim jacket over the front of her, slipping her arms in the sleeves. *Brrr. How dumb are they? They want access to my trunk to look for the typewriter. All they have to do is pull the backseat out. Even I know that. They had the damn doors open. My car better start, too. If it doesn't, I'll check the coil wire. They're playin' with the wrong person.* Growing up, she had spent a lot of time in the garage with her dad, looking at coil wires, points, plugs, breathers, fan belts, oil caps, distributors, dip sticks. He can fix anything, her dad. He is a first class machinist at the sprawling Sun Oil refinery. Hell, he taught her how to drive stick. *Nothin' like a manual transmission—nothin'.* And he taught her: "an ounce of prevention is worth a pound of cure." Standard maintenance goes a long way.

"You And Me Against the World" begins. A song Leora sang with her son. Leora turns the key in the ignition from accessories to off, but it was too late. Tears well as Leora's mind wanders through the memories. He filled her every waking hour, her boy did. Oh, how her arms had ached to hold him. What could have been? What should have been? Pangs of loneliness surround her. She is lonely. Of course she's lonely. That's a given. She breathes as if she's in labor, suppressing the lonely feelings until they sank back to the bottom of her heart. It was so much easier with a couple of drinks. *To hell with relationships. I should take a page from the guys' book. One night stands. Works for them! When in Rome do as the Romans do. It's a man's world. That's the hot set up. No more wearing my heart on my sleeve to be lied to and cheated on. Love 'em and leave 'em. Bad-da-boom, bad-da-bing. Talk to ya a little bit later. See ya! Any port in a storm, well, any port except lousy Griff. What does Gabe say? Eight to eighty—blind crippled or crazy—if they can't walk, carry 'em.* Leora giggles. *And Fidget would say Griff's a two-bagger. He's so ugly you need two bags in case the first one breaks.*

Leora laughs out loud. Sniffling, she blots her eyes with the bottom of her maroon unbuttoned short-sleeved blouse. She straightens her pink tank top as the girls show their high beams. This is the seventies. Burn your bra and free the girls, womens' lib and all that jazz. *Hell, a man invented it. Let him strap on a living one.* The window lights are still lit. Leora sighs. *Should I give her a couple more minutes? Is he in there?* Her mind drifts again. The parking lot begins to fill. She yawns. *That wedding reception must be over. Maybe Sydney doesn't have time to get to the window. I don't have time either, for a relationship or this!* Leora feels trapped like the two of them are backed against the wall, painted into a corner. *We're like up shit creek without an oar.* She is getting more and more leery of strangers and things that go bump in the night. And she is so tired she could sleep on a clothes line. She yawns again. Her eyes fly open, wide. *Oh, my God! SHIT! If they find stuff planted in my car, then they have that cause thing, probably cause, no, no, probable, probable cause! They can check the house! That's it! They wanna get in the house!* "The typewriter!" she blurts out loud then looks around to see if anyone heard her. She rolls up windows and yanks the keys out of the ignition. She has to go in the bar … now! She doesn't care who is in there. She doesn't care if the window lights are on or off. Screw the tag number. She doesn't want anybody crawling all over her house. She slips her jacket on, heading toward the bar then spins around and heads toward her car, then spins back around, heading toward the bar again and stops. *Wait a minute! Wait a minute! If they catch me at the car, I give 'em what they want. Wait a minute! Wait a minute!* She breathes deep. *Son-of-a-bitch! If I go in the bar and they're in there, I give 'em what they want. They can march my sorry ass right to my car!* She stares at the '64 Chevy. She feels damned if she does or damned if she doesn't. She almost hyperventilates. *Wait! Wait! Calm down, Leora, calm down.* She takes another deep breath, inhaling the hint of exhaust—French fries—and leaves in the chilly autumn air. *You're right! You're right! Check the car!* She blinks at her car then blinks at the traffic. She scans the street, the intersection, the straggle of people from the drugstore, the market, the Laundromat. Breathing through her mouth, she scurries double time to her vehicle in the last parking space down in front of the bakery. She walks around the front of the car to the driver's side, stepping down off the curb and cupping her hands to the window, peering inside. It is too dark. She tries to open the door. Her heart races, her stomach knots. Her cheeks flush as if all eyes were upon her. *Oh, my God! It's locked. They locked it!* She breathes deep. She digs for the keys in her pocketbook, watching the traffic, the parking lot, and the people in her peripheral vision. She is visibly shaken. Finally unlocking the door, she slips into her car, flooding the interior with light, then shuts the door as quickly as possible, drenching the interior with darkness. Slouching, she pulls the visor down. Nothing. She flips it up then checks the passenger side—nothing. She flips that side up and feels inside the glove compartment, first removing her one hitter to her pocketbook then feels for any unusual shapes. *I don't even know what I'm lookin' for, powder, pill, or plant?* Still no prize, she feels down the side of the front seat with her left hand, then feels all the way across the seat, finding nothing there or down the passenger side. She pulls the lever, pushing the bench seat back and feels under it from one side to the other, nothing. *Think! If I was a drug, where would I hide?* Headlights announce a car's entrance into the parking lot. Leora lies across the seat, paralyzed with fear; her eyes wide, holding her breath. Adrenaline rushes for flight or fright as she leans on one elbow just high enough to see a red car parking up in front of the bar and gives a sigh of relief. *I gotta get outta here.* She adjusts the front seat to its original position and checks one more place: the ashtray. No luck. *I'll go give Sydney her keys and come take my car for a ride. I gotta get to a gas station where there's some light.* She grabs her keys and pocketbook, exiting the vehicle quickly but not before her peripheral vision catches a flash of something in the backseat, perhaps a tiny reflection from the overhead light on a shiny surface. She locks the door in her hasty exit from the car. Curious, she cups her hands and peers through the window again. It's still too dark. She rolls her eyes and unlocks the car door again. The inside light blinks on as she pushes the back of the front seat forward. Stepping inside with one foot, she stretches to feel along the rear bench seat, locating a piece of plastic shoved in between the bottom of the back seat and cushion. It makes a crumbling noise when she pulls to remove it, but its contents remain jammed down the seat cushion, steadfast and unyielding. She puts pressure on the seat cushion, forcing it down and freeing the plastic bag. Pills tumble inside the bag, piling into the corner when Leora holds it up and glares at it for a split second— which is about as long as it takes the girl to get out of the car—balling it up and shoving it in her pocketbook with her keys. She practically runs past the row of closed businesses slowing to a walk in front of the Laundromat lights. *Thank you, Heckle 'n' Jeckle, you dumb son-of-a-bitches.*

"How dumb are they? Where's Gene Reyburn?" she says aloud, laughing all to herself, pacing in front of Papa's. She is jittery and nervous. *What should I do? Put 'em in the trash, put 'em in the black van?* She continues to pace, all the while scanning the parking lot until satisfied, she puts lighter to cigarette, pulling two twenty dollar bills from her purple tip bag. She shoves the Jacksons into her left back pocket along with her license, and slips her blue Bic in her top jacket pocket with her cigarettes staring at the front of Papa's several minutes before realizing one of the window lights are off.

"What are ya, waitin' for a bus?" Jug Head yells, jaywalking with Tata across Ninth Street to their favorite watering hole.

"What's happ'nin'?" Leora yells to the friendly faces hustling out of harm's way around two cars pulling into the parking lot.

The pair shuffle their way to the barmaid. "Why aren't you in there workin'? No, wait what's tonight?" Jug Head asks, shaking his head, tossing his thick dark hair from his face, exposing his otherwise dark brown eyes, the color now hidden by evening shadows. He gives Tata a quizzical glance.

"It's Saturday night." Tata speaks, slowly shaking his head. "The girl don't work Saturdays, right?" Tata's smile lights his face under a balding head, smoothing the wrinkles in his cheeks.

Leora nods smiling at the little old man. "You're right."

"Yeah, see? She works enough all week. Give the girl a break."

"What do ya got, a date? He's pickin' ya up by bus, huh?" Ball buster Jug Head laughs, shoving his hands in his front pockets and shrugs his shoulders. It is a bit brisk.

Blinking, Leora smirks at Jug Head then stands in front of the tavern's patrons with her back to the bar, spreading her arms and legs as if to block their entrance. "Let me see it." Leora holds a hand out, wiggling her fingers at Jug Head.

Jug Head bucks his eyes, grinning ear to ear.

Leora knows what he's thinking. "You wish!" She walked right into that one.

With an ornery laugh, he tries to hold her arms to her sides and tries kissing the top of her head.

"Get your dirty mind outta the gutter."

"Tata shakes his head. "That boy . . ." His voice trails.

"Boy?" Leora folds her arms in front of her. Jug Head slips an arm around her shoulder. "Tata, the boy is older than me. I'll tell ya what, wish in one hand and shit in the other, and see which one gets filled first."

Tata nods. "Yep, yep." He chuckles with laughter in his blue eyes.

Leora holds her hand out again with wiggling fingers.

Jug Head fishes in his back pocket for his wallet, still grinning. "Man, you're tough. What are you, the doorman? You cardin' me?"

"Man?" Leora wiggles her fingers at Jug Head. "You see a man you kiss 'im." She turns to Tata. "Do I look like a man?"

"You're the prettiest man I ever seen," Tata answers.

"Doorman this!" she says, wiggling her fingers at Jug Head again. "I don't want you're license. I know you're old".

"Oh! That hurts!" He grabs his chest, mimicking Redd Foxx. You're killin' me. Well, if ya don't want my license, what do ya want?" He laughs with exaggerated nods. "Ohhh, I get it, you do want my body."

Leora tightens her jaw to stop from laughing. "Yeah, the second Tuesday of next week." She holds her hand out again. "Give me your permission slip."

"Permission slip?"

"Does your wife know you're here?"

"Oh, you're cruel."

Leora stands with hands on hips. "Hey, I know your phone number. Don't make me call Eileen." Jug Head laughs, slipping an arm around her shoulder.

A police car enters the lot down in front of the bakery, slowly cruising past Leora and company, stopping just past the front of the tavern. Leora turns her back to them and slips her right arm behind Jug Head. Two car doors slam as the city blues exit the idling black-and-white. Leora cringes, closing her eyes and putting a death grip on the back of Jug Head's shirt, wishing she could crawl in a hole and pull it in after her. *This is it.*

"Do you?" Jug Head asks again.

"What?"

"Damn girl! You're tough. You didn't hear a word I said. Relax, baby, they don't know you're holdin'. You're with me." Jug Head jokes, grinning at Leora.

No truer words were ever spoken. *If you only knew, you'd shit a gold brick.* Leora is beside herself, wide-eyed, expressionless.

"Them cops went in the bar," Tata states, pointing toward the glass doors. "Maybe there's a ruckus in there."

"Hey, maybe somebody called about the ruckus out here," Jug Head tells Tata, grinning at Leora.

Leora wasn't laughing. In fact, her stomach was doing backflips.

"Hey, baby, come on. Go handle this. Lay the law down." Jug Head holds the door open.

"Nah," Leora answers, swallowing the lump in her throat. "Sonny and Hank are probably in there."

"Yeah," Tata agrees, "the girl's off."

"And besides that I don't work tonight." She makes a half-hearted attempt at humor while her mind races; she does not know what to do. For a split second, she wants to run—but only a split second. Run where?

"Well, let's check it out," Jug Head offers his arm to her. "Looks crowded."

"It is," Leora says, smiling weakly. "It's a spill over from Shea and Wilbur's wedding."

"Yeah, it was either go to the wedding reception earlier or come here later." Jug Head smiles.

"Good choice. I'll write you a note in case you're out after your curfew."

"Hey, I don't have a curfew," Jug Head answers with a questionable look.

Leora walks arm and arm through the doors. "Oh, really?"

"That's right," Jug Head answers, opening the inside door.

"Oh, then what time is Eileen comin'?"

Jug Head laughs, throwing his head back as decibels of "Philadelphia Freedom" escape through the open door. Elton John smothers his answer. Leora nods a thank you on her way into the den of inequity, spotting a full prayer meeting of Yarborough, Jackson, the mayor, and the ever so dumb Heckle n' Jeckle at their usual table up by the jukebox. *I bet Jammer doesn't fly out the door tonight, the piece of shit. Oh, maybe he'll have to fetch the cops for—hmmm—where's Uncle Donald?* All the ducks gooseneck the front door. The two officers are on their way out the backdoor. Leora walks with a beat to her right, past the lattice room divider, past the pool table around the bar to the mirrored wall side, squeezing between acouple of jitterbugs up by the taps. They each offer their seat to the perky brunette. It was only about eight-thirty and half the bar was already sloshed.

"Yo, Chooch, what's up?" Sydney asks, leaning over the sink, drying her hands on her jeans. Chooch is a name they started calling each other at the club to find one another killing two birds with one stone, so to speak. No one else answers to it, and no one knows their real names.

"The sky," Leora answers, plopping on a bar stool. She pulls two sets of keys from her jeans bag, slipping hers in her right front pocket and placing the bag and Sydney's keys on the bar. "What's happ'nin'?" Leora taps her pocketbook, pointing behind the bar. Sydney takes her own keys and Leora's bag, placing it under the register at the far end. The bar is fairly busy. It is not as packed as Leora first thought, just clusters or groups here and there.

"I was gonna send out the Calvary." Sydney drops a coaster in front of her best friend.

"It's a bitch, ain't it? See? That's how I felt last night."

"Give Chooch a drink." The young wedding reveler holds a pool stick against him with his arm while laying a five dollar bill flat on the bar with two hands.

"Did ya see the light?" Sydney asks, referring to the window.

"Are you a born-again Christian?" The pool stick jabs the young buck under the right side of his chin, leaving a blue chalk mark.

This could be fun. "Is that a bad thing?"

"No."

Leora bucks her eyes at him. "Then can I get an Amen?"

"Amen!"

"I'll drink to that. Give me a shot of blackberry brandy straight up and a side of chemicals on the rocks."

"Chemicals? Wow! I'll have some of that." Jab, jab, jab goes the poolstick.

"It's H2O, water."

The young fellow smiles at Leora. "I knew that." Jab. Jab.

Leora smiles back.

"You smell good," he compliments this hot-lookin' chick, bobbing his head and giving her his best debonair smile. Jab, jab, jab.

Leora almost laughs out loud. She licks her hand. "I taste good, too. Taste." She makes a loose fist, holding it out to him. He blushes, gathering his change with two hands still holding the pool stick with his arm. Jab. Jab. She looks past him to the other end of the room, spotting Uncle Donald seemingly in a heated discussion with someone on the far side of the massive support column. She signals to Sister Syd. "Give . . ." She points to the flirtatious jitterbug. ". . . and give me a Rollin' Rock pony." She places the twenty on the bar. Sydney places an opened long neck Bud in front of "Don Juan" and twists the cap off a Rock nip, sitting it on a coaster for Leora.

"Who's up?" Lane Phillips yells, standing at the pool table. "Whose quarters?"

"Me! Me! I'm up!"

"Well, let's go, Mimi."

The jitterbug holds a bottle of bubbly in each hand, hurrying to rack the balls, dragging the pool stick still being held by his arm. Jab. Jab. He spins around and raises his beer as a thank you. Jab. Jab. Jab.

Leora glances at Lane for a split second, dismissing her ex-husband with a turn of her head. "God, they let anybody in here."

"Yeah, and Gregory's up the other end bullshittin' with Goo Goo."

"He's checkin' to see if we were lyin'. We're surrounded." Leora changes the subject. "Don't Shea and Wilbur have five kids? It's about time they get married."

"Yeah, better late than never, and you're drinkin' fire water. What's up? Who you lookin' at?"

"D—all the above."

Sydney leans in. "Goo Goo asked for ya and so did Papa. I said what you told me to say, you were out back. Griff heard me."

"Papa, where is he?" Leora stands on the foot rail and holds on to the bar, checking out the room.

"Griff's talkin' to him on the other side of the phone." Sydney leans in again. "Hey, Sis, I was thinkin' you have to get your car outta here. Griff and the mayor came in the back right after I got here. It's a wonder we didn't run into 'em. They were all loud and boisterous, making sure everybody saw them. I think we are right. It's a setup. Griff said somethin' to the mayor, and the next thing you know he's on the pay phone then the cops walk in right over to their table." Sydney looks around for empty beverages. "He musta asked them if they saw you out front. They just went out back."

"I know, I saw 'em."

Marcie comes down from the other end of the bar and places an upside down shot glass in front of Leora. "It's on Goo Goo."

Leora nods. "Tell him I said thanks, Marcie."

"They're talkin' about you," Marcie offers.

"Who is?"

"Shauny and Papa."

Sydney snaps her head around with a gnarled expression.

"Well, if they talk about me, they're leavin' somebody else alone."

When Marcie is out of ear shot Sydney loses it. "Shauny? What the hell's that?"

"She must be related to Rhonda," Leora answers, trying to lighten the mood.

"Yeah, her sister."

"I don't think Goo Goo's involved, do you? I think if he was, Rob the Verb would be here, the two-faced bastard. I really think its all Griff with the mayor's help."

". . . And Marcie's. See, gut feelings are always right. See, we had a feeling about her. Remember you said somethin' to Sonny and he defended her? Well, he gave her the benefit of the doubt."

"Yeah, what did he tell me? We might need a job in six years when we're her age, she needs a job, she's a widow, she's just bein' friendly. She's from up the line and doesn't know anyone. Besides it's only one night a week. What's she been here like three months, her and her Buster Brown hairdo?"

"Don't get me started."

"Who's Goo Goo sittin' with?"

"Oh, you mean besides Gregory, God's gift to women ev-v-very where? Doc and Chick," Sydney answers before going to handle the thirsty crowd.

Leora throws back a blackberry, washing it down with the Rollin' Rock. She places a five dollar bill in the beer well before shoving the rest of the change in her jeans front pocket.

"Are you leavin', Momma?" Sydney asks.

"Not if I can help it but listen . . ."

Sydney pours her another shot and puts another upside down shot glass in front of her. "That's on Jug Head and Dinky."

Leora waves a thank you, smiling her finest casual grin. "Listen, I got it."

"Got what?"

"You know." Leora nods her head vigorously. "I checked my car. I got IT."

"Are you shittin' me, Mister?" Sydney stands up straight as all the color drains from her stone face. "These people are nuts!"

"I thought it had to be out in the open for them to see it, to give' em a reason to open my car but let me tell ya somethin', Sis, ya can't see anything inside. It's too dark."

"What are we doin'? What do ya want me to do? What should we do?" Sydney is rattled. She throws back Leora's shot and refills it for her best friend. "I should be done by eleven. Where we goin'?"

"Hey, we're goin' schminkin', right? Plan A. I should be propped in a corner by then, right? But if they cart me outta here, take my pocketbook home, and if they tell me to get my things, give me yours. Get ready, okay?" Sydney nods.

Marcie walks around Sydney, putting another upside down shot glass in front of Leora. "It's on Goo Goo. He wants to know if your new friend would like to meet his new friend."

Leora is not in the mood for head games. "Tell Goo Goo I'll think about it." She does not like talking to Marcie and waves hello to some regulars, a welcomed distraction, engaging in small talk and joke cracking.

"Hey, why don't sheep shrink when it rains?" Gordon asks, licking his stirrer.

Everyone responds with a lot of I-don't-knows and shoulder-shrugging. Gordon drinks his drink.

"Well, why?" George yells across the bar. "What's the answer?" Everyone mumbles in agreement.

"Oh, I don't know. My wool sweater shrunk in the washer." There is a bunch of eyes rolling, heads shaking, and moans.

"Yeah, well answer me this," Stewart starts. "Why don't they make planes out of what a black box is made out of?" More moans can be heard.

"Why don't psychics win lotteries?" Barbara questions the crowd.

Low laughter can be heard. Leora laughs, too.

"I always wondered why is it what doctors do is called practice?" Pamela asks.

"I got one and it comes with an answer." Jug Head yells, "Why are hurricanes named after women?" He looks around. "No takers?" He looks around again. "Cause they're wet and wild but when they leave they take the house and car with 'em."

Mugs and glasses clink as a few of the guys cheer and toast. Leora yells, "Yeah it's an old man's world, isn't it?"

"Whoaaa!" The crowd murmurs. Jug Head bucks his eyes smiling at his favorite barmaid shaking his head.

"Hey, God made Adam first, right?" Leora's announcement is met with a resounding yep, yep, yep. "Yeah, well, there's always a rough draft before the masterpiece." Pamela and a couple other girls roar, toasting and drinking. "I'll drink to that." Leora chases another shot with Rollin' Rock. Through her peripheral vision, she catches Lane leaning against the lattice, staring at her. *He must be fightin' with his new wife. I wonder if he found out she's runnin' on him yet? Karma's a bitch.* She locks eyes with him for a split second. *I'm out. You get one shot at me, my man.*

Sydney takes one of Leora's pyramid shot glasses for a blackberry refill. Leora gives her another for a Rock nip. "I must say, Sis, once we've hit 'em, they've been hit," she says, referring to Lane and Gregory.

"Oh, yeah, ya see 'im, do ya?" Leora asks, feeling mighty relaxed. "Can I have a witness?"

Sydney raises her hand. "Ya can't miss him. I think I see a bit of a drool," Sydney answers, leaning over, washing some mugs and glasses.

Marcie comes down and places another upside down shot glass in front of Leora. "This is on Goo Goo," Marcie continues. "And he says his new friend really wants to meet your new friend."

Leora is not in the mood to be around people she finds distasteful. *This broad sucks!* And she is more than sick and tired of being on guard. She blinks slowly at Marcie while speaking in an almost monotone voice. "Oh, and who is his newfound friend?"

"The Verb," Marcie answers. "Yeah, he said for me to tell you the Verb."

"The Verb?" Leora sits up straight. *Rob!* "The Verb wants to meet my new friend?" She pulls the ten from her front pocket. "Give Goo Goo a drink and ask him who my new friend is."

Sydney pours a shot, lingering in front of her best friend. "This is on Chooch," she says, referring to herself wiping the bar to eavesdrop on the conversation.

Marcie brings Leora her change, reaching in front of Sydney. "Your new friend is Sarah Treet. That's who the Verb wants to meet." Marcie thinks. "Oh, yeah, and Goo Goo said the Verb wants to meet her at Red Run Cove, whereever that is."

I'm Out!

Marcie's sandy color page-boy style hair bounces with each arrogant step she takes toward her end of the bar. The thirty-something-year-old had no clue of the magnitude of the bomb she dropped on the girls until she saw their shocked faces. It makes no-never-mind what-so-ever the actual cause or reason. In her smug world, she is the cause, she is the reason. She is delighted.

Sydney waits on a few customers while Leora leans backward and forward, looking along the wall, up the front end, at the tables, down the far end. "Did she say what I think she said?" Leora asks, throwing back a shot with the beer chaser.

Sydney loads the stainless steel drain with clean shot glasses, beer glasses, mugs, and chaser glasses. "Well, Sis, if you're drunk I am, too, 'cause I heard the same thing: Sarah Treet," Sydney whispers. "That means there's a rat, and Red Run Cove that means undercover, right? Goo Goo had to have told her what to say. Nobody knows it but us, right? He's playin' a game. He's testing us, right?"

"I don't know." Leora closes her eyes for a second or two. She is so fed up and tired of always being on her toes. Polluted and propped in a corner sounds inviting. The natural curly brunette covers her mouth with her hand, outlining her top lip with two fingers masking her speech. "Maybe we should fill 'im in on what's happ'nin', you know, tell 'im exactly what we found out about his verb. Speakin' of which," she continues masking her speech, holding either side of her mouth with her thumb and middle finger then smoothing her philtrum with her forefinger using a downward motion glancing across the bar at faces, "Do ya see Rob around anyplace?"

"Would he be sittin' at the table or with Goo Goo?" The combination of the wooden slats and Sydney's height is quite the advantage. She leans back, looking around. "So far all I've seen are two ex-husbands, cops, jackasses, and now a bitch."

Leora sighs. "What about a Sarah Treet? Anything?"

Sydney looks at face after face. "I got nothin', my vibes are asleep."

"Mine are workin' on it. So if Marcie doesn't know what Goo Goo's talkin' about, then it doesn't impress her, right? Ya get my drift? This has to be for our benefit, right? I'm out. Why the hell's he got ta play head games right now? That's not funny. He's got a warped sense of humor." She pulls her lighter and cigarettes from her top jacket pocket, placing them on the bar after lighting one and chasing a shot with water.

Sydney refreshes the water with loads of ice. "No, it doesn't impress her, but he's probably tryin' to make her feel important like she's his little secretary, ahem, I prefer gopher. She copped an attitude earlier thanks to Goo Goo, the instigator. He kept callin' me down her end of the bar. Blaze, give me change. Blaze, give us a drink. Blaze, where's Irish? He was drainin' his drinks and wavin' to me, shakin' the ice cubes. Let me tell ya somethin', Sis, the girl is slower than molasses in January goin' uphill. No wonder it's not busy on Saturdays. She doesn't even have the TV on. Aren't our Broad Street Bullies playin' at home tonight? The Flyers will be rockin' the Spectrum. And look at this place. Look how bright the lights are! And ya can hardly hear the jukebox unless you're sittin' on it! She had her eye on Gregory, too, until Goo Goo yelled, 'Blaze, give me and your ex-husband a drink.' And I yelled back, 'Marcie can get it, she can talk and chew gum; she's ambidextrous. Goo Goo gets this shit-eatin' grin on his face with bug eyes and yelled, 'Oh, she's a switch-hitter.' Everybody laughed except her. She is so pissed. She stood there with her arms crossed like she's gonna stomp her feet, hold her breath, and walk out, like quit, see ya." Sydney snaps her fingers. "Damn it, but Goo Goo jiggled his glass of ice cubes and smiled at her. He's been tippin' her every time she waits on 'im now. Keep an eye on her, Sis, the catty-ass bitch better look like rememberin' we're splittin'."

"Where's Hank and Sonny?" Leora yawns, leaning back and forth several times gawking at the far end. She inhales, almost gasps, when she realizes the figure sitting two stools away, behind the taps, is leaning not out of her way anymore but rather in synch with her forward, backward, forward, backward motion. She blinks at the unexpected, her only defense, as pink tinges her cheeks. Caught completely off guard, she avoids eye contact, trying to regroup as her peripheral vision presents a man dressed in jeans with an unzipped black leather jacket exposing a gray Henley and holding up a folded piece of paper between two fingers. She breathes deep, puffing her hair along her forehead when she exhales. *What's this another pawn of Griff's?* She shakes her leg from displeasure, unwilling to engage in empty conversation, annoyed with the thought of yet another useless encounter. A quick peripheral blink captures features similar to a mature Freddie Prince and slight hints of a dashing Clark Gable. A dark mustache accentuates a friendly smile.

"Here," he says, offering the paper to her, interrupting her physical survey.

Leora rolls her tongue around in her mouth, slowly inhaling, then turns only slightly toward his direction as she exhales, not forced or deliberately but subtle, nonchalant. She does not want to dance the tango or the bed spring waltz for that matter. She just wants to get drunk, emulsified. She closes her eyes, dismissing him more or less, but not dismissing his detailed silhouette now etched in her memory. *This guy's givin' me his phone number. Could this be our Sarah Treet? Here we go.* The chip on her shoulder stands at attention.

"Yo, Chooch." Sydney interrupts Leora's train of thought. "Papa told Hank and Sonny not to bother comin' in. He'll handle it."

Leora stares at her open hand, nodding to Sydney, offering her appendage to this stranger. She feels his eyes upon her as she breathes intoxicating scents of leather and aftershave, becoming almost pleasurably lightheaded from the manly concoction.

A masculine voice pulls her back to reality. "You dropped this." He reaches over and cradles her hand in his own, laying the paper flat in her palm. His touch is intentional and warm—warm as his smile, warm as the blush on Leora's cheeks.

She feels ridiculous and grateful he isn't a mind reader. She opens the folded paper in front of him, hoping to distract his piercing gaze from her rosy red humiliation.

"Thanks," she utters stupefied. She feels geechy, placing the paper on the bar, giving it a disgusted look. *Oh, yeah, our backward names. Its mine.*

"It is yours, isn't it?" He now sits sideways, facing her, resting an arm on the bar and the other on the back of his stool, unwilling to end the conversation. Her affirmative nod answers his question.

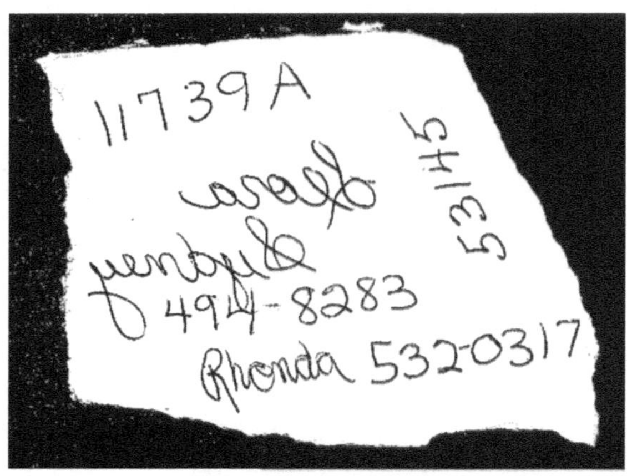

Leora holds the piece of paper with both hands, leaning left, leaning right; holding it above her head, finding herself wishing it was Freddie Clark's phone number. Finally she leans toward the mirror roughly twenty-five inches away and stands with Bic in hand. She would like to continue the dialogue and what better way than to have something to talk about other than the weather. She lights her Bic, placing it between the paper and mirror. The flame flickers as she moves the lighter back and forth and up and down, revealing the contents. There is her and her best friend's name written backward on the paper and now reflecting in the mirror as forward cursive writing. And above their names in the mirror are the letters: A P E r i l, "What?" she hollers and sits, dropping the paper on the bar as if it were on fire. Red flags and caution signs flit around her mind. She feels faint and sips some ice water, deciding a shot would be much better. *"Who makes an E like that?"* She throws back the shot, seeing flashes of

Rhonda's jiggling head. In a pearl, with a pearl, pearly gates resonate in her ears. A chill crawls up her spine. "Yo, Sis!" Leora calls.

Sydney is busy with customers gravitating to her end of the bar for faster service. Not to say she is the world's greatest barmaid. And she is still learning the system of what goes where. But even with fumbling in the speed racks and rooting in the coolers, she is still faster than her counterpart. She gives change and bags a six-pack, singing along with Fleetwood Mac.

"What does this say?" Leora waves the paper as Sydney walks over.

Sydney stands in front of Leora, talking out the side of her mouth with a wide smile. "It doesn't say anything. It can't talk!" She laughs out loud, slapping her leg. She bombs, except for extracting a genuine smile from the stranger. "That's so funny I forgot to laugh," Sydney mimics Gilda.

"No, really, what does it say?" Leora is adamant, tilting her head, all expression absent save for eyes bugged, lips pursed.

Sydney takes the paper and leans down to the light at the sink. She sees phone numbers and tag numbers, including Griff's tag number over top of their names in mirror writing for Rhonda's benefit the night before.

"You-u-u know-w-w," Sydney says, also leery of strangers, aware of the guy in the leather still sitting sideways, facing Leora who's watching the scenario. Now it's her turn with the eyes and lips. "Our names written backward . . ." she continues, throwing him a forced smile followed by a concerned look at Leora, ". . . and who-ja-cotch's what-cha-ma-call it. Why? What's up?"

"Well, the E is a backward three! I don't make an E like that! Do you?"

"Nooo, I don't make an E like a backward 3." Confusion clouds her face. "What E? There's no E in the" – Sydney catches herself – "the what-cha-ma-call-it. It's an A." She pinches the paper with her thumb and finger under the letter 'A' in Griff's tag number: 1-1-7-3-9-A. "See?"

Leora's eyes cross trying to focus on the paper. She sits back. "No. no, no, wait a minute. I saw an E."

"Where, Sis? What da ya mean?"

"I'm mean enough for anything." She guzzles her nip and stares at her best friend.

Sydney smiles, leaning on the bar in front of her. She pretends to pluck the chip off Leora's shoulder by its wings, releasing it into the air like a butterfly with a soft puff of air as if blowing a kiss. "Hey, Sis, ya ready for the corner or what?"

Leora takes a deep breath, smiling back at her favorite barkeep. "I guess, but I haven't seen any pink elephants just yet, only a backward three," she answers, feeling tranquil. "Oh, I get it. E is for elephant." Distrust teeters with tipsy and confusion. "You're tellin' me I wrote that, right, Sis?"

"Yepper." Sydney gives out cigarette change. "Would I lie to you, Momma? Isn't that what you wrote down when we were in the car?"

"Yeah, I did, didn't I?" Leora feels geechy again and very warm from a burning flush of embarrassment, wishing the lights were lower, the jukebox louder. She deducts she is reading more into the situation than is warranted and she should continue to lull her distrust into a liquid stupor, which is well in hand as she chases a shot with another big swig of Rock. In her peripheral vision, she spies Freddie Clark drinking his glass of beer with his left hand, which appears to be ring-less. She remembers the caterpillar. *"No!"* "Wait! Wait a minute! Yo, Sis, I saw it in a dream!" She hollers tongue-tied. "Oh, no, no, I mean the mirror, the mirror! I saw it in the mirror!"

She is on guard again, wary and anxious, shaking her leg, waiting with nervous anticipation while her partner in crime patrols the bar. Everything jumbles in her head: the pills, his silhouette, the bugs, the typewriter, Alice, the backward-looking three, his touch, the police, Virginia, Griff's ugly face.

Sydney finally returns and begins again, holding the paper up and lighting the Bic behind it. There is the tag number Leora jotted down above the backward writing. "You wrote that, right?"

Cantankerous Leora raises a shot in agreement. "Ah 'ight." She chases with a nip.

Sidney turns the paper over, lighting the Bic behind it again. Now their names appear written forward in cursive. The tag number above now appears backward. "Yeah, Sis, there's our names in cursive, oh-h-h, yeah-h-h, you're right. It is a curvy – Whoa!" Sydney reads the top of the paper and drops it on the bar.

"My tongue got wrapped around my eye teeth, and I couldn't see what I was sayin', right? Or could I? Ya see what I'm sayin'?" Leora s eyes are wide.

"I see what you're sayin' and see what you're seein', whoa-a-a!"

"And I wrote that?"

"Yeah, ya did, Sis!" Sydney looks at one side then the other.

"Where's Virginia give 'er a drink. She blitzed me!"

"Me, too, Sis!"

"I'll drink to that!" Leora throws back another shot, chasing it with ice water.

Marcie leans over, showing some cleavage while reaching for Freddie Clark's empty glass. "What's your pleasure?" she coos.

"I'll have a Miller and whatever they're smokin'." He smiles, dropping his eyes to her free show.

"I got it, Marcie." *You snake with hair.* Sydney places a fresh glass of beer on Freddie Clark's coaster, taking the used glass out of Marcie's hand before she has time to think about it, then points to the other end of the tavern. "Goo Goo's empty," she states, wanting to tell her to slither back up her end of the bar.

Leora feels almost giddy, armed with the knowledge she is correct in all categories—she is not drunk, only crazy; she is not seeing things, he is not a pawn and Virginia is right on as usual; (D) all the above. She slides one of her many upside down shot glasses to Sydney for Freddie Clark's beverage just as he throws more money on the bar, asking Sydney to give Leora a drink. Sydney takes the shot glass from her best friend.

He lifts his glass to Leora who in turn raises her nip. Glass and nip clink for a toast. Each sips their respective beverage. "Thanks."

Leora mimics Curly of the Three Stooges, "Soytenly!" She points to the pyramid, slipping him another shot glass, turning it right side up. "You want a shot?"

"Oh, no thanks, beer is fine."

Leora turns the glass upside down, leaving it in front of him.

"Oh, thanks. But I want to buy you a drink." He signals to Sydney, finishing an array of drinks. She dances over to him, singing "Walk this Way" with Aerosmith and playing her air guitar much to the delight of several patrons.

"Give her a drink."

Leora drains the rest of her nip, placing it in the beer well for replacement. "Thank you."

"I'm sorry. I didn't catch your name."

"Well," she states with a smile, "that's because I didn't throw it." She loses her nerve to look in his direction. "Leora. My name is Leora."

"Leora, is that French, Mada-my-zul (mademoiselle)?" He murders the French language on purpose.

Leora's negative answer swirls in hilarity. "Nooo."

"Parlez vous, hum-ma, hum-ma?"

Leora smiles at him.

"Can I interest you in my etchings?" It is cryptic. He smiles back.

It goes over her head. "Oh, you're an artist?" She feels stress-free, light as a feather, tension and trepidation lulling rather nicely in blackberry brandy, the chip on her shoulder now fluttering lazily at ease. She thinks whether Virginia had mentioned anything about an artist.

Freddie Clark chuckles all to himself. "So, what kind of language is on that paper?" He pulls her back into conversing.

Leora lays the paper on the bar, almost between them. "It's wonderful," she says, tongue-tied again. She rolls her eyes, shaking her head, laughing at her ineptness. "I mean Wonderland."

He stands, leaning over the empty stool, peering at the paper intrigued by Chantilly. "You mean like Alice in Wonderland?" he says, caught in her laughter. "Well, I like your first answer. It is wonderful. Kiss me quick."

She reacts without hesitation, indifference quickly diminishing as their eyes finally meet; his alluring gaze drawing her nearer as she raises her lips to his. She closes her eyes, surrendering to the magic, again feeling the inviting warmth of his touch as he lifts her face guiding her to him. Not quick or impulsive but rather unhurried, very unhurried, meaningful, exploring, savoring; lost in each other.

He brushes his lips softly against hers, bringing them back from wonderment. Leora slowly opens her eyes. He is there, a kiss away. She blinks, tingling from head to toe, not realizing her hand is entwined with his until he raises it over the top of the bar stool, pulling her to him as he stands beside her. "What did you say?"

She smiles, diverting her eyes, her telling eyes, as blush begins anew.

"What did she say?" Sydney interjects. "I heard that all the way over here," she says, drawing a pitcher of beer, smiling at the two of them. "It was in French, too, wasn't it, Sis?"

"I'm talkin' to you, Humpty Dumpty! What? Ya didn't hear me? I"ll say it again. I always repeat myself for assholes like you … you liar!" Goo Goo shouts. He flies off the handle, pointing at Griff, popping off his stool like a bottle rocket. Chick and Doc brace him against the bar. Standing next to Papa by the phone Griff leans on the bar, stirring his drink with his finger. He glares at Goo Goo with a self-satisfied cynical sneer on his face. Papa raises an open hand to Goo Goo, trying to calm him. Hector and Jammer join their boss, displacing patrons now sliding around the curved bar to the drop leaf section in place across the opening or move to the other end of the tavern altogether, away from the epicenter. Gregory, Chick, and Doc brace Goo Goo against the bar a second time as he lunges for freedom.

Papa raises his hand to Goo Goo again, shaking his head as Griff rants on with his false accusations. And Goo Goo, along with everyone else for that matter, had heard Griff's public spew. The mayor returns from the payphone, joining Griff and his stoolies.

"This ain't got nothin' ta do with you!" Griff yells. His demeaning attitude feeds his arrogance. He feels comfortable in his usual coercion, surrounded by his puppets; now with additional protection of Gregory, Doc, and Chick so to speak.

Goo Goo is livid. "Oh, no, well, then who's it got to do with, you piece of shit?" Chick and Doc have their hands full as Goo Goo points with his one free arm, leaning as far as he can. "Let me go, let go!" he tells his goombas, trying to loosen his other arm. "You step on my friends, you step on me, ya skirt! I'll rip your head off and shit down your neck!"

Papa shakes his head raising an open hand to Goo Goo once more, trying to calm him down.

"No! I wanna know! Got ta do with who? Fire her or face the consequences? Fire who?"

"No, that's not what he said." The mayor adds his two cents.

"How the hell would you know? You were on the payphone callin' the cops again, and I know that's what he said, I heard him. You callin' me a liar? You phony bastard!" The mayor backs out of the pissing contest, avoiding eye contact with ballistic Goo Goo. Sydney rushes to the chaos, past Marcie backing up to the taps. Leora hurries to the commotion along the mirrored wall.

"Goo Goo!" Leora calls, reaching him and grabbing his arm. Conversations cease. Patrons gather near and around the aperture and tables. "Goo Goo!"

"Get outta here!" he says under his breath, continuing to scoff at Griff with narrowed eyes and clenched teeth. He removes her hand from his arm. "Get outta here!"

"Come on, Goo Goo," she pleads, "the more you stir shit the more it stinks." She does not want Goo Goo flagged for protecting Marcie. *She sucks. Split the tips and send her packin'.*

"Who's gettin' arrested?" Goo Goo screams at Griff.

Oh, my God! She's a thievin' no bartendin' bitch! Holy shit!

"Shut up! None of your business!"

"Yeah it is, it's everybody's business! You made it that way! You and you're big mouth, you scumbag!" The veins in Goo Goo's neck bulge.

Papa waves a hand to Goo Goo. "It's ah okay. There's ah no gonna be no problem."

"Yeah, there is!" Goo Goo tells Papa. "If you don't fire her, he's gonna have her arrested!" He glares at Griff.

"It's ah nothin'." Papa does not want any trouble. He does not want to be labeled a nuisance bar.

"I know it's nothin'." Goo Goo speaks calmly to Papa glaring at Griff. "I'm talkin' to nothin'!"

Leora squeezes in beside Goo Goo. "Come on, Goo Goo, let it go."

"Get outta here, Irish, I mean it! He's gonna have you arrested. Leave!"

"Me?" For a split second, Leora's mind focuses on Marcie. Taking up for the bitch is no longer an option. *Hooray!* She would rather bath a cat. Now Goo Goo's words crash down, settling among bits and pieces of the day—the bugs, the diner, Alice, the pills. *Oh, yeah, the pills.* The pills are a means to an end, the end to Griff's manipulations before he ever gets started. For an instant, a fleeting moment, she was detached from this never-ending nightmare, lost in wonderment, which is also no longer an option as she stares at the empty stool behind the taps.

"Yo, Sis!" Sydney watches Leora's metamorphosis.

"You all right?" Gregory asks.

Leora meets Gregory's eyes with a glazed over look. "No, I'm half left. How da ya like me now, harem hubby?" Gregory bucks his eyes in silence, turning his head.

Plastering a smile on her face, she chooses her words, carefully enunciating each, repeating nothing, casting aside vulgarities; a symptom of rage, well, her rage anyway. Smoldering under her facial charade, the rage puts some whoop-ass on Leora, snatching up the chip on her shoulder by its wings and bitch-slapping it simple. She did not anticipate spectators. *Whatever. Who cares?* She breathes deep, closing her eyes. The image of poor Papa sits under her eyelids. *Upset Papa like that.* Anger implodes, dunking the chip on her shoulder into a sea of beer. She wants to punch Griff in the face her damn self.

"Yo, Sis!" Sydney reaches over, stretching as far as she can and tugs on Leora's jacket to get her attention.

"Give us a drink." Leora looks at Sydney, bearing her teeth with a fake smile, waving a finger back and forth, casting an ominous glare at the peanut gallery surrounding Papa.

"No, Irish, get outta here!"

Leora pats Goo Goo's arm and leans forward into his face, giving him a convulsive flurry of winks. "I got this." She looks at Sydney, continuing the flurry. "Give us a drink."

"Gaw head, Momma." Sydney sets up a shot with a tall water chaser, no beer, for her best friend. Goo Goo pats his money, starting all over again.

"Did ya hear me? He's gonna have you arrested!"

Leora stares at Sydney, sighing heavily while leaning her head to one side, then the other. "He's not gonna have me arrested," she purrs, jiggling her head like Rhonda honing in on Griff, "are you, Shauny?" Her voice is raspy; her stare deliberate. He devours her attention, watching her, undressing her with his eyes, a red blush of new skin still on his forehead.

"Yo! Sis! I'm pointin'!" Sydney points in their direction, the go ahead. "D—all the above."

Leora toasts Griff with her shot. "Goo Goo's a liar." She taunts Griff. Ain't he, Shauny?" She looks right at him, licking her lips and sucking on her finger. Sydney's eyes are huge. She smiles. Griff stares at this bitch of a nemesis.

She now turns her ire toward Mayor Evely. The girl is a lose cannon. She has had enough. "Nobody was found dead in my car." Her words slap the smug look right off the mayor's face just as if she physically backhanded him. Contentment washes over her. It is not as though she is accusing him of murder. A dead man was found in his car. Read the paper. Everyone in the bar knows it, why not say it?

Her comment evokes a response from the mayor. "Are you insinuating I killed Mr. Lister? Wel-l-l-l, you better be careful of your public innuendos, sister."

"What?" Leora cocks her head, cupping her ear.

This broad is beneath him, and he will make an example out of her. Conceit returns to his face as he raises his voice to implement a civic reprimand. "Let me rephrase that so you can comprehend, excuse me, I mean so you can understand." He speaks down to Leora, down and slow, "Are you saying I killed Mr. Lister?"

"Wha-a-at?" She wrinkles her face with confusion, giving him her best dumb broad look, playing right into his hand. "I said you what?"

Evely mumbles his degradation of this dumb bitch extracting chuckles from the peanut gallery "...I killed Mr. Lister!" He booms, slowly, enunciating, his voice dripping with disdain.

Leora smacks the bar. "I knew it! Derelick! I knew it! And I ain't your sister!"

The crowd ooohs and ahhhs are drowned out as the mayor lets fly expletives, raunch of another level. Jammer, Griff, and Hector form a circle around him as even Jackson and Carl abandon the table by the jukebox and shuffle to the bar.

Two patrolmen appear from the backdoor, walking to the mass confusion surrounding Papa. The buzzing and whispering in mini groups of people produces a collective gasp. Sydney turns the jukebox down. The situation is taking on a life of its own. "Get outta here!" Goo Goo pulls Leora to him.

"It's ah'ight." Leora tells her favorite bookie. 'Now that's how ya stir shit. Smell it?" She yawns, watching Chester's finest speak to poor Papa with constant interruptions from the mayor. "Give us a drink." Leora winks at her best friend.

Sydney pours her a shot. "I'm tryin' to listen to what they're sayin'."

"Who cares what they're sayin'. They suck big time." She grabs Sydney's hand. "I am sooo sick of all of this. I'm in!" She throws back the shot.

"There's ah no problem. They gonna leave," Papa explains.

"Yeah, get out." Leora laughs and licks her finger, pointing one by one at the mayor, Griff, Hector, Jammer, Carl. "You're flagged, you're flagged, you're flagged, you're flagged, you're all flagged, ladies." The chip on Leora's shoulder is doing the backstroke.

"Come on." Gregory pulls Leora to him. "We can take my car."

She gives him a piercing look. "No. Everything's swell." She is far beyond caring, unhinged, so to speak, and continues her verbal deluge. "Take me to your leader," she yells to the officers putting her wrists together. "Oh, there he is." She points at Mayor Evely. "Hey, wait a minute. You're public servants. You work for me. Hey! He does, too. Well, you're all fired!" She wants so much to scream out loud about the sneaky injustices endured by her and her best friend but bites her tongue. She does not want to blow it. She is feeling no pain, but she is not stupid. Besides, letting off steam has felt so good, and it did take some of the edge off. She snaps her head around, winking and nodding at Sydney.

Papa is beside himself. "He say ah no truths. What's a matter for you? I know this ah girl many of the years," Papa pleads.

"Its okay, Papa. Cheaters never win and losers."—Leora looks at Griff and points—

"Look like that!"

"Who owns a 1964 Chevy?"

Leora walks around the curve of the bar, away from Goo Goo and his explosive temper, raising her hand like a school girl. This is her baby, no one else's.

"Leora Wells?"

You damn well know I am. "Yes, I am! You got ESP or what?" Shit could melt in her mouth. She leans forward, reading his badge number. "Yo, Sis! Badge number twenty. That's one of my lucky numbers. Remember?" She looks at the stonefaced officer. "You're kiddin' me! Did you find my car?" Leora plays really stupid.

"Was it stolen, Ma'am?" He looks confused. The question does not jive with his instructions from his puppeteer.

"You're the cop. You tell me."

"Ahh, Ma'am, we have a report it was involved in several drug transactions."

"Ohhhh, my goodness, it was, was it?"

"Come with us, Ma'am."

"This is ah no good. This is ah wrong." Papa walks toward Leora and the officers.

"Oh, Papa, it's okay. These nice officers are gonna help me. I'll be right back," she tells her forlorn employer, following the city blues to the back parking lot. In less than five minutes, Leora walks in ahead of the officers with an announcement for her audience. "My car's not out there! It's gone! It really was stolen! Call the cops!" she turns to number twenty and his partner with tears actually welling in her eyes. "Oh, wait … you're cops! Help! Please!" She turns to the puppet show, batting her eyes, deliciously content. She deserves another Academy Award.

Filled with disgust, Griff slams his drink on the bar, not hard enough to break the glass but hard enough to slosh the contents all over. The mayor waves the officers over.

Sydney waves Leora's lighter and cigarettes at her. Leora struts over to where Papa now stands next to Goo Goo. "You okay, Sis?"

"Piece o' cake." She smiles, turning to her boss. "You okay, Papa? Stand by your convictions, that's what you say, that's what I'm doin'. It'll be all right."

"Aw-w, you work ah for me." He pats his chest. "It's ah okay. Between ah me an' ah you. I run ah my biz-ah-ness, jus ah my hands nobody else."

"Thank you, Papa." Leora leans over, looking at Goo Goo. "Give us a drink."

Goo Goo pushes money into the beer well to cover Leora's beverage, leaving the balance as a tip. He is leaving this den of inequity out of respect for Papa, pulling the plug on the electrified situation. He shakes Papa's hand before gathering the remainder of his money off the bar and nodding to the girls. Doc, Chick, and Gregory follow Papa and Goo Goo to the rear door. Sidney hooks her best friend up then leans on the bar, cupping Leora's ear. "I told Goo Goo about the pills. I had to. He woulda got arrested. He told me Marcie is Sarah Treet. Rob called here earlier and asked to talk to Shaun. He didn't know Goo Goo was home. They kicked the shit outta him, tied 'im up, and threw 'im in the black van after they ripped the equipment out of it. Goo Goo said somethin' about his place bein' bugged. I didn't say anything. Maybe they were buggin' both of us."

Leora stands like a mannequin. She could catch flies with her mouth. Sydney is not done. She grabs Leora's arm. "Hold on, Momma!" She leans in with her hand to her mouth again. Still stunned, Leora affixes her ear to Sydney. "Marcie is Griff's sister!"

"Excuse me, Ma'am."

"Huh?" Leora turns to the officers in a daze. "What? Oh, ahhh . . ." Leora regroups. "Ahhh, can you do an ABC, or XYZ, whatever that thing is to find my car?"

"The vehicle in question has been located in the front of the building."

"Wow! You're good! And you never left the building! But I saw your lips move!" Sarcastic Leora smiles. "Well, then never mind," she says in her best Gilda Radnor voice, following her blue escorts.

Stetson's

$\mathcal{L}$eora shivers, standing on the pavement in front of her car, partly from the chill in the sobering November air but more so from nerves. She had performed the gamut of being surprised, helpless, upset, and dumb; even going so far as to offer her keys to the patrolmen only after their discovery of locked doors. Now she watches the officers rooting through her Chevy, thinking maybe they themselves would be capable of planting something. Deeper in thought, she comes to the conclusion they can very well be capable if she had given their puppeteer cause for doubt, but there is no cause. Inside the tavern, the mayor wallows in his haughty world none the wiser. She had performed perfectly. *He ain't got a clue, the self-righteous shithead.* She casts a look-see past the closed businesses to the gawking bar patrons watching at bay just past the Laundromat, spilling occasionally off the curb onto the macadam. *If they were really lookin' for drugs, they'd have to arrest half the bar at least.* She smiles all to herself, watching Chester's finest, both on the driver's side, both with flashlights, taking turns in their search. Number twenty walks around to the other side of the two-door sedan, opening the passenger door, leaning in, continuing the search.

"Does my tag number match the number involved in the drug deals?"

Number twenty stands. "Negative, we have no plate number to compare it to."

I figured that. I betcha don't have a color description either. It's all a set up. You guys are puppets. They're suppose to be right *there, aren't they? But they ain't. So ya gotta root, so root.* "Yesss," she whispers, mimicking W. C. Fields, "The elephant of surprise." She sighs. "I guess I'm gonna have to be more careful." She speaks aloud, her voice soft with an apologetic tone. "I usually leave her unlocked because I don't need windows broken on top of a theft." She lies right to their faces. All's fair in love and war. This is war. Besides it was locked by Heckle and Jeckle, not her. "My dad installed a kill switch above the ashtray." That part is true. "I musta forgot to turn it on." That part is a lie. She forgot nothing.

Number twenty leans into the clean '64 again, then emerges, closing the door. He nods to his partner, confirming Leora's half-truth.

"Did you find anything?"

"Negative." The police are all business.

"Are wires hangin' out all over?" She plays stupid one more time.

"Negative, ma'am."

"Oh, so it's drivable?"

The second officer steps up on the pavement. "Affirmative, ma'am," he answers, handing the keys back to her. There is no proof her car was involved in anything.

"Thank you," she says, staring at the prized possession in her hand. The officer steps aside. Leora stands frozen in place a second or two, then moves in what feels like slow motion around the open door, tossing her cigarettes and lighter onto the passenger seat and sliding behind the wheel. She can hardly breathe. The patrolman closes her car door, giving a raised open hand as a good-bye gesture. *You don't have ta tell me twice.* Leora gives a feminine wave, fluttering her fingers. She pushes the clutch in, shifting the column stick to neutral and pumping the gas pedal twice. *Come on, Gal.* She turns the key. The Chevy purrs. She feeds it octane. Oompa! Oompa! The city blues make their way to the tavern where the onlookers scurry inside. The girl pulls on her headlights, revving the 283, then throws it in reverse, gripping the top of the bench seat, holding herself in position to look toward the rear as she pulls straight back out of the parking space. She cuts the wheel to her right, shifting into first gear. Oompa! Oompa! She drifts through the parking lot, past all the stores. The officers disappear into the barroom. *Thank God!* Just like that she is home free! And gone! She exits the lot while watching the front of the bar in her rearview mirror before making a left onto Ninth Street. She thinks about going home, but not alone. Besides she wants to drive and drive she does cruising down Ninth Street, rolling the window down and turning

WIBG way up. She sings oldies with The Four Tops, Aretha Franklin, The Four Seasons and thinks. Her mind races as usual. She is alone, isn't she? She makes a right on Market Street then bears left at the Y-intersection onto Chichester Avenue, taking a scenic cruise through Boothwyn and Ogden. *I wonder if Griff is screamin' at the cops.* She laughs aloud. *Maybe he's goin' after Heckle n' Jeckle, maybe not, but when he sees that van, he's gonna wanna go after somebody. I can't believe Goo Goo ripped all that equipment out. That is so neat! It means no bugs in the house. Yes, yes, yes, yes. Maybe we shoulda told him we were bein' bugged. Nah, we don't wanna involve him just like he didn't wanna involve us. Whatever. Maybe they did bug his apartment. Griff's a greedy sleezebag. What's Goo Goo gonna do? Go to the cops and tell 'em he's tryin' to take his illegal gambling business? Yeah, right! B-r-r-r.* She rolls the window up, leaving it cracked for her cigarette, joining Barry White in a duet. *I wonder if Papa flagged his ass. Whatever. Maybe he shouldn't. Keep your friends close and your enemies closer. Maybe I should take off a couple days and get the hell away from there. I don't wanna see Papa closed down.* Her mind jumps from subject to subject. *So Marcie is puke face's sister. I wonder if Goo Goo told Papa.* She sucks her breath in. *"I wonder if she got fired. The plot thickens.* She thinks about Charlie Chan, the Pink Panther, and the Thin Man as she belts out songs with Tony Orlando, The Commodores, John Denver, Dionne Warwick, and Roberta Flack on WIBG with Hy Lit's live Dance Party broadcasting from Vineland, New Jersey. She circles back onto Chi Avenue, hanging a left onto Meetinghouse Road to its ending, a T-intersection with route 452. At the stop sign, flashing hues of reds and blues light up the darkness, announcing a police car before it comes tearing past with its siren blaring, interrupting her and The Carpenters. She regroups, taking a deep breath and laughs. *Maybe number twenty called for back up. Oh, shit! Maybe it's for me!* Hanging a left on to 452, the opposite direction of the black and white, she cruises on down the road, singing with The Rolling Stones, The Supremes, Elton John, and Marvin Gaye. *Maybe I really should stay away from the bar. Maybe Goo Goo should. Griff is gonna be pissed at him for tearin' that van up and kickin' Rob's ass, let alone how pissed he is about the typewriter. Shit! The typewriter! What the helll are we gonna do with it? Hell, I don't know. I do know one thing though: I can't go back to the bar.* No way! *I gotta call Sis.* She pulls into Stetson's parking lot on the left, finding a space all the way back in the next to the last row. On the other side of Stetson's are six dilapidated one-room bungalows used by patrons for sleeping it off, for rendezvous, or as a stop over for truckers drivin' through. Live music can be heard as Leora walks to the secluded establishment, patting her backpocket for her money and license and shoving her keys in her jeans' front pocket. Leora feels safe, well, her vibes feel safe anyway. A bouncer asks for a two dollar cover charge, giving her change for a five, a ticket for one free drink, and pointing at a phone booth to her left.

"Papa's," Sydney states.

"'ello, 'ello, is that chew?" Leora questions her best friend.

"No, no, that's chew, this is me!"

"What's happ'nin'?"

"Yo! Sis! I was almost snoorin'. This place died when the cops came back in. All the wedding reception people are gone. It's dead, but Marcie thinks it's crowded. Oh, my God, Sis! Did you ever miss it! I figured you were out of here because that number twenty cop said they gave you back your keys. Griff went berserk! He accused 'em of bein' on the take. Talk about the pot callin' the kettle black! Griff grabbed number twenty by the front of his shirt and called 'im every frickin' name in the book! He was screamin' at the top of his lungs. The cops were gonna arrest him for assaulting a police officer. Jackson, Carl, and the mayor left with the cops after the mayor smoothed things over. "It took some doin' but," she sings soprano, "I think somebody's goin' to the Baha-a-m-as-s! Oh, my God, I said to Hector and Jammer, yeah, what's a dirty penny made outta? Copper! And when Griff walked back to the bar didn't Hector say that to him? I couldn't believe it! I thought Griff was gonna pop a vein! He chased both of 'em out the backdoor and I must say Griff is quite the tipper because they never came back! But I think it's 'cause they found their surprise in the van."

"E-gads! Ya know if they had found those drugs in my car tonight, that coulda been probable cause, and they could a got a search warrant for the house."

"Oh, wow, and ya know what else? They coulda went through my car too 'cause I live there. Hey, listen up. When Goo Goo left earlier he told Papa about Griff tryin' to set you up and how you said ya had it covered. Papa was so disgusted he went in the storage room. He didn't want to talk to any of 'em. He came out when Griff was goin' after Heckle n' Jeckle. They practically ran him down on their way out with Marcie close behind. I told him she's Griff's sister. He already knew it. That's another story. Anyway, listen, he was talkin' about when he bought the house off of Alice after that Lister guy died. Hold on a minute, Sis." Sydney waits on customers. "Ya there?"

"Yeah, Papa was talkin' about the house?"

"Oh, yeah, Papa said when he bought the house he got everything in it, too. He said Alice just got rid of everything. So when I went to get the rest of my stuff, Papa gave it all back. He asked me if it was okay, and I said sure. He needed room for the furniture from the beach property he bought and all of Gina's shit anyway. Papa said when he was talkin' to Griff tonight he offered Griff the apartment upstairs. He said he was gonna empty it and asked Griff if he was still interested. Griff said no. So I was thinkin'—hold on, Sis, hold that thought." Sydney handles a few clienteles. "I'm back. Ya there?"

"I'm here. You said Griff didn't want the apartment . . ."

"Oh! Yeah! Yeah! Yeah! Listen, does this make sense?"

"Oh, nooo!" Leora imitates Mr. Bill. "Do I have ta think?"

Sydney laughs. "No, no, listen. Papa offered Griff the apartment, and he said no. I think it's because there's nothin' up there he wants now. Remember when Crow and his buddies went with me to get the rest of my stuff? Papa called you later and said Griff was bore-assin' him for the apartment."

"Yeah, and Papa told 'im no."

"Well, Griff wanted it so bad because all that stuff came outta that Lister guy's place, our house. Griff wanted to go upstairs and root."

"But he watched you load up."

"Not the whole time. He was in the bar, tryin' to work Papa. They were already loadin' my car by the time he came out. Heckle was out there watchin'."

"Yeah, Heckle was watchin' all right, he was watchin' your ass!"

"Yeah, we'll have to toast horny dumb men again! See, when we were hidin' in Eva's car we heard Rob say he saw it, but he couldn't remember where. That's 'cause he didn't put it in my car, Crow or one of the jitterbugs did. And when Rob worked on my car he rooted through it and saw it, the son-of-a-bitch. He couldn't keep his cars straight. Goo Goo did a shakedown on Rob when they kicked his ass and threw him in the van. Rob told Goo Goo there wasn't anything wrong with Chick's car when they first met at the mall. Rob took the coil wire and when Goo Goo and Chick came out of the mall to leave, Rob timed it to where he just happened by. He did the same thing with Alice. And besides rootin' through my car, Mr. Helpful rooted through the house plus bugged it! It was all an act, rank-ass bastard."

"So, ya think he really forgot where he saw it?"

"Yeah, I think so. He was probably in the mayor's trunk, Carl's trunk, everybody's trunk! Where are you?"

"Oh, I'm at Stetson's."

"Stetson's? Plink-a-plink- a-plink! Are ya a honky-tonk angel tonight?"

Leora peeks through the accordion phonebooth door. "Well, I don't know about angel, but if I was a honky-tonk woman . . . this'd be the place to find a honky-tonk man. What time is it?"

"It's almost eleven."

"Are ya done work?"

"I don't know yet. Papa's in the back talkin' to Marcie. I wish he'd get rid of her. Hey, he knows Marcie is Griff's sister. That's why she's workin' here. He gave her a job and let Griff and his croonies meet here only if he left you alone. I don't think Papa knows the real reason Griff wanted the apartment. He never thought anything of it. And did you know her and Hank were, uhhh or are, uhhh . . ." Sydney whistles two notes like a cuckoo. "I mean like there's Back Alley Sally, Alice, and then there's Marcie."

"You're kiddin' me. The gigolo!"

Sydney laughs. "Cheese n' rice!"

"Yo, Sis, come get me when you're done, and I'll follow ya home. "I ain't comin' up there and I ain't goin' home by myself."

"I'll be there, Momma, for sure I ain't goin' home alone either! And I'm not goin' to the club. I think we oughta just sit on the note we typed."

"Oh, yeah, the note, I forgot about that. You might be right, Sis! Then again," Leora mimics W. C. Fields, "there's the elephant of surprise."

"Yaass," Sydney mimics him, too, "water, never touch the stuff, fish fuck in it you know."

"Hey, speakin' of notes, did you see the note I had with the tag numbers and Rhonda's phone numbers on it?"

"No, you don't have it?"

"Hell no! What else is new? Listen, when ya come out, don't forget my pocketbook, please."

"I got it, oh, here comes Papa." Leora listens to the distant conversation. "I did that."

"Which ah one, Cindy," Papa pronounces Sydney as Cindy, always has.

"Doesn't matter. Either one, Papa, under the register." Sydney's voice becomes louder as she picks up the receiver. "Yo, Sis, I told Papa you're okay. He was worried. He wants me to close. I told him it's not a problem."

"Holy shit! He fired her!"

"No, she's upset. She wants to leave." Sydney watches Papa walk back to the office. "He asked about the tips. I told 'im they're split under the register because I was supposed to be done at eleven. She's in the bathroom."

"Oh, my God, the van! Ya think Papa knows about it?"

"Nah-uh, I don't think. He said it's his business, you worked for him a lot of years, and he don't work for anybody. I don't think he realizes Lister was part owner of the house, or knows anything about the Feds, the typewriter, or even the van out back. I don't think he knows any of it. I think he really believes Griff wanted the apartment for his sister, and he's been hangin' around to get in your pants, and he set you up because you jilted him. I think that's all he knows. Goo Goo wouldn't involve 'im, and I ain't sayin' nothin'. That leaves Marcie. She ain't gonna blow her brother's cover. That's about the only thing! She sucks! Oh, let me go, Sis. She just came outta the bathroom. Here comes Papa."

"See ya later. I'll be here. I ain't goin' no place. It'll be me and the guy with the guitar pick in his teeth. Yee-haw!" Leora hangs up and passes the stallion bathroom to the filly bathroom then finds an empty stool at the bar in the crowded establishment. Exhaust fans fall short of their purpose in productivity as the smoke-filled room announces a shoddy performance. She pulls the stool closer to the oval bar, dragging it across the worn wooden floor, detecting a strong odor of hops and yeast. Her eyes adjust in the dim lighting as she takes in the room, noticing first the old, faded paneling on the walls then pool tables to the right, far right—three to be exact. Clear across the room, straight ahead from where she is sitting, is a slightly raised platform with a microphone, keyboard, guitar, and drums. Small round pedestal tables with chairs can be found along the left wall, along the wall behind her, and along the three-foot-high wrought-iron fence outlining a large square dance floor in front of the "stage." She keeps her bearings straight. *The front of the tavern is behind me.* She smiles back at one of the bartenders, ordering a Rollin' Rock and a shot of blackberry while placing the ticket and a twenty dollar bill on the bar. He pours a shot in a small chaser glass, filling it half full, his version, and a longneck Rock, taking only her ticket as payment. He winks at her. She smiles then throws back the shot, well, half of it, chasing it with Rock. She pulls money from her backpocket, separating a couple of one dollar bills for a tip, sliding them into the beer well and slipping the twenty and the remaining bills back in her pocket.

"Give the little lady a drink. Can I buy ya a drink?" a bearded wonder calls with a deep Southern drawl sitting a few stools away, signaling the bartender. The bartender points to the bearded wonder for Leora's benefit, pouring his version again of a shot. She raises her drink as a toast, a thank you. Four men, each in one-of-a-kind-styled cowboy boots, take to the platform dressed alike in jeans and long-sleeved brown shirts to begin their medley with B. J. Thomas's "Somebody Done Somebody Wrong" song sparking a sing-along. Even Leora sings along with this group – The Flatwoods. And when the dance floor fills, it includes Leora line dancing and two-stepping with the bearded wonder.

She is no stranger to country music. She had a transistor radio. She watched variety shows: Roy Clark, Glenn Campbell, Ed Sullivan, John Denver, Jimmy Dean, Hee Haw, etc. Didn't everybody? She had a record player and stereo. Didn't everybody? She grew up listening to country, Motown, rock n' roll, jazz. Walking with the bearded wonder back toward the bar, she detours to the ladies' room, holding high hopes the shifty character she saw standing by her stool at the beginning of the set has tired of the waiting game and has since wandered away. No such luck. The unsavory character sits on her stool as if glued to it. *You got a better chance of seein' God.* She pauses, straightening her shoulders, chewing hard on her double mint gum offered to her by a friendly Southern belle, continuing to her destiny.

The shifty character stands, giving Leora her seat. "I saved it for ya." *Yeah right, and I'm a virgin.* Leora nods a thank you. The bearded wonder waves to the bartender pointing to Leora, his dance partner.

"Oh, no, thanks. I'm good." She mouths the words, shaking her head, pointing to her drinks, then does a quick double take at a second bottle of Rock and a second glass of blackberry. The bearded wonder acknowledges Leora's response with a slight nod and a touch on the rim of his cowboy hat. Leora stares at the group of drinking vessels. "Really," she says softly under her breath. *Now what?* She refuses to look at Shifty.

"I bought you a drink."

Leora nods her head slowly. "So ya did. Thanks!" She sits the warm bottle of Rock in the beer well, ordering a beer glass full of ice and water, mostly ice.

"I never seen you before."

And what, that means you win finders keepers? Gimme a break! She enjoys a cool refreshing swig of clear liquid, making it impossible to respond.

"Where y'all from?" Loretta Lynn belts out "You Ain't Woman Enough" from the jukebox. Leora remembers this one and sings along with everyone else. "Where ya'll from?" He begins again, this time moving closer to the brunette and leaning on the bar next to her, bringing some manly smells that have nothing to do with cologne.

"Are you from around here?"

Leora shakes her head, breathing through her mouth. "No."

"Me neither. I'm from Memphis. I drive truck through here all the time."

"Hey, Luther!" An older woman greets the rough aromatic patron with a smile. "I didn't see you last night." She saunters over.

"Hey, Charlene."

"My God, Luther, a pole cat smells better 'n you!"

Luther chuckles. "I just got in a little bit ago. I got my room and everything next door, but I heard the boys playin'. I come right over here. I dropped a load in Memphis. I shoulda been here last night, but Billy Bob broke down and I stayed and helped. It's all good." He signals the bartender, ordering her a drink.

Leora seizes the opportunity to dismiss herself. "Here, sit here."

"Oh no, that's all right, honey," Charlene says apologetically.

"It's okay. I'm gonna play the jukebox." Leora finishes one glass of blackberry and stands, gathering the other blackberry and an ice water refill. "Any requests?"

"Yeah, Sugar, He'll Have To Go, thank ya."

Leora exits stage right, slipping away from the conversation into the crowd toward the pool table end of the bar, working her way back up the other side between the bar and the tables lining the dance floor. A couple vacates one of the small tables. Leora plops in a chair, watching the singing group mingle with its adoring public. They really are good. And their boots are to die for, even if you are not into cowboy boots. They are gorgeous. She is sure one pair is snake skin. She gulps her brandy, exchanging the empty glass for the ice water, and yawns. Two fellows appear at her table, one sits, one stands.

"Hi, ya need a ride?" the one sitting asks.

"No thanks." Leora leans against the wrought-iron fence to her right and yawns again. *The front of the tavern is to my left.* "I'm waitin' for somebody." It is not a lie. She is waiting for somebody—Sydney—and she plans on sleeping in the car while she waits. That's why she basically guzzled the glass of brandy, a nip and tuck. One nip and they tuck you in for the night.

"Here let me git cha a drink." The one sitting grabs her empty brandy glass.

"Oh, no thanks, really . . ."

"Mada-my-zul! Hey!" Freddie Clark leans on the back of her chair. Leora turns to her left as he now leans on the table and her chair surrounding her. She sits back, gazing into familiar eyes, friendly eyes; a sight for sore eyes. "Kiss me quick," he says once again. And once again she complies.

"A kiss to last." She said it out loud. She didn't mean to.

He looks at her, his smile mixed with perplexity. "What does that mean?"

"Oh, nothin'." She feels the blush. "I was just leavin'."

His smile is warm, inviting. "Well, so was I." He leads her through the crowd out into the cold still night, a light snow falling, his warm hand enfolding hers as he escorts her to her car. "I've seen this car around. I wondered who owned it. Nice car."

"Thanks." She unlocks the door, scooting over to the passenger side, placing the ice water on the dashboard then slipping the key in the ignition.

"Are your legs tired?" He slides the seat back for some breathing room.

Leora laughs. "Oh, you mean from dancin'?"

"No, you've been runnin' through my mind all evenin'."

Leora giggles. "Is that like I should be arrested 'cause it's illegal to look this good?"

Now Freddie Clark laughs. "No, you should be arrested for stealin' my heart." His kiss, too, is warm upon her hand.

She blushes in the dark. "What are ya doin' here? And don't say waitin' for me."

"I was shootin' pool. They were playin' partners over there where you were, so I came out here for a little action. I was getting' ready to leave when I came outta the men's room and saw you. You sure there's no boyfriend or husband waitin' around?"

Leora chucks her cigarettes and lighter on the dash. "Nah, just me," she answers, turning toward him. "So who's home waitin' around for you?"

"I'm sorta between homes. I rented my house out and was stayin' with my mom and stepfather. I'm on my way to visit my sister in Texas. You wanna come along?"

Come along? Leora rolls the window down, tossing her gum. "You visitin' or are you movin'?"

"I'm kickin' it around. There's a job down there if I want it."

She rolls the window up, shutting out the cold, the dusting of snow melting on the warm windshield. She stares into the darkness. Running from the bullshit sounds mighty inviting to her. *Can I bring Sydney?* She bites her tongue. "You don't have a job here?"

"Yeah, I'm a mechanic. I fix motorcycles." He repeats the question. "So, ya wanna come along?" Leora is uncomfortably silent. She can hear herself breathe. *Can he?* Thank God there are no arc lights revealing her blushing like a school girl, making her warm, very warm. She throws her jacket in the backseat and cracks the window. He senses her discomfort and changes the subject. "So you're not a gangster's moll, right? Nobody's gonna show up with tommy guns?"

"Well, if they do you can drive stick, right?" Leora answers him with a question, her voice throaty; her mouth dry. She sips the refreshing liquid, holding the cold glass against her temple in the darkness before returning it to the dash.

"Yeah, I can drive 'em, and I can fix 'em." He runs his hand around the steering wheel. Leora breathes deep. He turns the key to accessories. The light from the radio blinks on right before "Born to Be Wild" about blasts them out of the car. They both fumble for the volume knob. "Are you hard of hearin'?"

"Huh?" Their laughter fades to comfortable silence.

Freddie Clark changes the radio station to WMMR for the midnight block featuring Bob Seger and The Silver Bullet Band. "Someday, Lady, You'll Accomp'ny Me . . ." Freddy Clark sings the chorus, reaching for her hand. "So you're not a moll and you're nobody's wife or no one's girlfriend. That's hard to believe."

Leora shakes her head, but there is no shaking the butterflies. "Nah, I'm just a barmaid."

"Not just a barmaid, a smokin' barmaid." He smiles, leaning toward her for another kiss. She complies. "Ahh, speakin' of smokin' . . ." He pretends to hit a joint.

Leora nods. "I'm in."

"I'll be right back."

Leora is relaxed, stress-free again, feeling warm, tingly with tickling butterflies in her stomach. Freddie Clark returns with a long-sleeved green and brown plaid flannel shirt with a bag of stash in the pocket. He passes a dark brown wooden pipe for Leora to hold while he removes his leather, tossing it in the back. "Do you like hashish?" He pinches shake from the bottom of the bag, adding it on top of the hash in the pipe.

"It's ah'ight. I smoked it before."

"Well, this is weed and hash, a salad." He digs his Bic from his jeans pocket.

"A salad?" Leora laughs. "Who made the salad?" she mimics the commercial. He puts flame to salad, then passes the smoldering bowl with a distinct aroma of skunk. She refuses the offer. His quizzical features glow in the light from the radio as he exhales. "So who might I be smokin' with?" she asks, meeting his gaze.

"Me." He smiles with laughter in his eyes. "Ginn." He hits it again and passes it. "Hello, what's your name?"

She plays along. "Hi, my name is Leora." She puffs on the pipe as he covers the top of it with two fingers then releases it like a shot gun. Leora coughs laughing. "I usually smoke joints. What's your last name, Ginn?"

"That is my last name. That's what my friends call me." He pulls a cotter pin and a nut from his shirt pocket, placing them in her hand. "Here." His touch is warm, still warm. He watches confusion play upon her face in the dim light. "It's a roach clip, look." He pushes the two ends closed sliding the nut onto them. He moves the nut toward the other end. The two ends open. Then as he slides it back toward the split end they pinch closed.

"Ohhh, that's neat! Thanks!" She exchanges the pipe for the trinket, slipping it into her cigarette pack. Bob Seger is kicking ass. They make small talk—pleasurable conversation about mutual likes, dislikes, jokes and such; nothing deep, certainly nothing personal. She did not tell of Red Run Cove, Sarah Treet, the loss of her son, the heartache. And he did not speak of atrocities serving his country, the less-than-admirable qualities of an unfaithful spouse, the messy divorce, the loneliness behind his smile.

"So what's your real name?"

"That is my real name." He smiles. "Daniel."

"Well that's not so bad, Dan-yul-l-l-l-l." She lets his name roll off her tongue, a tease present in her voice. "So, you named after your daddy or what, Daniel Ginn?" She sips the water, playfully offering him a swig. "Can I call you Ginn?"

"Sure," he answers, taking a gulp of water, throwing the flannel shirt on the dashboard. It dangles over the radio, extinguishing what little light there had been. He leans over, placing the glass on the dash and turns to her. "Daniel Orrin Ginn, Jr."

"Ohh." Leora swallows hard, breathing that intoxicating leather and aftershave again. "Junior, huh?" she half whispers. He is a kiss away . . . again.

"Uh hum-m," he whispers nuzzling her hair. She leans away from him, trying to get her bearings. Her head is spinning, her breathing labored. He leans closer to her, slipping his right arm in the small of her back, his open hand climbing, burning against her flesh as he pulls her to him his warm breath, trailing kiss after kiss after kiss. She sighs, shrugging her shoulder to quell the chills from his searing lips.

"Leora," he whispers.

Bob Seger begins, "I know it's late . . ."

Ginn brushes his lips softly against her cheek, embracing her, wanting her, calling her, "Leora."

Once again Leora surrenders to the magic, lost in wonderment his lips finding hers, inflaming desire, igniting the passion. They sail the sea of splendor upon wave after wave of ecstasy. No misgivings, no promises, no expectations. Rising and falling, rising and falling enthralled, enraptured, swirling with breathless abandonment . . . drifting on tranquil tides . . . floating among spent embers of desire . . . washed upon the shore of afterglow.

A Fly on the Wall

"Ginn," Leora murmurs. Half-awake, she leans on one elbow, tasting her cotton mouth, moistening her tongue. She opens one eye to blackness, trying like hell to open the other. Defeated, she lies back down on her right side, rolling on to her back, then stretches, shivering from her half-nakedness in the cold car. She sits up disheveled, adjusting her clothing; pulling down, pulling up, blinking wide-eyed in the dark, groping for her platforms, sliding behind the steering wheel. Her feet are like ice. *I wonder what time it is. Is it today or yesterday or is it tomorrow?* She is alone. She feels around for her keys, locating two more pieces of clothing. *Oh, my Gawd!* Her teeth chatter as she moves the front seat to its original position, hanging on to the steering wheel. Keys jingle in the ignition. She starts the car in neutral, blasting the heater, then examines the extra clothing by radio light. The first one is her denim jacket, which she puts on immediately. The second is a green and brown plaid flannel shirt, both used to cover her while she lay sleeping. She has to pee like a race horse. She turns the radio off, which extinguishes the light, then winds the window down to scope out the parking lot. It is deserted. Her breath condenses in the cool air. The bar is closed. She tiptoes behind her car. On the far side of Stetson's, shanty doors and voices interrupt the quiet. She listens, blinking in the darkness and, of course, shivering. She stands just as a car whips into the parking lot. Leora scrambles into her safe haven, rolling the window up and locking the door. Headlights drench her car as Sydney pulls up next to her, driver side to driver side. Leora rolls down the window.

"Yo, Sis!" Sydney yells, turning her radio down. "I made it! And I got coffee." She moves the sixteen ounce Wawa go cup back and forth. "Four creams, two sugars."

"Yes, you did! Oh, God! Yes, you do!" Leora shivers.

"Were ya comin' to get me?"

"I don't know. I just woke up, maybe. What time is it?"

"Past three thirty. Sorry I took so long, but I stayed with Papa. He was by himself. Mr. Mac is off tonight. Tomorrow's Sunday, well, I mean today is, well, it's Sunday. Hank and Sonny weren't in, so I stayed."

"Did ya get busy?"

"Well, yeah, sorta," Sydney answers, hesitating and taking a deep breath, "not with customers though, Griff came back. I wanted to leave before they did, so they couldn't follow me, but I didn't wanna leave Papa alone with 'em so I stayed."

Leora gestures wait a minute, rolling up the window and shutting off her car. She yanks the keys from the ignition, feeling along the dashboard for her lighter and cigarettes, knocking the empty water glass to the floor. She makes sure not to bump the coffee and tea sitting on the open glove compartment door as she climbs into the passenger seat of Sydney's T-Bird.

Sydney reaches in the backseat, retrieving Leora's pocketbook. She turns off her car, too, cutting the lights and rolling the window up, leaving it cracked. "He is pissed squared."

"Who?" Leora swigs her coffee. "Griff, at us? What did he say to ya?"

"Oh, he didn't say anything to me. They got there about quarter of two. I only had three customers. I had given last call about one thirty. Papa and I thought we were gonna get outta there early, but the front door opened and in they walked."

"What? Him and Heckle n' Jeckle?"

"No, him and his snake with hair sister, and if looks could kill, I'd be dead. He sent a chill down my spine with his cold stare. I didn't look at 'im, just a glance. That was enough for me. Papa was doin' the registers. Of course, he said give 'em a drink."

"Did he ask Papa about me?"

"No, he never mentioned you, but Papa did. Papa finished the registers, and I locked the front door when the customers left. Then, Papa proceeded to ream him a new ass. That intimidation bullshit that went down earlier with the mayor and the cops didn't fly with Papa. He told 'im to stay away from ya. He said ya can't force yourself or your ideas on anybody. This is America! He don't want that shit in his place of business. He told Griff to look around and see how his business had suffered tonight. And the next time him or his clowns, including the mayor, threatens to close his bar or threatens any of his employees, they will hear from his lawyer. He handed me a business card and told me ta read it to Griff, twice: Garland D. Cherry, Jr., Esq. And ya know what else? Papa wasn't yellin'. I heard most of the conversation while I was cleanin' up so to speak. That's only 'cause of Papa's accent. He had to repeat himself all the time so Griff could get it. You could see veins starting to bulge in Griff's neck. He wanted to scream, but he didn't. He stood there grittin' his teeth. Marcie played it to the hilt. She boohooed all over the place. I kept busy wipin' down the bar, the tables, closin' curtains. He told Papa she really needs the apartment."

"Yeah, right! What she needs is some wall to wall counseling."

"Hey, they gave Papa a song and dance about how she had some kind of emergency and she had to leave and how she really, really needs the apartment and how he shouldn't a said he didn't want it. Oh yeah, and she got a part-time job a couple nights a week on top of her Saturdays, blah, blah, blah. She gets on my nerves. I wanted to put my finger down my throat."

Leora breathes deep, closing her eyes and holding her head with both hands. "Do we look like our heads twist off? Of course there's another job."

"Yeah, workin' for her piece of shit bru-th-h-er. That's her other job. But she made it sound like she just got a job at a drugstore or supermarket or somethin'. If I didn't know any better, I swear Papa wanted to put his finger down his throat, too. He just kept noddin'. Oh, yeah, Griff said he's not comin' in the bar anymore."

"He's not? What's he gonna do, sit in the parkin' lot?"

"No, he'll bug the bar then just sit upstairs and listen."

Leora bucks her eyes. "Nah-uh!"

"Hey, would I lie to you, Momma?" Sydney's hands shake, lighting her cigarette.

"You ah'ight? Put the heater on, Sis. Here, drink some tea."

Sydney starts her car, turning the heater on full blast.

"Hey, we always feel better with a plan." Leora tries to calm her down. "We'll think of one. Holy shit! My feet are freezin'!"

"Yepper, mine, too. It's time to pack these Dr. Scholl's away."

"Yeah, it was tryin' to snow earlier. Time to break out the argyles." Leora slides her feet closer to the heat. "Yo, Sis, we'll figure it out. Remember, strength in numbers." She digs for a cigarette, finding the outside cellophane wrapper of the flip top box inside stuffed full of weed. "Whoa!" It makes a crinkling sound when she removes it, bringing with it the scrap of paper with Rhonda's number and tag numbers, compliments of one Daniel Orrin Ginn.

"Oh, you found it!" Sydney says, retrieving it from the floor.

"So I did!" Leora smiles all to herself, stuffing the piece of paper in her top jeans jacket pocket. "And look at this." She pulls the cotter pin and nut from the cigarette pack, giving a demonstratingof its function. "It's a homemade roach clip."

"Wow, a treasure trove! I'm impressed!"

Leora funnels the clip back into the pack. "Oh yeah, smell!"

Sydney closes her eyes and takes a whiff. She leans over, groping in the glove compartment and pulls out the old stand by. "Whew! It smells like a skunk."

"That's what I thought." Leora loads Lucky Pierre, putting Bic to pipe. She passes to Sister Syd.

Sydney hits it, coughing when she exhales. She hits it one more time, holding her breath, rolling the window all the way up before passing the pipe back to Leora.

"What are ya doin'?"

Sydney exhales. "We ain't wastin' none o' this, Sis. We're goin' for a contact, too!" The girls laugh, relaxing in the safety of Sydney's car in a dark, deserted parking lot a world away from sinister aggravation.

"Hey, we can always give 'em the typewriter."

"Oh no, Sis. If that shows up now, he will definitely know it's us."

"He didn't threaten you, did he?"

"Nooo, like I said, he didn't talk to me. And that's probably 'cause I didn't look at 'im. I didn't give 'im a chance. I just kept busy cleanin' up. My vibes are a wreck. I couldn't breathe let alone think. Papa went upstairs with 'em and told me to lock the outside door. That's when I got ta thinkin', I wish I was a fly on the wall."

"You didn't!" Leora squeals. She takes a big gulp of the sixteen-ounce.

"Yeah, I did, and I must say what a fine fly I made!"

"You're shittin' me, Momma!" The girls toast with their coffee and tea.

"Nah-uh. Would I lie to you, Momma? And I didn't hear anything muffled either. I heard voices clear as a bell, and then some. I only had to crack the door a tiny bit to take the edge off. And they helped, too, God bless their little pea-pickin' hearts. They ended up standin' in the kitchen talkin' shit right on the other side of the door! I left the key in the deadbolt instead of puttin' it back under the step. That way I could turn the key and close it real quiet. I didn't catch much of the conversation at first 'cause Papa's got the Godfather voice goin' on plus was walkin' 'em through the bathroom, the two bedrooms, and the living room. But I heard Griff's big mouth joking about how he could crawl upstairs if he got drunk."

"I thought he wasn't comin' in the bar anymore?"

"Exactly. And if she had such an emergency, what's she doin' comin' back to the bar when her shift is over?"

"Yeah, I get your drift. They're gonna try a plan B."

"Speakin' of drift, he let an S. B. D.—silent but deadly—rip. It could gag a maggot and choke a roach. Whew! I almost coughed. He could fumigate buildings." Sydney takes another sip of the warm liquid. Her shivering wanes. "I'm glad he whispers like he has a megaphone. I really didn't need to crack the door open with his big mouth. Wish I'da known, he stunk! Anyway, they flicked the kitchen light on. Thank God, the door opens toward the wall. Griff asked if any furnishings came with the place. Papa said, 'Sure, if you want a furnished apartment'. And of course Griff spews all kinds of shit he wants like he's shoppin' at Levitz. Papa went to the other rooms, checking what furnishings he could supply. Griff and Marcie whispered in the kitchen, well stood in the kitchen comparing notes. She asked 'im how his hand was. He said he thought he messed up a knuckle. He thinks Heckle n' Jeckle put the bag of drugs in the wrong car. They kept tellin' Griff the cops got it. He said he knows one thing: Heckle n' Jeckle better not have it. He's gonna talk to the mayor. Griff and Marcie compared places each one of 'em looked when Papa walked 'em around and agreed the typewriter isn't upstairs and neither is the safe."

"The safe. Didn't Alice mention a safe?"

"Yeah, Sis, she threw it in Carl's face."

"It's probably as big as an oven and weighs three thousand pounds. Who the hell can pick that up?"

"I don't know. I know we didn't load one that day."

"So if they're lookin' for a safe that means nobody at the prayer meetin' has the money. Hmmm, verdy interestink," Leora says, mimicking Arte Johnson.

"And they were buggin' Goo Goo! He found that out tonight, givin' Rob a little wall to wall and sendin' 'im packin' with just the clothes on his back. From the way Griff and Marcie were talkin' Rob, lifted shit every time he did maintenance work for Goo Goo or worked on his car. He was always rootin' over there too, even in the trash! Now the slime balls have ta start all over again to set 'im up. But he told Marcie they ain't doin' it now. They can blackmail everybody and their mother after he gets his hands on the ledger and typewriter."

Leora winds her window down, inviting the cold morning air. "He's out for blood, the power-hungry bastard."

"How come we don't feel the power? We can't blackmail anybody. Hell, we have to keep it a secret. We got muckus."

"Yeah, ain't it a bitch? We can't turn it over to the Feds. They won't protect us. We'll be live at eleven on Action News. And we can't give it to Third Eye 'cause…"

"Third Eye?"

"Yeah, Griff."

"Leora roars. "Third Eye, that's too funny!"

Sydney laughs, too. "Sis, the stitches did make it look like a closed eye with eyelashes. Anyway, if he gets his hands on it, we become part of his magic act."

"Not if we have somethin' else he wants."

"You mean like leverage, power? We don't have any of that, Sis."

"But he doesn't know. He's got tunnel vision. He's greedy."

Sydney sighs. "Yeah, and he didn't wanna hear anything Marcie was sayin'. She was even gettin' on his nerves. He told her to shut up about Goo Goo. He said Goo Goo's business is the least of his worries. What good is ending up with Goo Goo's business gonna do 'im if he ends up rottin' in jail? He said he ain't doin' that again. They argued over her apartment—do this, do that. She said no. She asked him if the Feds were still diggin' and Griff said hell, yeah, and there is still fallout from flowers or somethin'. I didn't get it. He said his sources say every now and then the Feds stir things up and bring somebody in to compare their handwriting with the signatures on the phony documents. He said they'll never figure it out. And when they do it won't matter. He said she'd take it to her grave and not even know it. How 'bout that?"

"Take it to her grave . . . her?" Leora stares out the window, lost in thought. "And not even know it . . ." she mumbles.

"Yo, Sis, you go. Take up my slack. I wracked my brain 'til I can't think straight. I thought she must be blond. And the only person I could think of is Alice, but they checked her out already, didn't they? Besides, down at the diner, she told Carl the house was a place of business. She didn't know everything that went on in there. I was hopin' they'd delve into the subject a bit longer or deeper, whatever, but no such luck. I mean, we don't know everybody Griff knows, but associatin' with broads just doesn't seem to be one of his strong suits. More than likely he paid somebody. Oh yeah, they're gonna bug the bar."

"Why?" Leora turns to Sydney. "They won't be able to hear anything."

"'Cause that's what Marcie wants to do. I'm tellin' ya, she beats a dead horse. You can tell they're brother and sister. And I think she's more involved in Griff's shit than she lets on. Griff freaked! He said he didn't care about Goo Goo right now. His priority is his neck. He said just put the damn thing on the inside of the bar by the sink where Goo Goo sits and be done with it, but Marcie said that was too enclosed. She wants to put it on the outside, right under the bar where they all sit. He said he didn't care. He was basically yellin'. He said he'll worry about Goo Goo later."

"Did he say where he thinks the typewriter is?"

"All he said was he is gonna take care of her. She'll give him what he wants or he'll beat it outta her. That's when I shut the door. I couldn't breathe. I was done."

Leora gasps. She feels nauseous. "Rob remembered! I think I'm gonna throw up!"

"I know, me, too, Sis. I heard Papa's voice and cabinet doors slammin'. I imagine it was Marcie lookin' around the kitchen. Then I heard Griff ask Papa where this door leads to, and he turned the doorknob. I heard it spinnin' around and around, you know, it doesn't really work from that side, it's just for show. I held my breath! I heard Papa walk toward Griff, his soft spoken explanation muffled, then the distinct word wall and Griff said to Papa, 'You built a wall?' I heard Papa say the word no, then another muffled explanation. Griff tried repeating what Papa said, finally coming up with the pizza shop owner next door did it. Thank God, he can't whisper and has a hard time understanding Papa's broken English. I put the key back under the step and went down to the bar. I was gonna make myself a drink, but my stomach still had other ideas, so I paced in the foyer until they showed up. Griff's Continental was backed up right in front of the door. I cussed that stupid tag number. Marcie's Torino was parked next to it. I went back in the bar. Papa stood outside, talkin' a few minutes before comin' inside."

"Oh, they didn't come back in?"

"No, I peeked through the curtains. Marcie left her car there. I watched 'em pull outta the parking lot and go toward Highland Avenue."

"Yeah, he's got somethin' up his sleeve all right, and it ain't his arm."

"We should buy a gun."

"Yeah, ya know, we can't go to the cops. Hell, they probably got all the hitmen tied up, too."

"Hey, we got number twenty and his partner. They can't stand 'im a little bit."

"Yeah, that'd be neat, wouldn't it? But they'd bust them down to desk duty."

"I think you're right, Sis." The girls sit in silence, lost in their thoughts.

Leora sighs. "He's gonna beat it outta her. Is that what he said?"

"Yeah, with anger all over his face."

"You saw 'im?"

"Nah, he was grittin' his teeth. I saw what that looks like, Sis."

"Maybe our only option is to hope it all goes down at the house. Joe and Bill ain't gonna put up with it."

"Ooh, what's that? Our new guard dogs?"

"No, no, Trainer's finest. They don't want any trouble in their sleepy little borough. I don't think Griff has them in his backpocket. Maybe he'll think twice."

"Is that before or after he finds out the key doesn't work?" Sydney yawns.

"Well, if he's gonna beat it outta ya, then maybe he's gonna try and jump ya, you know, get ya alone some place."

"Me?" No, you, Sis!"

"No, you, Sis! Rob remembers seein' it in your trunk!"

"But they bugged your house! They even had a key!" Sydney exhales a moan, staring into the darkness

"Oh, my God, my nerves!" Leora taps Sydney. "Hey! If Heckle n' Jeckle are outta commission and Griff's hand is messed up, not to worry, right?"

"I don't know. He can still reach in his pocket to pay off a goon or two. I'll just show up about one-thirty when you're workin', and you can show up one-thirty when I'm workin'. We'll be a tag team. Your work, I sit. You sit, I work."

Leora thinks a minute. "What are ya gonna do 'til one-thirty, sit at another bar, warmin' up their stool?"

"Or," Sydney answers, "Maybe I'll sit in a parkin' lot like here for instance. This is a nice parkin' lot."

"Yeah, it is. Quiet. This is beyond keys or bugs. He's gonna step on us."

"Hey, Papa's fed up. Maybe Griff'll back off."

They look at each other. "Nah!" they say in unison.

"Papa said he's gonna try and get me some hours."

"Well, you can have my Monday or Wednesday."

"Okay, it'll go with my Saturdays 'cause it's just a matter of time before Marcie wears her welcome out. Hey, she told 'im she can't work this coming Saturday. She's goin' outta town for Thanksgiving and won't be around all weekend. He asked me if I wanted it. I told 'im I'm in."

"Gees, is it a family affair? Is Griff goin', too?"

"I don't know, hope so. Even Jack the Ripper had a mother. Papa told Griff Marcie can move in the beginning of next month, and he jacked the price up. Griff didn't even flinch. He handed 'im cash."

"Yeah, keep your friends close and your enemies . . . upstairs!"

Sydney takes a sip of tea then lights the pipe once more, puffing on it several times before passing it to her best friend. Leora hits it several times as it smolders, sizzling one last time before extinguishing itself into ashes. Leora is drained. Sydney yawns. "Hey, should we give 'em a house warming gift?"

"Oh, I can't do the Godfather thing with the poor horse's head! How 'bout cement shoes."

"Yeah, one size fits all."

"How many pairs ya think we need?"

"Never mind. That ain't gonna work. We need a cement company."

"Hey, leverage! Leverage! We can give 'em the typewriter without the ribbon!"

"Oh, yeah, 'cause everything that was typed should still be on it!"

"So we'll replace it with a new one and hide the old one."

"And they'll have ta let us go, or it will be mailed to, ah, somebody in a white hat." Leora yawns. "So where should we hide this incriminating evidence?"

"I don't know. We gotta think." Now Sydney yawns. "I can't do that right now."

"Yeah, me neither."

"Ya ready to hit it or what?"

"Yepper! I gotta put it to rest. You want me to follow you?"

"Whatever. It doesn't matter."

"Well, I wanted to ride by and see if the van was still there."

"Oh, I did, Sis, on my way over here. It is. I don't think it's drivable. Goo Goo did a number on it." Sydney yawns again.

"Then let's go home the back way up Township Line to Chestnut."

"Sounds good. Then we can both park on the street. They won't be able to block us in."

"You mean sometime today?"

"I don't think they're gonna. I'm not gettin' any bad vibes, are you?"

"No, but that's probably because our vibes are asleep, as usual. I'm in!" Leora climbs into her car, revving the engine and blasting the heater. They make the uneventful ride home in the wee hours of the crisp morning, pulling up in front of the house. The only sound heard is from Wheezer calling to them from the porch roof. He descends the old maple still, calling to his returning comrades sitting in front of the porch steps, purring and rooting on the pavement.

"Tiger!" Sydney runs her hand down Wheezer's back to the tip of his tail on her way up the steps to the front door. "Oooh, you're cold. Ya miss me?" He flops.

"Oh, Wheezer!" Leora lifts the young cat cradling him in her arms, kissing him on his head and rubbing him under his chin. He pulls himself to an upright position, trying to wrap around her neck like he did with Pete, then settles for just being held purring in Leora's ear. She kicks her shoes off next to Sydney's, locking the front door following Sydney up the "wooden hill." She pours the contented feline on her bed beside her pocketbook and the flannel shirt. After sitting the Wawa coffee on the night stand, she lies down across the bed and yawns.

Sydney appears in the doorway. "Yo, Sis. You done with your coffee?"

Leora holds a finger up, finishing another yawn. "Yes, I am."

"Well, here, I'll go throw 'em out and check Wheezer's food supply."

"That's ah'ight. I got it. You gaw head, un-lax and rewind. You gotta get back in the swing of things. You go get a shower. I'll get one after you."

"Oh, yeah," Sydney whispers, referring to the typewriter, "my bed partner is comfy cozy."

"Oh yeah, yeah, yeah!" Leora sits up, pointing to the ceiling light.

Sydney steps up on the bed, walking around, making Wheezer seek safer ground. She roots inside the cover, burning the top of her knuckle twice on the bulb before locating the bug. Of course that's hot, too, and she flings it; no particular place, "Ow!" It lands on the bed.

"Ow! Ow! Ow!" Leora hollers, juggling it like a hot lump of coal. She chucks it back on the comforter. Wheezer jumps up, joining the melee. He pounces on the hot item then tries to shake the heat from his paws. He bats the hot metal to the floor on the other side by the window. Leora crawls across the bed to retrieve the listening device, bumping into Sydney, knocking her down to a sitting position.

"What is that smell?" Sydney lifts the flannel shirt off the bed and chucks it to her curly-haired friend. Leora smiles. She holds the shirt in front of her, nuzzling it and breathing deep.

"That's testosterone."

"Nah-uh!" Sydney leans over, sniffing the garment. "Mmm, what is that?"

"That is skunk and after shave, here." Leora holds the pocket out for Sydney.

"Hmmm, where'd that come from?" Sydney's eyes widen. "Nah-uh!"

Leora laughs, throwing the shirt over her best friend's head.

Sydney speaks through the garment. "A honky-tonk man! Who knew?" She lifts the shirt from her face with both of her arms peeking at her best friend. "Go like this, Sis." Sydney bears her pearly whites with a wide grin, waiting for Leora to do the same.

"What?" Leora's gives her a half-assed smile.

"Oh, yeah, I see the guitar pick!" Sydney tosses the shirt to her best friend.

"No, no." Leora blushes. "Not a honky-tonk man. Well, not really. I mean I don't think." She looks at Sydney with a quizzical face.

"You don't think? You don't know? Oh, puh-lease! The next thing you're gonna tell me is you didn't get lucky!"

"I didn't!" Leora laughs.

"You got his shirt, for God's sake! I think it's a clue! It's evidence! No, wait! A trophy! You got lucky!"

"No." Leora blushes. "He got lucky!"

"Oh, that's right, Sis, I forgot. Love 'em and leave 'em. He got lucky. He got lucky you got, ahhh . . . his attire." Sydney laughs.

"It's the guy that was in the bar earlier tonight."

"You mean at Papa's? Ohh, yeah, the one who was talkin' French." Sydney bucks her eyes.

"Yeah, him. He was out there shootin' pool. He was leavin' for Texas. He has a sister who lives down there."

"Wow, he shoots pool, has a sister in Texas, he speaks French. What? No social security number?"

"Well, from what I can remember he's a motorcycle mechanic."

"Ya had 'im surrounded, huh?" Sydney throws a dig at her best friend.

Leora closes her eyes, sighing, holding the flannel shirt, and inhaling, "Yeah, I mean, no! I mean, what did you say?"

Sydney laughs. "Come back!" she says, acting like a hypnotist pretending to draw Leora back to reality. "You were surrounded by a grease monkey." A lightbulb goes off in Sydney's head. She stands in the doorway. "Oh! My God! A grease monkey! Dirty hands! A monkey!"

"What da ya mean a monkey? He's a mechanic. He fixes things."

"Virginia's monkey! Remember? Oh, where is Virginia? Where is that girl?" Sydney shakes her head laughing, heading for the bathroom.

"Well, he'll probably be a monkey in Texas," Leora hollers. "He's got a job offer down there," she adds. "I think he's tryin' to get his head on straight." Leora yawns and stretches, laying the shirt on the bed. "But what a nice distraction," she whispers. She steps gingerly through the hall and down the stairway, avoiding her furry friend underfoot. In the kitchen, she plops on a chair before flipping the one with the planted bug tapped underneath it. She rips it from the bottom of the seat then peels it off the duct tape. Wheezer demands attention, hopping on her lap as she lays the twin devices side by side in her hand for comparison.

"Leora, South Philly!" she says to the bugs, mimicking the kids from American Bandstand. She places the microphones side by side on the table. "I'm so glad we had this time together," she sings. "Hey, Wheezer, ya know why it's nice to have friends in high places? Because they all fall down and go boom!" She yells like Tweety Pie.

Wheezer bolts to the staircase, disappearing around the top of the steps. Leora replenishes his food out back and replaces his frozen water. She flips the kitchen chair right side up, scoops the useless metals off the table, then tosses them in the trash on her way upstairs for a relaxing shower before settling in for some much needed sleep, already being enjoyed by her furry friend.

Strength in Numbers

*F*razzled nerves keep Leora and Sydney on their toes, beginning with excessive knocking on the front door late Sunday morning, spooking them out of their peaceful slumbers. The girls are relieved to find Crow on the other side and indulge in chitchat, Mary Jane, instant coffee, and hot tea at the kitchen table. Crow recounts his escapades with Tom in Atlantic City, beginning with his winning wager on the Hagler/Monroe fight through the horse betting, crap tables, and the array of one arm bandits. The girls had had escapades too, and Crow resembles a spectator at a tennis match as the twosome relate some of their eventful weekend then drag Crow upstairs out on the porch roof, checking to find a hole for Wheezer's personal entrance into the structure to no avail. Standing in front of the linen closet with Crow, the girls feel a drft nip their bare feet.

"Wow! What the hell?" Sydney opens the thick door."

"Yeah, no shit!" Leora adds, "There's gotta be a hole someplace." Wheezer inspects, too, flopping and playfully feeling under the bottom shelf then scooting down the hall, disappearing into the bathroom.

"Well, I didn't see anything out front." Crow runs a lit match up one side of the shelves, across the top and down the other, extinguishing it with a quick puff before burning his fingers. "No draft here. It's all comin' in down there. I might as well check the patio roof out back. Are you sure he was in there, or is it like pink elephants, doll?"

Leora lunges at him. "Your sister!" she retorts, putting her tormentor in a headlock, giving him some noogies. He tickles his "use ta was babysitter" to escape her grip and hustles to one of the back bedrooms. He removes the screen, then climbs onto the patio roof for a quick inspection. "He can't get up here like he can out front." Crow shrugs his shoulders, climbing back inside standing once more in front of the linen closet. "There's definitely a breeze comin' through here."

"Yeah, well we didn't notice it when we were sleepin' there, right, Sis, when he was attackin' your feet from inside there?" Sydney moistens her cotton mouth.

"Sleepin' there? What, on the floor? What am I missin'?"

"Oh, that's another story." Sydney plays off Crow's questions. Or did she?

"Another story? I'm all ears."

Well, let me see, the typewriter, the bugs, the pills, she'll take it to her grave, a safe, he'll beat it outta her, outta me, whatever. Leora puckers her lips, rolling her tongue around in her mouth, her mind dismissing each untold issue, groping frantically for an answer. The more the merrier does not apply at this time but quite the opposite. Silence is golden, or as Leora tends to think, healthy. "Sydney snores." She blurts the answer, cutting her eyes to her tag team partner, who nods in agreement with the tall tale.

Crow tilts his head toward Sydney, mischief dancing in his eyes. "You saw wood?" He smirks at her, blinking wide-eyed.

"Where?" Sydney looks around. "I didn't see wood."

Crow shakes his head as he laughs. "No, not like see, saw with your eyes, but like . . ." Now the cohorts join in. Talk about changing the subject.

"I didn't see any wood." Sydney repeats herself.

"Hey, I didn't see any seesaw," Leora adds.

"No! No! No!" Crow shakes his head laughing.

"You mean like a teeter-totter, Sis?"

"Nooo!" Crow shakes his head. "Forget it! Forget it!"

"If I saw, would I what?" Sydney asks with hands on hips.

"No, like in the cartoons, a picture of a saw sawin' wood when they're sleepin'."

"Ohhhh, I get it! Never mind!" Leora mimics Roseann Rose Anna Dana.

"I didn't see a saw or sea wood or driftwood, whatever! Brrr, my feet are cold, daaamn!" Sydney heads toward the stairway.

Crow follows. "Hey, you think it's cold now wait 'til winter."

The subject is changed. Leora pulls a beach towel from the closet, stuffing the terrycloth under the length of the door with her foot.

"Crow stretches, standing at the top of the stairs. "I'll get Greg's ladder and check the roof out front over on the side by the tree. That's how he gets up there, right?"

Sydney abruptly halts, nodding while turning around on the stairs. "What, you mean today?"

Now Crow moistens his cotton mouth, almost walking into her. "No, the next time I come over."

Leora descends past both of them, striking a pose, holding on to the door knob. "You mean today, right?"

"No." Crow grins, bucking his eyes. "I'm gonna go hang out with Jenny."

"Well, you guys can hang out here." Sydney slips her arm through his. "Jenny, Joey, Chris, Pete, Greg—they like to hang out here." Sydney stands next to her best friend, nodding profusely.

Now Leora nods. "Do ya swear?" she asks, putting her hands on her hips.

"Swear what? Yeah, I swear, I'll be with Jenny." He blinks, beaming.

"No, nooo, swear you'll pop in n' out."

"Yeah, I'll be around other than a junkyard run to Jersey on Saturday."

"Around this!" Sydney leans on Leora's shoulder. "You really mean it?"

"I said, yeah." He looks at them, acceptance absent from their eyes. "What do ya want from me, blood?"

The girls badger. "You really, really mean it, for sure? You promise, right? Are you shittin' me, Mister?"

With an honor bright, a cross-your-heart-and-hope-to-die, and a fake spit, Crow earns permission to leave. Hesitating, he spins around at the door and walks back to them. He is bustin' at the seams. "Hey, I wanna tell ya somethin', but ya can't say anything 'til next Sunday."

"Yeah, well, I'm tellin', Sis." Leora nods toward Sydney.

"Yeah, well, I'm tellin', Sis." Sydney nods toward Leora.

Crow fishes in his pocket, pulling out an old blue velvet box.

"You shouldn't have!" Leora puts an open hand out.

"He didn't!" Sydney sticks an open hand over Leora's. They lean forward as Crow opens the worn box. Jaws drop as they stand, gawking at a brilliant, small, sparkling, pear-shaped diamond.

"Wowee!" It's beautiful!" Leora sighs.

"It's gorgeous!" Sydney removes the ice swirling in a white gold setting with two diamond chips. She tries sliding it on her ring finger. "Jenny has small hands."

"Here let me try!" Leora holds her hand out. Sydney pushes a bit harder.

"Yo! Yo! Yo! Don't get it stuck! Don't be pullin' a Lucille Ball!"

"Oh! It fits my pinky!" Sydney holds her hand out, admiring the twinkling stone.

"Here! Let me see it!" Leora slips it on her ring finger. It is just a little too tight. She holds her hand out, too, admiring the almost half-karat gem snug on the second joint. "I could do a force 'em!"

"A foursome?" Crow asks. He bucks his eyes. "Oh, a force 'em! No! No! No! Hell, I wanted you guys to keep it for me 'til next Sunday, but I don't think it's such a hot idea. Somebody's gonna end up losin' a finger!"

"No, no, no, it's okay."

"Yeah, you can leave it here. We'll be good."

"What a nice birthday present."

"Well, not really." Crow places the ring back in the box.

"Well, Jenny's birthday's comin' up, right?" Leora asks.

"Yeah, Monday. But it's not for her birthday."

"Yeah, well, we know that. You're gettin' engaged," Sydney states.

Crow smiles at her. "No."

"You're gonna marry somebody else? You brute!" Leora teases.

"Oh, no, a trollop from Atlantic City. I knew it. It's the ring girl, isn't it?"

"Oh yeah, the one that holds the signs up between the rounds." Leora looks at Crow. "How could you?"

Crow stands mute, grinning from ear to ear.

The girls stare with quizzical expressions.

"What's up?" Leora asks.

"Yeah, what aren't ya tellin' us that you're hintin' you aren't tellin' us?"

"We know where you live." Leora raises her eyebrows up and down.

"And we know your phone number." Sydney gives him an Oliver Hardy nod.

Crows hands the ring box to Leora and smiles. "We're already married."

You could knock the girls over with a feather as they stand like statues catching flies. "Say what?" Leora is dumbfounded.

"You're suppose to get engaged first and then married," Sydney explains.

"And then have a baby?" Crow asks.

"Yeah, and then have . . . say what?" Leora exhales.

"Oh! My! God!" Sydney holds her forehead with both hands.

Crow nods affirmatively as the two friends squeal jumping up and down.

"Puppy's gonna have a puppy!" The girls swarm Crow.

"We got married yesterday. Tom took us to elope and stood for us. As a wedding present he gave us the bridal suite. We told Jenny's parents this morning when Tom dropped us off. I told my mom a little while ago. She says we can live with her 'til we get our own place."

"Aww, that's neat." Leora gets him in a headlock for noogies.

Sydney pokes him in his sides. He wrestles loose. "Mom wants her over Sunday for a welcome to the family dinner. Then we'll tell my mom about, you know."

"Awww," Sydney coos. "About the baby. When is Jenny tellin' her parents?"

"We'll probably tell them this Thursday, Thanksgiving. We wanna tell them together." Crow is beaming. "You know, that's the first ring my dad gave my mom." He rubs the smooth Celtic cross between his thumb and index finger. "She wants me ta give it ta Jenny. Jenny doesn't know about it."

"Oh! Blackmail! Now ya have ta come back or we're tellin'," Sydney announces, patting him on the back on his way out. "So bring your jammies for a sleepover," she yells out the front door.

Even though Crow stands true to his word with his sporadic presence at the house during the day and nightly shenanigans at Papa's after work, the girls are on guard, wary, watchful. Waiting for the other shoe to drop gnaws in the back of their minds like a parasite—he'll beat it out of her; she'll give him what he wants. They are inseparable even when Leora works Monday night and Sydney works Wednesday. They warm a stool at the very beginning of each other's shift, citing strength in numbers. Griff is a no-show, which means thanks to Sydney's eavesdropping on the spiral staircase, Thanksgiving Day, straight through the weekend should be blissful. Yes, business as usual, like it was before they ever laid eyes on Griff. They breathe a collective sigh. Griff is a no-show, but so is Goo Goo. The curly hair duo does not realize that. Not right away anyway. Together they spend the delicious holiday shuffling between their family gatherings—stuffed. Their refrigerator is stuffed, too—stuffed with leftovers. And Crow had checked the front roof again in the beginning of the week and found nothing but a sound structure restored almost to its original regal state by its previous owner who had spared no expense before his sudden departure from the world.

Papa's reopens Friday, Black Friday, the start of the holidays; although in some eyes, the arrival of Santa Claus at the end of Gimbel's traditional Thanksgiving Day parade begins the mounting excitement and anticipation of the jolly season. The cooler weather adds to the festive atmosphere, evoking smiles and pleasantries among the multitudes. Papa's is busy as hell with a constant sing-along chorus of Christmas songs. Eva and Leora hardly have time to gab at their usual spot, standing in front of the taps and so gossip with one or two sentences as they pass each other like ships in the night.

"Did you say Trudy wants a divorce?" Leora scoots past Eva for a couple of chilled mugs.

Eva leans back away from the taps while drawing a pitcher. "Yeah, and Doc said he told her, 'Go for it'." She gathers three glasses on the way up her end of the bar, cracking her chewing gum.

Leora rings up a takeout at Eva's register. "So Doc's on the I-wanna-move-in kick again, is he?"

"Again, you mean still?"

"Yeah, I guess so, huh? He never got off it."

"Every three months, whether he needs it or not. He thinks if he's homeless, I'll let 'im sleep on the couch, you know, get his foot in the door," Eva answers, pouring a fruit loop. "Ain't happ'nin'. He ain't cheatin' on me."

"Well, isn't Mr. On-Again-Off-Again already cheatin' on ya with Trudy?"

"No, he's cheatin' on Trudy. He lives with her. He's seein' me."

"Oh!" Leora gives Eva her best Edith Bunker rendition.

Holiday merriment hangs in the air, producing a relaxing atmosphere already being enjoyed by the clientele. Dare Sydney partake? She sits toward Eva's end, just past the aperture, constantly glancing in the huge mirrors at the ever-changing faces up and down the bar. The idea of getting tipsy and bubbly begins to sound better and better to the redhead. After all she's off, Griff has not been seen since Saturday night, the typewriter is still resting comfortably, the bugs are gone, hell, so is the van, and all is right with the world. She mingles, dancing a little, playing shuffleboard, the jukebox, going out back for a couple of totes, shooting some pool, just plain kicked back, laid back—whatever. The prayer meeting table is replaced with beehive hairdo Mommas and sear sucker suited suitors. Sydney laughs all to herself, glancing around the bar at her comfort zone: Bopper, Fidget, Rocco, Pockets, Jug Head, Gabe, Skippy, Mort, Fat Cat, Moon Man, Lum, Tuna, and familiar second shifters trickling in. She grins, scanning the bar, then does a double take where Goo Goo and company usually graces them with his presence. She stares at the unfamiliar faces at the end of the bar, her smile fading to chiseled jaw.

"Where's Goo Goo?" she half-whispers, realizing the last time they saw him was also Saturday night. Now leaning forward, she tries attracting Leora's attention. It is too noisy. Leora is too busy; but not to worry. The girl can whistle. She can hail a cab in New York City a block away. So whistle it is. Heads turn in her direction. All speech ceases. For three and a half seconds, the only sound to be heard is Jimmy Dean singing Captain Santa Claus. Sydney hails Leora and waits. She glances at the clock: 12:20 a.m. Bad vibes crawl down her spine right to her gut feeling of uneasiness. She goosenecks Eva's end of the bar, swigging her Michelob as concern settles above her brow. She now does the same to Leora's end, waving at Crow, focusing past the full bar to the billiards. She has a funny feeling—a feeling of being watched. She blinks, again checking the mirrors, again scanning the bar. Then she sees him, Deep Blue Eyes from the diner, staring a hole through her, mixing it up with some of the second shifters down the front end of the bar on her side just as Leora places an upside down shot glass in front of her. "This is on him." She points to her left, smiling at her best friend. "Do ya see 'im?"

"Yes, I do!" Sydney gushes. "Tell 'im I said thanks." Deep Blue Eyes would go rather well with tipsy and bubbly. She blushes for what she is thinking, quickly switching back to matters at hand. "Yo, Sis, where's Goo Goo?"

Leora looks toward Eva's end of the bar. "Wow! I don't know." She stares at the strangers in Goo Goo's usual seat.

"Well, we haven't seen 'im since, you know," Sydney leans, forward cupping her mouth and mouthing the word Saturday.

Eva cracks jokes with George, Willie, and Harry on her way to the taps.

Leora questions the buxom barmaid, "Hey, E, where's Doc and everybody?"

Eva sits the empty pitcher in front of Sydney. "Oh, he ain't spendin' his money."

"Why, where's Goo Goo?"

"Oh, Doc said he took Angie to Vegas. It didn't cost 'im nothin'. He had a free trip from the airport, remember, from when his car was, ahem, stolen?"

"Oh, yeah, that's right."

"Chick's handlin' everything with Goo's long distance help, of course. Hey, Mutt and Jeff were here this afternoon when I met Doc." Confusion distorts Eva's face. She smacks Leora's arm. "You know, um, Griff's gophers, ah, yeah, Jammer and the other one. They're flyin' solo with Griff bein' outta town, too, and I do mean solo. Both of them together might make one person, although I think you might have to involve a third person for a brain." She draws a pitcher, yelling over her shoulder. "Can you imagine them in charge? One had a black eye, the other had a busted lip. I asked 'em what happened. They said they ran into a door." Eva lifts the full pitcher. "I said what, the same door? Both of 'em shook their heads yes! I laughed my ass off! I said the door won!"

"Yeah, they're dumb as a stump."

"Speakin' of dumb, what was goin' on Saturday night?"

"I'll bite. What was goin' on?"

"Well, according to Doc version, Goo and Griff got in an argument. The cops were called, you know, somethin' about messin' with Goo's friends. You know how I don't pay too much attention when Doc rattles on."

"It was a shoutin' match. I was here. Nobody was arrested."

Eva shuffles to the young, adoring trio, then leans forward to offer ample cleavage while pouring each one a drink from their pitcher and scoops their shower of tips, batting her deep brown eyes with a smile just in case they look at her face.

Leora resumes her patrol while Sydney racks her brain trying to think of Deep Blue Eyes's name. It is on the tip of her tongue. She leans forward, taking a gander down the end of the bar, hoping the sight of him will jog her memory. *I got nothin'.* She closes her eyes and sighs. *This ain't gonna work.* Her mind is in tipsy and bubbly mode. The only thought that comes to mind is General Hospital and the notorious Frank Smith. *I hope not. Ewww!* She scopes out the thirsty lot. Deep Blue Eyes is not there.

"Lookin' for your boyfriend?" A voice on the other side of her asks.

Surprised, Sydney turns to face him. She swigs her beer. *Oh, Momma!*

"Do you remember me?"

"Yes, I do," she answers through a smile, "from down the diner. You look different with clothes on." She wants to bite her tongue. Hell, she wants to chew it off. She clears her throat. "I mean without coveralls." *Not again!* She rolls her eyes.

"You don't look any different." His voice sounds deeper than Sydney remembers. "You come here often?"

Oh Momma! "Well, yeah, I work here."

"Oh, then you know a lot of the people comin' in here."

"Bryce! You're up!" His co-workers Nick and Manny wave. "Luke! Yo!"

He gestures a negative, shaking his head, leaning both arms on the bar, turning to Sydney resuming the conversation. "So what can you tell me about her?" He nods in Leora's direction, his penetrating stare into Sydney's eyes uninterrupted.

The importance of learning his name quickly takes a backseat to his immediate question. Sydney clears her throat a bit disappointed. "She's single." *There, I said it. Now move on.*

"Are you?"

Talk about playin' the field! What, just line 'em up? Not me, Luke the Kook! She stares at those questioning Deep Blues made deeper by a five o'clock shadow and a topping of dark brown wavy hair.

"Yes, I am," Sydney answers unimpressed, blinking him from her mind as a mere interruption in her fun-filled relaxing evening.

"Well, which one of you goes out with Shaun?"

Sydney throws a bewildered look at Lucas Bryce, swallowing hard to quell the grip of fear crawling up her spine, arousing adrenaline for fight or flight. "Shaun who?" She offers nothing. *You're not puttin' me in a trick. Let's play. I'm the dumbest blonde you'll ever meet.* There is no place in this redhead's conversation for the likes of Griff.

"Shaun Griffonetti, the guy who beat the shit outta my sister Monday."

Dumb goes out the window. Sydney is a mess, a stammering, stuttering mess. "Oh, n-no, you, oh, ah, mean, ah . . ." She draws a blank. "Ah . . ." She tries to think. "Um, the woman down the diner?" Sydney is aghast. *This can't be happ'nin'!* She feels nauseous. She tries to regroup. "That's a lie, neither one of us goes out with him."

"Well, her ex said one of you gave Alice somethin' that belongs to Shaun."

Alice! That's it! Yeah, probably right after you said you were gonna kick his ass! "That's another lie! You mean that day we were down there? You forgot your keys, right? He said he saw us give somethin' to your sister?" Sydney's stomach is doing backflips. "He didn't see muckus! We didn't give your sister anything. We don't even know your sister." Her voice is defensive. She locks eyes with Leora, who up until now has been all smiles. Alice was at the wrong place at the wrong time. Sydney's mind is spinning. *It's not our fault Griff went after her. We didn't lie and put her in harm's way. Carl did, that! What'd she call 'im? A Bic, yeah, rhymes with—*

Leora interrupts poor Sydney's train of thought, bringing Deep Blue Eyes his bottle of beer along with concern for her best friend.

"Why don't you ask Alice, really? We didn't give her anything, let alone anything belonging to Shaun Griffonetti. Ask her. She never met us. She'll tell you," Sydney announces aloud, a little "ketchup" for her best friend. So much for tipsy and bubbly, Sydney is stone cold sober.

"I plan on it just as soon as she wakes up. She's in a coma."

"Oh, my God!" Sydney speaks, sucking her breath in coughing and gagging. Leora almost hyperventilates as the raw truth stokes her adrenaline.

"I am so sorry," Sydney offers.

"Why? You said you didn't have anything to do with it." He leans on the bar, looking squarely at Sydney, his eyes void of expression, well, void of kind expression.

"What did the cops say?" Leora exhales the question, leaning on the bar in front of Luke. "That guy's nothin' but trouble," she adds, exhaling again. "He sucks!" She joins his ranks, thinking strength in numbers, hoping he realizes they are not part of the problem. *Please tell us he's in jail.*

Bryce turns a cold stare to Leora. "Guys like that are used to broads hangin' around 'em."

Say what? How dare you? Leora is not tipsy or drunk. And his attempted slap in the face deserves a retort. She leans closer, enunciating. "Yeah, those nasty bitches," she agrees, capturing his full attention. "You see a broad, you kiss 'er." She gives him a blank stare, watching her sarcasm settle, ready with a left-handed "punchline." He swigs his beer. "I didn't think so." She resumes her duties, handling the finally dwindling crowd.

"She's a hard ass."

"Yeah, she might be, but she ain't a liar or a thief. Neither am I for that matter," Sydney says. It is bad enough Griff has stuck them in the middle of everything, let alone having to defend themselves with strangers. The girl snatches her pocketbook off the bar, heading for the bathroom. Bryce grabs her arm. She glances at his grip then meets his cold stare with her own look of defiance.

He unhands her, draining his beer, sitting the empty bottle on the bar and sliding two dollars under the dead soldier. Leora replaces it with a full one. He digs for his keys. "Oh no, I'm done. I don't want anymore," he states with a voice tinged with regret.

"Oh, what's this, a tip?" Leora belittles him into admittance. "Thanks."

Sydney slides two ones on the bar. "This is on Chooch, the broad." Leora works the bar, not waiting for an acknowledgment. He has put her in the mother of all moods.

Bryce places his keys in front of him, folding his arms leaning on the bar, then stands tapping the cherry wood with his index fingers. Sydney studies his features, looking at him— really looking at him, past the angry chip on his shoulder. He looks drawn, weary, worried.

Chooch offers an olive branch, a little inside information on the up and up, something to win his trust or at least get his attention. "Hi, I'm

Sydney that's Leora," she starts leaning in his direction, pointing behind the bar. "Ya know he has a sister, too."

"Yeah." It is a short response, but a response none the less.

She tries one more time. "Ya know she works here." Sydney retreats, sitting up straight, sipping her beer. He can come to her.

Bryce corrects her, "She works for her brother." He swigs the bottle of brew.

"Who, Marcie, the no-bartendin' bitch?" Sydney watches his reaction in her peripheral vision. "She works here Saturday nights." The tidbit reels him in.

Bryce stands sideways, leaning on the bar, curiosity peaked. Silence reigns as he gulps his beer digesting her words.

"Her brother evidently misplaced somethin'or lost somethin' or can't find somethin'." The girl fluffs her hair, straightens her top; just downright refusing to look at him. "So says the grapevine." Sydney likes the grapevine idea, safe and generic. She runs with it, "And now maybe somebody found it or wants it or always had it or is sellin' it . . . I don't know, whatever." She pauses. "Anyway there's dissension in the ranks, a lot of finger pointin'. The jackass was comin' here with all the other little jackasses, includin' the mayor. They're gettin' desperate." She drains her Michelob, sitting it in the beer well, practically smug. Not once did she inject her or her best friend into it.

Still leaning on the bar, Bryce pulls a five from his pocket for the Mick, slugging the remainder of his for a refill. Sydney winks at her best friend.

"Did they get 'im?" Sydney asks. "Gaw head make my day."

"No," Bryce answers with an uneasy feeling of misjudgment. He takes a big swig of the cold beer, wishing he could make her day. He accepts her olive branch and opens up. "It was broad daylight, Monday afternoon."

"And nobody saw a thing, right?" She takes a long taste of Mick.

"Right."

"Not even the neighborhood busy body?"

"Oh, this didn't happen at her house. This happened in Media at her business."

"Oh." Sydney pauses, blinking. "Wait a minute. So let me get this straight. Your sister's in the hospital and nobody saw anything in broad daylight, in Media?" *Oh! We are so screwed!*

Bryce nods. "They think it was a break-in or attempted robbery."

"Say what? Was anything stolen?"

"Nah, nothin' was stolen. It's not about robbery. It's . . ." His voice trails.

Who don't know that? Sydney swallows the lump in her throat.

"They're sayin' they think she surprised whoever it was when she came back from lunch." He takes another gulp of liquid.

No doubt in my mind, Buddy Boy. You know what's up? "Well, I think the magic word here is the word 'think'. They think." Sydney swigs her beer. Bryce turns to her. She feels his eyes upon her as she continues, while looking straight ahead, mustering a professional voice, still keeping distance between her and downright concern. "I think if it was random, it would have been unusual, out of place, someone would have noticed. But it went unnoticed, it was usual." She mulls the words. Confusion clouds her face. "Did I say that right?" She captures Bryce's random glance with her warm smile.

"Yeah, I got it, somebody that ain't outta place." He throws her half a smile. She catches it.

"Yeah, like Griff." She takes a drink as if to wash his name out of her mouth.

"You mean Shaun? He wouldn't go around her place. She can't stand 'im. He doesn't have dirty hands."

"Not even for incriminating evidence?" She looks at him.

"Nah, he would send somebody. He always sends somebody. But she doesn't have any incriminating evidence. She woulda told me."

"Then are you thinkin'? Her ex-husband?"

"What? Beat her? No way. Don't let his size fool ya. He's a p—" Bryce checks himself. "He'd drop a dime to save his own ass."

"People do some crazy shit when they're backed against a wall." Sydney hesitates. "Did you back 'im against the wall?"

"You could say that. He dropped a dime – her." Bryce nods toward Leora. "Shaun's girlfriend."

"His girlfriend?" Sydney asks, shaking her head. *His girlfriend! There we are being thrown in the mix again, and we weren't even around! What is up with these people?* "She never was, is or ever will be his damn girlfriend!

He is the sleaziest son-of-a-bitch I ever met in my life!" Leora stops eavesdropping and just downright stands in front of the two and listens.

"Well, your boy told Carl to go to the diner and watch his girlfriend. He would be down later. But Alice distracted 'im, twistin' 'im with doubt like she always did, sayin' he's a fall guy, it's a set up and for him ta check his own trunk. He admitted to me he didn't see anything go down, but he was pissed so he lied."

"So he lied to Griff?" Sydney sips her beer.

"Yeah, and got his ass kicked." Bryce also takes a swig.

"Two times?" Sydney questions Bryce, looking at his solemn features while tapping his bottle with hers as a toast to something good in this whole conversation.

"Yeah, twice. He already had one blackeye for lyin'. I gave 'im another one," Bryce says in agreement now, tapping her bottle with his.

"Yes!" Leora says under her breath resuming her duties.

Sydney takes a sip, watching the crowd deep in thought. *Damn, the jig is up. She'll take it to her grave. Does that mean me or Sis?* The feeling of being watched creeps along the nape of her neck, bringing her back to reality. She glances around the bar and in the mirror. She turns, meeting those deep blue eyes—captivating, mesmerizing, absent of all animosity. She sighs, placing her denim bag on the bar, or so she thought. It topples off the edge to the floor, extracting her from the mystical blueness.

Papers, pens, chewing gum, lipstick, Bics are dumped. "Oh, shit!" She leans over to salvage her belongings, but not as quickly as Bryce, resulting in a full force collision: her face, his head. No screams, no choice words. She sees stars. Real stars taking her breath away. She gasps, sort of, there in a heap on the floor.

"Are you all right?" Bryce asks the stunned redhead.

She nods, groping the air, finding his outstretched hand. She accepts his strength, holding on to him to steady herself, nodding as he guides her onto the stool. And then it comes, a trickle at first, mostly unnoticeable until the warm red liquid drips on Sydney's hand. Peering through watery eyes, she leans over the bar, flailing to Leora.

"Jesus, Mary and Joseph! She's bleedin'! She's bleedin'!" Bryce yells, cupping his hand under her face, throwing an arm around her. "Holy shit! I'm sorry!" Customers gather Sydney's things, piling them on the bar as

Leora throws a dry bar rag at Bryce, grabbing another, filling it with ice. "I'm sorry! I'm sorry!"

Sydney sits with her head tilted back, the dry bar rag under her nose and the ice one on her face, making the okay sign.

"I'm sorry! It was an accident!" he tells Leora with pleading eyes.

"I know, I know," Leora answers, nodding. "You didn't mean it."

"Did it stop bleedin'? Is it bleedin'?" he asks the injured redhead.

Sydney slowly tilts her head in an upright position. The drip begins again.

"I'll take 'er to the hospital! Ya wanna go to the hospital? We're goin' to the hospital!" Bryce puts her head back to rest on his arm. She gropes for her pocketbook. "It's okay! It's okay! Don't move! You're fine! I gotcha! She wants her pocketbook stuff!" he yells to Leora. The two barmaids gather the contents off the bar, shoving it all back in the denim bag amidst mumbles and whispers.

"What happened?" Eva questions Leora.

"They butted heads—well, his head, her face," she answers.

"Oh, I'm really sorry!" Bryce tells Leora. He leans over Sydney. "You all right in there, Chooch?" He asks, lifting the ice rag just enough to look in her eyes. She gazes once more into those deep blues now filled with anguish and guilt.

"No, I'm half-left," she answers, still resting rather comfortably on his arm.

Bryce removes the rag full of ice, giving her a quizzical look. "Ya wanna go to the hospital?"

"Huh?" she answers, distracted by blueness. "Oh no, I'm okay," she answers. "I'll be fine." He helps her lift her head to the upright position.

Sydney never in her life saw so many eyes fixed on her, except for the time she lost her tube top doin' the bunny hop at the club. She pats her chest nonchalantly.

"Well, okay, if you say so. But if it gushes again, I'm takin' ya!"

She looks at her best friend with eyes already turning black.

"You wanna go home, Sis?" Leora asks her.

Sydney leans toward the bar, nodding slightly. It sets the room spinning. She lisps to the side, cradled against all of Bryce's six-foot frame.

"Whoa!" He throws his arm around her again.

"She wants to go home."

"I'll take 'er," Bryce announces. He signals to his comrades.

"Yo, Sis, is that okay?" Leora asks Sydney.

"Sure," Sydney answers, holding her head still.

"Are ya sure you're sure?" Leora leans on the bar, despondent.

"Sure I'm sure I'm sure."

Leora pats her hand. "Yo, Sis, maybe ya shouldn't be alone."

"She won't be. I'm gonna stay with her for a while. I'll drive her car, and Nick and Manny can bring mine and drop it off. I'm so sorry this happened."

Leora writes the bar phone number on a coaster and hands it to Bryce. He shoves it in his shirt pocket, grabbing the pocketbook, the ice-filled bar rag, giving his strength to a wobbly Sydney and holding a three-way conversation with his buddies.

"Bryce! Bryce!" Leora calls. He turns around slowly. "Your keys, you forgot your keys," she says, chucking them to him.

Listen Up!

. . . .

"Who was that masked man?" Eva asks, taking a breather, standing next to a forlorn Leora with her head resting on folded arms, staring at the front door. "So where the hell was she hidin' him?"

Leora stands up, cutting her eyes at the dark-haired beauty and smiles. "That, Momma, is Alice's brother."

"Brother? Who? Hank's Alice?"

"That'd be her. She's in a coma. Somebody bounced her brain."

"Oh, my God! What the—" Eva catches herself and speaks slower, "What the hell's goin' on? Waaait a minute, waaait a minute, maybe I don't wanna know." Eva holds her hand up like a traffic cop shaking her head, shuffling down her end to answer hooting and hollering from a couple of empties.

Leora handles her own end of thirsties, too not wanting to think about her best friend but unable to stop. She kicks it around—again. *This guy Luke Bryce seems nice enough. He seems sincere enough. He's just upset. I'd be upset, too. It's his sister, damn it!* She scans the whole bar for something, anything to occupy her run-away mind rushing to ring up a takeout at Eva's register. *Yeah, everybody leave.*

R-r-ring! R-r-ring! Leora grabs the telephone. "Papa's!" she yells above Robert Palmer, pressing a finger to her other ear. "Papa's!" She hears the dial tone dashing her hopes of an update on Sydney. *Guaranteed this is not the first time he went after his ex brother-in-law. He's been dealin' with these assholes longer than we have.* She waits on customers indulging in conversation of her best friend's mishap fueling her run-away mind. *Now look, Alice has been dragged into it too, by her ex-husband none the less.* She joins in a sing-along of "Sleigh Ride" by The Carpenters. Doubt creeps along the back of her mind. *Oh, my God! Maybe it's all a lie! Maybe nothin' happened to her. Maybe they're in cahoots, the lot of 'em finally finding a way to get into the house! We're in deep shit!* She wanders to Eva's end again, filling the funnel with used ice, throwing away used straws, saturated coasters, spent lemons and limes, draining beer glasses and pitchers, lining the beer well with a parade of the used glassware, her hands almost as busy as her mind. *Wait, wait! The nose bleed was an accident. That wasn't planned, not at all.* She takes a deep breath, waving good night to Jim and Aggie. *Hey, wait a minute, maybe Bryce and Alice are the good guys, like on our side.* Leora had had a good feeling about Bryce earlier, when he first seemed interested in Sydney. Not one iota of bad vibes. Then shit hit the fan with all that he-said-she-said bullshit until he and Sydney started comparing notes. *But they're all in the same circle. They all know each other, so I guess that doesn't necessarily make 'em good guys. It just causes dissension among the ranks. But then again, Alice isn't stupid. She was at the house when Lister owned it. She coulda lifted the typewriter back then and put 'em all in jail. That's her goal in life. Hmmm, so if she really didn't know about it, then that means she doesn't know we have it. Nobody knows. Just me, Sis, and the lamp post. Geez!* Images flit through her mind: Goo Goo, Griff, the mayor, Crow, Papa, Rob, Hank, Sonny, Eva, Doc . . . She sighs. *Nope. Nobody knows. I wouldn't imagine Alice would know Papa resold the house either, let alone I was the buyer.* Her eyes fly open along with her mouth. *Damn! I hope Bryce can't put two and two together! Nah, nah! He probably doesn't even know all the properties his sister unloaded when her boyfriend, or lawyer, or partner, whatever he is, or was, when he croaked!* She is frustrating herself big time!

"Nurse!" A customer rescues Leora from herself. She passes the taps, pulling Jack Daniels black label out of the speed rack at her end, robotic motions of bar tending, sort of like autopilot. A smile here, a thank you there, she handles the left over crowd, creating a glass parade on her own beer well. *Hell, Alice's brother is the least of our worries! Now that Griff knows Alice isn't holdin', and he's gotta know, doesn't it all come back to us again?* She gasps, scoping out the patrons while adding hot water to the washing and rinsing tubs. She sinks used shot glasses in the sudsy liquid to soak, then begins her task of diminishing her glass parade. *Hey, why didn't we just march our sorry asses right to the authorities?* She thinks. *Well, 'cause we haven't known all that long. Besides, march to who? Which one do you give it to? Who do you trust? What if whoever you give it to gives it to Griff and tells him where it came from? Tom said there's a slew of nervous Nellies out there. On the other hand, if we gave it to the Feds they would brag big time and announce us on television. We'd end up buried on exit eight.* Leora thinks hard. *Why didn't we just give it to Griff? Because dead men tell no tales. Neither do dead women. As soon as we give it up we're dead! We'll end up buried on exit eight along with the typewriter.* Leora's mind continues. *Hey, we should just give the damn typewriter ta Bryce! Alice deserves it. She told Carl if she had it she'd put 'em all in jail! Yeah! Payback's a bitch!* She scrubs glassware satisfied with new direction. *No, wait, maybe we should keep it. Bryce seems nice but not* that *nice. Not nice enough to hold my life in his hands. Besides, what if Bryce blames us for Alice gettin' hurt? What if he runs right to Griff? Griff probably has a reward out for the damn thing. Why can't we collect it? Yeah, right.* Leora has an anxious feeling. She takes a deep breath. *No, we'll just keep the damn thing and think about this. Maybe we should just keep it quiet.* She fishes three shot glasses out of the first sink—dunk, dunk, drain. *Why hasn't one of 'em called?*

Eva leans over the triple, sinks next to Leora lost in thought. "I changed my mind," Eva tells her coworker, "Give it up."

"Huh?"

Eva brings Leora back to earth. "Give it up. Tell me what's goin' on."

So Leora does just that, and only that, relating their first encounter with Deep Blue Eyes and Alice down the diner. No biggie," the curly-haired brunette says. "We were in the booth behind the register. He was in the next one with Alice and a couple workers. When we played the jukebox it got stuck on loud or high, whatever. It was funny. It really was. First he shook it, then I thought he was gonna rip it outta the wall. Marie came over and shut it off. We moved to the back booth." Leora switches gears. "Oh, yeah, Greg came in and paid for our food."

"Who? Sydney's Greg?"

"Yeah, the harem hoarder anyway, Alice was alone when they all went back to work. She said her brother thought Sydney was hot to trot. He tapped on the window when he came back for his keys." Leora skirts the main issues, racking her brain for more unrelated tidbits to feed her coworker instead of some of the detailed earful her and Sydney became privy to. "Oh yeah, Carl came in tryin' I guess, to rattle her slats, push her buttons, or pump her, whatever. Boy, does he suck at it. She called 'im a Bic! I laughed my ass off! Every time he tried to pump her she had a come back. Sydney and I turned the music down just ta listen. I bet when he left he was talkin' to himself. I thought Carl beat her up, but Bryce said he ain't built that way."

"Does Bryce know who did it?"

"He didn't say anything to me. Maybe he told Sis. Or maybe he's waitin' for Alice to tell him."

Sonny and Hank finally show their smiling faces at about twenty of two. The crowd has dwindled considerably along with the glassware parade.

Why doesn't one of 'em call? I knew it! It was just a ploy to get in the house! Her mind continues as usual. *Maybe they're at the hospital. Maybe she had another nose bleed. Egads!*

Leora retrieves used glasses Sonny gathers off the tables. "How's Alice?" she asks, standing in front of them, getting right to the heart of the matter, pulling no punches.

"I don't know. It's not my turn ta watch 'er." Hank leans on the bar, nodding an acknowledgment to waves and hollers.

Leora's heart sinks to her stomach. *Now what'll I do?* She watches Crow pulling cases from the walk-in and begins again. "Ya haven't seen her?"

"Why is it important?"

What in the hell is with the attitude? I don't need it. I got my own.

Sonny looks around, waving to a few of the customers. "It's been slow, huh?"

"No, not really it's closin' time." She gives him a stupefied look. "We already gave last call." Leora suppresses her attitude of telling Hank to go forth and multiply taking a different approach with Sonny. "It's late. Where have you been? Where's your note?"

"I've been to London to visit the queen." He bucks his eyes, blinking at her a smirk, tugging the corners of his mouth.

"Hey, we need a keg of Miller tapped," Eva reports, standing with Leora in front of the managers. "It just blew. You guys are just in time." She smiles.

"You're closed, aren't ya? Didn't you give last call? Mac will get it." Hank stands, facing Sonny his back in Eva's direction.

"Is that right?" Eva stands with hands on hips, cocking her head back and forth.

"Yeah, that's right. Give us a drink!" Hank barks.

Eva's smile fades. "Yeah, well, Mac can get that, too. We're closed." She turns up the lights, grabbing the tips and Leora, pulling her to the end of the bar before the girl could put her two cents in. Leora plops on a stool. Eva mixes herself a vodka and Coke. "You want a drink?"

"Not really. Tell ya what I'll have a wine, a Catawba Pink on the rocks."

Eva hands Leora her beverage, taking the stool on the far side of her, away from the opening, eliminating any possibility of a recurring argument with pleasant Hank. She licks the swizzle stick, blinking with defiance at Hank, sauntering through the opening, and gives him the pinky, the Hallmark finger which translates to: when I don't care enough to send my very best, which is just plain giving him the finger. He squeezes past Crow to make a couple Cutty and waters, mixing it up with the sparse clientele.

Sonny meanders down to the opening drink in hand. "Was it busy tonight?" he asks, hanging his suit jacket on the back of Leora's stool and rolling up his sleeves.

"Yeah, it was weird though." Leora counts out dollar increments of nickels, dimes, and quarters, aligning them in two rows snaking along the bar. "It was mobbed earlier instead of now at closing."

"We emptied the front register and put it all in this one." Eva counts paper money. "We didn't ring it out. We know how ya can't stand comin' in here and doin' absolutely nothin', especially him." Eva's statement reeks with sarcasm as she nods at Hank speaking out loud, "Maybe we should pay Crow or stop 'im from helpin'."

"So is the queen in the hospital?" Leora gulps her wine.

"You mean Snow White?" Eva chases an ice cube in her drink, popping it in her mouth, nodding toward Hank again. "Isn't that Grumpy, one of the dwarfs?"

Leora tries a different approach. "Hey, there were a lot of regulars missin' tonight, even Goo Goo. And there was no prayer meetin' tonight. Ahhhh, it was rather nice."

Eva pumps. "Yeah, did they finally get arrested or are they hidin'?"

"How can they get arrested?" Leora questions. "Who the hell is gonna arrest them? They're hidin' under a snake."

Sonny attempts a smokescreen. "Well, I guess, you know, the holiday weekend. Everybody's busy, you know, things to do."

Leora is done with the head games. "Oh, give it up, Sonny. You guys are wearin' suits. What's that about? Oh wait, I'm drunk. It's a figment of my imagination."

He puts on a Stan Laurel smile, watching Hank busy playing star down the front of the bar. "Well, Alice is in a hospital in Philadelphia."

"And . . .?" Leora is agitated.

"Were the two of you in Philly tonight?" Eva throws a question, too.

"Oh no, only the family is allowed in, and cops, lots o' cops. We were out at the Trade Winds."

"Well, how did you find out?" Eva questions. "You guys aren't family and certainly nobody at the Trade Winds is family."

Sonny eyes Hank sucking up the phony attention being displayed for the free drinks he and his ego doles out in his few and far between appearances behind the bar. "We went to get somethin' to eat earlier down the diner, and what's-her-name was there with Jammer. What's her name?" He rubs his forehead with his thumb and fingers. "He's got a black eye. What's her name? Ahhh, oh, yeah, Sally. She was goin' to the ladies room and stopped to say hi to Hank and started blabbin'."

"Who? Back Alley Sally, with Jammer? Move over Hank. No wonder he's miserable, replaced by a grape."

"Shhh, shhh," Sonny checks Hank in his peripheral vision. "Yeah, she told us Shaun went on a rampage, kickin' the shit outta Jammer and Hector."

It wouldn't have anything ta do with pills, would it? "Why?" Leora is all ears, cocking her head and blinking like a dumb blonde.

"She didn't say. We didn't ask any questions. We just listened. She said he kicked the shit outta Carl, too. When we went out to the Trade Winds, he"—Sonny points over his shoulder referring to Hank – "went after Carl right in front of Shaun."

Wide-eyed Leora sucks her breath in. "Shaun? He was out there?"

"Shh! Shh! He was out there, the mayor was out there—all of 'em, even Marcie. Yeah, Shaun sent Carl to take a powder. Shaun said Carl's really upset, and they're tryin' to find out what happened to Alice."

"Oh, and of course he ain't got a clue? He doesn't know anything."

"What? Did a boyfriend do it?" Eva asks.

"Yeah right, who are they blamin' Hank?"

"Wait, wait, wait," Sonny says, turning to take a glimpse at Hank. "He said Alice's brother is on a rampage. He already got Carl and told Hank to watch his back."

Leora is dumbfounded. "Are you kiddin' me? What a sicko! Did ya tell 'im ya know he's the one who did it?"

Sonny pauses, looking at the barmaids.

"Ya didn't, did cha? He lied right to your face, and you didn't say anything?"

"Nah, nah, nah, listen."

Eva jumps in. "What did he say he's gonna get you fired? Did you get paid off?" Eva slaps Leora's arm. "See, money talks, bullshit walks."

"He can say and do whatever he wants." Leora is glad she and Sydney kept the typewriter a secret.

Sonny stands in the opening of the bar, making sure Hank remains out of earshot down the other end of the bar while he speaks freely to Leora and Eva. "No, listen. I let 'im talk. Hank walked away like he was all pissed off, but I think he went lookin' for Carl. He never found him. Griff was drunk, loose-lipped. He mentioned Goo Goo. He got in an argument with Goo Goo last weekend. He doesn't know what the problem is. He just comes down here to have a couple drinks."

Leora glares at Sonny. "Poor little innocent Griff, a victim of circumstance, just havin' a couple drinks, he ain't botherin' nobody. His shit is sugar and everybody's runnin' after it with a spoon! Yeah, right!"

"He mentioned you, too. He said he told Salvatore he doesn't know why you're so upset with him. He's never done anything to you." Sonny smiles at her with a puppy dog face blinking.

Leora is beside herself. "He tried to get me fired! He tried to get me arrested!"

"When?" Eva blinks at Leora.

Leora clams up, afraid she's already said too much.

"Now, now," Sonny throws a quick look at Hank. "He told me he's been mannerly with you." Sonny bucks his eyes at Leora and continues, "He made it a rule never to go out with anyone that has an addiction. You're not use to bein' dumped. You are vindictive against him 'cause everybody and the mayor saw you pocket money from the business, and nothing was ever said even when Goo Goo tried to pin it on one of them. Oh, yeah, and he never called the police."

Leora breathes through her mouth unable to respond. All the girl can do is blink.

"What? Your boy is nuts! He's scary! Boy, he is pissed at your ass!" Eva looks at Leora. "They're all pissed at your ass! How can one person be allowed to do that let alone a group?"

Leora wants out of this conversation pronto. "One lies, the others swear to it. Consider the source."

"That's right," Sonny states, patting Leora's hand, "That's right." He makes a shushing gesture to the girls checking out Hank. "He said Carl is thinkin' about callin' the cops on Alice's brother. He looks like a raccoon."

That piece of shit! Bryce was tellin' the truth! I hope he's still at the house!

"I'd kick his ass, too, if it was my sister," Eva argues.

"Well, isn't that somethin'? Now Hank's gonna have ta play nice when that asshole comes in here, isn't he? See how he likes it." Leora changes the subject, glaring at the back of Hank's head totaling out the front register as the last of the customers call it a night, turning off the pool table light on their way out.

"I told 'im you can't come apart like that down here at the bar. You have to stay focused on business. You have to keep your personal life separate or Salvatore will can your ass. He won't be comin' in here that much anyway." Sonny pats his hair.

"Who? Griff? How do ya figure?" Leora stirs her wine with her finger.

Sonny explains. "All that trouble last weekend. Shaun apologized and said it won't happen again. Salvatore is none too happy."

"I don't know about that. I think Papa's smilin' all the way to the bank."

"As usual, you girls don't know what you're talkin' about," Hank appears, injecting himself into the conversation. "He's not blackmailin' anybody."

Leora snaps her head in Hank's direction with a disgruntled look on her face. "No shit, Sherlock!" *Correct this!* "Who the hell said anything about anybody blackmailin' anybody? Pay attention!"

"Who the hell is talkin' to you?" Eva is stoked.

Why don't ya stop actin' like broads?"

"Why don't -you- shut the hell up?" Eva gives him the real finger.

"Why don't -you- shut me up?" Hank is like a bear with a sore paw.

"Why don't cha listen up!" Leora talks above the verbal exchange. "Marcie rented Sydney's old apartment." She speaks in monotone then tilts her head back, doing a bottoms-up swig on her wine, sitting the glass on the bar amidst gawking from her three coworkers.

"That's bullshit. Salvatore would have said somethin' to me," Hank announces the chip on his shoulder just as shiny as ever.

'Why? He wasn't bangin' you." Eva sneers. "Oh, Marcie didn't tell ya?"

"Why would he tell you about his personal business?"

"Yeah, like he told you about that apartment building in Jersey? Did you give him permission to buy it?" Eva asks softly, demurely. She gazes into Hank's eyes, going from angel fish to piranha in one second. "Gimme a break!" she growls.

"What, Papa made you a landlord? Sydney never paid rent to you."

"Who the hell do you broads think you're talkin' to?"

"Nobody!" They yell in unison.

"Oh, excuse me, it's Mr. Nobdy!" Eva retorts.

"Leora slides off the stool. "I stand corrected!" She stares at Sonny immersed in his task of clearing the register, ignoring the whole scene.

"Oh, I know," Eva continues, "that's because he couldn't find ya. You were with Back Alley Sally. Oh, no, wait, that wasn't you; that was Jammer."

Hank throws the readout tape from the front register on the bar, stomping off to the head. Leora slips behind the bar, past Sonny to clean up the last remnants of the night, washing the last of the glasses, wiping the bar, draining the sinks. Crow continues filling the coolers with bottled brew.

"You've been awful quiet," Leora leans with him as he fills the cooler on the far side of the taps. "Ya gettin' cold feet?" She smiles. "You'll be fine, Daddy."

"What about your feet?"

"My feet aren't cold." She puts a foot on the opened cooler.

"So what did you step in?"

Leora inspects the bottom of her shoe. "Nothin', I didn't step in nothin'." She watches Crow peering into the cooler with vim and vigor as he loads a case of bud nips, throwing the empty box on the bar behind him and pulling another off the bar, continuing the process, refusing to look at her. Leora's smile evaporates into apprehension. She is not going there. "Nothin', I'm fine, my feet are fine."

"How 'bout Sydney?"

Leora hears uneasiness in Crow's voice. She tries to play it off. "Her feet are fine, too." She skirts the incident. "What a freak accident. I don't think her nose is broke, but she'll probably have a blackeye or two and a headache. Eva said she'll work tomorrow night for her."

"And Bryce?"

"Bryce? Oh, Bryce. What about him?" Leora asks nonchalantly.

"Do you trust him?"

"I don't know him."

"So you don't trust 'im."

"Trust 'im with what, Sydney? She's a big girl."

"So is Alice, and look where she is."

Leora is uncomfortable.

"Well, what about Griff, doll?" Crow is adamant.

Leora snaps her head at Crow. "What da ya mean? I can't stop him from comin' in here." She is defensive.

"Would you stop somebody from killin' him?"

"Would you?" Leora bucks her eyes, feeling really uncomfortable with the direction of the conversation.

Crow loads the rest of the nips and stands, tossing the empty box on the bar then turns, looking Leora square in the face. "Well, I wouldn't, but the question is, would you?"

"Leora tries her damnedest to smooth things over, to lighten the mood, to bring an end to the discussion. "Cool your tool, ya fool. It's fine. We got this."

"And just what is it you got?" Crow squints at her, leaning on the open cooler.

Leora looks at him with pleading eyes. *Please let it go, Crow.* "Personality!" She speaks around the lump in her throat.

"Trouble." Crow corrects her response. "I listened to this Bryce guy and his buddies talkin' tonight. There's a woman in intensive care because of her ex-husband's mouth or fist or both. Everybody's lookin' for somethin' that would put her ex-husband and the mayor, oh yeah, and Griff, the wannabe love of your life, in jail. And this guy you don't trust is at your house with your best friend."

Leora swallows hard, gazing at Crow in silence. She wants to cry, she wants to scream, she wants it over.

"Yes, or no? Given the chance would you stop somebody from poppin' that piece of shit?"

"You wouldn't." Leora straightens up, closing her eyes, breathing deep.

"I didn't." Now Crow stands. "Your boy's got a gun." He pulls full cases of empty longnecks from under the front end sinks, piling them on the aperture, glancing at Leora with disbelief still registered on her face.

"Says who?" Leora swallows hard, folding her arms in front of her.

"Says me, that's not hear say. I saw it tucked in the back of his pants."

Leora pinches her bottom lip, staring at the end of the bar, watching Eva finish up cashing in their tips to Sonny, then meets Crow's hazel eyes.

"No."

Crow leans on the top of the cooler. "No what? You don't believe me?" He blinks wide-eyed at her.

"No, I wouldn't lift a finger."

Crow pulls his keys from his pocket, removing his house key and laying the Chevy keychain with his truck key on the cooler. "Here, take my truck home. If your car's not there, maybe they can have a shoot-out someplace else this weekend."

"Nobody knows he's at my house. Sonny just said Carl might be tryin' ta have 'im arrested for kickin' his ass even though Griff did it first. He's safe at my house."

"Are you? What if the cops show up for a showdown? The whole bar saw him leave with your girl. Now what? What if Griff shows up all amorous? Your boy will plug 'im in a New York second. What da ya want, high noon at the Oh, Shit Corral?"

Leora closes her eyes, holding the back of her neck. She exhales, puffing her hair on her forehead. The girl is so fed up. She studies his solemn expression, meeting his concerned stare; this new side to Daddy Crow.

His features soften. "I'll grab it Sunday when I swing by for, you know," he leans forward whispering, "Jenny's surprise."

"Ah'ight, deal, but only because I love ya," Leora answers in agreement, scooping the key off the cooler. She fishes her keys from her pocket. "Can you get that off there?" she asks, handing them to him for some help.

Crow slides the GM key off the keyring and hands them back to Leora.

She smiles at him, speaking in a Shirley Temple voice. "Thanks, Daddy. Give us a kiss ta last," she teases, cutting her eyes at him, offering her cheek.

He kisses her cheek then grins, ducking through the aperture for more cases to continue refilling the other depleted coolers. Leora checks the bar one more time before pulling her pocketbook and jacket from the cabinet under the register.

"Here." Eva points to Leora's split of the night's take on the bar.

"That's good," Sonny says, holding the two money bags filled with paper money and coins.

"I told ya we were busy earlier." Leora shoves the tips into her purple pouch, looking around. "Where's Hank, still in the head lickin' his wounds?"

"Hopefully he stuck his head in the toilet and flushed it a couple times."

"See ya." Leora slips into her jacket. "You're workin' tomorrow, right?"

"Oh. Why? What's wrong with ..."

"Yeah." Eva answers, interrupting Sonny. "Sydney's under the weather." She turns to Leora and winks. "She should be better by Wednesday."

Leora nudges Eva. "Yeah, she should be. Thanks. Aren't you leavin'?"

"No, I'm gonna aggravate some more," Eva answers just as Hank emerges from the men's room.

Leora nudges her again. "Well, here he comes now."

"Is his head wet?"

Leora laughs, raising her hand as a good-bye gesture on her way to the front door, then changes direction walking over to the bar to talk with Crow on the down low. Crow abandons the cases, walking over to her.

"Listen, don't you get that for him," Leora states, nodding at the taps.

"It has ta be tapped anyway for Mister Mac," he says smiling.

"So tap it for Mister Mac. Don't tap it while Hank's here." She glances at the end of the bar where Eva is giving Hank a run for his money.

Crow shakes his head laughing. "You are bad."

"Well, loadin' the beer cases isn't Mister Mac's job. If it wasn't for you, miserable Hank wouldn't have time to stand around pickin' his ass."

Crow laughs out loud.

Leora spins around at the front door. "Hey, Puppy, there's two in the ice for ya!" she yells mouthing the word 'daddy'when he looks at her. She waves good night.

The Linen Closet

It is almost two thirty in the morning as Leora makes the right onto Chestnut Street. A black GTO faces Sydney's car parked on the left in front of the darkened house. She coasts the truck into the driveway. The conversation with Crow flies through her head as she walks to the porch. "Wheezer," she calls, her breath condensing in the air. The only sounds she hears are of her pounding heart and her anxious breathing. Even the distant refineries nightly hissing is absent. She jiggles her keys, putting the dead silence at bay. A faint meow catches her attention. She walks down the steps and looks toward the roof. "What are you doin', Wheeze?" She blinks, trying to adjust her eyes in the darkness. "You're not in the house with Sis?" She backs toward the street. "Wheezer," she calls, staring at the roof. She walks to her left into the grass, flipping her collar against the early morning chill. Shaking her keys, she calls louder, "Wheezer!" A faint meow dissipates with movement around the side of the house toward the back. "Wheezer, it's me. What'sa matter?" Leora feels uncomfortably alone in the cold, still dark. She jiggles her keys at the darkness again, walking to the front door. *What the hell is up?* Her mind begins again. She bungles with an uncooperative key at the keyhole, now leaning over using two hands for this major operation just as Sydney opens the door. Calm washes over Leora.

"Shhhh." A soft melody from the stereo escapes the den, along with the faint glow from the television outlining her best friend's almost angelic silhouette in her nightgown, gesturing toward the stairs. Leora chucks her shoes to join Sydney's and Bryce's on-the-throw rug behind the door before closing it then hits the hall light switch for her trek up the "wooden hill" to the bathroom.

At first they stand, squinting at each other in the bright light, the bathroom still slightly humid; Sydney's curly red mop practically dry.

Leora drops her pocketbook. "How are ya feelin'?" She drapes her jacket on the tub, focusing her eyes to study Sydney's face.

"With my hands." Sydney's response exudes relief. She turns toward the light for Leora's assessment, pulling a doobie from behind her ear and handing it to her. "It's nothin'. I look about this bad once a month," Sydney announces, inspecting the discoloration under her eyes in the medicine cabinet mirror. "The only difference is I don't have any cramps."

Leora lights the J, passing it to her best friend. "You're a little pale-lookin', and it's a bit swollen, but I must say it doesn't look as bad as I pictured."

"Yo, Sis, my nose coulda fell off and it wouldn't look half as bad as where your mind takes you!" The duo laughs.

"Well, Momma, you're off tomorrow night, Eva's workin'."

"I'm probably good to go," Sydney says, exhaling and passing.

"Well, Eva volunteered. Now you won't have to use a whole stick of cover up. You'll really be good to go on Wednesday." Leora takes a hit, flicking ashes in the toilet. "Eva's got this vendetta anyway." She hands sister Syd the burning ember.

"Nah-uh, who?"

"Hank."

"No doubt. I knew that."

"Eva was nice and Hank was nasty, again."

"She'll aggravate the shit out of 'im, again."

"Yeah, she pushes his buttons." Leora inhales. "She was still pushin' 'em when I left, somethin' about stickin' his head in the toilet and flushin' it." The girls laugh. "Hell, Sonny and Hank didn't show up 'til closin'. They were out the Trade Winds tonight. Griff was there with everybody from the prayer meetin', and so was Marcie."

Sydney chokes on a hit and passes the joint. "You're kiddin' me." Her mouth waters with distaste.

"Would I lie to you, Momma?" Leora inhales.

"I knew it was too good to be true."

"Yeah, ya believe it?" Leora hits it again before passing it. "They went out there 'cause they ran into Back Alley Sally down the diner. She was blabbin' about Griff, kickin' the shit outta Jammer, Hector, and Carl AND she told 'em about Alice bein' in the hospital. Hank went after Carl out there. Sonny said he thinks Carl might be pressin' charges against Bryce for hittin' 'im! Are you kiddin' me?"

"Are you for real?"Sydney exhales, rolling her eyes, shaking her head. "And Griff wasn't named for his handiwork, right?"

"Hell no. He wasn't named for his handiwork on Heckle 'n' Jeckle either. Remember? They told Eva the door did it. Sonny said Carl looks like a raccoon. Bryce was tellin' the truth. I was hopin' he was still here. The cops might be lookin' for 'im.'"

"So Sonny and Hank know about the set-up?"

"What, the pills? Nah-uh." Leora exhales the words, scowling. "Not to my knowledge. I asked Sonny why Griff was nailin' everybody, and he said they didn't ask Back Alley Sally any questions they just listened. I figure she would a told that, too, if she knew it. So I don't think she was told anything."

"Cheese and rice!" Sydney sighs. "How does this happen? Stink it up, Sis!"

"No, shit! We step in it, don't we?"

"Damn, we're gonna be needin' some hip boots pretty soon."

"Hip boots my ass, we need a wet suit! Oh yeah, listen ta this: Sonny said Griff told him I'm a drug addict. He doesn't go out with drug addicts. I don't take rejection well" Leora snaps her fingers. Sydney bucks her eyes. "Wait, wait. What else? Let me think. Oh yeah, I'm a thief, too. All of 'em, you hear me, all of 'em saw me pocket Papa's money. But my secret's safe with them! What da ya think of them apples?"

"Well, for one thing it sounds like the apples are full of worms. For another thing, the jig is up. What secret? He blew that! I'm surprised he didn't ask Sonny if he saw a typewriter layin' around."

"Is it still . . . ?" Leora nods in the direction of Sydney's bedroom, taking one last toke then, holding it for Sydney before dropping the roach into the toilet.

Sydney exhales. "Yepper, it's still sleepin'.'"

"Oh, and where's, uh, he at?"

"Oh, he's sleepin', too, downstairs in the den. He cooked me eggs and cleaned up the kitchen, can I keep 'im, Sis?" Sydney smiles at her roommate. "He sat at the other end of the couch, earlier rubbin' my feet in his lap. Next thing I know, I'm all snug in the afghan, and he's placin' a cup of tea on the coffee table. Please, can I?"

Leora smiles at mirror Sydney. "Does he know we have it, or that we know who has it?"

"Nah, Sis. I thought about tellin' 'im." She leans forward, inspecting her face closer up. "But what if he blames us for what happened to his sister?" She blows stray ashes off the lacy bodice.

"I know, I was thinkin' the same thing earlier." Leora crinkles her face. Her mind is in overdrive. "Yo, Sis, we didn't make Carl lie on Alice. Hell, we didn't even know who Alice was, let alone that she'd be there. They bugged us, they planted pills; they tried to get me fired. And ya know what? I thought about givin' Crow a heads-up, but I ran everybody I could think of through my mind. You and me, me and you, Sis. Nobody else knows, nobody."

"Yeah, well, now that Alice is outta the picture Griff'll be gunnin' for us. Seriously, who else is left, Momma?"

"Speakin' of guns, he has one."

"Yeah, and he's gonna come show it to us!"

"Not Griff, Sis, Bryce. Bryce has a gun."

Sydney's eyes pop. "Bryce!!!" She swallows his name.

Leora thought her best friend was pale before. No, now she is pale, and she sits on the side of the tub.

"He seemed like such a nice guy."

Leora puts the lid down on the toilet and sits leaning forward to talk. "Hey, Sis, he probably is. And he's probably sick and tired of dealin' with these lame people. We are, and it's only been, what, a couple weeks for us? Havin' a gun don't make you a bad person. We like Goo Goo, he has a gun." Leora thinks, nodding her head up and down. "Papa, we like Papa."

Sydney sighs. "We should just wait and calm down. Mums the word."

"Yeah, I'm gettin' bad vibes, are you?"

"Yeah, not before. But now, just talkin' about sayin' somethin'. I mean we haven't told anybody. But sayin' that . . ."

"That's where I'm at. Ya can't 'un' ring a bell, ya know? Let's let sleepin' dogs lie. We've got enough problems. No sense in complicatin' it."

"Works for me! Ya can't take it back once ya spill it."

"Did Bryce hint around or anything?"

"You mean about who would do somethin' like that?"

"No names? Huh?"

"No, but I didn't push. We didn't go there. I thought he was waitin' for his sister to give 'im a name. But now that you told me he's got the"—Sydney steps around the word—"you know what, maybe he's tired of waitin'. After all, he went after Carl; he came up to the bar to confront us. I'm glad we talked though. It's nice ta talk to someone who doesn't bullshit all the time."

"… Or talk down to ya."

"Yeah, you got it. I don't think he's involved with those people, Momma. I mean like deep. I think he's only involved because of his big sister. She married into it, well, divorced it and it's his sister. He's just lookin' out for her, and now this. I think he blames himself."

"Awww, he's a puppy, Sis, a puppy. Oh! Speakin' of puppies, Crow is the one who told me about the gun. He saw it. He over heard the conversations between Bryce and his buddies, too. He doesn't think Bryce is gonna be safe here. I asked 'im why not? None of those jackasses know Bryce was at the bar. Crow's answer was everybody at the bar saw him leave with you. I said, 'Well, nobody at the bar knows the cops might be lookin' for 'im'. Then Crow argues, 'What if Griff shows up or what if the cops show up?' That's when he gave me his truck key. You believe it? We switched vehicles. He said if they think I'm not here, then nobody will show up at the Oh! Shit Corral."

Sydney giggles. "Oh, Daddy Crow, Oh, my God, can ya stand it?"

"He told me he'll get it Sunday when he swings by for Jenny's ring."

"Oh yeah, Bryce did tell me the doctors put her in a coma on purpose. Somethin' about it protects her brain 'til the swelling goes down."

"Oh yeah, we heard of that before. Remember that girl was kicked in the head by a horse and they did that?"

"Yeah, I remember. And she got better."

"Let's go wake 'im up, Sis. We gotta tell 'im about the cops." Leora gathers her coat and denim bag.

Sydney reaches for the door, turning to her best friend. "Yo, Sis. Did I mention he's been here before? He thinks we're rentin' off of Papa. I left it at that. He said Steve had ta do a few renovations ta change this place back to a house."

"Steve?"

"Yeah, the guy that died? Isn't that his name?"

"Oh! Oh! Oh! Oh! Lister, hmmm, Steve is it?"

"Yeah, Bryce said he used ta stop by here and see his sister all the time." Leora catches flies. Sydney puts her hands on her hips. "Do you know Alice has the same canister set as us, and we keep 'em in the same place she did? Hooray for mushrooms!"

"Didn't she tell Carl this use to be a place of business? She didn't come here all that much."

Footsteps along with the sound of jingling keys are heard ascending the stairs. The girls stand straight as pokers with eyes wide and breathing abandoned.

Sydney takes a deep breath, opening the door. "Hi," she sings to Bryce. "You need to get in here?' The friends exit the bathroom.

Bryce blinks at Leora then the black nightgown, then at Leora, now the black nightgown again while slight fragrances of body lotion and powder dissipate in the hall. "I was comin' to see if you were all right," he says with a sleepy voice, stretching, yawning. He runs his fingers through his hair. He scratches his five o'clock shadow.

"She's good ta go thanks to you, Dr. Bryce, a doctor who makes house calls."

"And cooks." Sydney smiles at him.

"Well, that's hearsay," Leora states, "I don't believe it." She smiles at him, too.

"Well, believe it when I say that couch is comfortable." Bryce yawns again.

"Yepper, its hard work stayin' mad when you're exhausted and comfy."

"Comfy?" Bryce raises an eyebrow.

Sydney shakes her head. Leora blinks. "Oh, sorry, I mean snugly."

Now Bryce shakes his head, stepping sideways to the bathroom with his back away from the girls. "Snugly?"

"Well, yeah," Leora deepens the tone of her voice, "snugly." She jiggles her head like Rhonda. "Did anyone ever tell you, you talk in your sleep?"

Bryce tries to hide a quizzical look. "Why, what I say?"

Leora glances at Sydney. "Well, somethin' about Philadelphia." They watch Bryce for a reaction. Nothing.

Sydney brings it. "You have a gun."

That stirs a reaction, a big one. Bryce snaps his head at Sydney, placing his hand behind his back for a quick check with a face full of tell.

"Listen, I heard the cops might be lookin' for ya." Leora displays a nonchalant attitude, adjusting her pocketbook on her shoulder. "Carl might be pressin' charges."

"Shaun don't want any cops sniffin' around. He's got enough problems what with the Feds on the side lines. Besides I ain't the only one that hit 'im."

Sydney nods. "Yeah, we know Griff did, too. We already have a witness."

"Actually, several if ya count Heckle 'n' Jeckle," Leora adds.

"Heckle 'n' Jeckle? Who the hell . . . ?" Bryce's face contorts with confusion.

Sydney laughs. Leora joins in.

Bryce folds his arms in front of him. "Oh, so a little birdie told ya?"

"Nah-uh, they're real witnesses!" Sydney answers.

"A Heckle and a Jeckle are witnesses?" He tries to make them sound important, but it is what it is.

"Yeah, plus Griff kicked their asses, too."

"He did, did he, with what, a scarecrow?" Bryce decides to play. "You wanna sell me a bridge too, don't cha?" He asks, half smiling, shifting glances back and forth at the two of them, trying to hide confusion running amok on his face.

Sydney smiles at this very likable guy who has been nothing but brutally honest with her all evening.

Leora smiles, too. "Hey! As a matter of fact, we do have a bridge right up the road! And it only costs two eggs scrambled, toast, jelly, and coffee!"

Bryce's smile fades as he straightens his arm out in front of the girls, herding them toward the steps behind him. They follow his piercing gaze to the linen closet where the towel along the bottom of the door moves about eerily.

Leora screams, "Wheezer!"The duet runs to the door, calling him. An orange and white paw appears from under the door attacking the terry cloth.

"He's stuck in the wall again!" Sydney and Leora run past Bryce in full throttle to Leora's bedroom.

Pocketbook flies, jacket flies as both sprint across the bed, maneuvering behind curtains and sheers. A swoosh of cold night air invades the room as the girls open the window then fumble with the screen.

Bryce appears in the doorway. "What are ya doin'?" Confusion seems to be a steady fixture on his face around these two.

"It's Wheezer! You saw Wheezer!" Sydney explains. "He's stuck in the wall!"

"What wall?" Bryce is so confused.

"We don't know how he gets in there." Leora leans out the front window calling, "Wheezer!"

Sydney pokes her head out. "Come on, tiger!" They listen. "We looked, but we can't find a hole."

"Wait a minute, let me get this straight. You're sayin' he climbs through a hole in the roof and comes out behind the linen closet, right?"

"You mean behind behind?" Confusion now clouds Leora's face. "You mean in the wall?"

"What wall?" He asks again, rubbing his stubble, thinking he might actually be missing something.

Sydney takes up the cause. "Well, first there's the door, then the linen closet then the wall, behind behind—that's where Wheezer is, in the wall behind the linen closet behind the door!"

"There's no wall there. Why don't cha just let 'im out of the closet?"

All three stand with confused faces gawking back and forth at each other.

Leora eyes are wide, shifting back and forth as she thinks. "I don't have a sledgehammer?" Her answer is a question.

"You don't need a sledgehammer."

Leora bucks her eyes. "How do ya figure that?"

"Yeah," Sydney joins in, "what would you use?"

"Just unhook the slide bolts." Bryce walks back to the closet where the towel seemingly tries to escape under the door with the help of a certain feline. The girls follow. He swings the solid wood door all the way open to the right. "If I remember correctly," he states, feeling the door jam along the inside where it meets the thick wooden cabinet. He locates a heavy duty slide bolt roughly six inches from the top. "Yeah, here it is. There should be one about the same distance down the bottom."

The hallway light would be more than enough with the daylight pouring through the second floor windows, if they only knew what they were looking for.

Sydney stoops. "Got it."

Bryce reaches down, meeting Sydney's hand, moving the slide bolt into an upright position then pushing it up. Bang! "Steve kept folders in there along this wall. I saw him closin' it up a couple a times. I was never in there though." Bryce guides Sydney's hand to the other over sized slide bolt. "Didn't you ever wonder about the hinges?" He points to the rather large brass hinges on the left supporting the cabinet.

Sydney turns to an adoring Bryce, peering into his face inches away. "No," she answers pertly.

"Ya know, you can never have too . . . much . . . closet . . . sp . . ." Leora's voice trails, bearing witness to a lip lock thrown on her best friend.

Leora rolls with it. "Hey! Wait a minute! Yo, Sis, is he speakin' French?"

Sydney laughs. Bryce shakes his head. "What am I gonna do with the two of you?" He pushes the top slide bolt down. Bang! "The story goes Mr. and Mrs. Cummins lived here, and after their kids grew up, they made it into two apartments givin', 'em a supplement income. They lived in the bottom. When the missus died, Mr. Cummins just rented out rooms to foreigners on the ships or to out of state longshoremen. They were here a couple days, then they'd ship out again. Then when Mr. Cummins died, the kids sold it. That was Steve's bedroom." Bryce points to the backroom on the left. "You can't really see that bedroom light from the street 'cause of the tree out front. As far as anybody knew, this was just another place he conducted business from. He made this linen closet for Alice for when she showed up, which was pretty much all the time. He said it was cheaper than rippin' it all out. Those folders shoved behind here turned out ta be all of his legal papers, includin' a few more properties he added my sister's name to and his last will and testament. Alice gave the will to his daughter Corrine."

Leora peers, between the two of them, bobbing and weaving, trying to get a good look at the slide bolts.

"Should we unload it?" Sydney asks.

"What the shelves, nah, you don't have to."

Bryce shoves the enclosed cabinet once then shoves it again. The slide bolts separate like puzzle pieces as the massive cupboard without so much as a groan slowly opens to musty darkness. It would have forced Wheezer toward the left wall into the twelve-inch space formed by the width of the shelves, keeping him safe from being squished. He would have then scooted to the open end and dropped onto the first step on the stairway, ducking under the cabinet to hop up onto the open floor, escaping down the hallway. He would have if he was there. But he was no where to be found.

"Wheezer!" Leora calls. The almost stagnant cool air separates from the dark, creeping along the floor.

"Come on, Tiger." Sydney leans in to listen.

"He's not here." Leora sticks her bottom lip out in a pout.

"I think the slide bolts got 'im. They were pretty loud. Cats don't like that. If I remember correctly, there's an old stairway back here." Bryce steps inside feeling with his stocking feet lighting his Bic. He spots the railing on the right hand side. "Yeah, here's the railing. You can put weather stripping inside on the bottom of the door to stop that draft. It's already on the sides and the top, see? But I wouldn't do that 'til I found out how he's gettin' in here. What's his name?"

"Wheezer," Sydney answers.

"Wheezer, come on, pal." Bryce steps down, bending over to peer down the stairway. "Hey, I think some steps are missin'. Be careful when you decide to come in here. Bring a flashlight."

"He's not there, is he?" Leora asks.

"No," Bryce answers, exiting the enclosed stairwell, "he booked."

"The roof!" The girls run again to the bedroom

"Kitty-kitty-kitty-kitty-kitty-kitty-kitty-kitty-kitty!" Leora calls on the way.

Over the bed to the window, the girls sprint again, taking turns sticking their heads out calling his name.

Bryce stands leaning in the doorway again. "He went that a way," he says, pointing to Sydney's room.

"Where?" Sydney stands up turning around.

"What?" Leora bangs her head on the bottom of the window. "Owww!"

Bryce laughs. "You guys are accidents lookin' for a place ta happen!"

Leora snickers, rubbing her head. "Yeah, and I'm happ'nin'!"

Sydney places a hand on his chest, meeting his deep blue eyes before ducking under his arm to head for her bedroom. "Wheeze, come on, Tiger," she calls.

"Nice get up." Bryce speaks to Sydney, spinning around, watching her walk to her bedroom.

In the meantime, Leora wrestles with an uncooperative screen, finally sliding it back into place. She closes the window. "So you can hang out here for a while if ya want," she calls to Bryce, reinstating the sheers and drapes moving to her bureau, retrieving a change of attire.

"Yeah, you can hang out here if ya wanna." Sydney appears in the hallway with Houdini the furball in her arms. The closer she gets to Bryce the more Wheezer squirms in her arms for release, jumping to the floor and escaping down the stairs.

"That's weird," Sydney says, smiling. "Maybe you can't stay here. You know how that goes. Love me, love my cat."

Bryce heads toward the linen closet. "Here kitty, kitty. Nice kitty," he calls sarcastically.

Sydney laughs.

"That is weird," Leora agrees, "but come ta think of it, when I pulled up tonight, he didn't want anything ta do with me either. He wouldn't come ta me."

"You're kiddin' me, Sis!"

"Would I lie ta you?"

"Oh my, he must be jealous."

"Yeah," Leora agrees, "he is the man of the house."

They tag along with Bryce to the linen closet, glancing over the railing. No luck. "Wow, he's usually on the step. He's really pissed at you." Sydney walks behind Bryce.

"Yo, Sis. He thinks he's mad now, wait 'til we get rid of his entrance."

"Yeah, I'll have ta stop callin' 'im Tiger and call 'im Wildcat!"

Bryce pulls on the encased shelves. "Here," he says to Sydney, "feel." Sydney blinks at him blushing.

"What? No!" He grins at what she's thinkin'. "Hey, did I ever show you where the horse bit me?" He looks to his right, sliding his T-shirt off his shoulder with his left hand while goosenecking to see as far as he can down the back of his shoulder. Sydney moves in for a good look-see. He watches the trust and concern in her face change to eye-popping surprise as he tickles her thigh instead of, well, he tickles her thigh.

"What is it?" Leora asks Sydney, who by now is at the banister all the way over by the steps.

"I'll tell ya later," Sydney mutters, beet red, slightly shaking her head.

"Here," Bryce says to Leora, "grab this." Leora tucks her clean clothes under her arm. He guides her free hand, almost halfway from the top to an opening carved into the wooden structure, a sort of hidden handle for easy closure.

"Oh yeah, that's pretty neat."

"Pull," Bryce instructs her.

Leora pulls. The hardware meshes together effortlessly. Bryce slides each deadbolt, locking them in place. Bang! Bang!

# Snow Business

"Did I hear the phone?" Leora asks, hitting the bottom step.

"Yeah, Sis, it was Mrs. Bryce." Sydney locks the front door, turning off the porch light. "He called her from here earlier tonight to check on Alice when he brought me home and gave her our phone number. Alice is awake."

"You're shittin' me!" Leora follows Sydney to the kitchen.

"He was all about stayin' until he got the phone call. Want some coffee?" Sydney places the flashlight back in the tool drawer.

Leora nods, feeling really anxious. "Soitenly! I was ready to 'unlax' and rewind from my nice warm shower. I couldn't sleep now if my life depended on it." She removes a mug from the cupboard then digs in the silverware drawer for a spoon, scooping two teaspoons of instant coffee into her cup.

"Is he goin' over his parents or the hospital?"

"Well, his mom's on her way to Philly."

"I guess he said he'll call ya?"

Sydney nods. "He better. I gave 'im a handful of change for the payphones up there. Yo, Sis," she counts on her fingers, "he gave me his mother's number, his other sister's number, what's her name? Oh, yeah, Jeanie, Nicky's number, Manny's number. Oh, and Alice's home number. Wait! Wait! Wait! Oh yeah, and his work number!" She points to the folded piece of paper on the table. "Extension: thirteen twenty-four!" The tea kettle whistles for attention.

Leora gives her best friend a cheese smile. "I hope he goes straight ta Philly."

"He's better off, especially packin', you know what. At least it's still dark out."

"I hope he's not a hot head."

"He doesn't seem ta be. I mean even down the bar. He coulda shot first and asked questions later. I told 'im don't let 'em bring you down to their level."

"Until she gives him a name then —" Leora's voice trails. She changes the subject. "Well, at least he didn't forget his keys."

"Yeah, he did," Sydney answers, smiling.

"Nah-uh!"

"Yeah, he did! Tiger was wheezin', purrin', and floppin'. He even got up on the couch with us. But as soon as he heard keys jingle he was gone. So Bryce 'unclipped' 'em and sat 'em on the end table. The clip is from Alice. She gave it to him in August for his birthday 'cause he can never find 'em!"

"So this is the first time he used it?"

"Well, it was suppose ta be!" Sydney shakes her head. "You believe it? It's been on his keychain the whole time, even when we met 'im down the diner he had it!"

Leora shakes her head laughing too. "He just wanted another goodnight kiss."

Sydney raises her eyebrows and sighs. "Actually, he said good morning."

Leora does a shish-per shame on Sydney, drifting into thought. "Hey, who else do we know who clips?" she asks, stirring her Sanka.

"Clips?"

"Yeah, you know, hooks their keys, clip their keys on to belt loops."

"Vipers," Sydney answers, right off the top of her head.

Leora laughs. "Okay, let's start there: motorcycle gangs."

"How 'bout carpenters and electricians?"

"Yeah, the one that came in the bar when we lost electric—oh, Momma!"

"Then there's a bunch of customers." Sydney sips her tea.

"Yeah, includin' nitwits like Heckle 'n' Jeckle."

Sydney replaces her tea cup on the saucer halfway on the spoon, almost spilling the contents. "Rob!" She looks at Leora wide-eyed.

"Damn! I jiggled my keys tonight 'cause I heard Wheezer meowin', but he wouldn't come ta me. He ran. Now I know why, them bastards. You didn't hear anything tonight, did cha?"

"No, funny you should ask. That's what I was doin' with the flashlight. I checked the house key under the glider. It's still there. I don't think they'll do anything when one of us is around."

"Yeah, they're more like pillagers and rooters."

"I didn't close the keyholder tight this time. That way, if they come around, we'll know it 'cause they'll snap it shut. God only knows how many times they were in here."

Leora shivers from a chill running down the back of her neck, scratching her head from the creepy crawlies. "Yo, Sis, they'll probably only try it once, then they'll freak out and break a window."

"But they already checked here and came up empty-handed. Maybe they'll start lookin' at each other again."

"Oh God, you mean another prayer meetin'?"

"I guess. I don't know but I've been thinkin'. If we just keep up the front, you know, actin' like we think he's still after ya and he just won't take no for an answer, he'll call us all kinds of dumb bitches and leave us alone. That was Papa's beef for him ta stay away from ya. Besides, they don't know we have the pills, look at Jammer and Hector."

Leora nods. "Yeah, I've been thinkin', too. We got lucky when Number Twenty and his buddy escorted me out back, and I told 'em my car wasn't there. That's when they surmised it must have been stolen, and I went with it. So, at that point, even if they had found the pills, they couldn't have tied 'em to me. Griff was livid!"

"Yo, Sis! I thought his head was gonna spin around!"

"Think we should ask Hank and Sonny if Rob was out the Trade Winds?"

"Nah, remember, they were off there when I worked with Marcie that night. Papa closed. I don't think they have a clue Rob was workin' both sides."

"Well, I never said anything, and you didn't say anything." Leora blinks. "Goo Goo wouldn't say anything."

"And Marcie, look at her. She's not there ta kiss and tell. If anything, she's pumpin' Hank."

"Yeah, she's behind the bar to get information, not give any up." Leora scrunches her face. "Use and abuse, that's her motto. Well, she's usin' and abusin' the wrong one. Hank doesn't know anything, even though he thinks he knows everything. Talk about heads spinnin' around. You shoulda seen him when I told 'im Marcie rented your old apartment!"

"You know what, Sis? If Goo Goo didn't break Rob's arms, I bet Griff has 'im workin' overtime rewirin' that van."

"Yeah, now they got ta start all over ta get Goo Goo in a trick. He's gonna be real careful now. We should hook Goo Goo up with Simon. He makes everything purr—cars, motorcycles, lawnmowers, such a nice guy. Him and his little black Volkswagen. Papa uses 'im, poor Papa."

"Don't feel bad for Papa. He's got it covered. You gotta watch the quiet ones! I'm tellin' ya, I saw it in his eyes! That wasn't a threat when he told Griff ta stay away from his employees. That was a promise! You can take it to the bank!" Sydney takes a gulp of tea. "What's his favorite saying? Keep ah you friends close . . ."

Leora joins in, "And ah you enemies . . ."

"Upstairs!" They say in unison, toasting with their coffee and tea.

"That greedy wad," Leora announces. "He wants the whole package— the money, the typewriter, the ledger, Goo Goo's business, Pa –"

"The fair maiden," Sydney interjects.

"Fair maiden?" Leora looks at her best friend with eyes wide as her mouth. "Fair maiden this!"

"Well, okay then, Papa's business." Sydney yawns.

"Yeah, well, you can bet that's one thing we're sure of." Sydney's yawn is contagious. "He ain't got a snowball's chance in hell of gettin' that!" They do a high five at the kitchen table.

"Especially if Papa says he's takin' a trip ta New York. Then it's all over but the shoutin'!"

"Yeah, I'll call ah you two jackasses and raise ah you a hit man!"

"Can you imagine? I hope I'm not workin' that night!" Sydney nods, staring off into space. "Hell, I hope I'm not workin' when Goo Goo gets back! Once is enough for me!"

"Oh, don't forget we have ta tell Goo Goo Griff wants ta bug the bar right underneath where he sits."

"Yeah, he should be comin' back pretty soon. What's the date today?"

"The twenty, um, fifth, isn't it? Wait, when was Thanksgiving? The twenty-second, right?" Leora counts on her fingers. "The twenty-fourth, today's the twenty-fourth."

Sydney counts on her fingers, too. "That means next Saturday is December first, move in day."

"Maybe Marcie will want you ta work."

"Or she'll work so she can plant the-you-know-what." Sydney blinks, yawning.

"How are you feelin', Sis?"

"Ah'ight. Tired but ah'ight."

Leora yawns, squinting at the clock. "Well, no wonder. It's past five." She glances at the window. "It's daylight almost."

"Yeah, it's startin' ta get light out. I gotta put it to rest." Sydney yawns.

"Yeah, I wanna look at the inside of my eyelids, too. Gaw head, Sis, I got this," Leora tells her best friend. She tidies up the kitchen in a matter of minutes, replenishing Wheezer's food supply on the patio, then heads to bed. Upstairs she runs into Sydney, lugging her bed partner through the hallway. "Yo, Sis, I was just thinkin' the same thing. Oh! Oh! Oh! Wait a sec!" Leora yells on her way back downstairs. She reappears with a can of Hartz Mountain cat flea and tick spray, meeting Sydney at the linen closet.

Bang! What's up?" the redhead asks. Bang!

"Well, we can kill two birds with one stone. We'll hide the typewriter in it, and then spray the shit out of it with flea spray. Wheezer won't go in there any time soon!"

"Good thinkin', Momma! And they said you couldn't dance! I'm gonna sleep like a baby now!"

"*Me, Ta!*"

Sydney swings the heavy typewriter case by its handle, swaying it forward and backward; directing it behind the wooden shelving on the backward swing, then changes her mind, plopping it on the second step. "Hey, and if we ever hear from Bryce, again I'll just tell 'im we found out how Wheezer was gettin' in, and it's all taken care of."

"You'll hear." Leora sends a mist of flea killer into Wheezer's hideaway.

"You think so, huh?"

"Would I lie ta you?" Bang! Bang!

The girls settle in, awakening to Wheezer's call of the wild in the overcast rainy late, late afternoon. When nature calls, the orange and white tabby almost always sounds as if he has something caught in a vice. The best friends are perturbed until realizing the day was very restful, to say the least, and no wonder the poor thing's eyes are yellow.

Leora sets him free, out the backdoor, putting on the tea kettle and preparing her mug before running upstairs to get dressed.

"I can't believe it's so late," Sydney says, passing Leora on the stairs.

"Yeah, and so cold," Leora adds, heading into the bathroom.

"I thought I was only asleep about an hour," Sydney yells on her way down the stairs.

"Me, too," Leora yells back. "What a dreary day! It looks like its still tryin' to be daylight when its actuallyworkin' on night time."

Leora hears the phone ring, pulling herself together, then finally joins her cohort in the kitchen. She smiles at Sydney whose dark eyes—one more so than the other—are slightly visible through the cover stick, the liquid Cover Girl makeup, and the compact.

"I give up," Sydney laments, twisting the end of a doobie.

"Is he comin' over?"

Sydney fires it up. "Who?" She takes a hit.

"Wasn't that Bryce on the phone?"

"Oh no, Sis, that was Eva." She exhales, passing to Leora.

"Is there a problem?" The brunette takes a hit. "She's workin', right?" She takes another before passing it back.

Sister Syd inhales. "Oh, yeah, thank, God." She exhales, coughing. "I told her I look like who did it and ran!" She passes the bone and sips some tea.

Leora studies Sydney's features through a puff of exhaled smoke and passes. "Yo, Sis, it doesn't look so bad." She pulls the nut and cotter pin from the small inside zipper pocket in her jeans bag.

Sydney inhales, trying to blow smoke rings while affixing the cotter pin onto the dwindling J. She slides the nut forward, tightening its grip. "Yeah, that's what you say. You're just partial." The quizzical redhead blinks at Leora and smiles. "It doesn't look as bad as compared ta what?" She hits and passes.

Leora inhales, studying Sydney's features, then exhales, passing the roach. She musters a cheesy smile. Her answer is inaudible, a whisper.

"What'd ya say, Momma?" Sydney asks, holding her breath for three seconds—well, maybe four—she exhales, passing the roach clip then holding her hands in front of her face. "Yo, Sis, where'd ya go? Whip it on me, I can take it."

Leora smiles, blinking and shaking her head. "It doesn't look as bad as compared ta no nose." She takes a final toke then drops it into the ashtray.

Sydney stands, coughing and gagging. 'Who don't know that? I knew you were gonna say that!" She glances out the window, over the kitchen sink on the driveway side of the house. "Yo, Sis, it's snowin'!"

Leora hustles to the window coughing, too. She mimics Oliver Hardy, "It certainly is." Large wet snow flakes fall quickly in the still air, beginning the transformation of a dull gray Saturday into picture postcard scenes.

"I'm in!"

"Uh-huh! Me, ta!" Leora stands on her tiptoes, peering out at the grass and trees already outlined in the white magic.

"I hope it keeps it up. It should get colder as the night wears on."

"It sure is pretty."

"Let's eat!" Sydney opens the backdoor for Wheezer. He is no where to be found on the patio. She catches an adorable glimpse of him outside the screen door, busily chasing snow flakes. "Are ya comin' in or what? We'll be back." He stands on his hind legs, peeking at her from outside the patio door, busily distracted by falling flakes. He peeks again, this time being attacked by the white culprits, flicking them from an ear, now his tail— batting, pouncing; chasing the fluffy enemies. "Ah'ight, Tiger," Sydney yells. "Have fun, see ya later. No sleddin'." Leora peers around Sister Syd. "Somebody else likes the snow."

"I guess this beats the hell out of apartment livin', huh?"

"Yeah, he really hated apartment livin', kitty litter and all." They shut the door, watching through the yellow pastel kitchen curtains. He attempts one last quick peek before scurrying into the white wonderland. "Oh!" Leora gushes. "And guess what? If it keeps up, we get ta spin circles in a Chevy truck!"

"Oh, that's right!" Sydney says in agreement. "I'm in! Penn Fruit parkin' lot here we come!"

"Yeah, let's go eat. Goody! We can fishtail all the way to the diner." The girls leave a small light lit in Sydney's bedroom to give the appearance of residents on the property before locking up and climbing into Crow's ride.

"Brrr. Maybe we should a broke out our winter apparel."

Leora guns the 283 engine, trying to speak through chattering teeth. "Y-y-y-o-o-u-u m-m-mean our-r-r l-l-leath-th-thers?" She shivers, locating the switches for the lights, the heater, and the windshield wipers. "I know one thing: no more sizzlers and pantyhose 'til spring."

"Ya know what else, Sis?" Sydney asks as her best friend backs out of the driveway. "If it keeps snowin' like this, we won't have ta check the key under the glider. There'll be footprints."

"Well, if we pull up and see those damn footprints, we're gonna just keep drivin'," Leora answers, cutting the wheel to her right, backing into the street. She straightens the wheel, shifting into first, heading for Ninth Street past Sydney's 'Bird parked on the street. Sydney glances at her car and does a double take.

"Wait! Wait! Wait!" Sydney stares at Leora. "Did you see that? Hold up!"

"What?" The truck idles in neutral.

Leora gawks out the truck's back window, watching Sydney in the street behind the 'Bird. She opens the passenger side door, then closes it and walks around the back of the car in the street again to the truck's open door. Leora throws it in first.

"Wait!" Sydney yells, hopping in. "Wait!" Leora revs the engine. "My trunk isn't shut tight!"

"What do ya mean?"

"It won't close, Sis."

"Did Bryce or Manny or somebody get anything out of it?"

"Nah-uh, I don't think so. I didn't need anything outta there."

"Hang on." Leora throws it in reverse, backing past the Thunderbird then shifts into first, pulling up behind the car, putting on the high beams. Sydney jumps out while Leora pulls the emergency brake on and shifts to neutral. She turns off the windshield wipers, radio, and the heater; winding down the window before joining her best friend. "What's happ'nin'?"

"Feel, Sis." Sydney guides Leora's hand over the hardware on the trunk lid. "Now feel this." They move to the bottom.

"They feel the same. Where the hell's the thingy?" Leora feels the top again. Large, wet snowflakes have since been replaced by smaller, dryer flakes, a more serious snowfall. "Is the hook on the top or the bottom?"

Sydney slams the snow-covered lid. It pops open then slowly closes, assisted by gravity. "Whatever. I can't remember."

Leora tries picturing the trunk of her car and shakes her head. "I can't remember either." She blinks at the blacktop behind the car; the snow not yet covering the macadam but outlining everything else. She inspects the top and bottom parts of the trunk latch again, this time slower and more precise. "Oww!" her fingers find the jagged metal in the bottom part. "It came off of here."

Sydney feels along the inside of the T-Bird's trunk under the hardware. "Here it is!" She holds the broken steel hook tightly in her fist, fishing for her Bic. Leora flicks hers shivering. Sister Syd lays the cold metal in her hand, leaning over with Leora staring at it. The broken end sparkles in the light from the flame.

"You got anything in there to hold this stupid thing shut?"

"Hey, if it snows long enough that'll do it." Sydney digs out her Bic, lifting the trunk lid. The girls lean inside with lighted Bics chasing darkness, revealing a great disturbance among the contents. Broken knickknacks and cluttered kitchen items are strewn about. Leora no longer shivers. Sydney gags.

They stand with Bics extinguished, defeated, violated. The sound of sleet dancing on all surfaces brings them back to the task at hand. Leora taps Sydney, nodding. They shuffle flat-footed on the slippery surface back to the pickup. Leora blasts the heater, rolling up the window, turning off the lights. They sit quietly.

"I'm glad Tiger's outside." Sydney breaks the silence.

"Wish I had a gun."

"You'll go to jail, Sis."

"He'll go to hell." Leora reaches behind the seat, feeling around. Sydney reaches behind at her end feeling around. They each find the end of a bungee cord.

"Hey, I found one of those stretch things." Sydney pulls.

"– Me, ta, shit, it's stuck on somethin'."

"Mine, too."

Leora sighs, exiting the truck and stoops, reaching behind the seat up to her shoulder, feeling for the cord. She feels it slip through her hand.

"I got it!" Sydney announces, pulling on the elastic cable snaking out from in back of the seat.

"You believe it! I think we were pullin' the same one." Leora shakes her head.

The best friends return to the trunk. Lighting their Bics for guidance, they hook the cord to the trunk lid, pulling it taut over the bumper. They then take turns leaning over, swinging the other end until finally hooking it somewhere underneath.

They take baby steps back to the truck where Leora revs the engine, blasting the heater again. Her hands are like ice. "We're gonna catch pneumonia." She shivers.

Sydney stares at her car. Her hands are also cold as ice. "Yo, Sis. Thanks."

"Thanks for what? Another fine mess?"

"We didn't ask for this. It ain't you, Momma, it's them."

"We should just give 'em the typewriter." Leora is beyond disgusted.

"What, and tell 'em you can trust us we're not gonna say anything?"

Leora shoves one hand under her thigh to warm it up. "I guess Crow was right. We'd a probably had a shoot-out last night."

"They're probably gonna know we're not home and rummage. They're gonna see right through our fake 'we're home, stay away' ploy."

"I was thinkin' that."

"They're desperate, huh?" Sydney breaks out Lucky Pierre retrieved from her glove compartment.

"Yeah, I think they finally narrowed it down."

"Maybe Bryce was the only reason they didn't make a move." She finishes loading the bowl and fires it up.

"I was thinkin' that, too." Leora switches hands. "We're in deep shit." She leans her elbow on the door armrest, rubbing her forehead.

"Yo, Sis, they can hang me up by my toes. I will never mention Wheezer's hideaway, pinky swear." Sydney offers her little finger to her best friend.

Leora locks pinkies with her. "You and me, Momma."

"Yepper, we just play stupid. I think that's why they haven't gotten right in our faces. They're not for sure we know anything about it. They don't wanna spill the beans, but I think in order to check thoroughly, they're gonna have ta confront us." She relights the pipe and passes.

"Should we put Crow's ring in there? I don't know. I can't think." Leora puffs a few times then cups the bowl in her hand. She takes a deep draw then uncovers the glowing embers. She coughs from the shotgun, offering it back to Sydney.

Sydney takes a hit. "Well, my dad always says if it ain't broke don't fix it," she says exhaling.

"Ah'ight. So we'll leave it in your throw rug's mouth, right?"

"Yeah, Sis. It's okay even when I trip over it."

Christmas lights add color to the black and white scenic cruise on their way to the diner, bringing a pang of sadness to Leora's heart. They pass Pierre a few more times in silence, listening to the moldy oldies, the golden gassers.

"I swear if one thing is out a place, I'm callin' the damn cops," Sydney confesses, singing "Dancing in the Street" with Martha and the Vandellas.

"Yeah, then it will be on record. Good thinkin', Sis. We gotta start bein' the hunter, not the hunted." The sleet changes back to the small dryer flakes as the twosome park in the back. They walk toward the diner.

"Yo, Sis. Where's everybody at?" Sydney does a three-sixty in the sparsely filled parking lot.

Leora glances around, too. "Well," she answers with her best Southern drawl, "Thur scare-t."

"Well, run n' hide 'cause here we come, ready or not y'all."

"Anyone around our base is it!" The best friends high-five on their way into the diner, choosing the empty seat they had occupied before with the panorama view, although this time self-conscious Sydney faces the windows with her discolored eyes. They still stick out like sore thumbs. Who cares? Besides the jukebox works. And they feed it, exchanging pleasantries with Carol and Lefty, then enjoy his grilled pork chop platter with mashed potatoes, applesauce, string beans, and dinner rolls replaced with Kaisers—a nice hot meal on a cold snowy night.

"Yo, Sis, where do ya wanna hang out 'til later?" Both sip a cup of hot tea.

"I don't care, Momma," Sydney answers her finally warmed partner in crime.

"Do you still have the note?" Leora asks.

"Yepper, and you still have the pills, right?" Sydney gawks at a car, pulling into the parking lot then another. She sips her tea.

Leora roots in the bottom of her denim bag, slightly touching the corner of the plastic baggy. She nods to Sister Syd glancing out the window, at the crawling traffic exposing the falling snow in their headlights.

"Ah'ight. So what do ya wanna do? Go up the line or down the road?"

Leora pretends to think really hard. "Hmmm. It don't matter ta me. We're incognito. We have a 1962 pickup."

"Oh yeah, we can really go shminkin'!"

"Nah-huh! This might turn out to be like a fly-on-the-wall kinda thing!"

"Yeah! The worm turns." They wave goodnight to Lefty and Carol.

"Hey, we'll ride by and see if Goo Goo's back yet." Leora leaves the tip.

"We can look for the van, oh, and Griff's car. You have the paper with the tag numbers, right?"

Leora feels in the front pocket of her jacket and nods. "We can check the club, too." Leora sighs. "So much ta do, so little time."

Sydney holds the door for her best friend. "Yeah, we only have all night, so pleasure before business. We have ta party and spin circles yet."

"Down the road it is."

Night Crawlers

The pair stops for gas before popping in at a deserted Stetson's due to the inclement weather conditions, not that Leora was hoping to run into a certain someone. The girls decide to keep it local and "go to Hook to take a look", Marcus Hook, for its array of established watering holes. Just over the bridge, the municipality offers meter parking on the right side of the two-lane street all the way down to the Delaware River during business hours, afterwhich parking is free for the many patrons, foreign and domestic, feeding one of the livelihoods in this tiny town. Leora passes two snow-covered cars, readily finding a few empty meters together making parking simple. She pulls in, taking the farthest one, straightening the truck. The best friends head to Lefty's catty corner from them in an almost whiteout, just in time to hoist a drink then off with a group of diehard partying barhoppers hoofing it to the Turf Lounge, Cameo Room, Saint George's, Four D's, Clank's, Paradise, Fat's, Captain Jack's, not in that order but ending at the Star Hotel and Bar across from Lefty's at the beginning of the trek. Some had bands, some not, some had food, some not—all conducting business as usual with nary a shortage of people, who are also keeping it local, a great portion of which were familiar to the partners in crime, tipping their way around the borough. By 1 a.m. the miserable weather presented a night cap of rain topping the four- to five-inch blanket of snow with a frozen crust. And to add insult to injury, the temperature begins to rise along with a fog in the still of the night or the wee hours of the morning, depending on one's perspective. To the curlyhaired duet it is the still of the night, time to spin circles before heading up the line. They say good night at the Star Bar, dispersing a tip and sitting their upside down shot glasses for free drinks in front of Simon. With choice of drink in hands, they walk to Crow's truck in the spitting rain.

"Should we ride by the house?" Sydney asks, standing on the curb, scooping snow from her side of the windshield. The white fluffy flakes under the thin, frozen crust pack together, sliding off easily in a clump.

"Whatever!" Leora stands in the street, unlocking her side, the tips of her shoes disappear into the dirty snow plowed down the length of the truck up to the door. She reaches across the windshield as far as she can. The snow also packs in a clump although not quite as large a clump as Sister Syd's reach or grasp creates. "Do you wanna do that before or after we spin circles?" Leora engages the clutch, shifting into neutral, pumping the gas pedal twice, then turns the key. The pickup growls as if clearing its throat before purring as Leora revs the engine, feeding the liquid to the 283.

"Here's ta Penn Fruit!"

They sip their drinks. Leora hands her tall glass to her favorite barmaid.

"Ready or not, here we come. Anyone around our base is it!" Leora cuts the wheel left, shifting into first and guns it. The red truck climbs the "Zangari-water-ice mound," its front wheels crunching through the thin frozen crust, crushing the pile in its path, pushing the bumper deeper into the barricade of plowed mixture as the left back tire spins, making a whirring sound that polishes the packed water ice as smooth as glass. "Hang on!" Leora yells. She winds down her window for some air, cutting the steering wheel to her right, shifting into reverse to reposition the rear wheels. The truck descends. Again Leora cuts the steering wheel left, throwing it into first, giving the truck a steady dose of fuel. The pickup lunges forward. She jams it in reverse, whipping the steering wheel right, fueling the stock engine, creating a sort of rocking motion. The right rear wheel meets the curb. Now, whipping the steering wheel to the left, she again shifts into first, climbing the small icy pile, feeling the front of the vehicle slide slightly toward the right. She engages the clutch, permitting gravity to do its dirty work one more time, then pops the clutch. The left rear wheel bites, joining forces with its counterpart and the forward motion. The Chevy crawls through the concoction, the frozen mound scrapping the underside of the truck. Leora cuts the wheel to the right as the vehicle emerges from its encasement. Yelling and whistling can be heard coming from two Star Bar patrons watching and willing to help with the girls' dilemma. Leora toots to them.

"Yo, Sis! I'm in!"

"Me, ta!" Leora answers, breathing heavy. "Thank God, you're drivin'!"

Sydney laughs hysterically as she hands the VO and water to her best friend.

Leora engages the clutch, drifting to the intersection's red light. "Damn!" She wets her whistle, taking a big gulp of the VO and water, then pours a bit out, straining it with her finger to save the ice cubes.

"Yo, Sis, how'd I do?" Sydney holds her hand up for a high five. Leora sits the tall glass between her legs and high-fives her, putting the column shifter into neutral.

"You were outstanding!" the brunette answers, still breathing heavy, blasting the heater and turning on the windshield wipers.

"I was out standin', where? I've been ridin' shotgun the whole time!"

Leora laughs with her partner in crime. She revs the engine before shifting into first, making a left at the intersection's now green light. Wipers fling melting pieces and chunks of frozen snow dribbling down the warm glass. Leora rolls her window up, denying them entrance into the cab. They ride through Marcus Hook into Trainer at a slow steady clip, the fog continuing to rise.

"Wow! What are we, the only people out tonight?" Sydney looks around.

"Yeah, us and plows."

"Well, I hope they didn't plow the parkin' lot."

"Not a chance. We're talkin' Chester here. They're gettin' their beauty sleep."

"Don't say that, they're gonna have ta sleep 'til noon."

The girls ride straight up Fourth Street, cruising through three green lights, beacons in the thickening fog. At Fourth and Booth in Chester the duo catch the red light.

"We should go grab Crow." Sydney swigs her Michelob.

"I was thinkin' that, too. But it's Saturday night. He's probably with Jenny." Leora turns the heater down.

"Yeah, they're in lo-o-ve." Sydney runs out of breath.

"And married!"

"And pregnant!" Sydney adds.

Leora makes a left then downshifts to second, engaging the clutch. Oompa Oompa! Echoes as she revs the engine drifting under the railroad trestle.

"Oh, this truck sounds sooo healthy! Thank God, it's red."

"Yo, Sis, you don't like red. Isn't blue your favorite color?"

"Yepper, and this would be my truck if it was blue because Crow would be my boyfriend!"

"Yo! Sis! Bring 'em up the way ya want 'em!"

Sydney sings "Havin' My Baby" with Paul Anka. They laugh at their silliness, cruising by the two-way stop where Sixth Street crosses Booth on up to the Seventh Street T-intersection, thus making a left, entering Penn Fruit's slightly inclined parking lot behind Papa's and the little row of businesses. She rides to the right across the incline and stops. They sit, facing the rear of the shopping center, inspecting the massive lot with its melting snow and splotches of black top.

"You're kiddin' me!" Sydney sighs in disgust, winding down her window, leaning over, looking at the ground. The arc light pierces the fog, slightly reflecting off wet macadam, adding to her revulsion.

"I guess the ground was too warm. Damn it!" Leora shifts to first, driving left, circling the eight parked vehicles to exit the way she came in, dismissing the idea of the throughway between Penn Fruit and the end of the shopping center leading to the front.

"Wait! Wait! Wait!" Sydney taps Leora with a continuous pat.

Leora brakes, staring at Sydney, thinking the girl is wearing her beverage.

"Look! Look!" The redhead goosenecks around her best friend leaning to and fro and pointing. "Isn't that it?"

"What? Where?" Leora winds her window down, glaring at a black van sticking out like a sore thumb.

"Is that it?"

"I don't know, but there's one way ta find out. Hold on." Leora circles back around, facing the building again. One of them is Goo Goo's blue Cadillac. But there is no white wall tire on this van. They circle again, this time looking for Griff's white Lincoln or the mayor's BMW. "Oh! Wait! Wait! The tag number!"

"Ya got it?"Sydney asks, referring to the piece of paper from Rhonda.

"Do I, got, it? Does a bear shit in the woods? It's right here!" Leora jams two fingers in the top pocket of her denim jacket. "I'm so glad we wrote it down!" she states again, circling the cluster of vehicles in first gear. The truck jerks back and forth while the girl drives and digs for the evasive piece of paper. They glimpse the van's tag awash in the truck's high beams for a split second on their jerky ride, catching the last two numbers: 4 and 5. "Right there!" Leora hands the piece of paper to Sister Syd pulling up at the far end of the row facing Booth Street, cutting the lights and engine. Adrenaline prepares for flight or fright.

Sydney lights her Bic, turning the paper around and around, finally spotting the tag number 5-3-1-4-5—van. The last two numbers are the same, 4 – 5. "Yo! Sis! That's it!" She hands it back to Leora for safekeeping.

"Ya think Griff is in there, too, you know, parked out front?" Leora asks, pushing the paper deep into the hiding place it came from.

"Didn't he say he wasn't goin' in there anymore?"

"Yeah, well, didn't he say I was stealin' money?"

The girls sit in silence listening, becoming very aware of their surroundings.

"Ya wanna ride out front and take a look-see?"

Leora sighs. "Not really, do you?"

"Hell, no." They notice the tavern's unlit rear entrance. "Well, anyway, Goo Goo's back." Sydney makes small talk, glancing around the lot, listening to trickling water running to Booth Street. A lone car's spinning wheels at the go-ahead green light on Ninth Street can be heard. "What if they're all fightin' again?"

"Yo, Sis, ya wanna leave 'em a note or what?"

The redhead gasps. "I'm in! It just so happens I have one right here." Now it's her turn to root. "Right" – she roots in her denim bag – "here!" producing the holey ransom paper.

"Ya think it's unlocked?"

"I'll letcha know in a minute." Sydney slips out of the adrenaline-filled truck, leaving the door ajar. She walks with a stealthy gait to the black van four or five vehicles away, disappearing around the back to the driver's side. Leora sits in anticipation, watching and waiting for what seems like a lifetime. Her best friend scurries back to the truck, hopping in the passenger's side, holding the door shut. "Let's roll!" she squeals. "Go! Go! Go!"

Leora shifts to second, engaging the clutch, turning the key to the on position, drifting down the incline to Booth Street, gaining momentum. "It was unlocked, wasn't it?" She smiles, almost laughing out loud.

"Yes, it was, Momma!" Sydney slams her door shut.

The brunette pops the clutch, nailing the gas pedal. Crow's truck roars as she whips left onto Booth Street punching third. She turns on the headlights and heater, downshifting to second, making a left on to Ninth Street as the intersection light turns green. They gawk at the snow-covered front parking lot with a handful of snow-covered vehicles.

Sydney points. "There's Eva's car. Yo! Sis! We left there just in time. Look they're closed. The lights are off."

"Wasn't the one on the end Hank's car? Oh, that's too funny."

"Yeah, he's stuck with Eva again tonight."

"Nah-uh, I was thinkin' what if Jammer's in there on a date with Back Alley Sally?"

"Yeah, in the ladies' room! No, wait! It's a double date. Hank in the men's room!"

"Oh! That's a screamer!"

"Which one?"

"Yo, Sis, so where'd ya put it?"

"What? Oh, the note! I folded it in half and draped it over the steering wheel. They can't miss it."

"That's what you think. We'd be better off stapling it to one of their foreheads, then the other one could read it when he looked at 'im." The girls laugh themselves silly, burning excess adrenaline.

Sydney pulls out Pierre. "We shoulda went in the bar and told Goo Goo about the bug."

"We'll go down here and check out the house. If everything's hunky dory, we can head to the club and see if he shows up. If he doesn't, we'll go midnight knockin'."

"Well, they couldn't find anything in the house, and they didn't find anything in my trunk, so what's left? Oh, and we left a light on in my bedroom. Besides, Griff's gettin' ready to move into the apartment and Jammer's checkin' out bathrooms."

"He sure in hell wouldn't put Hector in charge, would he, the little gopher? The van is up and runnin', which means Rob's around some place. How'd it look?"

"Dark, the light didn't come on when I opened the door but –"

"But what? What's up?"

"Somebody was snorin' in the back."

"Oh! Lord! You're shittin' me!"

"Would I lie ta you, Momma?"

They cruise past the house and the Thunder Bird with its trunk still closed, the blanket of snow untouched even by Wheezer's footprints, making the girls feel better, knowing he is snug in his cat bedroom. They make a right onto Township Line Road down to the T-intersection at Highland Avenue, making a left, then bearing right for the entrance to I-95. Sydney passes Pierre to Leora one last time.

Leora takes a hit and coughs. "Do ya think when we tell Goo Goo about Griff tryin' ta bug the bar we should give 'im the pills while we're at it?"

"I think we should hang on to 'em, they're versatile."

"Well, listen ta you with your twenty-five cent word."

Sydney laughs. "Yo, Sis, I'm not just another pretty face."

Leora joins in. "That's right. You can talk and chew gum."

"Take it to the bank! And don't forget the cherry stems!"

Leora laughs. "Oh! The cherry stems! That was too funny! What was it Goo Goo said?"

"Oh, Sis, let me think. It was when we first met 'im, funny as hell."

Leora thinks, too. "That's right. It was his birthday, July." She blinks through memories. "What was that, four years ago? No, it's five!"

"Has it been that long? I remember like it was yesterday."

"Yeah, remember, Fidget and all of 'em had a giant cake wheeled in."

"Yepper, and a girl named Babette popped out of it in a leopard bikini."

"And somebody said somethin' about tyin' 'im in a knot."

Sydney thinks. "No, it was a pretzel. Somebody said that girl would twist 'im like a pretzel"

"That's right, and you said it's better than bein' tied up in knots."

"Yeah, and Goo Goo made a comment about thunder thighs and a scissor hold. That's when I laid the knotted cherry stem on a napkin and handed it to Eva to give ta him. He didn't believe I tied it with my tongue at first. Remember? He bet me twenty dollars he could tie one in a knot with his hands faster than I could say tongue-tied."

"Yeah, and you sucked 'im right in."

"And remember, Eva even gave 'im an edge fishin' for the longest cherry stems she could find. I remember him rollin' up his sleeves and doin' knee bends." Sydney laughs. "It took 'im forever! I let 'im win. Then he got cocky and said he'd give me a chance ta get my money back."

"And you lost again."

"Yeah, accidentally on purpose, and I acted all bent out a shape. I said double or nothin', and he said let's make it an even fifty and dinner, winner's choice." Sydney rolls her eyes. "Men."

"Yeah, that's when he said Vegas, here I come! I'll never forget the look on his face. My sister took Tink for the weekend, and we took a train ta New York City for dinner at the Copacabana."

Sydney laughs. "Yeah! Vegas this! Hey, wait a minute! That's why he's at the bar! I'm suppose ta be workin'! He got me a gift from Vegas!" Sydney sticks her bottom lip out in a humungous pout.

"Yeah, Sis. A Chippendale! He got you a Chippendale!"

Sydney looks at Leora wide-eyed, her pout morphing into an ornery smile as she taps her best friend. "Yo, Sis! And a washboard! I love washboards!"

"And a friend!" Leora adds.

"Yeah, a friend." Confusion clouds Sydney's face. "Oh, you mean a gun?"

"Nah-uh! Me! A friend for me! Treat me like a step sister!"

Sister Syd laughs, patting Leora's arm. "Yeah, Sis, he got you one, too."

"Thank you. Hey! He can have a gun! But where would he carry it?"

Inside the club The Blues Brothers belt out "Soul Man" on the jukebox while the stage sits empty, draped in darkness, akin to the dormant rear bar curtsey of the evening's snow fall. The curly duo readily finds seats at the first bar against the wall overlooking the sparsely filled room. They gooseneck with strained eyesight at the second bar, cast in obscurity by the absence of stage lights. A girl stirs her drink while three men huddle around the bar stool next to her. They spot him sitting on the stool in the middle of the standing bodies; Griff, dominating the conversation as usual.

"Is that Hector?" Leora asks.

"Yeah, but I don't know who the other two are." Sydney stares. "Is that Marcie?" The two try to blink away the layer of shadows clouding their vision. "It's Rhonda! It is, look, she jiggles!" They both now watch squinting, blinking. "See! She did it again!"

"Oh, this is gonna be fun."

Sydney turns to Leora. "What's gonna be fun?" She blinks wide-eyed. "What are you doin'?"

"Gettin' in trouble, what else?" Leora asks, placing a tip in the beer well for Tony. "But its okay, you are, too. Come on."

"I'm in! But let's hit the ladies' room on the way." Sydney takes her Mick from the bar, catching up with her best friend. From the ladies' room, they walk to the second bar, plopping four stools away from Rhonda, stirring her drink in silence. Sydney sits with her back to the jiggler facing Leora. They order two shots of Galliano from Nino.

"Hi-i-i!" Rhonda gushes. "How are ya? You believe this snow?" She jiggles.

Leora peeks around Sister Syd. "Oh, hey-y-y, what's up? I didn't see ya, it's so dark. Where's Dana?"

"Oh, she doesn't like to drive in this stuff."

Yeah, I hear ya. Our sled's double-parked." Sydney takes a sip.

"Have you heard from Virginia?"

"We were just talkin' about that yesterday." Sydney says, faking surprise in her voice. "Are you in or what?"

Rhonda giggles like a squeaky mouse. "Yes, yes, yes! By all means! When?"

"It probably won't be 'til after the holidays."

"Well, you have my number, right? I gave it to you, right?"

"Yes, you did," Leora answers. "You're gonna come early and check out wonderland, aren't cha?"

"Wonderland?" Rhonda jiggles.

"Yeah," Sydney says leaning toward Rhonda, eyeballing Griff. "You know, the mirrors. The caterpillar, remember? The twins! Oh! The twins!"

"Oh! Yeah!" All three laugh uproariously. Sydney sits up straight against the bar, reaching back with her right arm tapping Leora's knee, adrenaline at hand.

Leaning back against the bar stool with his arms crossed in front of him, the bar behind him, Griff takes a breather from the boisterous conversation and glances at Rhonda, his arrogance in place as usual. He leans toward her on an elbow, demanding her undivided attention, resenting her participation in some kind of interaction with a couple of broads.

"You want another drink, doll?" He interrupts her conversation with his controlling attitude—smug, intimidating, aggressive; overbearing.

Leora rat-ta-tats Sydney on her butt, adrenaline overflowing. "Look! Look!" she whispers like a ventriloquist, their eyes glued to the back of Griff's head.

Griff sits up straight, raising his arm, signaling for Nino behind him. He reaches in his right rear pocket for a wad of bills, pointing to Rhonda. "Give her another drink. Give them one, too." He points with his thumb toward the two broads throwing a Franklin on the bar, yawning while shoving the wad back into his pocket. "Will ya shut up!" he spews at Hector, affixing a conceited smirk on his face to present to Rhonda's little dumb friends who may also become cheap trysts for the ignorant, self indulgent, egotistical, calloused man.

"Thank you, Shauny." Rhonda jiggles. "I want you to meet some friends of mine." Rhonda's introduction falls on deaf ears. Griff is not listening. He is thinking about a threesome, flashing his best smile as he turns, coming face to face with the broa – the bitches!

The barmaids sit in a freeze frame, Leora grasping the back of Sydney's jacket, their breathing shallow, their eyes wide, glaring at Griff, the nemesis, the putrid power hungry bastard, his face awash with sheer disbelief as angry red drains to anemic white.

Rhonda leans toward the curly tops, continuing her intros, oblivious. "Remember I told you about my lawyer friend from California?" she whispers, jiggling, "I want you to meet Shaun Taylor, Esquire." Griff bolts from the bar stool through Hector, and the two unknowns hustling past the girls who in turn are, themselves, ready for flight. They spin on their bar stools, watching him head toward the bathrooms in the dinky crowd.

He removes the payphone receiver from a young girl hanging it up, waving some green at her. Of course she accepts.

"You wanna leave?" Sydney turns to her best friend, the epinephrine rampant among them, hearts pounding. She glances in Griff's direction, shrugging her shoulders.

"Oh no, you gonna go?" Rhonda jiggles, clueless.

Blinking wide-eyed at Sydney, Leora shrugs her shoulders, too. "Ah, yeah, I think I saw them," Leora answers, raising her shot to Rhonda. "Cheers!"

"Cheers!" Rhonda says, raising her drink.

"Salute!" Sydney offers as Hector now whizzes by. The two unknowns follow, though not as fast, deliberately not as fast, mind you. The dark-suited unknown purposely stares at each barmaid, a gaze emanating terror, stirring fear with his earless profile as does the second unknown now with his chilling stare, unblinking, unwavering, his long black hair unable to hide an ugly, raised scar snaking down his left cheek, a gold chain dangling from the watch pocket of his gray three-piece sharkskin suit.

"Oh, but you just got here." Rhonda jiggles.

"Oh no, we've been here a while." Leora swallows hard. Her voice is raspy. "We're waitin' for some, ah, friends." She licks her fingers.

Sydney pivots to check out Griff busy at the payphone, then pivots back to face Rhonda. She tries to speak, clearing her throat and tries once more. "Where'd you say your lawyer friend is from?"

"California, he's from California."

"Yeah, well, when's he goin' back?" Leora slides from her stool to stand between Rhonda and Sydney.

"Soon probably. He finally located his ex girlfriend. He's been waiting to hear if they got everything she stole from him."

Sydney moves over a couple of stools closer.

"What did she steal?" Confusion is apparent on Leora's face. She glances at Sydney who is throwing a confused look of her own to Leora while running Alice, Bryce, her trunk, the note— everything and everyone she can think of —through her mind.

"They were suppose to get all his money and important documents she stole."

"Why would she steal documents?" Sydney can't wait to hear this one.

"From what I heard, they were like deeds to property they both owned. She was going to forge his name and sell them right out from under him. Do you believe it?"

Hell no! What a crock of shit! It sounds exactly like what he's doin'!

"He asked me out to dinner after work yesterday, and said afterward he was going back to his hotel room to wait for an important phone call and didn't want to be alone. In fact, this afternoon, he took me back to my work to get my car, followed me home to drop it off and grab a change of clothes." Rhonda jiggles. "We went to dinner about seven o'clock tonight in Philly. He is so nice. He's still upset. See?"

"Why? Did she get arrested?"

"She wasn't arrested. She was in a real bad accident. I heard him on the phone at the restaurant when we were waiting for our reservation."

Leora and Sydney glare at each other. "Did he get his stuff back?"

"No." She jiggles.

"Well, then he might as well go home. They aren't married. The police will confiscate all of her things."

"The police aren't involved. A private investigator he hired found her in New Jersey. What's his name?" Rhonda jiggles, thinking.

"But the police are involved now if there was an accident. Did he talk to the police?" Leora glances at Sydney, her face full of disbelief, mouth agape.

"I don't know."

"Is the car in her name?" Now Sister Syd looks at Leora catching flies.

"I don't know. Oh, what's his name?"

"Well, if the car's in her name, he can't touch anything." Leora scratches her head, turning to Sydney who looks totally perturbed.

"Well, there wasn't anything. Even the trunk was empty. Angelo! That's it! That's his name, Angelo, his private investigator and his partner, uh, Tito. They're from New York, only the best, Shauny says. I should have introduced you to them." Rhonda jiggles.

Both girls perform bucking of the eyes at each other. "Is she in the hospital?" It is a reasonable question. Sydney waits for a reasonable answer.

"I think so."

"What's her name?" Leora hails Nino.

"Nino, can we have another shot and give one to her." She points to Rhonda. "And take it out of there." Leora points to Griff's pile of money.

"Oh no, I can't drink that."

"What da ya mean you can't? You're not allowed? We're celebratin'."

"Oh, is it your birthday?"

"Nah-uh, it's mine," Sydney answers. "In a couple of months," she says under her breath. *We might as well blow smoke, too.*

Rhonda jiggles. "Oh, okay then, just one. I never did a shot." Nino holds three short high ball glasses in one hand, pouring each Galliano separately, skillfully so as not to drip the syrupy liquor. Rhonda takes a sip. "Mmm, I thought it would taste bitter. It's actually quite tasty."

"I think it tastes like more. Cheers!" Sydney stands, leaning forward, holding her glass out for a toast. Three glasses clink.

Leora turns toward Sydney and whispers in her ear as she places her empty glass in the beer well. "He's got more bullshit than Carter's got liver pills."

"Yeah," Sydney whispers back, "but look who's swallowin' it. If she was on her way to Hershey Park and the sign said Hershey Park left, she'd go home."

"Dumb is good in her case!"

"Nino," Rhonda calls, "give us one more and take it out of there." She points to Griff's money and jiggles.

"See!" Leora whispers.

"Okay, one more than we gotta go," Sydney tells the naïve girl.

"Ohhh, do you have to?"

"Yeah," Sydney answers, waving frantically toward the first bar.

"Oh, I see them." Leora joins in the waving at no one.

"Okay, it was good seein' ya. Cheers!"

They toast one last time, leaving a tip in the beer well.

"You gonna be all right?" Sydney asks.

"Oh sure, Shauny will be right back, business, you know."

"Yepper. Busy, busy, busy. What's his girlfriend's name?"

"Who, Nancy? She's his ex-girlfriend."

Sydney rubs her nose, whispering to Leora. "Is he blowin' smoke or what?"

"Don't forget to call me about Virginia." Rhonda jiggles.

"We will," Sydney calls.

"I'm gettin' the creeps." Leora whispers, leaning into Sydney, walking across the empty dance floor.

"Speakin' of creeps, did you see the scar on that creep's face?"

Leora nods. "Private investigate this! If looks could kill, we'd be dead. Did ya see the first one?" Her voice squeaks. "He was missin' an ear!"

"I'm out! Let's leave."

"I'm in!"

The girls walk through the growing throng of patrons, eyeballing Griff at the payphone—screaming, with veins bulging, drowning out Styx singing "Come Sail Away" waving a paper in Jammer's face. Angelo taps Tito, nodding and pointing at the curly-haired best friends.

Nightmare on Chestnut Street

. . . .

The duo weaves past patrons trickling down the stairway into the club. Outside, Sydney bends forward, leaning her hands on her knees, filling her suffocated lungs with the cool air, darn near hyperventilating. Leora shuffles past her, tapping her best friend to follow suit only to rush back. The girls are visibly shaken by the unknowns with their identifiable battle scars and deliberate cold-blooded stares.

"Where the hell are we parked? What the hell am I doin'?" Leora is in a stupor. She jams her hands in her jeans pockets, producing a single key. *The truck.* "The truck! Where's the truck?"

"Ummm, ummm – Sydney gathers her thoughts – "Over there! We parked over there!" She joins Leora on a sprint to the safety of Crow's truck three rows away, hitting the locks. They stare in silence at the front door of the club, both of them shivering from lack of sleep, fear, the weather . . . D—all the above.

"I don't wanna play this anymore." Leora states, now on the verge of tears.

"Me neither." Sydney's eyes fill. "Let's give it all ta Goo Goo: typewriter, ribbon, pills. All of it."

"Did you see Goo Goo?" Leora asks, blinking tears away.

"Hell no, I wasn't lookin' for 'im, did you see 'im?" Sydney sniffles.

"No, all I saw was Griff wavin' that piece of paper Jammer gave 'im—our piece of paper!"

Sydney roots for a cigarette. "Yeah, with Happy and Bashful starin' a hole right through us! I had ta get the hell outta there!"

"Thought I was gonna die!" Leora mimics her girl Gilda.

"Shout was runnin' over there. Maybe Griff's head exploded!"

"Will wonders never cease?"

They each pull a cigarette, ready to light up when Hector emerges from the club. Needing ample legroom for her long legs, Sydney slides immediately to the roomy floor, laying her head on the bench seat facing Leora who keels over sideways. She takes a quick peek. "Where'd he go? Oh no!" she whispers. Sydney stirs. "Oh no, there he is," Leora states, lying back down. "He's lookin' for us."

"I hope he don't remember Crow's truck when he helped me move."

"Think about it, Sis. He knows Griff's car, too, but he's lookin' for our cars. Two of 'em, that's quite a feat 'cause he can't talk and chew gum. Besides, we can barely see him in this soup." Leora leans up again for a gander. Hector remains steadfast in his objective, scoping the parking lot in between the feminine distractions in dresses, miniskirts, seamed nylons, and sizzlers; until three young girls smiling and giggling, faun over him mistaking him for a bouncer of all things. It is all over. Chivalry holds the door then follows with a limp back inside.

"He's gone! He went back inside!" Leora sits up, starts the truck and turns the radio off. Rolling her window down, she listens for any approaching vehicles that might appear out of the fog. Screeching police cars are heard in the distance.

Sydney climbs on the seat. "Whew! Momma! Well, we wanted a confrontation." She winds down her window, turning the heater up.

"Nah-uh, we thought we wanted one. I don't wanna do that again!" The sirens become increasingly louder as Leora putters through the sloppy, slushy parking lot to a red hue at the intersection just in time as four police cars burst through the fog with flashing lights and deafening wails, fishtailing into the shopping center's parking lot.

"Maybe Griff's head did explode!"

"I don't see any ambulance." Leora turns left on the green hue. "I think maybe we messed up."

"What? We shouldn't a sat over there, huh?"

"Nah-uh, I was thinkin' about the note. We should have done it some place else instead of in the parkin' lot where we both work."

"Yeah, but neither one of us was workin', Eva was," Sydney reasons. "Jammer probably was suppose ta be watchin' and spyin' instead of bein' passed out."

"Oh! God!" Maybe Jammer's a liar, too, like Carl. Maybe he told Griff Goo Goo did it to avoid another blackeye and ended up gettin' one anyway!"

They ride through Chester and Upland, passing Pierre; the warm temperatures melting, the sewers draining, the fog thickening. Leora turns left onto Kerlin Street over the creek, past Crozer Park, winding up windows before catching the entrance ramp of I-95. "How 'bout Griff's face when he saw us? He looked like he saw a ghost or some facsimile thereof."

"Yeah, for a minute I thought he was scare-t!"

"Yeah, even with those goons as back up."

"Goons, you mean Handsome and Gorgeous?" Sydney names the unknowns again. "If they're private detectives, I'm the queen of England!"

They drive the main highway, a lone car enveloped in fog exiting at Highland Avenue. Leora revs the engine, breaking the eerie quiet at Township Line Road, a blush of red in the fog now below a blush of green.

"Wanna go home?" Leora asks.

"I'm in!"

Leora takes a right. "Goo Goo can wait."

"Yepper, he's a big boy."

"He's got his hands full."

"Yeah, he's gonna need two," Sydney says, agreeing with her best friend.

"He's gonna need to what?" Leora blinks, perplexed, driving at a snail's pace through the dense cloud.

"He's gonna need two hands for two guns."

"Oh, how'd we ever get mixed up in this shit?"

"Because of shithead, that's how. If we tell 'im we know, we're dead. If he finds out we know, we're dead."

"Yo, Sis, got any ideas?" Leora asks her partner in crime.

"What, like how ta get out of it alive?"

Leora turns onto Chestnut. "How 'bout Rhonda? She's in the dark."

"Yeah, this is Shaun Taylor, Esquire," Sydney mocks the young jiggler. "Shaun Taylor this! She ain't got a clue of his lies upon lies upon lies."

"I guess it's a good thing, safer anyway. I hope she doesn't ask any questions."

"Oh, you mean like about Nancy? Is she real or is she Memorex?"

"Yeah, ya gotta have a girlfriend before you can have an ex-girlfriend. "Yuck!"Boy, he just makes up lies as he goes along. A lawyer from California. I guess ya can't really say she's naïve. She only knows what that clown tells her."

"Maybe that's a good thing. Think about it, Momma. We were naïve. We thought he wanted ta take you away just ta get in your pants and then stumbled upon his scheme ta get in the house … and they had a key! We were clueless. He planted bugs while I rode around with evidence loaded in my trunk!"

"Yeah, if he'd a gone over there when Alice told him to, he coulda had the damn thing. She had no idea. But, oh, no! The arrogant bastard!"

"He probably said to the mayor and everybody: 'Eyy! Listen up. I got this!" Sydney mocks Fonzie. "But he didn't. He thought she got it. She thought he got it. So Alice sold it, Papa emptied it, which brings us ta us." Leora pulls up behind Sydney's car. The trunk is still closed. "Hooray! We did somethin' right!"

Sydney grabs Leora's arm. She winds her window down, leaning out, gawking at the ground, listening; her heart in her throat.

Leora is a little edgy cutting the lights, hesitating to cut the engine. "What? What's up?"

"Look at the snow, Sis."

Leora sits up straight, goosenecking. "What am I lookin' for?"

"Well, does that look like meltin' snow or does it look like we had company?" Sydney swallows the lump in her throat.

"What da ya mean?" Leora half-whispers, breathing through her mouth, suppressing panic. "Wait a minute." She backs up past the driveway then pulls forward, turning into it, and stopping on an angle. Headlights flood the front of the property. She tries the high beams rendered useless by the fog. The parking lights are also of little use. They sit mesmerized by the disturbing sight ogling the snow; untouched, virgin just a few hours ago now melting but definitely trampled, downtrodden from foot traffic. Wheezer rushes from the porch, slinking to Sydney's car, disappearing under it.

"Oh! My God! Wheezer!" Leora pulls into the driveway. They exit the truck, calling him frantically.

"Come on, Tiger! We're here! It's okay!" Sydney whips around the back of the truck walking to her car.

Leora stoops calling, coaxing, pleading. Wheezer answers.

"Maybe Bryce was here," Sydney whispers, "with Manny and what's his name. Come on, Tiger," she calls the young tabby, also stooping. "You're gonna get all wet. Let's grub." Wheezer answers.

"Look at you out here in the snow. Why aren't you snugly?" He crawls out from under the back of the Thunderbird, shaking a wet front paw and jumping to the sidewalk. "Oh! Wheezer!" Leora calls. Overjoyed, he forgets himself, flopping in the melting snow, but only for a split second before darting up the three steps to the porch. The girls walk to the house, checking water ice footprints in the grass on the sidewalk, on the steps, listening to the quiet. "Maybe it was Crow and his buddies wantin' ta spin circles at Penn Fruit."

Sydney yawns. "Well, I know it wasn't Santa Claus. It's too early. Besides, I don't see any pawprints."

"Or sled marks."

"Or reindeer poop." The girls giggle, slipping inside the house after Wheezer shakes a front foot then a back foot, scurrying into his sanctuary first.

They lock the door and un-gear—shoes, jackets, pocketbooks. "Well, I don't think it was Angelo or Toto." Sydney walks toward the kitchen, yawning again. "They don't look like schminkers ta me."

"Tito." Leora laughs. "Rhonda said Tito, Sis."

"Whatever."

"You know what ya call somebody like that?"

"Sir!" They say in unison.

"Yo, Sis, I bet if they took their suit jackets off, you'd see the batteries on their shoulders."

"You mean like Robert Conrad?" Now Leora yawns.

"Yeah, and I ain't knockin' it off."

"That makes two of us." They palaver around in the kitchen drying Wheezer's feet, filling his dishes out on the patio looking around a bit like nervous Nellies. Leora flicks the den light for a quick check, returning to the kitchen.

R-r-ring! R-r-ring! Sydney is closest to the phone. She screams at the phone, wide eyed, mouth agape, as she about rips the receiver off the wall. She takes a deep breath, smiling and glancing at the clock: 4:45. "Maybe its Bryce," she whispers to wide-eyed Leora grinning back at her.

"Hello." She swallows the lump in her throat, paralyzed by fear; terror twisting her face, diffusing her smile. "Wait, I can't understand you. What did you say?" She gazes at Leora despondently. "Calm down. No. No. Yes. Yes, I'm sure. Don't cry. Here." She hands the phone to Leora.

Leora stares at Sydney, her lips pursed, deep concern etched on her face. She mouths 'who is it' to the redhead.

"Eva," Sydney says aloud.

"Hello?" Eva becomes hysterical just hearing Leora's voice. "What's a matter?" Leora's eyes dart back and forth with every syllable spoken by her coworker.

"What's up?" Sydney asks. "What's happ'nin'?"

Leora stares, sucking air, unable to breathe, dropping the phone.

"What? Sis, what is it?" Sydney asks, eyes wide with fear watching Leora, emotionless a blank stare, mouth agape and wobbly, so wobbly. "Yo, Sis, you're scarin' me." She grabs Leora's arm, steadying her, pulling her down on a chair, reeling the receiver in by the extension cord. "Yo, what's goin'—?" Sydney listens, her eyes, too, dart back and forth, back and forth. She has no recollection of hanging up the phone. She is sitting down. She has no recollection of that either.

The best friends sit in shock, statues for all eternity, but for a knock at the door stirring each of them into life, forcing movement, a response. Sydney opens the door to Joe Sill, Trainer Police Chief and Officer Donnelly. She turns to Leora, standing behind her with eyes, oh, so swollen, her face soaked in tears. Sydney unravels a paper towel, wiping her own soaked face.

"Come in," Leora says, blinking tears, wiping her cheeks with her hands.

The chief gasps. "Oh, my God! You're here!"

Leora wakes in the dark in her bedroom to Wheezer's announcement of potty call. She stumbles from the bed fully dressed; her eyes nothing but slits trying like hell to adjust them in the hall light glare as she staggers to Wheezer at the top of the steps.

"Wheezer. Come on, Tiger. I gotcha," Sydney responds, rounding the staircase doing a double take at the sight of her best friend. Yo! Sis!" Her eyes fill as strong masculine arms hold her steadfast.

"Are you okay?"

Sydney nods, leaning on the banister.

"I got her," Bryce whispers, kissing Sydney's head, nuzzling her hair.

Leora sways, her legs are weak, her stomach unsettled. Her mind in a fog and then it floods over her, drowning her. She cannot breathe. "Oh! No! Sis! Oh! She tries so very hard to see past the horridness, to hear her own words. She gasps for air. "No! Sis! Sis!" She is queasy, light headed, faltering then crumbles into Bryce's strength, guiding her down to Sydney with arms outstretched, waiting until Leora fills them as Sydney in turn fills hers collapsing together on the stairs sobbing. Bryce gathers them, leading anguish and sorrow to the den.

"What time is it?" Leora's voice is raspy, whisperlike.

"I don't know," Sydney exhales the words, turning to Bryce beside her on the couch, water and medication in hand.

"It's goin' on five." He opens a clenched fist, dropping two pills into Sydney's cupped hands.

"In the morning?" Confusion settles on Leora's face.

"No, no, no," Bryce answers. "It's dinner time."

"What's today?" Leora is lost.

"It's Sunday, Sis," Sydney answers. "It's still Sunday."

"Oh, no."

Sydney consumes a valium, handing the other to Leora. "Here, Sis."

Leora swallows the pill, waiting for the illusion of calm the little blue crutch spews forth; paralyzing the grief, numbing the pit of her stomach, strengthening her buckling legs, dulling the massive heartache.

"I'm gonna go get us somethin' to eat," Bryce announces in the doorway. "You need anything?"

"Oh, I don't know. Are ya hungry, Sis?"

Leora shrugs her shoulders.

"Cheese steaks. Yeah, cheese steaks." Sydney nods.

"Nah, I was goin' down the diner. I have some dinner vouchers."

"Oh thanks, well then, a salad, huh, Sis?"

"Yeah, thanks, that's good."

"Two garden salads, two Kaiser rolls and blue cheese on the side. Oh, can ya stop at Wawa for a half gallon of milk for coffee? You're gonna have some, right?"

"Yeah, sure, by the way," Bryce remembers, "I put the water on for your coffee and tea."

"Okay." Sydney leans on the arm of the couch to steady herself as she stands.

"You gonna be all right?" Bryce moves toward her; ready, willing, and able.

"Sure, just a little rusty," Sydney says, taking a deep breath, meeting his eyes.

"Yeah, her and the tin man," Leora's stomach finishes her sentence.

"I should hurry, huh?"

"No," Leora answers with a half smile. "Just get extra blue cheese."

Bryce grins back at her. "I'll be back." He glances at Sydney. "Ya sure?"

"Sure I'm sure," Sydney answers.

"Be careful on those steps. Keep the door locked."

"Oh, wait." She follows him slowly to the front door, fishing her keys from her pocketbook. "Here."

Bryce takes the keys, embracing her, kissing her. He pulls the gun from the back of his pants. "Here."

There is no argument. Sydney takes the Smith & Wesson, gripping it by the barrel. She walks into the den. "Company!"

Leora blinks, watching Sydney lay the piece on the coffee table, void of expression. The tea kettle whistles. The brunette tries her hand at standing, lisping to the right. She puts her arms out for balance.

"Yo! Sis!"

"I'm ah'ight! I'm ah'ight!"

"Ya sure?"

"I got this."

Sydney herself walks a bit gingerly to the kitchen, gathering cups and spoons, tea bag, coffee, sugar, and the last of the milk.

Leora appears, her sea legs subsiding, along with the queasiness as she slides into a kitchen chair. Her stomach growls again. It is so embarrassing.

"Are ya hungry, Sis?"

"Not really, but my stomach is. When did Bryce get here?" Her mouth is dry.

"Oh, I guess about three o'clock." Sydney pours hot water into their mugs and sits across from her best friend.

"How long was I asleep?" Leora gives her mug a dose of moo juice.

"About two hours longer than me. What's the last thing you remember?" Sydney squeezes her teabag.

Leora thinks. "Talkin' to Eva." She sips her coffee once, twice.

"You don't remember Chief Sill?" Sydney takes a sip.

Leora shakes her head.

"I didn't think so. That's when I went through your pocketbook, which I apologize for, looking for the bag of pills from the set up."

Leora takes a deep breath, exhaling through her mouth. "What did he say?"

"He didn't say much of anything. He was concerned about you, but you were here. We couldn't offer him any information other than the title to your car with the VIN number . . ." Sydney's voice trails. "He said he'll make a copy of it and give it back."

"And what about . . ." Leora starts. "What about . . ." she breathes through her mouth.

Sydney grabs her arm. "I don't know anything, Sis. He didn't say. All I know is your car was found someplace, and they came here lookin' for me and were really surprised ta find you." She reties her robe.

Leora stares at Sydney with unblinking eyes full of sadness. "How did Eva know?"

"She heard on her police radio when she got home from work, Sis." Sydney breathes deep. "They found a '64 Chevy, like a light green color. She called the cops."

"Oh! Carrie!" Leora's eyes fill. "Oh! My God! Jenny!"

Sydney pats Leora's arm. "The footprints we saw were from the chief and Officer Donnelly. They came here twice. This last time is when they saw the truck." She blinks, taking a breath for composure. "I told 'em you and I were usin' it since Friday night, and he asked where your car is, so I gave 'im Crow's name. You told 'em his address, Sis. They radioed Chester ta tell 'em they located the owner of the car and gave them Carrie's address and . . ." Sydney sighs. "Whatever."

"Did they arrest 'im?"

"Who? Oh, that's all I know, but the chief did say he'd be in touch."

"Has anybody called?"

"Actually, I took the receiver off the hook and put it back on when Bryce showed up. Carrie called. The police and a couple federal agents told her they located the truck here. She said it stands ta reason if he has your car, you have his truck. She said she coulda told 'em that, but she didn't know they were lookin' for it. We weren't home the first time they came by. She told 'em ta leave it be right where it is 'cause it's in her name, you know, insurance is cheaper. She thinks it's safer here anyway as compared ta the project's track record. She doesn't know a whole lot either. All she knows is there was a one car accident, and your car was unnoticeable from the road, especially being covered with snow. The police told her she would be updated as they are updated. Chief Sill told me to try and keep a lid on it, I guess, because it was your car and you're here. He said he'll be back."

Leora shivers with closed eyes and shallow breathing, pushing her hair from her forehead. It feels like a rat's nest. She feels grimy. "I need a shower. I gotta get a shower."

"Ya need help gettin' up there, Sis?"

"No, I'll be all right. If I get dizzy, I'll sit down and go up backwards."

"You goin' ta bed when you're done?"

"Nah-uh."

"You want another cup of coffee?"

Leora nods, putting a teaspoon full of freeze dried Folger's coffee in her cup along with two teaspoons full of sugar and filling it a quarter of the way full with milk. She stands, leaning on the table, stabilizing her swaying.

"Ya ah'ight? Tell me what ya need, Sis. I'll follow ya up there and get it for ya and twist us a couple." Sydney smiles at her best friend, placing the miniscule amount of milk back in the refrigerator. She walks slowly to the stove, grabbing the tea kettle, then walks slowly to the sink, filling it then slowly back, placing it on the lit burner.

"Shit. You're askin' me if I'm ah'ight, are you?"

"Ain't we a mess? The blind leadin' the blind."

"I see, said the blind man as he picked up his hammer and saw." Leora recites, smiling at Sydney. "Ya ah'ight?"

"No, I'm half left." Sydney smiles back.

Leora meanders to the stairs; Sydney right behind her, ready to break her fall so they could both break their necks. Ushered into the bathroom, Leora puts the lid down on the toilet to sit for a minute or two. In the meantime, Sister Syd gathers a nightgown and robe for her before retrieving the shoebox lid, rolling papers and the film canister on her hands and knees from under her bed. She hears the shower start, scooting onto her bed from a kneeling position and sits a minute. She stands, ready to continue with a slow stride but a stride nonetheless, finally reaching the bathroom door. She knocks. "Yo! Sis!"

"Yo! Sis!" Leora answers. "Come on in!" She yells above the running water.

"Here's your robe and nightgown." Sydney places them on the toilet seat.

"Okay, thanks."

"I'll put your clothes in the hamper."

The tea kettle begins as the redhead maneuvers through the hall and on down the steps. "All right, shut up!" By the time Leora appears, Sydney has rolled two, let Wheezer in, loved on him, and given choice seating to their "company."

"Oh, Sis, I thought you woulda called me for backup."

"That's for when you're goin' up, you sit down and back up, comin' down its feet first."

"Awww, Sis." She pours hot water in Leora's mug.

"What? I'm okay." She pulls the chair out across from Sydney.

"Oh, not there, sit here. That's for our 'company'."

Leora looks at the gun, then shoves the chair to the table and sits in front of her coffee mug. Wheezer hops in her lap, purring, ready for some serious pets.

"Chief Sill did ask me about my dark eyes. I told him it was from my period. That was the end of that."

"Ya think Bryce is okay?" Leora sounds anxious, cradling the orange and white tabby, softly stroking his face with eyes closed, purring his ass off.

Sydney starts a joint. "Yeah, he was gonna check around ta see if anything is in the wind. He had no idea when he got here. He's been in Philly the whole time."

"Alice? What about Alice?"

Sydney breathes deep, averting Leora's eyes—empty eyes, sad eyes about to be made sadder. "She doesn't know what happened, Sis, she can't remember."

Tossing Cookies

. . . .

R-r-ring! R-r-ring! The phone interrupts their mutual nightmare.

"Hello," Sydney answers, clearing her throat dabbing her eyes.

"Sydney? Hey, have ya heard anything?"

"Hey, Eva." Sydney clears her throat. "We heard from Carrie a little while ago. She wants us ta keep the truck here for now. The police were wantin' ta tow it outta here, God only knows why. It must be a clue." Sydney is being sarcastic. "It's been here all weekend. I told them that earlier. Carrie told them there is no reason in the world to confiscate – and that's the word she used — to confiscate her truck. It's in her name. She showed 'em the title. The cops backed off. When they were here earlier, they told us ta keep everything on the down low like we know somethin'. What the hell are we gonna tell? We know they found the car, that's about it."

"Yeah! Right! Keep it on the down low. Why don't they? They got diarrhea of the mouth. They keep talkin' on the scanner, the truck—in question, the vehicle, in question, the address—in question. I heard a little while ago on the freakin' scanner they dispatched an ambulance to the address in question; ten-twenty-four Ganster Place over there in the village."

"Oh! My God, the baby!" Sydney shrieks.

"What?" Leora stands wide-eyed, hands on her hips, mouth agape.

"The baby? What baby?" Eva is in the dark. "His mom's gonna have a baby?"

"No, Jenny! Jenny's pregnant! They eloped! They got married!" Sydney had struggled to be strong, keeping it together. Not anymore. She looses it.

264

Leora takes the phone from Sydney along with a deep breath, hugging her best friend. "Yo, Eva."

"Leora? Oh, God! Leora! If there's anything I can do . . . you want me to work tomorrow night?"

"No, no, no, thanks," Leora answers.

"Hey, I musta called your house twenty times this morning. I got done work early because of the snow. I just heard a few minutes ago your car was found out of state. I don't know when, just that they said the car in question—affirmative, it was found in New York. They shouldn't be tellin' shit on the scanner!"

Leora gasps and sits. She is completely rattled. Her hands are shaking, her stomach, oh, so queasy.

Sydney blinks tears. "What?"

"They found my car in New York."

Sydney parks her ass in a chair, too.

"I'm tellin' ya, they're as bad as a hen party! I heard the description of your car earlier and called the cops. I musta called your house twenty times," Eva repeats herself. "And when Sydney answered the damn phone, I lost it. And they're still runnin' their faces. They said the license plate was missin' off the car in question. They shouldn't be sayin' shit on the damn scanner! Ohhh! Yeah! And they found a wallet in the car in question. That's why they first thought it was stolen from Chester because they found a wallet with a Chester address belonging to a Mr. Sheppard. That's Crow, isn't it? He was drivin' your car?"

"Yeah," Leora answers, wiping tears.

"Somebody was after 'im? Who would wanna hurt him?"

"He was playin' big brother."

"Oh, so nobody wanted ta hurt 'im? Oh! Shit! You! You! Somebody wanted to hurt you? No! Oh! My God! No! That piece of shit!"

Leora swallows hard for composer; her breathing labored, her voice just above a whisper, "a lull in the action." She clears her throat, taking a deep breath. "That's all he was tryin' ta do. He was worried because of Alice. He wanted ta put a lull in the action. He figured if the asshole didn't see my car, then he wouldn't come around."

"Yeah, well, the asshole takes everything personal and acts like he's livin' in the 1920s. Evidently, he's trouble, big time! He thinks money can buy anything and anybody. His father was a big wig or somethin' up in New York, and Griff was nothin' but trouble. He went after cops, took bribes; threatened his own family. He went to jail! He's a keeper, yeah, right! He's basically nine cents short of a dime. Wait a second." Leora hears whispering. "Ya there?" Eva speaks to Leora. "Doc's here."

"Yeah, I'm here."

"The families ignored 'im, you know, like ostracized 'im. What?" Eva whispers again. "Yeah, I'm back. Doc said he set up shop on the main line with some guy he met in jail . . . huh? What?" Eva whispers again, "Noodle? Because why? A what?" Eva turns back to the phone to speak to Leora. "Some guy they call Noodle, low profile, way worse than Griff. He's not a partner, he's more like a right hand man or whatever. He's more trouble than Griff. Thank God he stayed up the line runnin' everything while Griff's been tryin' ta branch out. He's basically the only one Griff trusts." Eva rambles on, trying to remember everything Doc has spilled. "Oh, yeah, Goo Goo called Doc from Vegas. He's not comin' back 'til later today. He told Doc Papa escorted the extra furniture from upstairs over to Jersey late last night. It's a front! Who don't know that? I mean he did, but come on, with an accent like that, well, even Chrissy Snow can figure that one out. He's got connections, and I ain't talkin' a friend of a friend of a friend. I got it out of Doc. Papa's related to one of the families on his mother's side. He's breakin' bread in New York." The girls suck air, gawking at each other. "I mean, think about it, he drove his own car. He ain't ridin' shotgun in a movin' van! Ya know Papa rented that apartment upstairs to Griff and his sister and that guy Rob was actually workin' for Griff. Doc said Rob sabotaged Goo's car then turned around and came along and fixed it, gettin' in good with Goo Goo to get shit on 'im for Griff so he could have 'im arrested and get 'im outta the way. Rob bugged Goo's apartment, his office, his car. He's very electronically inclined. He even went through Goo's trash. But Goo found out and sent 'im packin' empty-handed right after he kicked the shit out of 'im, right?" Eva whispers to Doc again, then speaks to Leora. "Are ya there? Hello?"

The best friends listen intently, wide-eyed, catching flies. Leora turns the receiver slightly toward herself. "I'm here. So's Sydney. She's listenin', too."

"Look how Griff lied sayin' he turned you down, you're stealin', you're an addict. I'll tell ya what, I wouldn't put nothin' past 'im. Look at those two, the ones who told me they ran into a door? What do ya call 'em, oh, yeah, Heckle 'n' Jeckle. Look at Alice, and those meetings, yeah, those prayer meetings at the bar." Eva takes a breath. "He oughta go back up the line where he belongs. Better yet, he oughta go back to New York. Oh! Sorry. I bet it's all tied together."

And then there's the typewriter, the key to my house, the bugs, Griff's private investigators, the pills. You just don't know how tied together it all is!

"He's got a favorite four-letter word, and it don't begin with F, it begins with `M` for mine! He's a sneak, liar, bully, thief, murderer, shit! He don't seem ta take rejection well either! For that matter, I don't think he's above rape either. Hey, girl, you never led him on. You never liked 'im, and you never even pretended you did. It's all about him and what he wants."

Leora wants to tell Eva everything—everything about the bugs, the threats to Papa, Goo Goo's involvement, the pills the prick planted in her car to give probable cause for a search of her house where they would have found the damn typewriter. She wants to tell Eva how she and Sydney were in the dark, two naïve flies on the wall, learning Griff was never really into her, just circling her for the incriminating evidence, the damn elusive incriminating evidence she and Sydney are not suppose to know about. She wants to tell Eva how they never said anything, never involved anybody—sparing them, protecting them. She and Sydney had hopes they all would have killed each other by now. She wants to spill her guts about Alice, how her memory has been beaten into silence and how Crow has paid for their friendship. It was all her fault. She wants to confess.

A knock at the door startles the despondent girls, sucking in their breath, popping eyes simultaneously. They know it's not Bryce. He has a key.

"I gotta go, Eva. Somebody's at the front door," Leora half-whispers.

"I'll stay on the line 'til you find out who it is. Just say help and hang up. I'll have the cops there with bells on! What's your address?"

"Nine hundred Chestnut." Leora eyeballs their "company" on the kitchen chair as she walks with Sydney toward the front door, stretching the phone cord as far as it will go—which is practically past the dining room doorway—her adrenaline hot on the trail of panic. She takes another two steps, stretching her arm behind her, gripping the receiver. Sydney turns the porch light on opening the door.

Leora stands sideways, slightly swaying with feet apart, ready to spring toward the kitchen if need be. There is no need. Chief Joe Sill, chewing on an unlit White Owl, enters with Officer Donnelly and two detectives. "Let me go, Eva, it's the cops." Leora walks back through the open archway, hanging up the phone and placing their "company," ashtray, cardboard lid, and whatnot into the oven. She walks gingerly to greet the group of authorities stalled by Sydney in the foyer. Leora winks at her best friend, calming her wide-eyed stare, leading them to the kitchen. Chief Sill hands her the car title.

"Here, let me get another chair," Sydney states, walking toward the archway.

"I'll get it." Officer Donnelly follows, disappearing to the left with her retrieving the desk chair from the den, and returning before Sydney. He places it at the corner of the table next to Leora pointing at it with an open hand for Chief Sill. Sydney sits across from her best friend.

Dry-cleaning chemicals, starch, and Skin Bracer sit down with supposedly New York's finest. "This is Federal Agent Les Talbot," Chief Sill begins, "and Federal Agent Donald Black."

"It's your car?" Agent Talbot dives in with a pronounced New York accent, pointing to Sydney. Adjusting black-rimmed glasses sitting between bushy Italian eyebrows and his schnozzola, he lays a folder on the table then gropes the inside pocket of his trench coat, pulling out a notepad with a pencil shoved through the spiral wire top.

"No, it's hers." Sydney points to Leora, distaste ever so present in her mouth.

"And you are?"

"Sydney." She glances at Leora.

Agent Talbot leans forward, staring at Sydney until she looks at him.

"Sydney," she reiterates louder, meeting his cold, almost calculating stare.

"Okay, Cindy. Ahhh, what's your last name?" He readies pad and pencil.

Now the redhead leans forward, staring, waiting for impatience to get the best of him, and it does. He glances at her. She enunciates slowly. "Syd . . . ney. Sydney Nethery."

"Wait, wait." The chief interrupts. "I've got all this information." He hands Leora her title.

"What's that?" Agent Black questions, his accent unmistakable laying his folder on the table, also producing a pad and pencil from the inside pocket of his suit coat.

"That's the title to the car that was found in New York State," The chief speaks softly, enunciating, staring at this, this, well, dick for lack of a better word.

"Here." Agent Black waves his hand in a flurry at Leora taking the title.

Chief Sill switches the White Owl from one side of his mouth to the other. He retrieves the title, folding it up and handing it back to Leora. "You already have a copy in your folder." The chief hones in on Detective Black's face. "And a copy in his folder, too," he enunciates, speaking softly, pointing in Detective Talbot's direction with furrowed brow above eyes still fixed on Agent Black.

Detective Black cuts his eyes at the Trainer police chief. "This is an ongoing investigation. It's federal because it's over state lines."

"Well, good," Chief Sill pats Agent Black's folder. "And this is papers pertaining to . . . well, will you look at that? Papers pertaining to an ongoing investigation over state lines!" Officer Donnelly stands, cheesing with arms crossed in front of him.

Agent Black snaps his head in Leora's direction. "What's your name?"

Leora clears her throat. "Leora Wells. You found my car in New York. Is it totaled?"

"I ain't at liberty ta say." He cuts her off. His bedside manner sucks. He is no Joe Friday. "Do you know"—he looks to the first page of his notepad for inspiration—"do you know . . ." He cannot read the writing, "Ander—ew Sheppard, J R?"

"No," she answers with a confused stare.

"Andrew," Agent Talbot runs his fingers through his coal-colored hair, his brown eyes darting back and forth over his own notes, "Andrew Sheppard, Jr."

Leora turns to Agent Talbot, nodding, swallowing a lump in her throat.

"When is the last time you saw him?" Agent Talbot pushes his glasses up his nose, leaning forward toward Leora. He is no Columbo.

Leora's breath puffs her hair on her forehead as she exhales through her mouth. "Friday night," she says in a half-whisper, clearing her throat, "Friday night."

"Saturday morning." Sydney interjects.

Agent Black, a distinguished-looking man with graying temples, brown eyes, a healthy head of dark hair, leans toward the redhead, the map of Italy all over his face—along with displeasure. "Well, which is it?"

Leora's breathing is labored, very labored as sweat beads on her forehead.

"It depends on your perspective." Sydney blinks at him. "If you're workin' it, it's Friday night, but if you wanna get iffy about it, then the shift ends after midnight, two o'clock in the morning." She leans forward, speaking slowly, enunciating, "The next day."

Agent Black studies Sydney's face. "And just what does this iffy mean?"

"Hey, they haven't seen their friend since Friday night or Saturday morning, pick one. Here, they haven't seen their friend since the end of her shift." Chief Sill points at Leora. "Does that clear it up for you? They switched vehicles. End of story, unless you want to enlighten them?'

"No, this investigation is ongoing." Agent Black writes in his notepad, his hands rough, calloused, actually not unlike his counterpart. He refuses to look at the chief.

"Yeah, you said that. Well, keep ongoin'. And this is suppose ta be a questioning, not an interrogation. I got their statements. Why don't you ask them something that is not in the folder, you know, like a brand new question?"

"Well, if you'd let me continue and quit interruptin'—"

"What are you talkin' about? You were supposed to be here"—Chief Sill checks his watch—"three and a half, almost four hours ago. Are you going to tell her about her vehicle? Do you know anything about her vehicle? If you had read anything in that damn folder . . ." The portly chief's voice is a tad bit edgy. He removes the White Owl. "His mother and his new wife said the last time they saw the boy was Friday afternoon, when he left for work. He works second shift. Doesn't miss a lot of time. The wife spoke to him on his lunch break or dinner break about eight o'clock Friday night, and then again on his last break at roughly twenty-two hundred hours. That's in the folder. Did you read that? He was reported missing

Saturday night with his truck. But he was driving a car—her car, which was found in New York." Chief Sill holds the White Owl between his first and second fingers, patting his shirt pocket for a pack of matches, his eyes all over the guy's mug. He thinks better of lighting it, popping the unlit cigar back in his mouth.

Leora leans an elbow on the table, holding her head and closing her eyes.

"Yeah, we know."

"You know? Well, then what are you talkin' about?" He removes the stogie, patting his shirt pocket again. "That was after these kids had any contact. What the hell's the matter with you?" Chief Sill smacks the folder with his open hand. "You haven't read any of this, have you?" He shakes his head, then pops the White Owl back in his mush.

Agent Talbot throws a question. "Do you know of anyone who would want to cause bodily harm to one Andrew Sheppard, say, like your jealous boyfriend?" He glances back and forth at the girls.

"I don't have a boyfriend."

"You are not in a relationship with Shaun Griffonetti?"

Sister Syd bursts out laughing. "Does she look blind to you?"

Chief Sill listens intently with furrowed brow and narrowing eyes.

Agent Black jumps in. "Well, what about infidelity? A love triangle? Did he find out his wife was cheatin'? Was he? Is he involved in say, organized crime, so ta speak?" His rough hands fumble, pulling a wallet size photo from the folder. He tosses it on the table. A smiling Crow stands alongside the mural on his pick-up truck. A picture Leora herself had taken. The girls burst into tears. Officer Donnelly shakes his head.

"Okay, we're done here." Chief Sill stands, straddling the kitchen chair, shaking his head, ending the whole shebang. Leora stands, too, but not soon enough. She looses her lunch in her hands, spewing on Detective Black's shoulder, down his back, the chair, the floor, basically everything between her and the sink.

"Oh! My God! Sis!" Sydney springs from her chair, tiptoeing to the sink, turning the faucet on. She pulls a clean hand towel from the drawer, wringing it out under cold water for Leora, leaning against the sink for support, her legs again wobbly. She rinses her mouth. Sydney snatches the dish rag off the hook, wringing it under hot water and chucking it on the table for the detective to fend for himself as she steers Leora to sit. "Are ya happy now?"

Poor pale Leora. She is as white as a ghost. She wipes her face with the cool cloth. Detective Talbot walks briskly, gagging all the way to the front door.

"Well, that's the end of this interrogation, I mean questioning," Officer Donnelly announces.

"You mean circus?" Chief Sill does not mince words. "We're gonna get outta here and let you get some rest."

The Chief watches Detective Black folding his suit jacket inside out after wiping it off as best he could, unable to remove the stench of sour milk, bile and gastric whatnot. "We'll do this another time." He heads for the door, carrying the reeking suit coat at arms length.

Chief Sill looks over the top of his bifocals, watching the two investigators make a quick, smelly exit. He removes the White Owl, patting Leora's shoulder. "Nice goin', kid, my exact sentiments." He snickers.

Officer Donnelly places a business card on the table with their home phone numbers written on the back. Sydney walks them to the door.

Chief Sill shoves his bifocals into his shirt pocket, exchanging them for the pack of matches. "If you have any questions, feel free to call. Chin up, Kiddo."

Sydney retrieves the wet mop and pine cleaner from the small utility closet under the staircase, also housing the washer and dryer, just as the kitchen phone rings, breaking the silence and her train of thought. Startled, she squeals, dropping the mop.

"Hello. Hi." Bryce's voice brings a sense of calm and a smile to Sydney. "No, just a half, we can't drink a gallon . . . Oh, you do, do you? …Yes, we do. … It doesn't matter what kind, we have both . . . My favorite? Puff wheat." She sits the bottle of pine on the counter, glancing at Leora. "Grab a bottle of Canada Dry, too, while you're at it? No, we're not makin' drinks. It's good for upset stomachs, too, ya know. Only if what? … Seymour who? See more of m . . . Oh! Ah! Ha! Ha!"

Leora pours White Cap into the plugged sink, swishing the dish towels in hot disinfectant water. She wrings one out, wiping down the chair, the table and the cabinet doors under the sink, chucking it in the sink and reaching for the mop. Sydney holds the handle tight, making Leora look her square in the eye.

"I'm fine," the brunette whispers.

Sydney relinquishes her grasp, indulging in conversation with her future husband. She feels it, and she knows it. "Nah-uh, it's ah'ight. Take your time . . . oh, we're fine, not too hungry right now . . . maybe by then . . . are you bringin' jammies? I know ya don't." Sydney laughs. "See what? Etchings. You draw? …You're bad . . . I'll tell her. Talk ta ya later . . . Bye." Sydney hangs the phone up and takes the mop from Leora. "Sit down, Sis, take a break."

Leora offers no argument. She sits, gladly actually. Her stomach is still a little floppy. "I pretended too real, huh?"

"You certainly did. You almost had me convinced, too, but I knew you weren't really sick to your stomach." Sydney shakes her head, giving Leora half a smile before finishing the floor and the sink. She retires the cleaning aids to the closet, throwing the soiled dish towels into the washer. "Bryce won't be much longer. He said all he has ta do is stop for milk."

"Oh, good, company." Leora sincerely means it. "Speakin' of company, where's ours?" She looks around the kitchen, smiling at her best friend.

"Oh, right here, Momma." Sydney pulls the box and the ashtray out of the oven, placing them on the table. She lifts the "company" by the barrel, laying it back on the chair.

"Boy, they had some rough-lookin' hands for detectives."

"Yepper, they're in dire need of Madge. What's she say, 'You're soakin' in it'? That should be their ritual."

"Could you imagine handin' the typewriter over to one of them?"

"No way," Sydney answers. "They'd have us arrested for conspiracy."

"Or receiving stolen property."

"Or withholdin', ahhhh!" Sydney goes blank. "Oh, withholding evidence."

"D—all the above."

"That Detective Black would probably have us shot at sunrise."

"Speakin' of shot, I hope Griff don't know that we know what he knows that they know." Leora sits with confusion on her face her eyes dart back and forth. "Did I say that right?"

"Geez! If Griff knew that we knew what he knows, well, let's just say I'll never look at spaghetti the same way ever again!"

"Yeah, Griff's hitmen detectives. They gave me the creeps. So do these guys."

"Yeah, sayin' Griff was your boyfriend. Are you shittin' me, mister?"

"Yeah, we shoulda told 'em he's Rhonda's boyfriend from California, the one and only Shaun Taylor, Esquire—gimme a break! And he was waitin, for a phone call, yeah, right!"

"Yeah, waitin' for a phone call and didn't wanna wait all alone, my ass!"

"Yeah, tellin' gullible Rhonda his ex-girlfriend was rippin' him off."

"That lyin' sack of shit! Yeah, ya need an ex ta have an ex, let alone one rippin' 'im off!" Sydney sighs. "And poor Alice! She was nowhere around and got put in it!"

"Did ya see him, all conceited and arrogant as usual until he came face ta face with us? He looked like he saw a ghost!" Leora laughs, lost in thoughts of a smug Griff, the-tell-all Rhonda, the death grip she had on Sydney's jacket, the shock on Griff's face—no, the fear. It really was a sight to behold.

"Yeah, he did, didn't he? He ran past us like his ass was on fire. I felt a breeze and smelled burnin' hair!"

Pleasurable expressions drain from Leora's face, along with color. She stands, knocking her chair over, grabbing her best friend's arm. "He didn't know I wasn't in the car! He thought I was in the car!"

Sydney blinks with a half-smile and a measure of perplexity, delving into her memories of that night: the rattling on and on of Rhonda, Griff's jaw-dropping, wide-eyed glance; the pure satisfaction of seeing whatever it was in his eyes. "What? Wait! What?"

"Rhonda! His ex was in an accident! She said over Jersey! The car was empty! Over New Jersey! Crow went to New Jersey!" It hits Sydney like a ton of bricks. "Oh! My God!" Sydney is beside herself. "Your car! The trunk was empty!" She shakes her head in disbelief. She can't breathe. Now she nods. She exhales, coughing and gagging. "My car." Her voice is raspy. "My trunk, your trunk."

Leora blinks tears. "She said his ex didn't have anything! She was in a bad accident! Me! Oh! Me! He thought it was me!" She leans an elbow on the table, holding her head up. "He checked every place. I shoulda known, every place but my trunk! Oh! My! God!" She crosses her arms on the table, laying her head on them. Sick to her stomach again, she leaps to the sink. Her head is spinning. She has the dry heaves. She rests her elbows on the sink, her legs are like rubber.

"Who should we call? Should we call somebody?" Sydney asks, rushing to her best friend. She wrings a new hand towel.

Leora finishes gagging then reaches for a glass in the dish drain, filling it with water, downing as much as is physically possible under the circumstances while leaning against the sink.

"Yo, Sis, ya wanna sit down?"

"Not yet." Leora wretches the water. "At least now I don't have the dry heaves." She rinses her mouth then downs more of the liquid.

Sydney picks up Leora's chair, sliding it to her.

"Good thinkin', Sis, thanks." Leora sinks into the chair, straightening her arms, leaning on her legs with her hands. "Maybe I'll have some crackers."

"You want a hunk of burnt toast?"

"Nah-uh, the crackers should stay down."

Sydney grabs a pack of saltines, placing them on the table. "Yo, Sis, what are we gonna do? I know he did it, had it done, is involved, Jim-in-notie!" Sydney picks her brain, searching for an answer. "They've been skirtin' us this whole time because they really not sure if we know what's goin' on."

"Yeah, you said a mouthful. We gotta figure out what ta do, ya know, like who are we gonna give this shit to?"

"Yeah, that's our problem. At one point it was Griff or the Feds. One would kill us, the other would get us killed! Scratch that. Now it's Alice, Goo Goo, Papa, Bryce . . ." Sydney thinks.

"The cops, the other cops, the mayor but no detectives." Leora moves her chair to the table. She is weak from the physical activity. She wants to lie down.

"You got that right, private or not-so-private, no detectives!"

"That goes for the Noodle guy and Earless; New York's finest." Leora chews a cracker.

"Yeah, my vibes were off the wall."

"Yeah, mine were goin' berserk, too, that is, when I wasn't pukin'."

"Yeah, between our nerves and walkin' around in the snow last night, we're workin' on nervous breakdowns and pneumonia! Maybe you should take another pill." Sydney is frazzled and concerned.

Leora eats another cracker. "I would, but I don't wanna waste it."

Sydney smiles. "Good point."

"Maybe Bryce shouldn't be here." Leora throws it out to her best friend. "You know, it's not safe ta be around us."

"Maybe it's not safe ta be around him. Not for us though. I, myself, like the "company" he keeps. They gotta know he wants a piece of somebody. They know he was here when they broke into my trunk. They didn't come near the house. Yours was next. Ya think now they'll leave us alone?"

"I don't know, Sis. I guess it depends on if they have somebody else in mind. Maybe they finally will kill each other. Or should the question be: who's next?"

Bryce turns the key, opening the door. "Honey, I'm home!" he yells with a smile.

Monday, Monday

The Monday night shift drudgery approaches. Not that Leora must show up for her shift this evening. Begging off is an option suitable under the circumstances, one which allows them to remain holed up, so-to-speak—sad, stagnant, kicking around and around and around questions which they have already turned over and over and over again and again and again. They are their own worst enemy, and they seem to have plenty of them. No sense in adding two more. Change is in order, a new perspective, idea, information, fresh air, something and/or somebody to light a fire under their asses. Besides, they are rested, as well as can be expected. And they have discarded useless thoughts of denial, moving forward through the painful turn of events. One need only, well, in this case, two need only to spy their "company" still occupying a chair in the kitchen to realize the depth of the situation heightening their somber awareness to a point of double-checking themselves and each other. No music, no television to mask an unfamiliar noise; a dangerous intrusion. Bryce's arrival from Philadelphia reinforces their sense of security, but it is short-lived as now he ventures out yet again; this time for his impending night job and this time absconding with the "company" the girls had grown to call theirs. Their acceptance of his take-it-to-the-bank promise to appear at Papa's later after the completion of his shift does absolutely nothing to quell the but-what-about-now quandary, brutally apparent as the door closes behind him. Comfortable feelings unravel in the quiet as fear crawls across skin, climbing up spines, triggering shivers, seeping into the backs of their minds, bringing flashes of the damaged trunk, broken knickknacks,

Mr. No Ear, Sir Spaghetti Face, magnifying sounds, distorting shadows, stirring the cauldron of apprehension.

Fire down below! Well, then drudgery it is; the hot setup, the shelter, the retreat, the safe haven in public. There ya go! So what if Leora's shift begins almost three hours from now? Strength in numbers, especially since their strength has dwindled from three to two. So what if they only take Sydney's car just in case she rides home later with Bryce? That is an acceptable idea. They go with it, getting dressed, settling Wheezer out on the patio, locking the backdoor, double-checking the backdoor, locking the front door, double-checking the front door, down the porch steps bracing against the brisk air, the looming uncertainty, turning toward the driveway, habit, heading for Leora's car, habit, always parked in the driveway, but wait – .The girls freeze, motionless, staring at the candy apple red reminder not so long ago filled to capacity, creaking, surrounded by laughter, now empty, draped in silence, idle, waiting.

And the world turns—uncaring, gray, empty, and foreign; with its cold air and sleeping trees. They take a scenic cruise and then some, the melted snow almost gone except for puddles here and there that more than likely will freeze with impending nightfall. They pass Pierre. They pass time, up Chester Pike Boulevard down Mac Dade Boulevard each lined with sprawling businesses and tiny residences intersecting at the Sixty-Ninth Street terminal. They stop on their way back for hot pork sandwiches, checking the bungee cord on the T-Bird's trunk. The absence of any new information, good or bad at this point, stifles conversation for the girls, alone yet together, as each carries this burden of loss, preparing to perform socially, straightening their game faces.

Jenny is holding her own, now back home under the watchful eyes of her parents. And Carrie, well, short of a basket case, Carrie flies in the face of bereavement, gathering Crow's siblings to her shattered heart, consoling, comforting, a mother's strength unwavering, steadfast as she leaves this very morning with her crushed hearts in tow to Somewhere, New York, to identify her first born, to bring him home accompanied by her late husband's brother Scott.

Condolences from patrons play second fiddle to the collection jug spotted along the side of the rear register, a pungent reminder of a harsh finality. Leora joins Eva behind the bar. She is sick of construed skepticism and answering I-don't-know for the umpteenth time. Besides, she only has half an hour more before her shift begins. She readily busies herself.

"Our first place pool league team is playing the second place team away tonight, and then they're on break for the holidays," Eva states, chewing her Double Mint. "It's gonna be like a ghost town here tonight."

"Oh, yeah, that's right." Leora washes a few glasses and wipes the bar down. "Hey, if you wanna leave, it's ah'ight. It's cool. I'm in."

"Yeah, well, I can dig it. It'd be stupid for me ta tell ya ta sit down. God, these people don't shut up!"

Leora speaks from experience her voice monotone, "They mean well." She knows the drill. *Been there, did that.* She will emerge herself in her work, too busy for small talk, hell, too busy for any kind of talk, assumption or otherwise. *Screw the weather. Screw the he-said, she-said bullshit.* She wants to throw the collection jug against the wall. *Screw the world.*

"Sonny will be in tonight." Eva fills a couple of mugs. "Papa still hasn't come back from New York yet, uh, I mean from Jersey, wherever, 'cause of the weather," she says, bucking her eyes. "But it was a blizzard when he went over there. It ain't snowin' now." She scrunches her mouth to one side.

"I wonder if he's still rentin' out the apartment." Leora removes the grate from the draft beer, busily washing it in the sudsy water and wiping the drain with the bar rag.

"Oh yeah, they moved in yesterday. Their movin' van pulled in just as Papa's movin' van headed out for his beach property. It was a little teeny thing, you know, what da ya call 'em, a box truck? The family was in here cleanin' as usual for a Sunday. Papa left instructions for Hank to supervise on Sunday and personally hand Griff the key to the apartment." The buxom brunette waltzes the filled mugs to a couple of clientele by the front register.

Leora hastily replaces the grates, then roots through the drawer for the flashlight, the whole time mulling over Sydney's fly-on-the-wall moment. She shoves the light into her right armpit, walking to the opposite end of the bar, folding the rinsed bar rag in the beer well before beginning an inspection for an electronic bug. She shines the flashlight into the space beneath the bar to the left of the triple sink, illuminating an electrical outlet with wires and cobwebs and such. She scans the underside of the wooden bar, continuing left as the flashlight floods the black void. Leaning over the trash can, she feels along the inside of the wood frame. Her posture draws several wolf whistles as she inches her way in, vying for a glimpse of whatever her hand has discovered duck-taped toward the top.

"What are ya doin'?" Eva leans an arm on her coworker's back. "What's up?"

Leora stands, blinking her eyes to adjust them. "I thought I dropped a dollar bill back there," she mumbles, pointing behind the trash can.

"Up there, underneath the bar?"

Quick thinking Leora, you got a give it to her.

"I was checkin' for critters, ya know, cockroaches, spiders." She shivers, thinking about a roach falling in her hair or a spider dangling in her face. "Forget it. They can have it."

"I'll get it," the brown-eyed barmaid announces, peering into the black abyss.

"That's ah'ight, leave it for Mr. Mac."

Leora walks back to the register, placing the flashlight in the drawer. With mouth agape and eyes bugged, she nods to Sister Syd, grabbing a couple empty mugs. Sydney appears despondent. "E! So you were here yesterday?" she yells, dislodging Eva from her curious inspection.

Eva walks past her to the front end of the bar to replenish some longnecks and nips. "Yes, I was. It just so happens I was gettin' a pizza next door, and those guys of Griff's were movin' everything in."

"Who, Heckle 'n' Jeckle?"

"Yeah, them and a couple other ones," Eva answers, rooting for a nip. "The family was here, cleanin' as usual on a Sunday so I popped in. They told Marcie she could wait in here out of the way. Hank sat on his ass as usual. Marcie didn't lift a finger ta help them either, but she was Little Miss Susie Homemaker behind the bar. She cleaned speed racks and sinks, hell, she even moved trash cans and swept. How 'bout them apples?" Eva hustles to patrons, unaware of the disbelief on her coworker's face.

"Yeah, she can't work a Saturday, but she can help clean, go figure," Leora hollers, rubbing her forehead thinking. She glances toward Sydney standing at the end of the bar, head bobbing in agreement to the surrounding gossipy conversations, listening to not a blessed word, wishing it was she who could retreat behind the bar. Leora waves, disrupting Sydney's blank stare, then points to Goo Goo's regular seat at the opening of the curvy wooden structure. She places a Michelob on a coaster for her best friend's arrival. The redhead squeezes through the group, practically unnoticed as patrons continue discussions of hearsay, assumptions, etc.

Sydney hangs her pocketbook on the back of the end bar stool, throwing her denim jacket over top and parks it. She breathes a relaxing sigh, watching the trickle of customers mesh with the hodgepodge of drinkers scattered mostly around the front end. The crowd will dwindle considerably as the pool league members and fans embark to their last match of this year, but for right now, right here is peace and quiet, she likes it.

Eva gathers her end of the shift tips, hastily cutting short any attempt to converse with a smile and a thank you, shuffling back down the far end. "I don't blame ya! See? People never shut up! Ya know, opinions are like ass—"

"Bellybuttons!" Leora stands behind Eva in the opening.

Eva leans sideways, tilting her head back. "Yeah, and everybody's got one."

Leora speaks slowly, "Yeah, with two exceptions."

"Yeah, two." Eva snaps her head around to Leora. "Say what?"

"Two exceptions," Leora repeats. "They found two mummies, Adam and Eve."

"Get the hell out a here! Were there pictures?"

"No, somebody showed me an article in one of those smut magazines. They found a male and female mummy, and it said without a doubt it was them."

"How the hell did they know that? What? Were their names carved on the crypts, here lies Adam, here lies Eve in hieroglyphics?"

Leora gives a negative shake of her head.

"Oh, I know, a toe tag."

"Uhhhhhhhhhhhh!" Leora mimics the buzzer on "The Price is Right." "Wrong, neither one of the mummies had a bellybutton."

"…A bellybutton?" Eva throws her head back cacklin'. "That's pretty good!" She dumps her tips in her Crown Royal pouch, fishing her fake rabbit fur jacket and pocketbook from under the register. "I'm gonna go." She roots in her pocketbook, finally locating her keys. "If I hear anything on the scanner, I'll call ya."

"Thanks," Leora answers.

"See ya, Momma." Sydney pivots her stool, leaning on the bar, blinking at Leora.

"Here!" Leora smacks the end of the bar, making a come hither movement with her finger for Sydney to follow her to the shuffleboard. "Ya really can't see it unless ya climb in there. It's up high. We gotta tell Goo Goo. I'll go after work." She goosenecks the bar, standing on tiptoes.

"I'll go with ya."

"Aren't ya goin' home with Bryce?" Leora talks quickly, wide-eyed.

"Oh, yeah."

"Yo, Sis, he can come with us. We can blindfold 'im or not blindfold 'im. I don't care, which ever. You guys can wait in the car. Three ain't a crowd to me!" Fudge waves paper money for change. "Well, actually four, he can bring "company". Get my drift?" she asks her best friend. "Strength in numbers," she adds, walking behind the bar.

Sonny gushes through the front door with a deliberate gait, checking the clock on his way to the rear of the bar. He stands in the opening next to Sydney's stool, placing his left arm around her. Leora immediately jams a hand full of ice in a tall glass for a Cutty and water. "No! No! No! No! No!" he tells Leora, standing at the end of the bar in front of Sydney. Sonny places his other arm around her. "I was talkin' to Eva out front. You didn't have ta come in tonight. I'm here."

"I know, it's ah'ight. I'd go stark ravin' mad anyway." Which is not a lie, she just left out the part where she and Sydney were scared shitless. "Besides, it's gonna be slow, no pool league." Leora dumps the ice in the funnel and puts the glass upside down on the drain. She truly does not want to mingle. Maybe she really shouldn't be here. Maybe she should leave. *It would be fine if everyone would stop asking me questions and quit bringing up my son. Remember? Remember? Are you shittin' me?*

"God forbid she gets busy," Sydney interjects. "I dare her. I'm in."

Leora sighs, scoping out the bar for empties, spotting Tom Dayton down by the aperture. In a bit of a rush, she walks to him, tilting a make-believe beverage. Tom nods, throwing a Hamilton on the bar. She dives into the cooler for a Michelob.

Butley calls to Leora. "Get it here." He pats his money on the bar.

Tom nods a thank you to Butley. "Give me a shot of ginger brandy." Leora complies. She takes Butley's money for the shot and places Tom's change in front of him for his bottle of beer. "I was gonna stop by yesterday, but I saw the police car and I thought better of it. I know this isn't easy." Leora's eyes fill. "I spoke with Carrie yesterday. What can I say? She's holdin' her own. Your car was found covered with snow down a small incline in a stream of less than a foot of water. They got more white stuff than we did. Three people riding their snowmobiles spotted it. Who knows when it would have been found? The local police are working with this federal investigation. There's nothing in the paper. It's on the down low. I told them there is no reason in the world why that boy shoulda been up there."

Leora closes her eyes, her breathing is labored. Queasy flutters.

Sydney and Sonny walk over to Tom.

"I'm gonna get some coffee next door, you want one?"

Leora nods, finding her voice, "I'm in."

Tom declines. He downs the ginger brandy.

"And you'll take a hot tea, right?" Sonny asks the redhead.

Sydney sits on the stool next to Tom. "You want me to?" she teases, nodding affirmatively to Sonny placing her untouched Mick in front of Tom. He orders another shot. The conversation is repeated. So are the flutters.

"Didn't you tell Shaun off down the club that night we spoke in the parking lot?"

Guilt bitchslaps Leora, twisting her heart. Once again, her eyes fill. Her pursed lips quiver, struggling against a frown pulling at the corners of her mouth.

Tom grasps Leora's arm, preventing escape. "Hey, I don't care if he's jealous or not jealous. I don't care if you were sleepin' with 'im or blackmailin' 'im. It ain't you're fault. The mothe—" Tom takes a breath— "he's a sick-o. Hey! Back in April, he told the Feds the New York fellas whacked Lister, remember? I think I told you."

Leora nods, glancing at Sydney.

"Listen, he was always a problem, even as a kid. I heard he killed animals, pets—you know, his pets; other peoples' pets. Out of respect for his father, he was made an enforcer, but they could never rein him in. He didn't follow their rules, he had his own, which was none. He showed no respect—to anyone. I don't care what anybody says; he's not nuts, he's mean."

Leora patrols the bar, refreshing beverages, giving change, answering the phone, serving the growing congregation of faithful pool league followers. Sonny returns, placing a cardboard holder containing a coffee, a tea, stirrers, handfuls of creamers, and packets of sugar. He lifts his coffee from the cardboard carrier. "I'll be in the office if you ladies need anything."

Leora mixes her coffee, doing a taste test before taking a few gulps of the hot brew. *Mmmm, tastes like more. Good to the last drop.*

Tom orders another shot. "I just wanted to stop. Well, Salvatore asked me to check on you. He'll be glad to hear you are working. He's worried about you and Sydney. He left for Italy this morning and won't return until after the holidays. It was planned a month ago. He's sorry to hear about such a nice boy and wants to apologize for bringing sadness to your doorstep." Tom chases the Ginger Brandy with the Mick.

Leora and Sydney glance at each other with narrowed eyes, pursed lips, torqued jaws furrowed brows; their facial features scrunched almost to a point of grotesque.

"He didn't do anything," Leora states through her distorted facial expression. She turns to Tom. "They don't bother me sittin' at that table. Business is business. Do what cha got a do."

"Yeah," Sydney adds, "their money's green wherever they sit. I'm in!"

"Oh, you mean the apartment," Leora says, glancing at Tom. "It's ah 'ight." She eyeballs the bar before turning to her dear friend.

Tom locks eyes with her. His gaze is solemn. "No. He said your doorstep. He said he should not have sold you the house."

Sydney stands. She cocks her head sideways, playing the blonde card. "Why? It's a perfectly good house. It has a hole in the roof someplace, but it's a nice house."

"Well, it's not so much the house as it is what's inside. The previous owner is believed to have left incriminating evidence behind from illegal activities."

"Illegal activities?" Leora swallows hard affixing a blank stare on her face. Her mind races. Her heart joins in. *Ya can't trace cash! That's what Tom had said before! Holy shit! Did Papa find the money? They know about the typewriter! Does he think Griff has it? Does he think we have? He can have it! I hope he comes back with a bunch of whoop-ass goombas!*

Sydney gets it, too. She is not just another pretty face. "Evidence? What? Wallpaper? There wasn't anything in the house when she moved in just walls and a roof." It is the truth. Back then it was walls and a roof. Just recently it became a half truth because they didn't know then what they know now. The best friends are cautious. The partners in crime go from dumb blondes to stupid broads and say nothing about the truck full of furniture. Let sleeping dogs lie.

Tom orders a drink for Butley. He sits back, crossing his arms, waiting for Leora to complete her duties. "Papa emptied the apartment upstairs Saturday and let Griff move in yesterday." He uncrosses his arms, leaning forward. "That is, after Gia and her friends got done picking through all of it." If Tom is fishing, he is out of luck because Leora and Sydney do not bite, flinch, or even blink. They do nothing to throw themselves into this mix; this ready-made nightmare.

"Stink it up, Gia," Leora quips.

"Yeah," Sydney adds, blinking, "I'm surprised there was anything left to move after she and her friends got done rummaging."

The tavern resembles closing time as first place Papa's and fans stream out of the establishment for the last match of the first half with the second place Fun House. Tom stands, adjusting his Wranglers, sliding the change from the Hamilton into the beer well. "Hey, listen, I want to give you a heads-up. Griff was dragged out of the club early Sunday morning and questioned." Both of the girls think back to the fog and the police cars. "He was in the club with his new girlfriend, giving the impression you are his old one. He was acting like a victim. He said he didn't do anything wrong and produced a note. The Feds verified it was typed on the missing typewriter. He probably sent it to himself, but he says it's a setup! The New York fellas did it! He's draggin' them into it yet again! Hell, he's draggin' them down here! Mark my words! And you! He told them you were the target because they don't know he dumped you!"

Leora and Sydney are beside themselves, mouths wide, eyes wide; their minds sorting the sordidly. The brunette attacks her duties like Grant took Richmond. It does nothing to distract her mind. *The note! The note! The note!* She is going to be sick. She rushes to the ladies' room.

Sydney pops from her stool, shuffling off to tend bar. *The note! The note! The note!* She washes the seemingly endless array of glassware; washing, thinking, washing, thinking. She fills the stainless steel drain. She empties ashtrays, wiping the bar down, patrolling the handful of patrons. Butley points to Tom.

Leora returns. "Thanks, Sis."

"Yepper," Sydney answers, pulling the ginger brandy from the speed rack, scooping a shot glass off the drain and standing in front of Tom.

Tom declines. "Are you all right?" He watches pale Leora leaning on the bar, giving him a masquerade smile. "You oughta go home and lay down." He glances at Sydney. "Both of you."

The barmaids stand in silence, afraid of saying too much, not enough. Their vibes are having a field day.

"I'm ah'ight," Leora states.

"Me, ta," Sydney adds.

"Well, in the long run it just might be safer at home. I think it's gonna get messy. He's out there where the air is rare. He does and says what ever suits his purpose." Tom looks at his watch. "Listen, he did seven years for killing his younger cousin, Frankie Flowers. When Griff's father, Serafino Griffonetti died, the families absorbed all of the man's, ahhh, holdings so to speak. But in Griff's greed-induced mind, what they did was steal his inheritance, not to mention the fringe benefits and elaborate lifestyle that came to an end with his father's passing. The cops started finding bodies on both sides of the fence. He was killin' cops and blamin' his own, killin' his own and blamin' the cops. He was ruthless. The families cut him loose. Like I said, he killed his own cousin, thinkin' Frankie got everything 'cause he worked closely with his Uncle Serafino, Griff's dad, while jackass Griff was out in left field most of the time, wreaking havoc and runnin' up lawyer fees. Frankie had maintained that position after his uncle's death, not only 'cause he knew the ins and outs, but he was trustworthy. He wasn't handed anything. His poor wife miscarried their only child two weeks after his murder. The families turned their backs on Griff. He had nowhere to hide. They practically handed him over to the Feds on a silver platter. He went to jail unprotected. But he did a safe and sound country club incarceration and continues his life of Riley. He's got'em by the short hairs. Told you he's not squirrel food." Tom pulls at his sleeve with one finger, exposing his watch. "Well, I'm gonna run down the Fun House before heading home. You guys be careful. Don't take any wooden nickels." He pats the bar, pulling keys from his black three quarter-length leather on his way out. Air pressure fills the foyer, forcing the inside door slightly open to escape as Tom exits the building.

The tavern resembles 2:15 a.m. with its handful of patrons. Leora doles out the scatter of upside down shot glasses abandoned by the pool league and their fanatical fans dispersing them to the minuscule sum of leftover customers.

"Boy, oh, boy. He's just a fountain of knowledge," Sydney says, folding her arms in front of her, leaning back against the taps.

"Well, he knows a few people. Yo, Sis, that's one thing about Tom, he don't blow smoke. I don't know if he was givin' us a heads-up or what? It's like Papa extinguished all paths to us, like coverin' our asses, 'cause now it could be anyplace—Gia, her friends, the beach, a friend of a friend."

Sydney breathes deep. "Maybe they do think Griff sent the note to himself! Oh, my God! I thought I was gonna throw up, too!"

"I swear if anybody comes in here with a New York accent, I'm pointin' upstairs!"

"I thought about runnin' home and gettin' the damn thing! Are you thinkin' what I'm thinkin'? I mean, like they might be thinkin' we have it and don't know we have it, ya think?" Sydney sighs. "Well, Papa trusts 'im, doesn't he?"

"Yeah, well, they go back a ways, hell, come ta think of it, eighteen, nineteen years. In fact, Tom told me he took Papa to his first Businessman's Annual Cadillac Dinner Banquet. It was like a hundred and fifty dollars a plate. If they pull your ticket, you win a Caddy. Papa won. No more sleepin' in the apartment."

Sonny emerges from the office. "I'll be back." He searches his pants pockets, his jacket pockets, coming across the bar keys, his house keys, finally finding his car keys.

Sydney heads to the ladies room. "Go Papa's!"

"I'll be here." Leora yells, slipping empty longnecks in the cases under the sink. "Usual time is good, really. See ya." She walks to the back register, lowering the decimals on Deep Purple a notch or two before serving Marie her usual glass of beer. The music seems louder in the empty room without piles of ears to absorb the sound. *Could be me. Who gives a rat's ass?*

All watering holes, from the finer establishments down to neighborhood joints, have their regulars: a helpful Crow, a lost Simon, a lonely Marie. Papa's lonely Marie neither drives nor smokes. She is a war bride, now almost sixty and a widow, with her cockney accent about as thick as when she first arrived. She holds on to the bar, sliding her Humpty Dumpty torso onto the stool, making herself comfortable. She slips her arms out of her black mohair coat, leaving it to hang from her bar stool seat, then pats her pale red-dyed hair as if utilizing the ten-by-ten mirror across the room on the far wall. The permanent from weeks ago still holds curls in need of relaxation and in need of new color as tell-tale gray frames a friendly face etched by time with its wrinkles of wisdom.

"Carrie's not back yet," Marie states, her faded blue eyes darting back and forth. She busily lays a flimsy palest pink acetate scarf on the bar to extract bunched up bills from her nurse's uniform. She carefully separates a one dollar bill from the heap of money for her glass of beer, then shoves the wad into her black patten leather pocketbook, snapping it shut. Her gold wedding band winks in the white light from the TV screen. Leora places sixty cents by the English woman's glass, then leans on the beer well in front of her.

Marie Coucci resides in Buckman Village in the same house she shared with her husband for thirty-four years; the home where they raised three children and in which Marie continues holiday traditions for her seven grandchildren. She is comfortable with her simple life, work, market, even her doctor within walking distance if need be. She knows a few things about a few things. She is in the loop—from her husband's relatives in Lennox Park, to her friends in Highland Gardens, to her coworkers at Sacred Heart Hospital; she hears the buzz, she knows the buzz, and she repeats the buzz if she likes you. She likes Leora.

"Little Quinn keeps checking for their black Blazer." Love light dances in her eyes, meeting Leora's gaze as the slightest of smiles brightens her face at the mere mention of her grandson, Quinn, Jr. He is eleven years old. He is friends with Carrie's youngest, Clem. Both were friends with Leora's son.

The English woman's wide mouth puts Leora in mind of Martha Ray while her voice sounds a little like Katherine Hepburn. "He's a bit upset.

He knows somebody stole Clem's brother's truck." She drains her draft, pulling a dollar bill from her pocketbook, snapping it shut.

Is it better for the young to draw their own conclusion, or is it better to tell them the real one? No, let them live in their world, their limited world, their innocent world. "Tell Quinn I borrowed the truck. I have it." Leora says from the tap, refilling Marie's glass.

"That's jolly good," Marie tells the brunette. She takes a swig of beer as Leora places forty cents by her coaster. "Over on Chestnut, right? Stephen Lister's old place, Nancy's son?"

English Manners

$\mathcal{L}$eora nods blinking, thinking, blinking, thinking. *Nancy, Nancy, where have I heard that name before? Why does that sound so familiar?* She eyeballs the ladies room, watching for Sydney.

"She was a very nice woman." Marie sips her draft.

"Oh. You knew her?"

"Oh, but she's quite alive, I believe. She's in Fair Acres geriatrics care. She's been there a while, I guess nigh on to six years."

"Oh, do you visit her?"

"Oh no, I only knew her from being brought to the hospital a few times, you know, for emergency medical care—a broken toe, pneumonia, or the time she broke her leg. Bit of a prude that one, but then again she had Alzheimer's." Marie drains her glass, sliding it slightly forward to the brunette. Leora refills her glass, taking exact change. "After the cast was removed, Mrs. Lister stayed with us about twelve weeks, you know, for physical therapy. It made sense, you know, instead of transporting her back and forth to the facility. That was maybe three years ago. She spoke of Stephen all the time. As far as I know, he was her only child." Marie sips foam from her glass. "And the Beatles, she loved the Beatles, too. That's all she talked about—Stephen, The Beatles, Stephen, The Beatles, she didn't want to forget them. Did I mention she had Alzheimer's? Stephen brought her a rather large picture of them, you know, The Beatles. She wrote their names above each one and had it hanging on the hospital wall across from the foot of her bed while she recuperated. She did the same thing with a photograph of her son, you know. She kept that by the telly. She was afraid she would forget him, too. She wrote his name above his picture. I imagine by now she doesn't even realize he has passed." Marie smiles at Leora. "She thought I was the Queen Mum."

Leora smiles back, spotting Sydney bent over between her stool and the bar.

"Wide load!" Leora yells, coming up behind her.

"Shit! Do you believe it? I dumped this pocketbook again, well, almost, well I might as well have, a lipstick rolled . . . (grunt) over . . . (grunt) here." Sydney stretches, grasping the Simply Mauve colored tube on the foot ledge. Thud! She bangs her head on the overlapping cherry wood bar.

"Oh, my God! What the—! Are you ah'ight?"

Sydney stands up straight with one eye tightly shut.

"You're an accident lookin' for a place ta happen!"

The redhead smiles. "I'm happ'nin'."

Leora places a finger perpendicular to her lips, pointing to the end of bar. Sydney nods in agreement. "Is it still in the cabinet under the charcoal pit?"

"Say what?" Sydney blinks her watery eyes, following Leora to the jukebox.

"What's in the cabinet?"

Leora shakes her head, slipping two quarters in the jukebox—two plays for a quarter, five for fifty cents. Nat King Cole croons the "Christmas Song." "I don't know what came over me. I'm so fed up. I'm disgusted. Let 'em chew on that a while. Yo, Sis, what do we know about a Nancy? Didn't we hear that name before?"

"Nancy, Nancy . . ." Sydney squints. "Yeah, Nancy . . . Nancy . . . Let me think."

"Marie was talkin' to me about Quinn. Remember Quinn, Tink's little buddy? Marie's grandson? He thinks somebody stole Crow's truck. I told her no, I have it. And she said, 'You do? Where, over at Stephen's, Nancy's son's old place?' She said this Nancy has Alzheimer's. She loves the Beatles. Why does that name ring a bell?"

Old man Slats waves and points to the television. It is nine o'clock, time for Monday night football.

Leora maneuvers behind the bar, aiming the remote at the television, changing the channel just in time for the kick off between the Baltimore Colts and Los Angeles Rams. She turns the volume up a bit.

"It is tails. The Baltimore Colts win the toss," Howard Cossell announces. "The Colts have opted to receive."

Leora patrols the remaining customers before joining her co-conspirator. She gives the finger to the buggd end of the bar and sits on the other side of the opening.

Marie waves a good night to the barmaids, almost running into Chief Sill in full uniform, including an unlit White Owl stuffed in his pie hole. He holds the door for her then walks to the bar. Leora meanders to him, trying to slow her pounding heart.

"There's nothing wrong, everything's fine. No one broke into your house." He glances at Sydney.

"Well, they gotta bring it in before they can take it out." Leora gives the chief a pasted cheese grin. "What are you doin' in this neck of the woods?" she asks, trying to lighten the mood. "What, are you lost?" She breathes through her cheese grin.

Chief Sill leans forward, removing his cigar, speaking in a low tone. The inquisitive brunette leans on the beer well. "No, no, no, I just wanted to let you two ladies know that our get-together the other night was . . . well . . . was . . . well . . . I was told the two detectives were . . . well . . . they weren't detectives." He stares at his cigar, rolling it between his thumb and two fingers. "The two detectives were . . . well . . . the two real detectives . . . well . . ." He stops rolling, bucking his eyes to look her square in hers. "Uhhhhhh, the real ones, uhhhhh, were found in the trunk of their car, somewhere in New Jersey." Now he stands up straight, patting his shirt pocket, rooting for a pack of matches.

Leora stands erect, pinching her upper lip, smoothing her philtrum, eyes bugging, breathing labored, concern awash on her face. She scans the five customers' beverages.

Chief Sill leans forward again. "Oh, no, no, no, not that. They were a little embarrassed and a little cold, but they were locked in the trunk nonetheless." He pops the cigar back in his mush.

Leora turns in his direction. "So who were we talkin' to the other night?"

Chief Sill removes the stogie. "Let's just say people you probably won't ever see again, but if you do, lock your door and call us. I don't want to alarm you, that's not my intention, just a little friendly advice."

The chief peers over top of his spectacles, meeting Leora's wide eyes. "I'm just sayin'," he says, looking around the immense room, "I'm on at midnight. Bill will be patrolling periodically. Four-nine-four—"

"Six-eight-double zero." Leora finishes the phone number.

"Yeah. Good," The chief stammers. "I don't expect they'll be back around. Well, not to your place, well, not them anyway. Like I said, if you hear anything or see any questionable activity . . . well . . . we're around, and you know the number."

Leora plasters a smile on her face, shaking her head affirmatively, watching Chief Sill head out the door.

"Touch down! Baltimore!" Howard Cossell announces.

How are ya gonna answer the phone if you're out patrollin'? Leora walks double time to the opening, tugging Sister Syd's sweater as she trots to the jukebox. She summons Robert Palmer, D-3, then repeats her informative discussion with Chief Sill.

"So its like Tom said earlier," Sydney states. "Shaun's a whack-o! Bad enough they wanna fit him in cement shoes, but now they wanna come down here and do it! And then there's noodle face and snake ear at the club! Holy shit!! We're surrounded!"

Goo Goo, Doc, and Chick walk toward the girls from the rear entrance. His somber mood is about to become even more somber as Sydney makes a shushing sign. She pushes C-9, "Free Bird", then begins. The girls are like a tag team; one catches her breath while the other continues, each injecting a detail here and there. Goo Goo stares at the floor, listening with jaw torqued, slightly rocking back and forth, heel to toe. He glances at Sydney then Leora, nodding his head with a forced half-smile, half-sneer. He is steaming. Upon his arrival on Sunday evening from Las Vegas, last night as a matter of fact, the sad news of Crow had been quite unnerving—there in the airport, to say the least, but now from the horse's mouth with details of an elopement, a baby, Leora's car in New York, the probability of dealing with yet another hidden transmitter. Well, now Goo Goo can hardly contain his festering anger. He refuses drinks, citing, just passing by on his way to something or other with keys in one hand and rubbing his forehead, his chin, his neck with the other. He jingles his keys, thinking. Leora walks behind the bar, stretching to snag Slats's empty glass sitting behind the taps. Two more customers depart. The brunette empties ashtrays, washes glasses, and wipes the bar down. She walks to Sydney, sitting alone, and plops on the stool opposite her. Goo Goo and company are gone.

"Goo Goo is so pissed," the redhead mouths the words to her best friend.

Marcie flits through the front door. She hustles to the charcoal pit, rooting in cabinets, slamming doors. She waves to the best friends on her way to the ladies' room. The girls pivot, facing each other with mouths open, blinking at the ladies' room, at each other, at the end of the bar, at the ladies room, at each other, at the end of the bar . . .

"Yo! Sis!" Sydney slaps the bar. "Ya know what I was thinkin'? Not at the charcoal pit, and don't even say BMW." Sydney shrugs, rolling her eyes.

"Oh, no?" Leora shakes her head, looking six ways to Sunday; the three patrons, the front door, the ladies' room.

"Yo, Sis! Remember?" Sydney nods. "Oh, hey, Momma, I didn't tell ya? Damn it! Stupid me! An empty beer box in the walk in." Now Leora shrugs.

Goo Goo reappears, walking to the bar while Doc and Chick slip a couple of dollar bills in the jukebox, playing albums of Frank Sinatra, Sammy Davis, Jr., and the big bands. They join their boss at the bar, who is offering condolences to the girls, ordering beverages, and smacking the bar in time with Tommy Dorsey's "In the Mood."

Marcie bolts from the bathroom, straight for the bar. "Hi." Her voice is demure, sickening demure. "Hi."

"Don't cha just love this song?" Goo Goo asks, clapping his hands.

Marcie squeezes through the gathering. "Excuse me," she tells Leora, standing on the end of the wooden slats at the opening, with a hand on either side of the bar, basically in Marcie's way.

"Oh, what cha fart?" Goo Goo chortles, grinning at Marcie with a fixed gaze.

Sydney turns her stool in Marcie's direction. She is so ready. She wants to nail her. *Gimme some o' this.*

"Hi, Goo Goo," Marcie purrs. She jiggles her head, shades of Rhonda, patting the bottom of her page boy do, basically ignoring her coworkers. "I seem to have misplaced my ring. I was in here cleaning on Sunday, and I thought I took it off over there." She points to the pit. "I guess I left it back here." She points behind the bar, squaring her shoulders, meeting

Leora's eyes with a cold, calculating stare just like her brother's. Leora's whimsical expression morphs into a solemn stare, jaw set, eyes fixed with a here-I-am answer. She scratches an eyebrow with her middle finger. Jammer enters through the front door, high-stepping, lisping, drawing all eyes, interrupting the stand off. Impressed with the lack of customers, he is almost distracted from his specific mission doled out to him four times by Griff. Marcie catches him in her peripheral vision, immediately shuffling to him, intercepting him in front of the walk-in box. She stands stiff as a board, arms straight down by her sides, hands clenched.

"He told me to get, um . . ." Jammer slurs his words a bit, swaying like a cattail trying to remember his mission, "I need, uh, space of beer, no, no, wait a minute, uh, a six pick but not really." He leans toward her, wobbling, giving her an exaggerated wink.

Marcie grits her teeth, pulling him to the front door, telling him to keep it down. She looks a lot like her brother, especially when the veins bulge in her neck. And she is a lot like her brother too, in more ways than one. With arms crossed in front of her, she leans forward, inches from Jammer's face, still gritting her teeth, telling him to whisper.

Goo Goo stands at the opposite side of the opening, clapping his hands and conducting Doc and Chick in another sing-along. He waves the girls over. Leora stands behind the bar while Sydney slides onto the end bar stool. "Listen," he says, watching Marcie and Jammer. "She's a nut case," he announces in a low voice, watching the one-sided argument. "She's as crazy as her brother. She don't need this job. She got money—her dead husband's. That's a different story." He reaches for his drink. "Her and her brother are from New York. He got in some really deep shit up there. But he covered his ass. That's why he lived through jail, why he's still breathin'."

"He was in jail a long time ago. Isn't that stuff old?" Sydney asks.

"Blaze, there's no time limit on murder. Murder's murder. You can get charged with that anytime."

Murder. Well, that certainly puts it in perspective. Just the word itself, ominous, let alone coming from Goo Goo's lips. He, well . . . Goo Goo is fun, funny, at the club, here at work, even when they stayed at the airport motel. Fun is fun, and business is business—the flip side the darker side, the ugly side.

"Look, the bottom line is he wrote down, you know, shit. Cops on the take, hits, payoffs, names, business details, you know, all the stuff like, you know,, tellin' shit like well, you know, detailing where bodies are buried and the guns that were used, well . . ." Goo Goo spies Marcie and Jammer, then leans closer. "You know, he kept a lot of the guns that were used. He never threw 'em in the river. They can be matched to any homicide in the last ten years or so in New York. All they need is a slug, and it sends the fuzz right to New York's doorstep. It's like he's untouchable. His apartment was tossed up the line. That's why he moved in with his sister. Her place was trashed, too. He was livin' in a motel room. Just a matter of time before they'll come sniff 'im out down around here."

"Well, they are down around here! They were at the house, sittin' right at the table with us and the Trainer police!" Leora swallows hard.

"Yeah, these guys had New York accents and said they were detectives. But the real ones were locked in the trunk of their car!"

Goo Goo's face announces disbelief.

Leora nods profusely. "Seriously! Trainer cops were here to give us a heads-up! He left not five minutes before you came in the first time!"

Goo Goo gulps his VO and water, concern settling across his face. "That ain't good. You know, the mayor hasn't been at his office for over two weeks. He calls in. What's that tell ya? You haven't seen 'im, have ya? Ya ain't goin' to. His family's AWOL, too. Shit is gonna hit the fan, I'm tellin' you. You'd think he'd get out of Dodge and take it with him. I'd be long gone." He glances at Marcie, hawking Jammer inside the walk in. "There's only one thing that would stop me from leavin' for parts unknown."

Marcie is out of patience, her arms crossed, tapping her foot, getting more and more perturbed watching Jammer inside, spending most of his time trying to keep his balance instead of checking for a six-pack, no, a case, no, what was it? She cuts her eyes toward the end of the bar. Doc and Chick sing "New York, New York" with Frank Sinatra as Goo Goo, clapping his hands in time with the music, pirouettes.

"Yeah, you couldn't leave Angie." Sydney smiles.

"What?" Goo Goo spins back around, facing the bar.

"The one thing that would keep you from parts unknown. Angie, right?" Leora questions.

"Angie? I don't think so, Irish. A woman is a downfall. Ask Doc." He glances over at Doc and Chick with a wide grin.

"Oh! I'm tellin' Eva!" Sydney taunts.

"They are. Look at Adam and Eve. Look at the movies, gangsters, politicians, even the cowboys. All done in by broads, except the cowboy who rides off into the sunset with his horse." Goo Goo smirks.

"What's so big about that? He ends up with a nag," Leora states giving Sydney a high-five.

Goo Goo shakes his head, laughing. "You girls. Oh, here Blaze." He pulls a ballpoint pen from the inside pocket of his coat, holding it in front of her. It is a Chippendale, blond, blue eyes, upside down in black and white, swim trunks and a black collar with a white bow tie.

Sydney cocks her head. "It's a Chippendale! Yo, Sis! He did! He got me a Chippendale! She takes the pen from Goo Goo. "Here, let me write you a thank you!" She writes in the air then holds the pen right side up by the tip, admiring the hunk. "Look a washboard! I love washboards! Look at his little bow tie and his little . . ." The swim trunks slowly peel away. Leora and Sydney bump heads, laughing hysterically.

Leora holds Sydney's hand still. "Look! A natural blond!" She stares at the little man. "Oh, well, I'd rather be tickled to death than choked to death!" All five roar with laughter, interrupted by the front door. A customer. No, just Hector. Beginning his message to Marcie, he, too, becomes silent, surveying the empty room. But he is buzzed, not pickled, and continues.

"What in the hell is he doin' inside there?" Goo Goo whispers.

"Tryin' ta stand up," Leora answers. "But if ya ask Marcie, she'll tell ya he's huntin' for her damn ring."

"Yeah, 'cause she's gonna say she must a lost it in there "yesterday" cleanin' up "yesterday" and loading the beer cases yester day!" Sarcasm raises Sydney's voice.

Leora laughs and tries drowning out her best friend. Goo Goo conducts his goombas in a chorus of "The Candy Man", eyeballing the fiasco at the walk-in.

"It's a load all right," Leora states on her way to the front of the bar.

Goo Goo drains his glass. Ice cubes tinkle. "Ah, Blaze, what's she lookin' for? What'd she lose?"

"Her teeth, if I can help it."

Goo Goo bucks his eyes, throwing Ben Franklin on the bar. "Ah, Blaze, calm down now. Come on, get us a drink. You too. Get everybody a drink."

Reluctantly, Sister Syd meanders behind the bar. She refreshes Doc and Chick, takes care of Goo Goo, and grabs herself a Mick. "Yo, Sis, give 'em a drink on Goo Goo. You in or what?"

Leora holds up a wait-a-minute finger, backing up her three customers—Slats and a young couple. But Sydney does not see Leora, let alone her finger. How can she when she is hawking the lowlife? She twists the cap from the bottle, lost in thoughts of fifty ways to rearrange Marcie's face.

". . . ze! Blaze! Spit it out," Goo Goo says.

Sydney comes back to reality. "What?" She sits an upside down shot glass in the beer well for Leora.

"Spit that bottle cap out!" Goo Goo tries to get her undivided attention.

The redhead takes a deep breath, cocking her head at him. "Twist-off. They're twist-off caps." She rolls her tongue in her mouth.

"Okay, Blaze." He smiles at her. "There for a minute, I thought you chewed it off like you were the Bionic Woman or somethin'." He smiles again.

Sydney makes a right-handed fist then a left one. "Six months or sudden death?"

Leora totals Goo Goo, ringing him up and placing his change from the C note at his seat on the other side of the opening.

Marcie opens the glass door of the walk-in, yelling at Jammer. "You gotta go!" Jammer turns, facing Marcie—well, in her direction. "Get out!" She yells, with all patience gone, flailing her arms, screeching like the Wicked Witch of the West. Jammer walks into the glass wall. He feels his way to the door, more so for balance than anything else, climbing out and shrugging his shoulders, already forgetting why he was ever in there in the first place. Still flailing and screaming, she points to the door, sending Heckle n' Jeckle on their way. "Two heads are better than one, my ass," Marcie mumbles. "Assholes."

"Did you find it?" Leora throws a coaster on the bar, sitting a gin and tonic with a slice of lime wedged on the rim. Marcie's answer is unimportant. "This is on Goo Goo," she yells over her shoulder. She would rather crawl on broken glass than engage in a conversation with Griff's sneaky ass, pompous sister.

Marcie cuts her eyes at Goo Goo, disgust and anger apparent on her face. Goo Goo gives her a thumbs-up, taking a slug of VO and water, never losing eye contact, staring her down, sending her on her way. The vacuum packed air forces the inside door open as she exits the building.

"She knows." Sydney talks softly. "We messed up."

"Yep." Leora sighs. "Hector just told her. Stink it up us."

"How stupid was it to bug this bar? Dumb bitch." Goo Goo walks toward the shuffleboard, summoning Chick.

It was pretty stupid. But what about the wild goose chase? That was pretty stupid, too. It's over here, it's over there! What were they thinking? They might as well have told them we got what you want. They should have played it cool, keeping them guessing. Hopefully, Marcie flew upstairs, ranting about Goo Goo. Or maybe Griff is screaming, "I told ya so!" Maybe he and Marcie are going at it. Maybe pigs fly.

Goo Goo and Chick walk back to the bar. "Like I said, there's only one thing that would stop me from bookin'," Goo Goo says in a boisterous tone, pointing to the end of the bar, nodding. Leora nods, moving aside for Goo Goo. "And it's the same thing that's stoppin' that dumb son-of-a-bitch upstairs. The money – he ain't got it!" He roots under the end of the bar, ripping the transmitter from its hiding place. He scrunches the duct tape and contents in his hands, passing the wad to Chic, patting his pocket for his firearm before sending Chick out the back for a disposal.

The girls are speechless, unable to move, twin statues with jaw-dropping expressions. "There, that's better. Ah, give us a drink." Goo Goo throws a fifty on the bar in front of Blaze. He smiles at the brunette. "Ah, you look like you could use one, too, Irish. Get one for yourself."

Leora becomes mechanical, reaching for Goo Goo's glass on the other side of the opening. She refreshes his VO, refilling Doc, then pours two shots of Galliano for her and Blaze, downing hers before walking to the front of the bar, giving rounds to the three patrons. Slats refuses. It is half-time. He will be at home for the second half of the football game. Three customers enter and stand at the bar. Leora flips coasters in front of each one.

"Where's everybody at?" the one with a beard asks.

"What were you raided?"

That's all I need. "Our pool team is playing away. They're in first place."

"Damn! What's the whole bar on the team?" He shakes his eggbeater hairstyle from his face.

"Would you like a beverage?"

"Oh, I don't know." The bearded man leans forward, looking at his co-drinkers. "This place is dead."

The front door opens. Two Chester police officers enter. One walks over to the bar while the other walks to Guiliano Giangiordano.

Leora slides her fingers through the front of her hair, holding the top of her head, assuming the position of statue again, watching the officer approach Goo Goo. She snaps her attention to the officer in front of her, catching the three would-be patrons, departing like yesterday in her peripheral vision.

"Can I help you?"

"No, thanks, I'm fine." He also proceeds to Goo Goo.

Leora spies Chick reentering the establishment, walking to the bar on the far side of Sydney. She makes a fresh Bacardi and Coke, placing it in front of him. Two officers appear from the rear entrance. Chick orders a shot for Sister Syd. Leora dumps Chick's drink from alongside Doc, washing the glass, stealing a look-see at Goo Goo as she wipes the bar, never giving the slightest inclination it belongs to Chick. The front door opens. Two more officers enter.

Leora hustles to the aperture. "Do you need something?" she asks. One officer raises his hand in a no-thank-you gesture while scanning the room. The other smacks his partner's arm, pointing to the back of the room. They exit the way they came in.

Leora gives a little quickstep to the end of the bar, breathing deep, eyeballing the uniforms.

Goo Goo stands alongside Sydney, placing both arms around her shoulders, pulling her to him sideways, kissing her on her head then letting go. "See ya later, Blaze." He leans against the opening now, wrapping his right arm around her, pulling her toward the bar, kissing her on her head again. She sits frozen in place. He turns to his seat, walking over, pushing his leftover money into the beer well. "I'm gonna follow these guys to the police station." He turns back to face Sydney, throwing a fifty on the bar in front of her. "Give her a drink."

Leora grabs the dry bar towel hanging on the end of the bar, running it through her hands over and over out of sheer nervousness, watching Goo Goo and the blue quartet walk around the end of the charcoal pit out of sight. "What the hell was that? Are you shittin' me, mister?""

"Are they gone?" Sydney is still frozen in place.

"I think so." Doc walks past the pit. "I don't see 'em." He walks to the back.

Leora is concerned. "Yo, Sis, are you ah'ight?"

"Where's Chick? Chick! Come 'ere! Get it!"

Chick moves over to the redhead. "What's a matter?"

"My lap! Get it off my lap! Get it!"

He bobs and weaves for an eye spy. Sydney leans back. Chick lifts Goo Goo's thirty-eight from Sydney's lap. It disappears into his leather.

"Sweet Jesus!" Leora glances up the bar at her only two customers. The young girl is waving. Leora's rushes to the couple, meeting warm and friendly dark brown eyes.

"Sorry. I don't know your name. I hate yelling, 'Hey you.'"

Leora regroups. "That's okay. I've been called worse. Leora."

"Hi, Leora, my name is Pauline. This is my husband Dave."

Leora nods a hello, reaching for Pauline's glass.

"Oh, no thanks. We have to go. Do you know Bryce, Luke Bryce?"

"Yes," Leora answers.

"Bryce is my cousin. Can you tell him we stopped by? We gotta go."

"Sure. Dave and Pauline, right?"

"We stopped in to see his sister, and she said he would be comin' here after work to meet his girlfriend. That's not you, is it?" She gathers her waist-length hair to one side, slipping her coat on and slipping her leather bag over her shoulder.

Leora shakes her head.

"Well, we live out in Chester County."

"That's a hike."

"Yeah, we gotta go. Just let him know we were here. Nice talkin' to you."

"Same here. I'll let him know." Leora cleans up, then joins Sydney at the other end. Doc and Chick have left, too. The girls are alone.

"Yo, Sis, we in deep shit or what?" Sydney washes glasses.

"I don't know." Leora empties ashtrays.

"Sydney turns to Leora. "How 'bout Goo Goo yellin': He ain't got it? You know, Griff, the money? Ya think Goo Goo has it? You think he's had it all along?"

"I don't know." Leora sighs. "I do know we were almost rich 'cause I liked ta shit a gold brick when he ripped that out from under the bar. Thought I was gonna die. Maybe we'll get lucky, and they're stranglin' each other as we speak."

"I'll drink ta that. Take it outta here." Sydney lays the Grant on the bar for two shots. Leora rings them up, laying the change on the bar. Sonny bounds through the door, glancing at the television talking in the empty room.

"The Fun House didn't win, did they?" Leora asks shakng her head and licking her fingers.

"No," Sonny answers. "Neither did Shaun. I just saw him in the backseat of a cop car in the parking lot—in handcuffs."

Yo! Sis!

R-r-ring! R-r-ring! Leora pats the night stand. R-r-ring! She widens her patting area. R-r-ring! She leans on her right elbow, opening her left eye. R-r-ring! "All right, already!" Lunging at the night stand, she hits her mark, lifting the French phone's receiver from its cradle before it can continue its incessant demand for attention.

"Hello, yo, Eva." Leora lays her head on her pillow. "Huh? Not anymore." Her mind is drifting, slowly drifting off to . . . "Huh? Uh-huh . . . I'm awake . . ." She rolls over on her back with the coiled receiver cord stretched almost to its limit across her face. "What time is it?" she mumbles in monotone. "Huh?" She rallies, consciousness switching ears. "Huh? Two thirty? Oh, ten thirty . . . In the morning?" She yawns. "You're at work? Already? What?" Her eyes fly open. "What!" She kicks and flings the bedsheet and comforter with her feet and her one free arm while the other keeps a death grip on the receiver. "What! What was hit?"

"No! A hit! A hit!" Eva is beside herself. "They're callin' it a hit, for God's sake! I was gonna wait and call ya later, but I couldn't. You have to get one! It's only a little article. Page three, right hand corner down the bottom! And a shitty picture! I had ta let ya know! No details, ya know, it doesn't say anything like that, they can't I guess! But we know what they're talkin' about! It's like a heads-up! We can read between the lines! Lock your doors! Call the cops! I don't know, move!"

Sydney stands in the doorway, slipping into her leopard print robe.

"It doesn't say what happened?"

"No, it's just a little article of a man found in a car! Wait! Let me find it . . . Here! Sources report manner of death consistent with previous ongoing investigations! That means hit, doesn't it? It doesn't even say where! Or what kinda car! Just his name! But we know! I don't even know why I called ya! Upset I guess!"

The loss of Crow washes over Leora. She is queasy. "Is Doc there?" She changes the subject.

"Yeah, so's Chick! They're callin' it a hit! What the hell?"

Leora places her hand over the receiver. "Somethin's in the paper."

The front of Sydney's leopard print nightgown billows as she takes a seat on the bed alongside of her best friend. Wheezer appears in the doorway. He stretches his front legs, lifting his rear end into the air. He stretches again, this time straightening his hind legs, then sits with his tail curled around his feet, blinking at the disturbing commotion.

"What happened with Goo Goo?" Leora keeps the subject changed.

"Goo Goo's not back yet."

Leora's eyes widen. "What, since last night? Was he arrested?"

Eva talks to Doc then speaks to Leora. "Are you there?"

"Yeah."

"Doc says he doesn't know 'cause he hasn't heard anything from him."

"But when he left he wasn't in handcuffs. He went willingly. In fact, I think he drove his own car. Ask Doc, he's the one who walked to the backdoor and looked."

The whispering on the other end of the line begins again. "Yeah, Doc says he drove off in his car, a cop car in front of him and one behind him like an escor—"

Boom! Boom! Boom! A pounding on the front door startles everyone, cat included. Wheezer books toward Sydney's room, passing Bryce hustling and hopping down the hall, stepping into his jeans while trying not to drop his "friend" on the floor.

"I'll call ya back."

"What? What's goin' on?"

Boom! Boom! "I gotta go. Somebody's here." Looking a bit like who-did-it-and-ran, Leora straightens her blue nightgown, slipping into her black acetate robe from the cedar chest. With a quick scan out the bedroom windows, she fluffs her hair with her hands then ties her robe closed on her way down to the foyer.

Sydney turns the doorknob with Bryce standing by. She gasps. It is Pete. Sydney is taken aback. Tears fill her eyes. He looks so much like his older brother. She opens the storm door for him. "Come on in." She pulls on his coat sleeve. He takes one more glance at the red pickup as Sydney surrounds him.

Leora surrounds him, too, bursting into tears there in the foyer, there in the quiet. A newspaper falls to the floor, from under Pete's arm. Bryce refolds the disheveled Chester Times tucking it under his own arm and shoving his hand in his pocket.

Leora does not want to hear when the services are. "Come on in and sit down." She breaks the silence, the sadness.

"No, I gotta get back. Mom wanted me to—"

"How'd you get here? You want somethin' ta drink?" Leora knows she is babbling. She cannot help herself. She feels faint.

"I walked. No, Becka's with Mom. I gotta get back. Mom's not too good."

Leora's eyes fill. Oh, how she wishes to be any place right now other than here.

"Yo, Sis! The ring! Upstairs! Remember!" Sydney lifts tears from under her eyes with a finger and sniffles.

"That's right! Oh, my God!"

"I'll get it, Sis!" Sydney bolts up the steps.

Leora watches Sydney scale the stairway. "Oh, I'm sorry, where's my mind? Pete, this is Luke Bryce. Bryce, this is our Pete." The men shake hands. Wheezer loves against Pete's leg, purring his ass off. "Oh, excuse me, this is Wheezer's Pete."

The feline encourages Pete—no, downright demands—the nineteen-year-old to scoop him up. He complies, cradling him in his arms. Wheezer wiggles into an upright position, loving on Pete's chin, gently patting Pete's face for some sweet nothin'. Pete obliges, whispering to him, gently rubbing his chin, his ears, his head; then lifts him, draping him around his neck. Wheezer purrs contentedly loving on Pete's ear.

Sydney smiles, descending the staircase. "Hey, Tiger, you're happier than a cat coverin' shit." She hands the ring box to Pete. He opens it.

"That's your mom's," Leora states.

"Yeah, she was wondering what, uh, if, uh . . ." Pete swallows, gulping air, ". . . maybe it was stolen or somethin'."

Sydney dances around his brother's name, too, as if not equating his name with this ungodly nightmare will make it not so. "We were asked to hang on to it." She sighs. "We forgot."

Pete offers Wheezer his hand. The young cat borders on berserk, purring full throttle, loving on Pete's ear and reaching for his hand with both paws. "We went to New York on Sunday. All of us."

Leora grits her teeth, practically holding her breath.

"Mom and I came back yesterday afternoon."

Leora is confused. "What, you mean Monday afternoon?"

"You stayed over night?" Sydney asks.

"Had to, Mom was in the hospital."

Gasp! Gasp!

Pete swallows hard. "It . . ." He inhales. The words stick in his throat on tears. He swallows again—this young buck, Crow's broken sibling. He takes a different approach. "We went all the way up there, uh, it, uh . . ." The words still stick, a lump. He clears his throat to speak, "It ain't him." He exhales the words, barely audible.

Bryce has his arms full, maneuvering the best friends to sit down on the stairs before they fall down. Pete wipes his eyes as Bryce squeezes his shoulders, then yanks him into a headlock, now a bear hug, finally patting him on his back.

"It was creepy," Pete states. "Mom screamed then fainted, so they kept her overnight. The police were called. I told 'em it wasn't my . . . that ain't him."

"Not . . ." Now Leora exhales. No equating here either. "Who is it?"

"I don't know. When we left, they still didn't know, or they just weren't sayin'." He remembers the newspaper. "Oh yeah, Mom wants me to show you this." He feels under his arm for the newspaper. Bryce feels under his arm, too. It lays disheveled on the floor again. Bryce gathers it a second time, handing it to Sydney. "Look on page three."

Leora leads the way to the kitchen, flicking the switch to flood the already bright room with light. Sydney lays open the paper on the kitchen table. Three heads sink lower and lower to read the small article and gawk at the fuzzy black and white picture with Crow's given name in bold print.

Leora breathes through her mouth. So does Sydney. Eva is right. Vague details: a car, a man, snow, the execution-style of death, and a picture. A horrible picture. The girls bob and weave to reposition the glare of the light. A terrible picture no matter which way you look at it.

Pete unwraps Wheezer cradling him. The orange and white tabby wiggles to an upright position again, ready for round two.

"I don't believe this." Leora stands up in disgust.

"Yeah, they need a new photographer. That's awful."

"That doesn't even look like him." Leora hands the newspaper to Sydney. "Here, hold this up," she utters, questionable concern etched deep in her brow.

Sydney complies. Her best friend backs up, steps forward, backs up, steps forward, stands up straight, now leans forward, glancing at the picture at different intervals, intrigued with her peripheral vision of a split second image.

"Yo! Sis! Look at it and tell me if you see anything unusual, like familiar." Leora takes the newspaper, moving the article to and away from Sydney.

"Whaaat?" *Unusually familiar? Are you shittin' me? What am I lookin'at? What am I lookin' for? Gimme a hint.* Sydney walks forward and gawks. She steps backward and gawks. "What am I seein'?"

"Who are ya seein'?"

"Who?" Sister Syd gives her best friend a questionable look and glances at the paper, turning her head back and forth. Wait, there! A split second image! She looks at Leora then the paper. Yeah, there! Her peripheral vision! There again! Her eyes pop. "Oh, my God! Qh! My! God!" She grabs the newspaper from Leora, tilting it back and forth, to and fro. "Rob! It looks like Rob, doesn't it? It is, ain't it?"

"You know that guy?" Pete asks. "Does my brother know him?"

Leora looks closer at the picture tilting it north, east, south and west. Her mind races through the past. Rob burned the candle at both ends, so to speak, with Griff and Goo Goo. He never came in the bar when Crow was there, not to her knowledge, and was a pain in the ass around the house for a minute or two. "No," she says with conviction. She meets Pete's stare. "No."

"But you know 'im, right?"

"From a gas station," Sydney jumps in. "He did some work on my car." Guilt slowly crawls across her heart.

"My brother woulda fixed it."

Leora smiles. "Come on, it's a Ford."

Pete throws his head back chortling, nodding; remembering.

"It wasn't broke or anything just maintenance." The redhead points to the paper. "And he bought everything it needed: points, plugs, oil, brakes all the way around." Sydney bats her baby blues. "It cost me a ten dollar bill, a six-pack, a pizza, and a promise." She glances at Bryce and smiles.

Pete bucks his eyes at Sydney. "You wanna see my tights?"

"Tights? Come on, Batman?" Leora flattens his turned-up collar, compliments of his furry friend. "You don't even wear skivies anymore for fear of wedgies."

Pete blushes, closing his eyes. Bryce tussles his hair as the four share a fleeting moment of laughter. Now is a perfect time to jump on Crow for repeating a confidence, a perfect time, but instead reality jumps on Pete. Heartache stirs.

Reality invades Leora mind, too. *What about Crow? Oh, my God!* Emptiness seeps into her heart. "So what are they gonna do?"

"Uncle Scott's been on the phone a couple o' times this morning. I don't know. They messed up. They put that guy's driver license mug shot with my brother's name."

"Incompetence runs amuck." Sydney's voice is terse.

"As usual," Leora spits.

"Now what?" Sydney asks. "What did they say? What happened?"

"They sorta drilled us when we got there, you know, like if we knew you guys, if you were his girlfriend. I said no way, she's too old."

"Hey! Hey! Hey!" Leora scrunches her face.

Pete gives Leora a half smile. "They kept at it, so I finally told 'em you were our old babysitter."

Bryce covers his mouth, hiding his laughter.

"They asked if he ever knew some other people I never heard of, uh, like a Shaun, a Stephen somebody, I don't know, I said I never heard of 'em. They asked me if you knew 'em. I said, 'I don't know ask her'. And other dudes with big Italian names. Do I know 'em? No. Does she know 'em? 'I don't know, ask her'. I told 'em I never heard of 'em, he never mentioned any of 'em to me. They asked if he had a gun 'cause they found one. I told 'em no and Mom looked at me, and I said what? Not that I know of. This went down on our way to the morgue. The hell with that shit." The unpleasant experience is forever etched in his mind. "It's like a giant refrigerated room full of giant filing cabinets full of bodies. Next thing ya know, Mom's on the floor. Everybody was runnin' around, nurses, cops, doctors. I kept askin', 'So where's my brother'?" His question remains unanswered as the three join in a chorus of silence. "I just wanna . . . I need . . . What happened to my brother? I gotta go. Mom's bad."

And you're good? Leora rubs the back of Pete's jacket as all three walk him to the door, four counting Killer underfoot. Bryce runs back to the kitchen, retrieving the paper Pete had brought. Pete declines it, picking up his comrade one last time, nuzzling him, petting him before placing him on the steps.

Leora feels for her pocketbook under her jacket on the coatrack, digging through it. The truck key jingles against the Chevy emblem on the keychain as she places them in Pete's hand, curling his fingers around it.

Pete opens his fist.

"Gaw 'head. We're okay. We don't need it. Thanks." He needs a distraction for his helplessness, his feeling of inadequacy the overwhelming anxiety. "It has gas. You're good ta go." Bryce shakes Pete's hand after the girls take their turn offering hugs, words of encouragement, and vows of constant communication.

The warm and cold clash condensing on the storm door glass. Leora reopens it, watching Pete hesitating, now walking, stopping, now walking to the '62 red Chevy pickup. He leans on the edge of the roof with both arms, his head bowed against his brother's truck, a picture forever etched in her mind. She closes the doors.

Bryce is slipping into his black car coat.

"What's happ'nin'?" Leora about chokes on the words. She is despondent.

"I'm gonna fix her trunk."

Sydney smiles. ". . . And?"

Oompa! Oompa! Tears well in Leora's eyes.

"What?" Bryce gives Sydney a shit-eatin' grin. "What, that it's only gonna cost ya a pizza and a six-pack?"

Sydney's mouth is as wide as her eyes. She backs away from him full of laughter, refusing his advances, shaking her head as she pretends to struggle against the chase until she catches him there in his embrace. He nuzzles her hair, whispering as she taunts, laughing again, their fingers entwined, she, now whispering, permitting a kiss, now another.

Leora daydreams of her own chase not so long ago—his arms, his strength, his breath upon her skin, her name upon his lips, the smell of aftershave and leather, the warmth, contentment, the afterglow. She sighs, mustering a smile.

"Gaw 'head, say it." Sydney half-whispers, brushing her lips down his cheek, gently, tantalizing, against his lips, teasing.

"No, wait, let me guess." Leora plays along, blinking copiously, her eyes darting here, there, here, there, there, here. "Um, I know, it's gonna cost a pizza, six pack and ten dollars."

"No! No! No!" Sydney blinks at Bryce and then at Leora, a conspiracy. She tries to contain her laughter.

Leora blinks profusely. "Well, I know the promise part is out. You done broke that several times, Ginger Snap."

Bryce throws his head back with a boisterous laugh. "What am I gonna do with you two?"

"Love us," Ginger Snap answers, their hands still entwined. "But first you can start with . . ." she bucks her eyes at him.

"Who made the salad?" He cuts his eyes at her, smiling, pulling her to him.

Leora gets it. "I'm in! And croutons . . . on the side . . . lots. Oooo! And a roll?"

"Oh no, wait a minute." He turns to Sydney. "You didn't say anything about a roll." The devil dances in his eyes.

"Sister Syd rolls her tongue in her mouth. "That's right, and I didn't say anything about a roll in the hay either."

"Got it!" He pulls her to him. "Extra rolls!" He kisses her, unlocking his fingers to surround her with his arms. "See ya in a bit."

The girls prepare for the day, especially Leora, anticipating the salad and the buttered roll. She settles Wheezer on the back patio, refilling his dish and replacing his frozen water with fresh. She makes a coffee and a tea, joining Sydney upstairs. The aroma of skunk permeates Leora's nostrils as she steps precariously up the wooden hill.

Sydney, all spiffy, meets her best friend at the top of the stairs. She exhales, stuffing the doobie in Leora's mouth in exchange for the hot cup of tea. "I just lit it, Momma."

They walk to Leora's room. The brunette puffs then inhales, holding her breath. She pulls attire from her drawers: a purple bulky knit sweater, jeans, under garments, argyle socks of lavender and pink, throwing all of it on the bed while passing the joint back and forth. She walks around in circles a few times dis-com-boo-berated. "I gotta call Eva back." She sighs just thinking about the future conversation of Rob, Crow, the unanswered questions and neverending hypotheses.

"Okay, but light some place first, would ya?"

"Maybe I'll get dressed first."

"There you go, a plan."

Leora swigs her coffee, gathering her clothes from the bed, heading for the bathroom. By the time she emerges, she finds Sydney closing up the linen closet, can of spray in hand. "What's happ'nin'?"

Sydney studies pale Leora. "Your eyes look like two burnt holes in a sheet. You ah'ight?"

"No, I'm half left." Puking is never a fun time.

"You want me ta call Eva?"

"Nah-uh, it can wait."

"Yo, Sis, Tiger was in there again."

"Where is he?"

"I don't know. I started sprayin' he took off."

They hear a thud coming from Leora's room and find Wheezer jumping and swiping at the philodendron.

"Wheezer!" The mischievous feline flops. "What are you doin'? You already done mangled it once. It's too short." Leora starts toward him. He runs to his hideout under the bed. She walks around the cedar chest to the plant. Out springs Wild Wheezer tagging her feet, eyes dilated, ears perked as he prances sideways, back in the air, scooting back under the bed, coming out the other side, sprinting past the cedar chest, jumping on the windowsill, and eyeballing the plant from a closer view. Movement to his right, two o'clock! Tree branches seem to playfully sway outside the window. He wiggles his tail.

"Oh, you can go out," Leora tells him, "but not from up here."

"Yepper, you won't be gettin' back in there too soon."

"I know, let's put 'im out and watch what he does."

Wheezer pretends to be preoccupied with the tree branches, cocking each ear as he nonchalantly listens to their fading footsteps until he can no longer stand it. He leaps from the windowsill, racing through the hallway, passing them in the middle of the stairway. He wins, running to the den, then slinking back to lie in wait with only his perked ears and dilated eyes visible above the bottom step.

"I thought we were friends," Leora tells the feisty feline.

The pair descend one step, now another, now one more, a little closer . . . now! Wheezer leaps on the bottom step, arched back, walking sideways, now running up two steps, tagging the stragglers' feet now down, disappearing into the den.

"Yo! No more catnip for you, Tiger!"

"You're not suppose ta stalk friends." Leora hollers to the mischievous fur ball. "Speakin' of friends, did Bryce leave his 'friend'?"

"Yepper, in the kitchen, same spot different day, but just as comfortable."

"Well, what are ya gonna do if ya need to use it, Sis?"

"What do ya mean?" Sydney follows Leora to the kitchen, perplexed.

"Yo, Sis, you couldn't even take it off your lap last night."

Sydney smiles. "That's okay. That's where you come in."

"Nah-uh!"

"Hey, Momma! All I gotta do is picture you with a gun in your hand. I'd run!"

Leora smiles. "Yo, Sis, ya think it was the right thing ta do?"

"What?"

"Pete, you know, givin' him the key to the truck."

"Yepper, I meant ta tell ya that. He is so lost. And if Carrie's not okay with it, well, we'll go get it. It's not a problem. He breaks my heart."

"Doesn't he? It's so sad. This is horrible. But that really does look like Rob. Maybe it's a good thing everybody knows I wasn't that asshole's girlfriend. We have nothin' ta do with him."

"Neither did Crow."

They become silent, lost in their own thoughts. *Poor Pete. Poor Carrie. Poor Crow. Where is he? What happened to him? Poor Jennie.* Apprehension feeds their imaginations: sounds of echoing gun shots, yelling, disturbing images of exit eights, watery graves, blood; snowflakes falling in eyes with the blank stare of death.

"Wheezer! Come on let's go out!" Leora ends it for both of them. The nightmarish thoughts dissolve into conversation.

"Yeah, come on, Tiger!" Sydney walks to the backdoor. "Come on, we're gonna play follow the leader! Tag! You're it!"

"You believe it? When you want him for somethin' ya gotta hunt 'im down." Leora starts for the den. Wheezer whips past her to the door. "There you are."

You have to let a feline think it is their idea. Sydney does just that. She stands over him with her hand on the doorknob. "What?" She makes him ask.

He meows.

"You do? Okay, then, there ya go." She opens the door for his quick exit.

They high-five, standing at the backdoor on tiptoes to sleuth over the cafe curtains. Wheezer opens the screen door and scurries to the left side of the house. "Oh, my God, it's on! Come on!" Sydney opens the door.

"We need our coats!"

"We don't have time, the little shit."

They hustle out the door, walking to the left of the enclosed patio, peeking for the tabby who sits cocking an ear, staring them right in their faces.

"Oh! Shit! Hi!" Sydney yells. She waves at him.

Leora backs up, covering her mouth, stifling laughter.

"Bye!" Sydney calls. "I'm gonna go now." She steps backward out of his sight.

"You believe this?" Leora whispers.

Sydney shakes her head, rolling her eyes. They stand with their arms crossed. It is getting brisk. "I wonder if he has any dead animal carcasses in here." She uncrosses her arms, opening the right sliding door, exposing his bed. Something smells. She cannot quite put her finger on it, but it is not of expired prey, more like industrial. "What is that?"

Sydney leans toward the door and sniffs. "It smells like flea spray." She pops her head into the closed space, sniffing again. "I didn't spray him."

"No, he didn't smell like that in the house." Leora slides the other side open. The chemical concoction is more noticeable.

"What the hell? It's definitely flea spray." Sydney roots through the boots, tools, and gloves. She smells her hands. Nothing.

Leora's turn. She jostles the leggings, coats, hats, and scarves hanging up. "Oh, oh, oh. Is it gettin' stronger or is it me?"

"Is it live, or is it Memorex?" Sydney asks. "Oh, I smell it. It's live!"

Leora removes the outer wear from the hooks, dropping them. She stoops, sniffing on her way down, following the odor. She pushes the garments away from the paneling, exposing the hole Pete made when he smashed Charlotte's cousin with his sneaker. The flea spray continues wafting through the hole. "Whoa! What the hell!"

"What is it?" Sydney stoops alongside Leora.

"It's the hole in the wall from Pete's size twelve."

"Oh! Wow!" Flea spray's comin' outta there?" Confusion covers Sydney's face. She stands.

Leora's legs are about to go to sleep. She stands, too. "Yo, Sis, ya think this is how Wheezer's been gettin' in?"

"By George, I think you've got it! That little heathen!" Sydney stoops again, pressing her face to the hole. "It's dark, I can't see anything."

"Wait a sec." Leora fetches a flashlight from the kitchen. "Here, Sis."

Sydney peers through the hole again. "It's still black in there." She turns the flashlight off. "Hey, wait a minute. Isn't this house made of stone?"

Leora pats her best friend on her head. "Well, it ain't straw."

"And it ain't sticks." Sydney smiles. "And it ain't bricks." She shines the light around the edge of the hole, removing a piece of the damaged paneling smashed inside by Pete. She stands up, offering the piece of evidence to Leora. "And it ain't suppose to be drywall." Sydney leans into the closet, slapping the wall above the opening with an open hand. It makes a hollow sound. She leans to the right toward Wheezer's bedroom end and does the same thing. It makes a thud sound, a solid sound.

"Oh, that's right! Alice said Steve changed it back to a house from apartments. This is an entrance to the second floor apartment that use ta be here! He had it dry walled and paneled over! There should be steps back there, right?"

"Oh! The steps in the linen closet. I'll open the door. You shine the flashlight in."

"And then what? You can't come down the steps. Bryce said they're broken."

"Well, I'll check it out. I'll take my trusty Bic."

Leora kneels in the closet waiting, waiting, and waiting. It seems like an eternity. Bang! Bang! "Yo! Sis!" She shines the flashlight inside the hole.

"Yo! Momma!" The lighter's flame dances. "I feel a draaaft!"Sydney sings.

"Whew! What'd I use a half a can?"

Leora hears shuffling and creaking wood.

"Yep, two steps are missin'." She flicks her Bic and pauses at the last step before the break. "Shine the flashlight in here for a minute. I wanna see somethin'."

Leora blinks, leaning forward. "What the hell? I am!" she yells alongside the flashlight. She wiggles the light like a strobe. "It's right here! See?"

"No, are you shinin' it in here? You see my Bic?"

"No!" Leora hears shuffling, creaking wood, a plank tumbling down. "Are you ah'ight? Don't step on any nails, for God's sake! Yo, Sis?" She hears movement, now silence. "Sis? Come on! Knock it off! Enough of "The Twilight Zone!"

She holds the flashlight at different angles, peering into the hole. "Sis! Yo! Sis! You ah'ight?" A left hand appears right in front of Leora's flashlight. She screams bloody murder.

"Yo, Sis! It's me. Look! This is why we can't see each other." She opens her hand and slaps the blackness. It makes a smacking noise. "Here, gimme the light." Leora complies, slipping it through the ten-inch or so jagged hole into the hand. Leora has no depth perception. Dark is dark.

"Here." She shines the flashlight from above. "Look, see this?" Smack. Smack. The best friend's hand stops in the blackness. "Yo! Sis! It's a safe! I'm leanin' on a safe!"

Safe n' Sound

"A safe?"

"You believe it, Sis? A safe! And the biggest safe I've ever seen, might I add!"

Sydney shines the light back and forth on the metal monstrosity.

"It's hug with an 'e'!"

"Yeah, Papa's is a little bitty thing compared to this badass."

Leora sucks air. "Oh! Wow! That must be the one Alice was talkin' about!" she hollers down the stairs.

Sydney sucks air, too. "And Goo Goo! Remember he said only one thing would make him hang around!"

"Nah-uh! Ya think it's full of money?" Leora squeals like a little girl. "It's huuuge!"

"We're rich! Come on down!"

"Wait a minute. I'll be right back."

Sydney stands on the fourth step from the bottom at the break, aiming the   beacon of light onto the top of the stairs. Shining and waiting, shining and waiting for Leora who finally appears in the glow of the night light she removed from the front window, another flashlight under her left arm with an extension cord. Sydney wiggles the beacon of light like a strobe. "Yo! Sis! You're the next contestant on finders, keepers!"

Leora leans forward, holding the seven-watt over the steps, casting a tint of light.

"Holy shit! Sis! Ya look like the Statue of Liberty!" Their voices echo a tad bit in the hollow space.

"Don't she have a blindfold?" Leora asks. "Oh no, wait, that's the broad with the scales. The one you're talkin' about is French, a mada-my-zul." She smiles all to herself, slowly descending as far as the extension cord permits, two steps short of the separation. "This is as far as it will go. And that's with both extension cords."

"Ya shoulda grabbed my flashlight."

"Yo! Sis! I did!" the brunette answers, yanking it from under her arm and waving it at her. "The batteries are dead, of course! Do you know who you're talkin' to? As Usual, that's who! As Usual!"

"Well, you're talkin' to: An Accident Lookin' for a Place Ta Happen."

"Gee, people are gonna say: Hey, there they are: An Accident Lookin' for a Place Ta Happen As Usual?" Leora laughs, sitting the night light on the fourth step from the top. She herself sits on the last one, stretching her legs, traversing the two empty spaces down to where her best friend is perched. She holds the railing, pulling herself to a standing position. "Brrrr! It's a bit nippy."

"That's because of the cold hard cash!"

"Yeah, watch, it's probably full of sheets and blankets."

Sydney spotlights the massive safe, filling the area, sitting only two feet or so away from the stairs with ten and twelve inches on the sides respectively—plenty of room for maneuverability if you're skinny as a rail and stand sideways. "You believe it?" She steps to the floor.

Leora looks down, holding the railing, blinking, feeling with her foot for the edge of each step as she descends to the floor, her eyes still adjusting in the dimness.

Sydney shines the flashlight on the front of the safe, illuminating its handle and its combination lock. "Look, Sis!"

"It's humungous!" Leora feels the cold metal surface on the top, resulting in a handful of dust. She claps her hands, wiping them together. Musty replaces flea spray along with the smell of dry wall and wood.

"Talk about an elephant in the room, huh, Momma?"

"In the room? It is the room!"

They face the stairs. "There's no way this safe came from up there."

Leora crosses her arms, watching the beam of light Sydney sends dancing on the railing, the walls; the steps. "Not unless it walked. Who in their right mind would drag this thing upstairs in the first place?"

"D—all the above." They share laughter.

"Yeah, elephant versus whacko! Well, I don't see any ivory."

"I hope they fed it more than peanuts!" Sydney giggles, leaning forward, shining the flashlight again up and down the stairwell, on the railing and walls, checking for scrapes or some other telltale sign of damage. She spotlights the floor in front of the safe for gashes.

"Here, Sis, shine the light here." Leora points at the center of the steps.

Sydney hands over the flashlight.

Leora inspects along the edges of each step. "Nope."

"What?" Sydney is very familiar with Leora's wild imagination. "Where ya goin' with this? What are we lookin' for?"

"Well, I thought maybe they tied a rope around it and slid it down the steps. But I don't see any scuff marks anywhere."

"Or blood. That thing would a pulled 'em right down the steps with it. What was that?" The girls listen. "It's the refrigerator comin' on in the kitchen." Sydney knocks on the wall. "Whew! I feel better."

Leora shines the flashlight toward the top of the staircase.

"We ought a get out a here. I wonder what time it is. Bryce should be comin' pretty soon."

"I'm in! My stomach thinks my throat was cut!" Leora hands the flashlight back to Sydney. "We'll come back after he leaves for work." The phone rings.

"Oh! Shit!"

"Speak of the devil!" Leora turns to the stairs.

"His ears must be ringin'!" Sydney shines the flashlight one last time—on the steps, the floor, the safe, the walls, the ceiling, just all around. She turns to leave when a glint of light shoots from the corner on the right hand side of the stairwell. She floods the object with her beam of light. "Yo! Sis! Check it out!"

"Whoa! Nah-uh!" Leora joins her partner in crime. "A light?"

Sydney squeezes sideways, between the wall and the safe facing the wall. "Yepper!" A light bulb protrudes above a square brass cover designed for four panes of glass. One is missing. The remaining three are dusty as all get out. "It looks like an outside light." She feels along the bottom of the outdoor light. "There's no pull chain. Hmmm. Then where's the switch?" She squeezes back out, pointing to the other side. "That side's tighter than this one," she says, squeezing back into her side, this time facing the safe and shining the light all over the opposite side of the stairwell, the wall, the corner now down the back wall. No sign of a switch plate. "Maybe it's at the top of the steps." The light of day streams through the hole in the wall Pete made, centered just below the top of the safe. But at such an angle Sydney's range of vision is limited. She sees to the patio floor. Big deal. Unimpressed, she abandons the idea, resting her elbows on the safe. She leans sideways, exploring behind the safe, making a whole new discovery.

"Oooww! The plot thickens!" Sydney announces.

"What?" Leora stands on tiptoes, squeezing in on the opposite side. "The butler did it!" She takes a look-see over the back as Sydney sends light to an array of stationery strewn about the floor, spotting a small black plastic waste can toward Leora's end. "Someone's been busy." The phone rings again.

"Let me guess. Is it bigger than a bread box?"

"Here, I'll give ya a hint. What's orange, white, and furry all over?"

"Tiger!"

They make quick work of stuffing the wastebasket full of their bounty then maneuvering their way up the steps.

"I'll put this in your bedroom"—Sydney bucks her eyes—"then I'm gonna grab—" She nods toward her bedroom.

"I'm in!" Leora reinstates the nght light on the windowsill, plugging it back in, and returns the extension cords to the utility closet under the steps on her way to the kitchen. She pours two small glasses of ice tea; one for her, one for Sydney. Downing hers, she glances at the time; one-fifteen. The tea is cold all the way down to her empty stomach. The brunette pours another, removing a wooden clip clothespin from a bag of cheese curls and grazes.

Sydney swigs her tea, rooting for batteries in the kitchen drawers with her coat on. "I put the can in your room," Sydney explains.

Leora takes a gulp of tea. "Where you goin'?" She sounds almost despondent.

Sydney pulls two D batteries from the bottom drawer, their sorta tool drawer. "Oh, I'm gonna run out to the car and get Pierre." She pops the batteries into the dead flashlight. "That way we don't need an ashtray."

She lays the readied flashlight next to the other on the counter, grabbing a handful of cheese curls for her trip.

R-r-ring! R-r-ring! Sydney waits. "Hello." Leora shakes her head at Sydney. It is not Bryce. "Yo! Eva. That was you? We were here. It stopped ringin' before we could get to it. What's happ'nin'?" She shoves a cheese curl in her mouth, stepping out to Wheezer's closet on the patio, stuffing a few knit scarves into the hole.

"Did I tell you earlier I heard Papa's in Italy!"

"He is?" Leora plays dumb. "When did he leave?" She closes the kitchen door, dipping back into the cheese curls.

"I don't know, but he won't be back 'til after New Years."

Sydney follows Wheezer to the kitchen, carrying two brown bags stacked on top of each other and gripping a third.

Leora covers the receiver with her hand, mouthing the words; I'm in! She holds the phone against her ear with her shoulder, sliding the square Styrofoam container out of the bag. Sydney dumps the bag with the plastic utensils, cups of dressing, croutons, two extra rolls, and pads of butter on the table. "Yo! Sis! It's Eva. She said Papa's in Italy. So, E, who's in charge and don't tell me Hank and Sonny?"

"Nah, Papa's son is, well, he'll be in and out. Sonny and Hank are still doin' their thing, but Mario is chief."

"Mario? Why Mario? Why not Salvatore, Jr.? He's like his dad. Nobody blows smoke around him, and he is sooo nice." Leora chews a slice of cucumber.

"I think Junior is takin' care of the shore property."

"The shore property? Really? Why? It's empty, isn't it? What's ta take care of? Hey! Wait a minute! Ya think Papa's passin' the torch, or what?"

"Oh, I don't know, I hope not. Not yet. I'll have ta find another job. Not Mario. I couldn't work for him. He's too young and kind of a hothead. Not that forty-four is young, but well, he just doesn't seem as street smart as Junior. I hope Griff doesn't get any ideas like, while the cat's away the mice will play and end up playin' him like a violin. I will quit!"

"Well, Griff don't look musically inclined except for the organ. Maybe Mario's gonna play him. I mean the guy's not stupid, he's a hothead. It's all about personality. Junior is more like his dad, quiet. Mario is like Griff.

Maybe Griff has met his match! Maybe Papa knows exactly what he's doin'. Hey! He's in jail. Maybe we won't have ta worry about 'im."

"Who, Griff? In jail? For what, pray tell?""

"Would I lie ta you, Momma?" Leora chews a piece of lettuce. "I'm serious as a heart attack. Sonny saw him in handcuffs last night. He pulled up from pool league and watched 'em drive away with Griff in the back of a patrol car, one of many I might add." She devours a slice of radish.

"They probably wanted ta ask 'im a couple questions, and he popped one of 'em! Maybe they found evidence ta hang his ass."

"Would that make my day, or what?" Leora sings, "All I want for Christmas . . . is his balls on my tree."

"I gotta go. A couple of customers just came in. Oh, and here comes Doc and Chick again with no Goo Goo. I'll talk ta ya later."

"Later." Leora dumps croutons and blue cheese onto her salad and delves in.

Wheezer jumps up on the kitchen chair with the "company." Sydney shoos him. "What did Eva have ta say?"

Leora comes up for air. "Just that she heard Papa's in Italy and Mario is gonna be in charge 'til he comes back." She takes another bite of roll and butter. "I didn't mention the picture. She don't know we have a paper. Oh" –the famished girl swallows –"she thinks Junior's babysitting the empty beach house. Yeah, right. Chick and Doc walked in with no Goo Goo. She said she'll call later. Is he fixin' your trunk, or what?"

"Yes, he is. In fact he's almost done. Men! Our food was sittin' on the roof of my car! Are you shittin' me, mister?"

"Hey! Everything happens for a reason. He was probably here when we were"—Leroa raises her eyebrows up and down nodding her head—"you know."

"Whew! That was close."

"But you coulda distracted him. No doubt in my mind."

The girls laugh.

"Oh, I told him last night his cousin Pauline was lookin' for him."

"Did ya mention Pauline was told he was meetin' his girlfriend?"

"Nah-uh, I just told 'im his cousin stopped in. He said he's got a lot of cousins. His mother is one of nine, not ta mention the four on his dad's side. He said she stopped ta see how Alice was doin'." Sydney smiles.

"Oh, so it did come from Alice. Remember? She said he thought you were hot ta trot. He musta told her it's the girl from the diner. Have your ears been ringin' lately?" Leora smiles at her best friend. "Ya think she knows?"

"Knows what? What are you talkin' about?"

Leora bucks her eyes, nodding.

"Oh, about the, who-ja-cotch? Nah-uh, it's you and me, Momma."

"Hey, maybe that's why the steps were broke, a detergent, ah, deturdent." Leora pretends to remove a piece of tobacco from the tip of her tongue. "A deterrent! Did I say that right?"

"Look at you with your twenty-five cent word! Where's Goo Goo?"

"Well, it took me seventy-five cents ta get to it!" They laugh. "Stephen probably said the steps are broke and left it at that. I think Alice accepted any explanation, at any time, on any subject when it came from Stephen."

"Yeah, Bryce doesn't know 'cause Alice doesn't know. If she did, she woulda told 'im 'cause they're tight," Sydney reasons. "Think about it. The hell with Bryce. She woulda been live at eleven if it stopped them from beatin' the life out of her."

"You're right, Sis, and we'd be goners." Leora chews on a crouton. "Stephen probably stuck the safe in there then put the dry wall up, ya know, givin' Alice a song and dance about not wantin' to spend all that money ta rip it all out, it's just cheaper to seal it up." Leora's mind takes off. "You know, he probably said he didn't need another entrance into the building. It's safer without it, and he built a cute little secret place that opens to a cute little linen closet at the top of the old steps where you can stick all those important papers, and the steps are broke so stay away."

"Ah'ight, I will!" Sydney answers, "Tomorrow!"

The girls share a laugh.

"I don't think Papa ever knew either." Leora's mind is still jumping around. "Whoa! Momma! You're thinkin' he knew? You think he knew and sold ya the house and didn't tell ya? Holy shit!" Sydney stares at her partner in crime, blinking profusely.

"Well, maybe. He did empty the place out." Leora blinks.

"Nay, he thinks he emptied it." Now Leora has Sydney thinking. "But you're sayin' maybe this thing is empty and just sittin' there collectin' dust."

"Well, maybe."

"They'd ahad to blow it up! We'd a seen it in the paper: Blast Levels House."

"Yeah, with a picture of the safe still intact." They laugh themselves silly.

"Oh, Bryce said he heard on the radio Bob Seger is doin' the Spectrum, December twenty-eighth. You in or what?"

Leora thinks long and hard. *Christmas, empty holidays. Lonely holidays.* Not that Leora was alone. There is always Sydney. And the fact of the matter is, over the last several years—goin' on four to be exact—Leora spends Christmas dinner at her sister's; a showing, somewhere between an hour to an hour and a half tops. Their mom springs for the turkey, the trimmings, the works, helping her sister prepare it. It is just a lot easier for everyone to pull up a chair at her house than to have her pack up her brood. Besides, she lives right next door to their mom. No, Leora isn't alone, her heart is.

"No, yes, hello, is anybody in there?"

"Huh?"

"You know Bob Seger, Old Time Rock And Roll, Main Street, Turn the Page . . ."

Leora thinks of Ginn.

"Yo! Sis! Is that a no?"

"Yeah. Huh? No." Leora blinks at Sydney. "No, it's yeah, yes, I'm in."

"Are you sure? Holy shit, Sis, ya ah'ight?"

Leora shakes her head. "No, I'm half left. I'm in. I'm in."

Sydney offers conversation. "Bryce and some of the guys down at work bought a bunch of tickets when they went on sale last week or the week before. Whatever. He said they sold out in two hours."

"We were gonna get some. Shit. We forgot."

"Well, we intended to. Time sure flies when you're havin' fun."

"Yeah, what's my mom say? The path ta hell is paved with good intentions? Well, tell Bryce my intention is ta go."

Bryce trots through the kitchen over to the sink, seemingly right on cue. "What? What I do?" He lathers his hands and forearms with Lava.

Sydney pulls a hand towel from a bottom drawer, tossing it to him.

Bryce dries off and pulls Sydney to him. "What Ginger Snap?" He puts his arms around her, kissing her forehead. "What?" He smiles at her.

Sydney gazes into his eyes, offering a kiss, her stomach doing all kinds of little somersaults.

Bryce accepts it and holds her in an embrace, laying his head on top of hers and winking at Leora.

Leora smiles, shaking her head, closing the Styrofoam containers of left over salads to store in the refrigerator 'til later.

"Thanks for lettin' me fix your car."

Sydney elbows him.

"Ugh." He chortles, releasing her. He leans over, holding his gut as if he were injured grinning like a Cheshire cat. "Come on, Ginger Snap, I mean it. It's an honor. What? What Ginger Snap? What, do I owe you a pizza?" Cantankerous is in full bloom.

"I got your Ginger Snap."

"Yes, you do, Baby!" Bryce smiles at Sydney with the orneriest look she has ever seen. Ginger Snap goes after him grab happy.

He covers up, turning sideways, blocking her hands until he can finally get a hold of one of her arms. "Now, now, you don't have ta thank me the pleasure is all mine."

R-r-ring! R-r-ring!

Lucky for Bryce, Sydney is closest. Saved by the bell.

"Hello . . . no, you have the wrong number." Sydney cuts her eyes at Bryce.

"Who'd they want?" Leora asks.

Sydney points at Bryce, crossing her arms.

He leans back against the counter, bucking his eyes at her. "Was it a girl?"

"Yes." Sydney hesitates. "They wanted somebody named Sara."

"Oh good. For a minute there, I thought it was one of my cousins."

Sydney goes for Deep Blue Eyes again. He finagles one arm now, the other wrapping her up in front of him. He pulls her backward, folding his arms with her arms in front of her, nuzzling her hair. "You don't work tonight, do you?"

"Nah-uh." Sydney turns around, standing alongside him. "Neither one of us do, why?"

Bryce is hands-on with Sydney. He smiles, easing an arm around her shoulders, pulling her closer, but holding her left arm nearest him in case of another elbow attack. "Should I come here after work, or are you goin' out and about?"

Sydney and Leora look at each other.

"You goin' some place, Sis?"

"Nah-uh, you goin' some place, Sis?"

"Nah-uh."

"Well, it's igmatimus!" Bryce glances back and forth at them, smiling. "That's what my little nephew said to me one time. We're all goin', Uncle Luke! It's igmatimus!" He chuckles. "Then I'll be over after work. Is that all right?" He pulls Sydney to him, giving her a hug and a kiss and a kiss.

"Ah'ight," Sydney answers.

Bryce heads for the front door.

"Oh! Oh! You forgot ah . . ." Leora pulls the kitchen chair out.

"No, I'll be back." Neither girl disagrees. Leora shoves the chair back in place.

Bryce holds his arm out for Sydney to fill, walking toward the foyer. She wraps her arm around him, shoving her hand in his back pocket, resting her head against him.

"Thank you for fixing my car." They share another kiss.

"Don't thank me yet, Ginger Snap." He smiles adoringly. "Not 'til you get my bill." They kiss again.

"Get a room!" Leora says, laughing.

"Ya got any for rent?" Bryce nuzzles Sydney's hair. "Hey, I know, why don't I just bunk with you?" Sydney looks into Deep Blue Eyes, smiling.

"Is that like save money shower with a friend?" Leora asks.

They laugh, all three. It feels good.

Bryce hugs Ginger Snap, rubbing her arm. "I'll call ya later." He kisses her hair. "Hey, you guys, answer the phone when I call. Don't be makin' shit run around my mind with you two." He opens the front door, locking it, then tests the outside doorknob. "I have your key. See ya in a bit." A quick kiss, and he departs. The door locks behind him.

"Ain't he swell? Bye! Pull away. That's it. Bye!" Sydney stares out the front window, shaking a leg full of impatience, watching and waiting for Bryce to pull away. She turns around and runs right into her accomplice. They laugh.

"Is he gone?" Leora asks, bending over to peer out the window.

"Yepper."

They walk to the kitchen. "He's got a bad case of Sydney-stones."

Sydney laughs. "It's a cute!"

They grab flashlights and beverages from the kitchen where the brunette exchanges her smaller glass of iced tea for a larger, one and the redhead opens a Mick.

"What time does he get done?"

"I think he's four to midnight. He's gonna go see Alice before he goes to work. She's doin' good, but she still can't remember anything."

"I guess that's a blessing in disguise."

"That's what I told him. He wants ta know who did it, but I think she's safer if she doesn't remember." They climb the stairs.

"Yeah, I think everybody's safer. Maybe she thinks that, too."

"You think she might remember?"

"I don't know, Sis, if it was me, I don't know, if my silence could keep my ass safe let alone other people, I think I'd take dumb blonde to a whole new level."

"Me ta, Momma."

Wheezer leads the way around the banister then sits in the middle of the hall. The girls walk around him into Leora's room.

"Wheezer," Leora calls. He flops. They laugh.

"Oh, wait a sec," Sydney sits Pierre, the film canister, the flashlight, and her Mick on the nightstand. She goes to her bedroom, feeling under her bed, on her hands and knees for the shoebox lid.

Leora hits the ceiling light, sitting her tea and her flashlight on the nightstand. She opens the curtains as wide as they can go then dumps the waste basket on the bed.

Wheezer stands three feet or so away from the front of the linen closet door, sniffing. He hears Sydney.

"Tiger! We found it. Took us long enough, huh? Well, we're only human!" Wheezer follows Sydney into Leora's room. She plops at the head of the bed, facing Leora sitting at the foot, deep into her investigation. Wheezer joins the pair of sleuths. He loves the sound of paper.

"Look, Sis." Leora hands a pale blue paper to her best friend. "It's a bill from Fair Acres for his mom in January."

Sydney scopes it out. "What's the date, what year? Oh, this year."

"Well, Marie said he has a daughter. I guess she's handlin' everything now. When did they say he dropped dead, April, March? Whatever."

"Here's a yellow, a doctor bill for January." Sydney lays it on the blue one.

Leora straightens one of the many standard sized crumpled pieces of paper. "Oh, here's a bill for flowers," she reads on. "It's for two arrangements." Wheezer can no longer stand it. He attacks, sliding across the papers, his rear end in the air. Leora ushers him to the hall. A paw appears under the door. "This one is from Marcus Hook Florist, February twelfth. Aw, Valentine's Day."

"Oh, what's this?" Sydney opens an unsealed envelope, removing four folded papers stapled together. "I think it's some kind of a contract." She lays the papers on the bed, holding the bottom to prevent it from folding back up as she lifts the top one and continues to read the next page, the next page.

Leora tries her hand at reading upside down. "A contract for a business? Isn't that what it says? Good, ain't I?"

Sydney flips through the jargon to the last page. "Blah, blah . . . Oh! My! God! She holds it up for Leora to read the signature.

Leora leans forward and reads: George Harrison. Leora gasps. "George Harrison!"

Forging Ahead

"George Harrison!" A chill runs down Leora's spine. The girl is not alone. Sydney shivers, flipping back to the first page. "It's blank, Sis. See? I mean you got the legal mumbo jumbo, but there's no business name or date or address or anything."

Leora pulls another thick envelope from the scattered pile. Sure enough, it reveals more of the same, fill in the blanks. She flips to the last page. "Look! Look! Look!" Leora hands Mr. Lennon's blank contract to Sister Syd and pulls another and another, four, no, five, no, wait, six, seven, eight. Eight more white envelopes of blank contracts with bogus signatures of a Mr. Starr, Mr. Lennon, Mr. McCartney, and Mr. Harrison. They place the phony contracts back into their envelopes, tossing them and the pastel bills onto the pillows out of their way. "Hank was right."

"Big time!" Sydney straightens a crumpled paper. "Look, this has John, John, John, John, John blotted umpteen times. Got a little carried away, don't ya think?"

"Practice makes perfect." Leora straightens another crumpled one." This one has George blotted all over it."

Sydney pulls one of the white envelopes, opening the papers to the last page. Wrong one. She pulls another. "Here," she says, handing Leora the blank contract with George's fake signature on it. She searches for a Mr. Lennon bogus signature.

Leora compares the readable signature on the contract to the blotted backward signatures all over the paper. Apples and oranges. "Wait a sec."

She moves to the bureau mirror, holding the papers up, leaning forward; blinking back and forth back and forth.

Sydney brings her evidence. She leans forward, peeking from the side of John's contract, now over the top now, the other side around, the blotter paper.

Leora laughs. "What are ya doin', Sis, sneakin' up on it?"

"Yeah, and it's on to me, Sis!"

The signatures blotted umpteen times are now readable in the mirror while the contract signature reflections are backward. Oranges and apples.

"Wait a sec." Sydney turns the contract around facing her, while holding the blotter paper facing the mirror. "Sis! Look! Hurry up!" The bottom of the contract folds up. She places the contract on the mirror still facing her, and spreads her fingers over the contract to hold it open, moving the blotter paper closer to the mirror. She leans sideways to get a good look-see. The top of the mirror tips forward as the bottom tilts backward from the redhead's pressure, allowing the contract to slide slowly down, doown off the mirror. Sydney chucks the papers on the bed and plops. "Breeaaaaak!" She leans over the cardboard lid fills, lights, and passes.

Leora sits Indian style, staring at the stationery mess, exhaling, passing, waiting for inspiration, finally deciding to begin her plan by separating the torn pieces into two groups: one a fountain pen pile, the other a typing pile which is the larger of the two. She removes the contract's stapled corners from the menagerie, nine in all, placing them on the side of her. Gathering a bunch of the typed pieces, she deals them like a deck of cards on to the bed in five-by-six rows, exposing any and all of the remaining corner pieces of the contracts. Placing them to the side with the stapled corners, the brunette scoops the used pieces into a pile on the other side of her, then grabs a fresh handful, beginning the process again.

Sydney exhales. "Puzzles! I love puzzles!" Sydney grabs a handful. "Remember, I found that letter to Gregory in his pants pocket from Gonor-Rita, his third wife, when I was washin' clothes? It was in smaller pieces than this. I'm in!" She finds a corner piece and places it in Leora's corner pile.

"Oh, you mean the letter Rita wrote when she found his Emeraude-scented anniversary card stuffed in his duffel bag?" Leora laughs. "She went on and on to him about goin' ta Houston ta kick your ass! That was funny as hell, well, not at the time 'cause you found out that Houston was where Judy, wife number two lived. But he told you, you were number one, even yellin' it when we were throwin' his clothes out the bedroom window!" Leora aligns four corner pieces beside a contract. "Yo, Sis, from the size of these pieces of paper, it looks like there's eight to a sheet."

"Eight pieces?" Sydney squawks like a parrot. "Pieces of eight! Pieces of eight!"

Leora chokes on a hit, laughing. "Dead men tell no tales!"

Sydney exhales, singing. "Two hot chick's on a dead man's sa-afe. Yo! Hoe! Yo!"

"And a bottle of Harvey Bristol!"

The best friends decide to concentrate on creating the first and the last pages of the contracts, the most important ones. The blah, blah, blah legal gibberish in between on the other pages is unimportant. The decision to locate only those pieces narrows their work considerably. So much so they complete one first page and the last pages of three different contracts: one George and two Paul. Leora throws the unused pieces in the small waste basket for reuse out of the way to prevent a setback stifling their progress. She loads, lights, and passes then begins sorting through the pieces again.

Sydney starts a smaller stack out of all the fountain pen pieces of paper, creating another disheveled deck to deal onto the bed, gathering corner pieces into a pile. "Yo! Sis! Look! Some of the names on here are written and some are blotted. See?" She exhales, holding one up for Leora, counting corner pieces as she finds them. "Four, ten, twelve, fifteen, eighteen. Busy man!"

Leora exhales. "Busy cat! Stink it up, Wheezer!" Leora's mind is cranking. Here she goes again. She flips to the last page of the George contract, exposing the signature. She adds the page with George blotted all over it and five fingers two, no, three of the four fountain pen pieces with George written and blotted on them already pieced together on the bed by the Puzzle Queen.

Sydney finds the two remaining fountain pen corner pieces, completing her pile. She inhales, glancing at Leora with that look. She knows that look. The wheels are turning. She exhales. "A lot of the pieces are torn the same size and shape. He musta ripped bunches at a time."

Leora stands. "Come on." She yawns and stretches.

"What's up?"

"I was thinkin'."

Sydney exhales again. "Wait a minute, Sis, don't do that!"

Leora laughs, walking to the windows. "What time does that clock say? It's gettin' dark."

Sydney leans over, sliding the clock radio in her direction. "It says seven fourteen. Oh, yeah, its 'lude time!"

"Time sure flies when you're hav—" Leora steps from in front of the window, back against the wall sliding to the floor.

"Up against the wall fother . . ." Concern slaps the smile off her face. She stops singing. "Yo! Sis!" she practically whispers, rushing to Leora. "What's wrong?"

Leora pulls her down into a stooping position. "Hear it? Listen." She too whispers only because her heart's in her throat.

Sydney meets Leora's eyes, cocking her head and listens. A car engine idles. "The car? You mean a car?"

Leora nods, swallowing fear, telling herself to get a grip. "Yeah, it's sittin' out front! Griff! His white Lincoln! It's him! I know it is!"

Sydney listens, looking around the room, thinking, thinking; thinking. She juts her bottom lip out frowning. "Wait a minute." She maneuvers to the bed, crawls across it and heads for the door.

"Yo! Sis! You goin' to the kitchen?" Leora's mind takes off. "You think he's tryin' the key?"

Sydney shrugs her shoulders. "I'll be right back." She slips out of the bedroom, closing the door behind her.

Leora sits on the floor, listening, waiting; waiting, listening. It feels like a lifetime. *Where the hell'd she go?* The Mark V is still running. No voices, no doors slamming, but the car continues to idle. It is a good thing. *What the hell is she doin'?* If the engine shuts off, Leora will swallow her teeth. *Thump. Thump. What was that?* She can no longer stand it. With papers in a death grip, the brunette crawls on the floor around the cedar chest to the door just as the redhead opens it.

The curly hair duo screams bloody murder. Wheezer was all for a play time visit. Not any more. He is gone.

"You scared the shit outta me!" Sydney shuts the bedroom door.

"No! This is me, that's you!"

"He's gone, Sis. Did ya see?"

"Nah-uh! When? When would I see? I kept waitin' for you! I thought he got ya! Where were you downstairs?"

"Hell, no! In my bedroom. I made it look like I wasn't alone. I turned the light on and stood alongside my open drapes with my back toward the window, then wrapped my arms around myself like I was being pawed."

"Nah-uh!" Leora's adrenaline finally begins to relax. She sighs.

"I guess it worked. He pulled away. I left the bedroom light on and ran across the bed and liked ta broke my neck on my tiger rug. I gotta move that thing!"

"Oh, that's what I heard." Leora shakes her head. "Did ya see anybody with him?"

"Oh, I didn't look, Sis. I backed up once and got a glimpse of the car. But I didn't wanna let 'im know I knew he was there. I heard him leave."

"You think Griff is pissed 'cause we ran Marcie around, you know, to the charcoal pit then the walk in?"

"I think it's worse than that!"

"Ya do?"

"Well, process of elimination. Maybe he's regroupin'. I mean Alice wasn't holdin', my trunk wasn't holdin', my old apartment wasn't holdin', your trunk wasn't holdin', the house wasn't holdin' because Rob rooted through it." Sydney sighs."As if that wasn't enough. He bugged the house, too . . . and Goo Goo."

"Well, maybe we're safe. Think about it. Goo Goo didn't make no bones about anything last night, even with Marcie. I mean, he got rid of the bugs they put at his place, kicked the shit outta Rob, ripped all the wiring outta their van then said a lot a shit last night, playin' head games with Marcie before throwing the bug out, she adamantly demanded her brother plant in the bar. Maybe the focus is on Goo Goo, and he knows it. Maybe Goo Goo's keepin' his distance, thinkin' he's keepin' us out of it."

"Don't we wish we were out of it? If he only knew! It's just a matter of time. He's runnin' out of options. We're next! I'm tellin' ya when he's for sure about us we're done! And I think he's for sure!" Sydney blinks. "Tell the truth, Sis, you really think that?"

Leora looks at Sydney. "I don't know what ta think. My vibes have vibes. Maybe that's why he was outside the house tonight, because he is for sure." Leora sighs. "Look at Rob. Look at my car. Don't ya think he did that? I do." Leora throws a flustered look at her best friend. "Yo! Sis! I can still see his face at the club when he saw us. He looked like he saw a ghost. He was surprised ta be lookin' at my smilin' face. Why? I'll tell ya why, 'cause he had it done ta blame New York, but there I was. And now Rob's found dead up there. Why? Ta shut 'im up or ta set New York up? Or is it all in my mind 'cause New York actually did do it?"

"But New York don't want anything ta happen to Third Eye . . . yet. Remember? That paper with all those incriminating details and guns. The guns, too, right?"

"Oh yeah, the hit guns Griff keeps usin', that he never ditched. He probably did do somethin' ta Rob. It's like everybody's in his way. Wait 'til he finds out we are—big time! And where's Crow? Did he use one on Crow?" Leora's eyes fill. "Or is he bein' tortured some place. He doesn't know anything." *Exit eight, cement shoes, the Pine Barrens.* Leora's mind is bookin'.

Sydney is almost sorry she asked. "Ya ah'ight?"

Leora nods, breathing deep. "Half left." The brunette tries unsuccessfully to stifle her thoughts. "Where's Rob's car? You think he was comin' after me? You think New York did it? Ya think Griff did it? Rob was his electrical man. Griff is off the wall."

"Yeah, you got that right! Griff would bite the hand that feeds 'im. I don't like him a little bit. He would eat his young. He probably did. He don't have any kids, right? Look at his track record, Sis. He does shit and points the finger at everybody else. People are disposable ta him." Sydney fires up Pierre and passes. "Well, we at least know the piece of shit is out and about. I wonder if Goo Goo is."

"We can always call Eva." Leora takes a long drawl then passes the bowl. "I wanted ta check these papers out in the bathroom light." She relaxes her grip on the papers, smoothing them against her bosom. "Ya in or what?"

Sydney exhales through her nose, coughing and nodding. "Yepper. Let's do somethin'." Her mind needs to be occupied. So does Leora's.

"Here." Leora hands the papers to her best friend. Sydney pops the pipe in her mouth, freeing her hands. "I'm gonna run downstairs and get some scotch tape." She opens the bedroom door.

"Grab me a Mick," Sydney says out of the side of her mouth.

Wheezer scoots past them into the bedroom, wondering why they are all fired up, going the other way. He sits blinking, watching Sydney disappear into the bathroom and Leora's head sink into the floor as she descends to the first level.

Upon her return, the brunette finds Sydney with Pierre still clenched between her teeth, well engrossed in her handwriting analysis.

"Da-a da . . . da-a da . . . da-a da . . . da-a da . . . da-a da . . . da-a da . . . da-a da-a-a . . . da-da-da-da," Leora sings "The Pink Panther" theme.

Sister Syd glances in Leora's direction, blinking. She breaks into a wide grin.

"Hi." Leora smiles back.

Sydney removes the pipe. "Yes, I am, I mean, Hellooo!"

"What's happ'nin', Charlie?"

"Huh?"

"Charlie, you know, Charlie Chan."

Sydney speaks in an Asian accent, blinking and bowing." Not to worry, my number one friend. Remember Confucius say, woman who fly plane upside down have crack up."

The girls burst into laughter. Leora sits on the side of the bathtub, wiping her eyes. Sydney drops the papers in the sink and takes a break, sitting on the toilet lid. She places Pierre on the tank next to the porcelain duck and sighs. "Oh! Look, Sis. There's one they missed. That's the only one I have left that isn't broken."

"Awwww, there's gotta be a couple in your trunk. We didn't look yet. Hey, if they break this one, we're knee-deep in holy shit!" She hands the Michelob to the redhead.

"Oh, thanks, oh, here, trade ya." Sydney reaches for the pipe, handing it to Leora. "Have a little ketchup." She pulls a Bic from her pocket, handing it to Leora, then takes a nice cold drink.

Leora exhales. "Hey, think about it, what's safer than puttin' your wrapped knickknacks in a box and keepin' 'em in the trunk of your car out of everybody's way?" She takes another toke.

"Evidently keepin' 'em in somebody else's. I'll drink ta that." Sydney swigs her Mick.

"Me, ta." Leora holds her hand out for a swig, placing the bowl beside the cold water faucet. She hands the Michelob back to Sydney, gathering the papers from the porcelain sink.

"Gaw head, check it out, Momma, but they don't match up usin' my eyeballs."

Leora blinks with a concerned expression. "So, you're sayin' he didn't sign these papers?"

"Yepper."

"Hmmm. Well, is it before or after? Did he come across somebody while he was practicin' and decided they were better and go with them or did he already have somebody and they quit or left, whatever, so he had ta do it himself? Did I say that right, or what?"

"So what you're sayin' is did he ditch his John Hancock 'cause it sucked?" She inhales. "Or"—she exhales—"or because whoever he had quit, died, or got arrested? Whatever!" She passes the bowl.

"Died!" Leora snaps her head toward Sydney, taking the pipe. "She'll take it to her grave! She won't even know! He said he was gonna beat it outta her! We thought he was comin' after one of us for the typewriter! He went after Alice!"

"She didn't know anything." Sydney thinks with furrowed brow, eyes darting back and forth. "Well, yeah, Sis, she almost did go to her grave. She was comatose. We thought he figured out we had it. But then found out he meant Alice."

Leora chokes on a hit, laying the pipe on the back of the sink. "She doesn't!"

"No, Sis, she doesn't."

Leora gasps for air again. "Rhonda!" She coughs.

Sydney pats Leora on her back trying to blink her eyes as wide as the moon. "Rhonda? What do ya mean, Sis, Rhonda signed it?"

Until she finds her voice, all Leora can do is shake her head no. "Marie! – She coughs again and again – "Marie Coucci!" She holds her arms in the air.

Sydney places her hands on her cheeks, holding her face with her mouth wide open. "What?" What are ya talkin' about, Sis?" She pats her a couple more times. "Ya think Marie did it? English Marie, the nurse?"

Leora shakes her head no and coughs. "Nancy!"

"Nancy!" Sydney pushes her hair off her forehead with both hands, then rubs her face with one hand while the other goes on her hip. "Are you shittin' me?" The redhead takes a long swig of Mick and hands it to Leora. "Here! Swig this!" Gripping the bowl with her teeth, she gathers the papers from the sink, looping an arm through Leora's. Leora takes a gulp. "Yo! Sis! Stop thinkin'!" They shuffle toward the bedroom. "Get a drink of tea, take a break, whatever!"

They make it as far as the bedroom doorway. Who plays well with others or by himself? Wheezer. Who is a busy cat? Wheezer. Who loves paper? Uh, yeah. He really does. Especially his stash. This was his stash first. Wonderful! But they can play, too. There's plenty to go around, right here on the bed. Well, there was. With his rear end in the air, front paws spread, Wheezer jerks his head around mouth agape, wheezing.

"Ti-i-ger!" Sydney stands with her mouth open, too, but for a different reason; basically shock. Leora shakes her head.

The tone of Sydney's voice sounds more like a barked reprimand than happy playmates come to call. The tabby leaps to the floor, scurrying under the bed.

Sydney chucks the papers on the bed, surveying the situation.

Leora places the Mick on the nightstand. She pulls the tape from her pocket, throwing it on the bed and leans over, looking in the waste basket. "Gee, he missed all this. Yeah, team!"

"I lo-o-ve puzzles!" Sydney exhales the words, crawling on her hands and knees gathering torn scraps, crumpled, and balled up pieces of paper, tossing them on the bed as she goes. She lifts the comforter, checking under the bed and ends up staring Wheezer right in the face. The feisty feline blinks his dilated eyes, crouching, ready to bolt if his name is yelled one more time. "Heel, not you, Tiger, your sister!" She climbs on the bed, careful not to agitate the air as Leora begins, creating the four typed documents again, separating the written and blotted ones into their own pile as she goes along. Sydney assumes her position to assemble the five standard sheets of paper starting with the four pieces they used in the bathroom. She removes corner pieces as she comes across them, starting the process all over again.

"What the hell are we doin'? We don't really need these anymore," Leora continues. "We already know he didn't sign 'em." She slips the bottom right hand piece of paper with George's name written on it into place, completing it a second time. "There. One down three ta go." Gathering all the pieces, she places them on her dresser with the scotch tape, spying a stray piece of blotter paper standing straight up between the leg of the bed and the cedar chest. She finishes her glass of tea on the nightstand, bending for the scrap and sits. "We don't need these either." She throws it on the bed.

"Yeah, but they're puzzles. Puzzles are addictive. I'm in! Besides, these are a lot easier ta do than those typed contracts. Check it out. I found twenty corner pieces, Sis. That's like five full sheets of paper, right?"

"Yeah."

"And they're ripped into eight pieces."

"Yeah." Leora gives her best friend a questionable stare.

"Well, eight times five is forty pieces as compared to one contract with four pages to a contract, eight pieces for each page. That's thirty-two pieces for one contract, and we have nine stapled corners so that's nine contracts, let me see, eight times four, thirty-two, thirty-two times nine," Sydney mumbles, wiggling fingers, multiplying to herself. "Screw that, Sis! Let's make these!" Sydney matches several of the torn fountain pen pieces by their ripped angle. "So what were you sayin', ah, about Rhonda? You think maybe, ah, she signed those names or maybe, ah, somebody else?" Sydney blinks at her best friend, waiting for a name. Just one name instead of three.

Leora begins straightening one of the papers crumpled into a tight ball. "Yeah," she answers lost in thought. "What?" She blinks at Sydney. "What? Rhonda? What did you say? Rhonda signed the papers? No! No! Nancy! Rhonda mentioned a Nancy. We kept tryin' ta remember where we heard that name before. We heard it from Rhonda."

Sydney completes a fountain pen, paper scraping all the pieces together, then placing them on the bureau. "Oh! That's right! Third Eye told her he had an ex named Nancy that ripped 'im off, and she was in an accident." She returns to the bed in her reconstruction mode, trying to erase Crow and Leora's car from her mind.

"And Marie mentioned a Nancy the other night at work, remember?"

Sydney stops what she's doing, giving the brunette her full attention, not quite getting it.

"What was it you heard the night you filled in for Marcie when Papa took them up ta look at the apartment after the bar was closed?" Sydney smiles. "You want me ta think? We get in enough trouble with you thinkin' let alone me." She thinks back. "Let me see, I wanted ta be a fly on the wall, so I listened at the door. Mmmm, he was bitchin'. He thought the pills were put in the wrong car, hmmmm, they fought like cats and dogs over the bug she wanted ta plant in the bar, oh, he said he was gonna beat it out of her, which we took as a threat to one of us over the damn typewriter, but it turned out ta be Alice. He said she'll take it to her grave, and she almost did."

"But didn't you hear him say she won't even know it? She'll take it to her grave and won't even know it?"

"Cause she'd be dead! Dead men tell no tales. Neither do dead broads." Sydney thinks out loud, "I don't know a Nancy, do we?"

"No, but remember Marie said to me you have Stephen's house, Nancy's son?"

"Yeah, but Griff didn't mention a Nancy that night, Sis."

"No, not by name. But he did to Rhonda. He lied to Rhonda about California, Noodle the investigator, his ex-girlfriend Nancy, who just so happens to have the same name as the mother of his dead partner."

"Yepper, 'cause he makes shit up as he goes along. I guess that's the first name that came to his warped mind. It was a safe name. Rhonda will never meet her. The real Nancy's in a home and by now probably doesn't even know it." Sydney eyes pop. *She'll take it to her grave and don't even know it.* She hears Griff's voice in the back of her mind. "She don't even know it!"

"Yeah! Yeah!" Leora nods "Yo, Sis! And those signatures are sorta girly lookin'. That's probably why his handwriting was so bad. He was tryin' ta write like a woman."

Sydney inhales. "We're gonna get killed!"

"So far so good!" Leora says with pursed lips.

"His partner drops dead and leaves him high and dry."

"Oh! Pierre." Leora spies the pipe. "I think Stephen told 'im what he was doin' but dropped dead before he could tell 'im where he was doin' it!" She lights and passes.

Sydney exhales, mocking Vito Corleone, "The Feds are gettin' close. But I got everything takin' care of—the ledger, the typewriter. Don't worry about it. I gave my mother an offer she couldn't refuse, she signed everything. I got a safe, too. Come over tomorrow. I'll show ya what we're doin'. I'll tell Derrick the Derelict tomorrow mornin' . . . ugh!" She grabs her throat gasping.

Leora laughs, laying the eight-and-a-half-by-eleven wrinkled paper on her leg to smooth it flat.

"Nancy didn't die and take it to her grave. Stephen did!" Sydney breaks into song. "Two hot chicks on a dead man's sa-afe!"

"Yo, Hoe ... look!" Leora finally takes a gander at the handwritten paper she had been so meticulously trying to smooth. "Look at this! All these initials and numbers written in the margins: cn – 1200, go – 900, jd – 1000, rs – 900, ww – 800, gm – 900 . . . and all these different addresses. Norwood, Darby, Holmes, Drexel Hill, Ardmore, Newtown Square . . . There's gotta be twenty-five, thirty properties here." She leans forward, holding it out for Sydney's benefit.

"They sure did own a lot of 'em." Sydney exhales and passes.

"These are fictitious, Sis, for that money laundering." Leora inhales.

"Oh, yeah, that's right. It wasn't Stephen and Alice, it was Stephen and them."

Leora exhales. "Yeah, the prayer meetin'." She taps the spent pipe on the ashtray.

"It's a shame. I bet the signatures are her handwriting. I don't want her ta go ta jail."

"Well, she wouldn't know it anyway, but I don't either. Maybe he was practicin' because she's really bad now. Sounds like the business was doin' good, growin'." Leora sits the pipe in the ashtray.

Sydney opens a balled up paper, smoothing it on her leg. It is basically the same. "Oh, look, I think this is a date—1-7, see, top right hand corner, January. How 'bout yours?"

"Oh, yeah, this one's 2-11, February. So the papers which are balled up tight as a drum hide names, payouts, and addresses. Maybe the ledger Griff wants has some of this. Maybe it really did happen that way. He didn't get a chance ta do anything." "Outstanding printing. Good penmanship. Very legible. And look. He makes his E like a backward three. Like in the mirror. This is original shit." Sydney hits Leora with a flurry of blinks. "This is! Really!" Sydney pours over the handwritten paper. "Yo, Sis, listen: DE-900, CY-300, SG-3100. Is that on yours? Look at the bottom. All capital letters."

Leora looks at the bottom of hers. "Oh, yeah. DE-900. Oh, wait, don't you have CY-300? This one says CY-400, SG-3000."

"Oh! Hey! SG, Shaun. That's Griff! Whaaat? Three thousand. That must be dollars! Three thousand dollars!"

"CY, that's Carl and DE is the mayor!"

"They sure weren't partners like I thought they were partners."

"What? They were in cahoots."

"Well, it ain't even."

"What, the numbers? Of course not. Griff's involved, isn't he? He has that only child syndrome. He takes his half outta the middle. Besides it was his business. The mayor gets his shake down money, Stephen pays himself, and Griff makes sure his buddy Yarborough was slipped somethin' ta keep him happy."

"Yeah, while Griff's partner slipped Yarborough's wife somethin' ta keep her happy."

The girls gather all the balled up paper, straightening them and putting them in a pile by date. On all the papers, the nine hundred dollar payout to the mayor stays the same. Property addresses change, figures next to the small initials change, and Griff's figures change. Carl's cut changes, but never higher than four hundred.

Sydney reaches for the contracts and the bills. "I think these were layin' on top of the safe. These weren't thrown away. Wheezer had a field day." She lays them on the stack of payout papers.

"Or two." Leora transfers the four finished fountain pen puzzle piles two at a time to her bureau. She walks to her windows, closing the drapes. "There. That feels better."

Sydney stands the papers in the waste basket. "We're gonna leave everything in here, right? Or do ya wanna put it in Tiger's playground?"

"Oh, I don't care, Sis. We can leave 'em here. I'm leavin' the light on. What time is it?"

They glance at the clock: 7:51.

"Almost eight o'clock. Bryce'll be callin' soon."

"Let's eat."

"Oh, that's right, we have salads ta finish. I'm in. I'm gonna go close my drapes. Wait for me."

Leora sits the ashtray on the nightstand, grabbing Pierre. "I think we're the only ones in the whole wide world who know about this, not that people aren't tryin' ta find out," she hollers, stuffing the wooden bowl. "Did ya notice those balled up papers, you know, the real deal ones? Anyway, did ya notice they were written with a ball point pen? We should a looked at them first. That's really Stephen's handwriting," she yells, gathering the Mick bottle and her iced tea glass, leaving the light on. "Sis? Yo! Sis!" She heads to Sydney's room. Apprehension tags along. "Yo! Sis!" The light is on. She swallows hard, peeking around the door jam, finding Sister Syd facing the bed, gyrating and shaking her ass in front of the one window with open drapes. She blinks wide-eyed.

Sydney throws her hands up, spinning around, doing a series of hand movements.

"Nice, Sis."

"He's back! I saw 'im when I closed the drapes in the atrium window."

"Who's . . ." Leora gasps. "Nah-uh! He's out there?" She drops to the floor.

Sydney stops wiggling and leans toward the bed. "Yo! Sis! How 'bout you come pull these drapes closed while I'm dancin' so he sees both my hands in the air. But first get Bryce's flannel shirt and put it on. That's believable."

Adrenaline feeds Leora's anxiousness as she crawls to Sydney's bureau, reaching for the shirt. Wheezer is amused, blinking, sitting encircled by his tail, wiggling the orange tip. His owner stands against the wall alongside the window.

"Wait a minute." Sydney starts flailing again, turning slowly toward the other side of the room as if holding a conversation with someone walking to the window. She nods to Leora. "Okay, now." She smiles, gyrating.

Leora faces the wall, shuffling sideways, hiding behind the drapery, exposing her flannel-covered right arm. She reaches across to the other side, pulling it closed then falling to the floor with her best friend. "Can't we just shoot 'im?"

The girls chew on rolls and leftover salad, discussing their agenda for the remainder of the evening, which may include a puzzle contest.

"Ya think the phone is tapped?" Leora bites down on a hunk of roll.

"No, we found everything, didn't we?" Sydney sticks a half of cherry tomato with her fork then a slice of radish, a piece of onion, and a chunk of blue cheese.

Leora swallows. "Yeah, but I mean do you think it's tapped tapped?"

Sydney finishes her mouthful. "Oh, you mean from them, the other them, the good guys! Well, it wouldn't blow my mind."

R-i-n-n-g! R-i-n-n-g!

Bryce's phone call informs Ginger Snap of his impending four-hour extended shift.

"It'll be late, so I'll come by tomorrow."

"Yeah, sure, so I'll see ya tomorrow." Sydney says aloud, glaring at Leora.

"He's not comin' over?" Leora mouths the words, blinking.

Sydney blinks back, shaking her head. "Well, you gotta take it while you can get it." She blushes. "I mean work!" She explains holding the phone with her shoulder while steering a crouton onto her fork. "Well, if ya can't sleep, you know, where I live . . . that, too." The tasty crouton crunches. "What?"

"Alice might be rememb'rin' shit." Sydney repeats his statement aloud, blinking again at her best friend. "What makes you think that? What did she say?"

Leora stares stonefaced.

"Well, it's not so much what she's sayin' but what she's not sayin', you know, she wishes she could remember. She ain't sayin' that anymore. I think details are comin' back."

"And they might be scarin' the shit outta her." Silence reigned, and they both got wet. "Ya there?"

"Yo."

"I mean, she was bad. Good Lord, she was in a coma. She might not want to remember. Besides, she really can't say anything because the authorities will go after the bastards then the bastards 'ill know she remembered and shut her up permanently."

"Well, I mentioned you guys before, and she had no recollection. I told her this afternoon about us. She said she remembers both of you from the diner."

About us. Sydney takes a deep breath. "What about us?"

"You know," Deep Blue Eyes sidesteps his heart, "how I blackened both your eyes and gave ya a bloody nose?"

Sydney laughs, keeping it light, also keeping it unsaid. "And did ya tell her that was just ta get my attention? The plan was ta steal my dog and bring it back sayin' you found it."

"You don't have a dog."

"I know." Sydney laughs again, shaking her head. "That's why you went fishin', you know, danglin' Bob Seger tickets. Hook, line, and sinker! I'm in!"

Bryce laughs. "A mermaid!"

"No, two. Leora's in!"

"Oh, good 'cause Manny and them wanna pile in. I'll tell 'em we're full up. I'll get one of my cousins ta ride with us."

"God knows you have several. Make it a rich one!"

Leora nods to her best friend with perplexity.

Sydney gives Leora a quick grin. "So it's a blind date, huh?"

"No, he ain't blind." Bryce laughs. "I'll buy her ticket, my treat. Hey, that's why I'm workin' overtime ta buy her ticket. There ya go."

Now Sydney laughs. "You're so bright your mother calls you son!"

Confusion still plays upon the brunette's face.

Sydney covers the phone with her hand. "Don't ask."

"I gotta go, lunch break."

"Ah'ight. Oh, and listen, if you call here later on your break and we don't answer, it's 'cause we're gonna run to the police station and see what's up with Leora's car. The chief's on second shift—oh no, he's not." Leora holds up three fingers. "He starts at midnight. He's on third."

"Who's on first?"

"I don't know."

"No, he's on third."

Sydney catches on. "What?"

They laugh. "What am I gonna do with you?"

"Love me." Sydney wanted to bite her tongue off.

"I'll see what I can do."

"If ya can't sleep, ah, park, ah, in the driveway, um," Sydney stammers with a warm flush on her cheeks. "You have a key."

"Yeah, so keep the doors locked. See ya in a bit."

She leaps at a change of subject. "Oh, speakin' of locks, does your company have a lock?"

"My company. I don't have a company."

"No here, your company, you know," Sydney tries a different approach. "O-day ou-yay peak-say ig-Pay atin-Lay?"

"Es-yay."

"Well, uhm, aybe-may ones-phay apped-tay. On the kitchen chair, you know, your company that's been stayin' with us?"

"Oh, I got it Ginger Snap, yeah, but not lately so be careful. What's wrong?"

"Oh, nothin', nothin'. It's no big deal." But it is a big deal. If something were to happen, the girls now know they can just blast somebody to kingdom come. Sydney plays it off. "We had a bet. We figured it'd be safer just ta ask. Yo! Sis! You won."

The curly duo finish salads, straighten up the kitchen, and situate Wheezer out on the patio in the still of the night. Sydney loads Pierre, passing back and forth while Leora makes a phone call to Carrie. *No news is good news* repeats in Leora's mind, trying to spin a positive on Carrie's negative answers of "I don't know" to most of Leora's questions.

Frazzled, the redhead runs upstairs, collecting the four fountain pen puzzles from Leora's dresser only to hear Leora say, "Oh, you don't know" yet again upon her return. She places the separated groups on the table, removing the scotch tape from her back pocket before sitting.

Leora replaces the receiver on the wall phone and sits. "She's a mess." The brunette lights the pipe taking a long draw.

Sydney lays two compatible pieces together, sealing them with the cellophane tape. "She don't know nothin', huh?"

"Yeah, you think our minds are goin' nuts, just talk ta her." Leora slides a pile in front of her. "There's no funeral, no memorial, no nothin'. Whatever."

Sydney maneuvers another piece of paper into place, sharing a thought. "Yo, Sis, what about your car?" She takes a hit, a good one.

"I didn't get that far. Basically it's an ongoing investigation and Carrie's sorta on the back burner. They've sorta clammed up and stopped givin' her details 'cause the guy they found shot isn't her son. Now they have no answers for her. Whatever. It was a hit they said so before they knew it was Rob. Carrie asked again if Crow was in the mob or if I know of anybody down at the bar that he mighta had a run in with." Leora shakes her head. "She was ever so grateful for the ring and thanked us four times, oh, and the truck. She said Pete has a purpose. He wouldn't leave her side before. She was so worried about him. Now he's down the garage with Joe, Chris, and Greg. She said she's payin' Crow's part of the rent. They're lettin' Pete keep the truck there. It's good for all of 'em. She said, 'Now if I could just find out.'" Leora's voice trails. *Did the mob really do it, or was it jackass Griff usin' one of the guns? How can we find out? Nobody 'ill tell us anything. And I certainly ain't askin' Griff. Besides, why ask for a lie.* Leora sighs. She dials Eva's number, checking the stove clock: 8:32.

"Hello, hi, is your mom there? Thank you." Leora begins her puzzle task, laying several pieces in place. "Yo! Eva! What's happ'nin'? Yeah, I'll hold." She tapes two pieces of her puzzle together, waiting for Eva, who runs upstairs to grab the bedroom phone.

Eva speaks into the phone. "I got it." She listens. "Got it!" She waits for her son to hang up the kitchen phone. "Richie!" She listens. "Richard! Hang it up! She yells at the top of her lungs. Click. "Ya there?"

"Yeah, I'm here. Ya busy?"

"No, I was gettin' ready ta call ya. Doc just left. A secret ain't a secret unless ya tell it. Just ask Doc. Listen, Marcie and Griff were in the bar arguin' like cats and dogs!"

"Why? Over what? Don't tell me let me guess. Ah, she found out he really is an asshole!!"

Eva snickers. "Well, ya know you said they took Griff in handcuffs last night. Well, he didn't get out 'til this afternoon. Marcie came in the bar around one-ish, and I asked her what was goin' on with Griff. Her eyes liked ta popped outta her head. They got in an argument last night, big time! She left and went over some guy's house. That's where she was comin' from when she stopped in the bar on her way upstairs. She had no idea. And after she flew down there ta spring 'im, well, let me tell ya somethin', they held round two right here in the bar. She came stompin' in with him followin' right behind her yellin' and carryin' on. He wanted ta go straight upstairs and she said, 'Why, so ya can scream and jump up and down like a Ubangi? You've been yellin' since ya got in the car! Shut up! Give it a rest!' Talk about your knickers in a knot, she was salty. She said, 'You think you're so God damn smart! Now what do we do? Now who do we get ta wire everything?' And he screamed back at her, 'You mean you! Who are you gettin'?' Eva talks in a deep voice. He yelled, 'I told ya before I don't give a shit! What good is any of it if I'm in jail? You're the one that thought it was so important! It ain't my problem!' Then Marcie shot back, 'who you talkin' to?' and told 'im ta go forth and multiply if ya get my drift. She told 'im she shoulda left 'im in jail. He was pissed. Then he got real nice to her 'cause he needed her keys ta get in the apartment. She said, 'It ain't my problem!' I thought he was gonna hit her. From what I gathered, they were hangin' out at the van and got into a huge disagreement. She stormed upstairs and got some of her junk and left. Next thing ya know, Chester's finest came by and you know cocky Griff. He got arrested. The house keys were upstairs. He had the van keys in his pocket. He kept callin' the apartment, but she wasn't there. And Jammer and Hector were stuck in the parkin' lot. They slept in the van and liked ta froze their asses off. They were in and out all day today. It's probably a good thing he was in jail all night 'cause he didn't have any keys ta get in the apartment after she locked up and left. But I figure even if they didn't arrest him, they woulda been there later 'cause he didn't have any keys to get in so he woulda probably shattered the glass door and ended up in jail anyway."

Leora and Sydney now know it really was Rob. But who did it? New York? Griff? If he wanted Leora's car, then maybe so did New York. The duo offer no tidbits of last night's round one of Goo Goo, the bug or Marcie's little treasure hunt. "Did they kiss and make up?" The girls stand with ears cocked toward the receiver between them.

"I don't know about all that. If ya mean did he act civil toward her, hell no! I asked him if he wanted a drink, and he got that frickin' sneer on his face yellin' and carryin' on like a two year old. 'Ya dumb broads. Do I look thirsty ta you?' And I said, 'No, so go sit at the tables. Ya can't sit at the bar unless you're over twenty-one and buyin' drinks.' He threw daggers at me, so I threw 'em back and said, 'By the way, if you see a dumb broad, you kiss her' then stood right in front of his sorry ass wavin' the air in front of me like he stunk, which he did. Marcie gave 'im the key ta go upstairs. She stayed in the bar, but I don't think it's 'cause she's scared of 'im.'"

"Did he show up all spiffy?"

"No, but in the meantime Goo, Doc, and Chick came in the back. He's such an instigator. He told me ta give Marcie a drink. He yelled, 'Ya know, she's ambidextrous,' grinnin' with that shit-eatin' grin. He is ornery as cat shit! She yelled he oughta keep his hands to himself. He said, 'I didn't touch ya. I just bought ya a drink! I'm over here.' She cut her eyes at 'im and hollered, 'I'm talkin about keepin your hands off of shit that don't belong to you!' Goo actually sneered at her then asked her if she meant the trash bag in front of his apartment. He said 'That was my shit. The bag at the curb in front of my apartment? The black plastic trash bag? Is that what ya mean?' She gave 'im a dirty look and didn't answer him. She was boilin', all red in the face, looked just like Griff with long hair. It really pissed her off. She stomped out of there. She's like a Jekyll and Hyde. I thought she was all quiet and mealy mouth. She did like a one-eighty. Coulda fooled me."

"Yeah," Leora agrees, "that's what she showed everybody. She kept to herself. She boohooed ta Papa. She needed a job, she don't know anybody, a poor little all alone helpless blonde . . . bimbo."

"Nah-uh, more like a high-maintenance bitch."

"Yeah," Eva agrees, "like she's in the dark about Griff. She came across like she had no idea her brother was such a nasty ass. They were different as day and night. That's how I saw it, but Doc told me Papa knew it from the get-go. He's known she's never bartended a day in her miserable life, and he's known she was Griff's sister. Doc said she even got away with murderin' her rich husband with the ol' radio in the bath water routine.

She is far from bein' helpless, innocent, or dumb. Hey, she went head ta head with Griff and he lost."

Eva is seeing Marcie in a whole new light with sinister shadows of malice and greed finding her as cold and calculating as her brother. A frightening thought which the partners in crime have already experienced firsthand and agree wholeheartedly.

"Doc also said the guy who fixed Goo's car—you know, bad-da-boom bad-da-bing—he's dead."

"You're kiddin' me!" Leora shrugs at Sydney.

"That's why they wanted Goo Goo downtown. They know Goo knew 'im, Rob, right?"

"Yeah, that's his name. What happened?" Both girls cock their ears to the phone.

"Well, they asked Goo a bunch of questions. He told 'em he knew 'im. He said the guy fixed cars and was a handyman around the apartment building. They asked Goo if he knew of anybody he hung around with. Goo told 'em no it wasn't his turn ta watch 'im. He didn't know what he did on his own time. He didn't keep tabs on 'im. He said he's only known 'im a couple months. He did tell 'em about the Chateau and an ex-girlfriend named Mabel."

Oh! Good! Send 'em out o' town. Leora blinks at Sydney, covering the receiver. "You didn't leave your name when you went out there lookin' for 'im, did ya?"

Sydney shakes her head.

"What happened to 'im?" Leora cringes.

"They found two cars. His car and another. He was in the other car. There were three sets of tire tracks in the snow, and they were all meltin'."

Leora talks into the phone. "Was he shot, stabbed, strangled, or what?" She cocks an ear.

Sydney also asks a question. "Did he OD?" She turns her head ta listen.

"I don't know, but that's 'cause Doc don't know. If he did, I'd a got it outta him. I told 'im don't tell half a story. Of course it went right over his head. So that's all he knows. Hey, did ya hear anything about your car?"

"Nah-uh."

"You think it'll be drive-able, or you think they're gonna tell ya ta junk it?"

"I don't know, in fact, Chief Sill is workin' midnight ta eight tonight. We were just talkin' about doin' some midnight knockin' at the police station to find out what's happ'nin'."

"I'm sure if ya gotta take a ride, both of you will go. Ya can't go by yourself. Let me know. I'll work Monday or Wednesday. I need the money anyway, Christmas is comin'. Unless you go on the weekend. But I don't think they'd be open, you know how the government works rather don't work."

"Yeah, like molasses in January goin' uphill."

"Well, let me go. I gotta get these kids situated. I'll call ya if I hear anything."

The girls have less than three hours to kill until they go midnight knockin'.

"Well, there's one thing: Eva didn't say anything about the picture in the paper resemblin' Rob instead of Crow."

"She didn't say anything about Rob workin' for Goo Goo and Griff at the same time either."

"I don't know if she knows it. You'd think she did 'cause Doc was there when Goo Goo said he kicked Rob's ass and threw 'im in the van unless Doc was excluded from the festivities 'cause of his big mouth."

"Come ta think of it, Goo Goo whispered it to me that night. That's the night he told me Marcie was Sarah Treet and Griff's sister. Goo Goo wouldn't offer information about Rob workin' for Griff, too. Why would he? Let them figure it out. It's their job." Sydney scrunches her face.

Leora shivers. "It's gettin' complicated."

"Yeah, ya have he said she said about this and that. Well, we're the only ones that know about Rob buggin' us, about the typewriter, the safe, uh, what else, Sis, think! What else can't we talk about? It's gettin' hard ta keep track."

"The fake businesses, the fake contracts, the practice papers, Mrs. Lister!"

Wide-eyed Sydney blinks. "Oh yeah, the payouts and all that shit!" Sydney gulps air, finishing her second puzzle, taping the last piece in place and heads for the backdoor full of nervous energy. "Yo! Momma! Ya think the little schminker is back in his cat cave?"

"I don't know, Sis. I stuffed scarves into the hole and there might still be a scent of flea spray hangin' around."

Sydney returns with an orange and white sidekick. "Look who's here." Wheezer scoots in, blinking in the glare of the light. "He was sittin' out there lookin' bored as hell. I told 'im I don't know how all that stuff got in that hole. Hey, Tiger, talk ta her." She points to Leora. Wheezer sits, blinking. "He's not used ta us bein' here." Sydney sits, beginning another puzzle.

"Yeah, we're suppose ta be out there where the air is rare." Leora sighs. "Yo! Sis! Do you think Griff is comin' around because he knows we typed that damn ransom note?"

"Oh! My God!" Sydney scrunches her face again. "I forgot about that! Yo! Sis! That's another thing we can't talk about!" Sydney joins two pieces of her puzzle with tape and sighs. "Ya know, I felt so guilty thinkin' about that night. I thought it was our fault Griff went after your car."

"Yeah, I did too, but you know the note was after the fact. It had already happened, Sis. That's why he thought he saw a ghost."

Sydney nods, working her puzzle. She sighs. "Your trunk was the last place he needed ta check. I mean Rob was all over this place." Her voice drops to a whisper, "There was no typewriter to be found, so maybe he'll put it to rest and become somebody else's nightmare. Good! God! If he is somebody else's nightmare, then all this ridin' up and down the street tonight means he's stalkin' ya! He's a frickin' prevert!"

Leora leans over, lifting the gun off the kitchen chair, holding it by the nozzle. "Well, he's gonna be a dead one!" She lays it lovingly back into its place of concealment.

"Maybe we should just give all those papers to the cops. They're original. If we wait too long, they might be obsolete."

"Ya think? Wait! Wait! Wait! I don't think there's an expiration date. But what do we tell 'em? We found it under a cabbage leaf? Somebody handed 'em to us because we're kind, considerate, adorable, and understanding? Yo, Sis, we couldn't say anything before about the typewriter, remember? The cops would tell and then we get killed, or we give it to Griff and then we get killed. Now we have a stupid safe." Leora finishes her puzzle. "Oh, plus there's the envelope, the one Griff is holdin' over the families or whoever they are? Remember? If the cops get that envelope, then they get New York then live at eleven we're whacked!"

Sydney blinks with a disgruntled gaze. "So we're back ta square one." The redhead puckers her lips, thinking. "Then if anybody mentions," Sydney counts on her fingers, "the typewriter, a safe, Nancy Lister, money, oh, the ransom note, shit, never mind . . . anything. We just say huh to everything."

"Yeah, everything and everybody, includin' Eva. She don't need ta be mixed up in any of this and if she does get mixed up in it, it won't be 'cause she heard it from us."

"Yeah, she can point to Doc."

Her completed fountain pen paper makes a crinkling noise as Leora smooths it flat on the table, looking over, 'Starr' written frontward and blotted backward. "I think he was just startin' this. I don't think he did this and then thought of usin' his mother. I think he was already usin' her until she was so bad he couldn't use her anymore. I think he was practicin'."

Sydney lays two more pieces in place on the final sheet of the fountain pen paper. "Yepper, 'cause he wasn't even close." She affixes them to the main sheet.

Leora smooths Sydney's first completed paper flat; 'Lennon' blotted and written. Now her second one, 'George'. "What's that one you're doin', John?"

"No, George."

"Another George? Wow."

"Practice makes perfect."

Leora shakes her head, studying the signatures. "He sucked. He had a long way ta go."

Sydney tapes the last two pieces in place, handing the paper to Leora. "It's time ta stink it up, see what else we can get into." She stands stretching, glancing at the clock: 9:58.

"You are the Puzzle Queen!" Leora flattens the final paper, laying it on the pile standing and stretching, too.

"Thank you, thank you very much." Sydney mimics the King.

Leora gathers the papers. "I'll take 'em upstairs and put 'em with the other ones."

"Good thinkin', Sis. Let's keep all Stephen's papers together. Should we put it all back in the cat cave, Wheezer's playground?"

"Get outta my mind." Leora smiles at her best friend. "Should we take the flashlights?"

Sydney leans sideways, tapping her head as if to empty it out of her ears. "Yo! Sis! Get outta mine."

The best friends reach for the wooden pipe simultaneously. "Pierre!" they say in unison.

Upstairs, the brunette places the puzzle papers into the wastebasket with all the other findings. Sydney runs back downstairs for drinks—a wine and a Mick, using an elbow to turn the kitchen light out and an elbow to turn the hall light on. She sets drinks on the nightstand, checking the bedroom with her partner in crime to make sure everything discovered behind the linen closet is on its way back in.

"Wait a minute, Sis." Sydney turns off Leora's bedroom light then peeks through the drapes, peering out the window. The outside world is still, quiet. "Ah'ight."

Leora begins the parade to the linen closet, hitting the hall light switch on her way, followed by Wheezer with Sydney bringing up the rear.

Bang! Bang! Wheezer is none too keen sharing his playground with anyone or anything, including his roommates, especially when he is not permitted to enter through his portal. After the initial opening, he returns reluctant, hating that disgusting noise. Besides, they might not smell anything but he does—flea spray.

"Hey, Tiger, what? Are you afraid of the dark?" Sydney feels around the door jam with the help of the hall light. "Let me find a switch . . . here . . . some place." Now she uses her flashlight.

Leora joins in. "What the hell? I don't see anything, Sis."

Sydney wiggles her nose like Samantha Stevens.

Leora laughs, crossing her arms and blinking like Jeannie. "Never mind."

The redhead slips into the back bedroom, unscrewing the light bulb in the table lamp sitting on the floor, yelling on her way over to the linen closet. "Here, Sis." She peers into the darkness. "Yo! Sis!" Sydney shines her flashlight down the steps. "Yo! Momma! Here ya go!"

Leora stands behind Sister Syd. "What?"

Sydney screams. From the waist up, her body wants to go this way while from the waist down it wants to go that way.

"Yo! Sis! It's me!"

"That's you! This is me! You scared the livin' shit outta me!" Sydney's legs are like rubber. "Where'd ya go?"

Leora leans over, placing her hands on her knees, almost hyperventilating. "I stuffed Pierre. Holy shit!" Her heart is none too regular either. She feels it in her throat.

"Whew! Momma, we ready?"

"If you say so."

"Here." Sydney hands Leora the bulb.

"What's this for?"

"Well, I've been thinkin'. You go in the cat cave while I go out back and look for a light switch or chain or rope, whatever."

"There's already a bulb down there."

"I know, but just in case it's burned out or broke, whatever. In case it don't work. I'm out. I ain't runnin' all the way back in here."

"Good thinkin', Sis, 'cause I don't feel like runnin' up and down the broken steps either."

Leora sets the wastebasket on top of the safe, shining her flashlight on Wheezer's portal. She pulls the scarves through the portal and waits to see her best friend's flashlight, and there it is.

The beam from Sydney's flashlight flits all over. "I don't see any switch, damn it!"

"Yeah, with our luck it's probably in the safe!" Leora squeezes between the metal monstrosity and the wall, shining the flashlight on the fixture in the corner. The square brass cover with only three of its four glass panes sits loosely in place on the base. A seventy-five-watt bulb protrudes above the dingy glass fixture and jiggles in the socket when touched. Leora twists it, flooding the space with light. Instantly, she looks away, now turning the fixture clockwise, facing the missing glass pane side toward the wall, seeing nothing but white. "Yo! Sis! It blitzed me!"

Sydney peeks in Wheezer's portal. "Wow, Momma. What is it a floodlight? Here I come!" She shoves the massive cupboard open, hearing a slight clanging of metal. The linen closet shelving moves effortlessly. Physics at its finest. She moves to the second step next to the typewriter, closing the cupboard and shining the flashlight as she descends the staircase. She shoves the flashlight under her arm, lifting a square dome-shaped brass fixture by its small spire.

"What is it, Sis?" Leora is still seeing white spots from her blitz.

"I think it's the top piece of that fixture. Whew! It's really dusty." Sydney tries wiping some of the dust off. She blows on it then places it in the wastebasket, making sure not to break the extra bulb.

"I take it there was no switch up there, huh?"

"Hey, maybe there isn't one. Maybe ya just tighten and untighten the bulb."

"Works for me! At least you found somethin'." Leora is frustrated. "I have been all over this safe. I didn't find anything. I didn't find any sign of a combination written on the damn thing or scratched into it. I rubbed all over it so much, well, let me just say if there was a Genie in there we'd a seen 'im by now. Stephen musta kept the combo in his head. Oh, by the way, ya still need a flashlight. The damn safe casts a shadow big time in the front and over there on the other side."

The girls search walls, base boards, steps.

"I quit!" Leora packs Wheezer's portal with the scarves. "It's gettin' a little brisk."

"It certainly is. We need a bonfire. Oh! Yeah! Fire it up!" Sydney takes a toke and passes.

Leora surveys the enclosed area. "Wow! All this and then drop dead before you can tell anybody." She passes. "Well, it coulda been worse. He coulda dropped dead in here!"

Sydney chokes on a hit. "Yeah, no wonder Third Eye is goin' nuts!"

"Don't I wish? And you know how that goes."

"What, the wish in one hand thing?" Sydney passes.

Leora nods exhaling. "Oh, if he knew about this, he'd kill us twice!" She smacks the safe.

Sydney lights and passes. "We can't move the damn thing." She kicks it. We definitely can't tell anybody. We can't even get a locksmith, we'll have ta kill 'im."

Leora rubs the side of the safe. "Open sez me. See. Nothing. That's what I thought. Well, I'm ready if you are."

"Yeah, that's enough fun. Let's go get in trouble." Sydney removes the dusty top piece of the fixture from the wastebasket. "He couldn't use this top 'cause the bulb is too big. See?" She points to the fixture with the bulb protruding out of the top. "But a regular size bulb isn't bright enough."

"It's a dim watt."

Sydney laughs, holding the intricately designed top above the bulb. It could sit in place on its brass frame if the bulb was just a hair or two smaller. "That's pretty. I mean if it weren't so dusty." She glances around. "Yeah, it's too dark with this on. We could use it as a paper weight."

"Or a murder weapon."

"Yo! Sis!" The redhead shudders admiring the almost completed fixture one last time. "Boy, these are really dirty."

"Oh, I thought they were frosted glass."

"That's funny." Sydney wipes the center pane with a finger, tilting the top part toward her away from the bulb as she rests it on the edge of the frame. The solid brass piece blocks the rays of light illuminating the wall. "Boy, these are really cruddy." She leans closer, wiping another, now the other, now the center one, wiping again and again and again. She licks her finger wiping again. "Oh, My! God!"

"What?" Leora squints, blinking. Along the bottom of each pane of glass are two letters in faded magic marker.

"Look, Sis! Look!" Sydney twists the empty side of the cover counterclockwise to begin her demonstration. She holds the cover over the bulb on the edge of the frame. "Watch! Watch!" She rotates the glass fixture clockwise. pi, er, re.

Leora blinks, holding her forehead. "P-i-e-r-r-e! Pierre!"

Finders Keepers

"Who woulda thunk?

Sydney smirks. "Who's on first?

"What?"

"What's on second?"

Leora blinks. "I don't know."

"I don't know's on third."

Leora gets it. "Chief Sill's on third." The girls laugh.

"The one out front isn't like this one."

"What out front?"

"The outside light fixture. It isn't the same design as this one, is it?"

"No, it's not as Gothic. But it isn't Early American either."

"Yeah, more like Early Addams Family." Sydney shields her eyes. She has been squinting the whole time. She lifts the top, laying it behind her on the safe. "We should change the light bulb. We don't need it this bright. What do we have ta read? Ya can't see the front of the safe anyway. It's in its own shadow. We need a flashlight or Bic. Maybe he put that light bulb in so he could see his writing on the cover. That is his writing." Sydney pauses. "It's the same writing that's on all those papers. You can tell by the backward three. Well, put it this way: whoever wrote the payouts and addresses wrote this."

"I saw one of them, too, the three, remember?" Leora thinks. "On our list." *The list Ginn found . . . returned . . . in the car . . . the music . . . his laugh . . . his arms . . . his kiss.* Leora sighs. "An E written like that, a backward three. Turns out it was Griff's tag number in the mirr—" Leora shades her eyes, blinking at the glass cover. She gasps. "Yo! Sis! Look! Look at the letters! They could be backward numbers! Think about it! PI! Is that nineteen? And here, look, seventy-three! And that's thirty-seven!"

Sydney sucks air with gasping sounds. "The combination!" She exhales.

Both perch on the steps, taking small sips of beverages, trying to swallow past the lumps in their throats.

"Is this how it felt ta open Pandora's Box?"

"I don't know. Good grief! Sis! Ya think we're gonna unleash somethin'?" Leora blinks.

"Sydney bucks her eyes. "Well, ya think this is a good thing?"

"I don't know. It's not a bad thing, is it?"

"Well, okay, then is it the right thing?"

"I don't know about right either. Is this wrong?"

"Geez, Sis." Sydney sighs, staring at the handle and the dial. "We're gonna open a can of worms."

"That's the biggest can of worms I ever saw in my life."

"I like worms," Sydney reasons.

"Me ta. Ya know a worm has ten hearts."

"Nah-uh, I didn't know. So a worm is all heart."

"But they're not all in the same place like a cluster."

"Well, that's good ta know."

"Yeah, five on one side and five on the other, like evenly spaced little ribs. One side's a boy and one side's a girl. But it can't go forth and multiply. It needs another worm."

Sydney stares, blinking profusely, catching flies.

"What? I got an A in science. What can I tell ya?" Leora continues. "That band you see on the middle of 'em in the spring is how they mate. And they only have one baby."

Sydney holds her face, leaning her elbows on her knees, blinking at Leora.

"If you rip 'em in half, they regenerate then ya have two worms. Farmers know that."

"Good a can of worms. They don't bite, and they can't see us. I'm in." Sydney raises her hand for a high five. Her best friend complies. "Finders keepers."

"Yeah, ya snooze ya lose! And that's the truth." Leora gives a raspberry.

The girls stoop in front of the safe. Sydney weaves her fingers together, stretching and limbering up. Leora laughs, aiming her beam of light onto the dial. "Okay, its right-left-right, right? Isn't that how it was in school?"

"You mean the school lockers?" Leora practices on an air combination. "Yes."

"It's showtime!" Sister Syd's hands are clammy. She begins at zero, turning the dial to nineteen, inhaling and exhaling as if in labor. "What's the next one? What's the next one?"

"Seventy-three, right? I mean to the left, right? Nineteen was to the right, right?"

Sydney nods, turning the dial counter clockwise to seventy-three.

"Okay now thirty-seven, right?"

Sydney turns the dial to the right. Thirty-seven aligns with the notch on the safe. She exhales, yanking the handle. Nothing. "Are you shittin' me, mister?" She does it again with the same result.

"Wait a minute. Wait a minute, Sis." The brunette checks with her air combination again. "You have ta go around twice or somethin', remember?"

Sydney's eyes dart back and forth as she searches her mind. "Oh yeah, somethin' about goin' past zero. Sydney begins again, starting at zero, turning right to nineteen then leeeft past seventy-five, past zero to seventy-five then right to thirty-seven. She exhales, pulling the handle up again. Nothing.

"Maybe for it to open, we have to do left-right-left instead of right-left-right."

Sydney moves out of the way. "Have at it."

Leora's turn. Left-right-left. She stands, yanking the handle. Nothing. She does right-left-right standing pulling as hard as she can. Nothing.

"Maybe I should pat my head with one hand, rub my stomach with the other, and hop up and down on one foot." Sydney stands with her fingers weaved together, holding the back of her neck.

"Sounds easier than this shit." Leora grabs the handle, trying to jerk it up and down.

"I'm done. I'm ready for some real trouble."

"Me, ta."

"Ya hear it, Sis?"

"What?"

"I got a secret. I got a secret," Leora sings in her little girl voice

Sydney kicks the safe. "I got one, too-o-o," she sings. "Well, a secret ain't a secret unless ya tell it. Give it up." She kicks the metal nemesis again, squeezing between it and the wall, facing the fixture to unscrew the bulb. "Ow!" She tries a second time. "Son-of-a-bitch that's hot!" She licks her fingertips. "Damn!" Between the hot bulb, the tight space, and her not-so-small hands, the redhead barely turns the bulb. "Shit! I can't get my fingers in there!"

"It was easy to twist it on. It wasn't hot." Leora holds her hands in front of her face, pretending to hide. "Yo! Sis! But can ya do this?"

"I certainly can." Now Sydney holds her hands in front of her face.

"Yo! Sis! Where 'd ya go?"

"Peek-a-boo!"

"Peek-a-boo to you, too!"

"Wow!" Sydney squints. "That wasn't such a good idea. My eyes liked the dark. Don't this thing come off?" She feels around the bottom of the glass cover with one hand and shades her eyes with the other.

"The one out front doesn't. Ya have ta reach in and wipe it out when ya change the bulb. It's all one piece." Leora shrugs. "This one moves 'cause I turned it when it blitzed me. The opening was facin' this-a-way." Leora points to the opposite wall.

Sydney turns the brass fixture counterclockwise. "Yepper, it's loose. It isn't on tight. Just think, he put this on here." The glass cover begins to wobble. "Oh! Shit! Sis! We can't take this off. We got ta take the bulb out first! It's too big ta fit through the bottom!"

"You're kiddin' me?" Leora rolls her eyes, shaking her head. "I am so ready ta get in trouble. Don't you have a baseball bat in your trunk?"

"Yeah, we need a break. Bryce'll probably be a no-show, but if he does show it won't be 'til after four tomorrow mornin'. We can come back in a bit for round two."

"My turn!" The girls switch places. Leora reaches in the opening made by the missing pane of glass. No maneuvering there. She feels inside the top of the square cover. "Hand me my wine, Sis."

"There ya go, Sis, get it drunk!"

Leora takes a couple of gulps before shoving the tips of her fingers into the cold liquid now holding her hand in an upright position. "Scalpel!" She hands Sydney the wine. Now with one, two, three quick twists the light bulb unscrews sending them into darkness.

"Whoa!"

"Yo! Sis! Move your hand. Where'd ya go? I can't see!" The girls blink and giggle in the blackness.

Sydney grabs Leora's lit flashlight on the safe to retrieve hers from the steps. "Here."

Leora squeezes out of the tight space. "Ready?"

"You wanna put the other bulb in first?"

"Ya want to? Might as well since we're already here and it's finally loose. Then we don't have ta go through all this shit again." She faces the wall again, aiming the beam at the fixture then doing touch testing on the bulb. "It's gettin' cooler." She gives it another half a twist.

Sydney takes the seventy-five-watt in exchange for the sixty.

Leora illuminates the socket through the open side of the square fixture, moving this way and shining the light, moving that way and shining the light. "Yo! Sis! It looks like he wrote numbers on the inside of this thing with a magic marker 'cause they're way darker than the outside. Look."

Leora leans toward the back wall, giving Sister Syd room to get a good look-see.

"Here hold my flashlight." Sydney turns the glass cover counterclockwise until it unscrews completely. She removes it with both hands, placing it on top of the safe. The girls inspect the brass with flashlights a blazing. "Yepper, look. From the outside, they look worn and faded."

"He probably wrote 'em in there in case he forgot. I mean, he worked with numbers all the time. He's the only one he had ta worry about." Leora blinks. "We were doin' it backward!"

"What ninety-one?"

"No! No! It's still nineteen, but it's last instead of first. Here, look. What did we say?" Leora shines her flashlight on the glass cover reading on the outside left to right. "We said Pierre, see: nineteen, seventy-three, thirty-seven. But from the inside readin' from the left it's thirty-seven, seventy-three, and nineteen! We don't have ta reverse or switch or anything! The numbers are numbers! That's how he wrote it! We did it backward!"

Placing the glass cover back in position becomes a two-man job, well, four hands. Leora shines her flashlight on the socket as Sydney threads the heavy outdoor cover into place. Leora hands Sydney the sixty-watt. She screws it into the socket, flooding the small area with instant light, although not as bright as before, it is better than two beams of light in pitch-black. "Sis, I was thinkin'."

"Oh, boy. That ain't good," Leora teases.

Sydney laughs. "No, listen. Maybe that pane of glass is missin' on purpose, so he knows where ta start."

The girls step away in silence. Sydney stands with arms crossed. Leora sets the flashlight on top of the safe. They have been mentally drained for a long time now – weeks. The metal monster will finally give up its secret, Stephen's secret.

"Watch when we open it up there'll be an IOU." Leora jiggles an ice cube into her mouth.

"I was thinkin' more on the line of . . . "Psych!"

Leora sighs. "As long as there's nothin' in there that says 'don't turn around'!"

Sydney shivers turning around shining her light up the steps. "Yo! Sis!"

Leora turns, blinking in flurries at the top of the stairs. "What is it?" Her voice cracks.

Sydney exhales through her mouth. "You scared the sh— what? You thought I was psychin' you? I thought you were psychin' me! You said don't turn around! You creeped me out!"

Leora shimmies with a chill.

Sydney takes a deep breath. "Ah 'ight. Ready?"

"Ready."

The girls sit Indian-style on the floor, lit flashlights in hand, Leora to the left facing their 'elephant'.

Both spotlight the dial as Sydney turns to each number in their new combination, ending with nineteen on the notch. The dial tightens slightly as the tumblers align. Two flashlight beams spotlight the front of the safe, shadowed by its immense size. Sydney pulls up. Nothing. She closes her eyes, shaking her head.

"You're shittin' me!" Leora shines the light on the dial.

Sydney pulls on the handle. Angrily she stands with a death grip on it. With each word she yanks as hard as she can. "Huckl-buckle-bean-stalk!"

Nothing. She forces the handle down. Down it goes! She holds it in place, afraid it will pop back up and lock itself. Her heart is pounding.

Leora's heart is in her throat. She springs to her knees, closer, shining the light at the opening.

Sydney pulls on the door swinging it open as she drops to her knees. Two beacons of light flit to and fro. Bundles and bundles of US currency fill the safe except for papers shoved onto the top of the pile and save for the space across the front occupied by three brown bags, a red velvet pouch, and what seems to be an ever allusive ledger.

Leora is speechless.

So is Sydney. She gives a soft wolf whistle.

They continue shining their flashlights on the contents, slower now, gawking, unconsciously shaking their heads.

"Yo, Sis, what da ya wanna do?"

Sydney smiles at Leora. "How 'bout we count it? Fifty-fifty."

Leora moves closer, peering inside, leaning side to side. "That's solid money, Sis, all the way to the bank, I mean back."

Sydney feels a paper bag, softly pushing, recognizing the unmistakable shape. She gasps. "That's a gun!"

Leora feels, too. "Are they all guns?" She feels the other two bags. "Yeah, Momma, they're guns." She does not want to look at them. Neither does Sydney. They believe their hands. "These are the ones, aren't they, the ones with the finger prints? These are what Griff is so gunge-ho about."

"You mean the ones New York's been lookin' for all this time? Yepper, I think these be the ones." Sydney pulls the ledger, slipping to a sitting position, leafing through the pages. "Yo! Sis! That's what he did, copied everything in here keepin' it up ta date. Look! There's scads of shit written in here. This goes back a ways."

Leora glances sideways, nodding, reaching for the top of the safe for the small stack of papers stuffed onto the top of the currency. They move slowly as she pulls them from the cramped area, careful not to rip any. "He . . . couldn't . . . fit another one . . . in here." The safe finally surrenders envelopes and photographs. She lays them on the top of the safe, pulling the largest one from under all of them, knowing it is a picture and turns it over. A black and white photo of The Fab Four smiles at her with their names written over their heads. "Whoa!" She turns the picture sideways.

Sydney clamors to her knees, throwing the ledger on the floor. With her hands on her hips; she goosenecks the photo. "She signed those contracts we found, huh, didn't she?"

"Doesn't it look like this writing? This is the picture Marie was talkin' about, you know, the one Mrs. Lister wrote on so she wouldn't forget their names. I wonder why he's got it." Leora blinks at Sydney. "She died."

"You're right. She died. He was practicin'." Sydney looks at a smaller black and white picture of a mother, father, and a boy about five or six years old, dated on the back 1940. Another is of a gray-haired woman dated 1974. A five-by-seven picture of Stephen, a younger Stephen, undated with his name written above his head. The redhead hands them to Leora, grabbing an unsealed manila envelope. She turns the plain envelope over and over in her hands, checking for writing, then reaches inside, pulling out a white sealed business envelope addressed to a district attorney's office in New York. She holds it in the air with her finger and thumb. "Yo! Sis! The letter! The third letter! This is the third letter!"

Leora stands eyes wide, mouth wider, arms to her sides. "It all makes sense now. This is what he's really been after all along. We just found his death warrant."

"Griff is probably the last person alive who knew Stephen had this. I don't think Marcie knows." She slips it back in the manila envelope. "Come on." Sydney lifts the paper bags one by one, placing them on the floor.

"We gotta find Goo Goo. He might know who ta give all this to. He's in the numbers. We'll see about your car then hit work and see if Goo Goo's around. If not, we'll swing by his place for some midnight knockin'. Good-bye, Griff."

"See ya." The girls lay the pictures on the safe. "We're leavin' this open, aren't we?"

Sydney places the ledger on top of them. "Yepper." She reaches in the wastebasket for the top piece of the fixture, sitting it between the safe and the door. "There, that's bett—" The spring on the back door interrupts.

"Listen! Will ya listen?" A voice strains to whisper on the patio. "It's fine. The kitchen light's off. They're upstairs. You saw the lights on up there. Well, just slip in, put it under the couch cushion then he can call the cops. I told ya ta let me try. You probably didn't have the damn thing in all the way that's why it broke."

Leora tries to swallow fear. She is afraid they will hear her. Sydney stands dumfounded, reaching over, twisting the light off. Not that it matters. The winter scarves block the cold air and the light. But darkness has become somewhat of a guardian. The girls lean on the safe, listening. One of their flashlights tap the safe.

"What was that?"

The partners in crime recognize Jammer's voice.

"That was your ass hittin' the floor if the boss finds out you screwed this up. They're gonna know somebody was here when they can't get their key in the hole. Don't say anything until we come back out. I don't wanna have ta shoot anybody with this," Hector states. "And don't touch nothin'. We ain't here ta party. In fact, maybe you oughtta just stand here and wait for me."

The best friends hear shuffling and jiggling. "It's locked! Now what? He's gonna be pissed."

"Should we go ask 'im?"

"He ain't there! You dumb son-of-a-bitch! Marcie and him went to meet Angelo and Tito out at the Chateau." The screen door squeaks as the spring stretches again. "What are ya doin'?"

"Lookin' for that damn cat. I hate cats."

"Shhhh! Shut up, will ya? At least whisper."

"What are we doin' now?"

"We'll put it in her car under the front seat, then we'll call and tell the boss they changed the lock so we couldn't get in. And stick ta the story. They changed the lock that's all ya got ta remem..." Their voices become inaudible as they walk out of the enclosed patio around the house.

"They gone." Leora whispers.

"I think so."

Leora grabs the envelope, shoving the pipe in her pocket. She grabs the Mick bottle, her empty wine glass, and one of the paperbag guns, shining her light on the other two.

Sydney shoves her flashlight under her arm, grabbing a gun in each hand. "Ready?"

"I'll go first, and then I'll light your way."

"Ah'ight."

Wheezer stands at the top of the steps, waiting patiently with a friendly meow.

"Wheezer!" Leora calls, climbing the stairs. He flops. "Oh! Wheezer! He wants ta hurt you!" She shines the flashlight, guiding Sister Syd up the broken staircase, laying the brown bag on the floor.

Sydney's brown bags join it. She pulls the linen closet shelves closed, sliding the dead bolt almost through into place.

In the meantime, Leora turns the hall light off, tiptoeing to her bedroom. Sydney follows. They spot two figures running across Ninth Street to a black van.

"We gotta go find out about your car. And we gotta find Goo Goo."

"You mean mean before you get arrested for a setup?" The van speeds away up Ninth Street toward Chester. "You know I was feelin' bad when I said this is his death warrant. But guess what, couldn't happen to a nicer guy."

"I don't like gophers either."

"'Specially the two-legged kind."

"'Specially the ones that hate cats."

It is after eleven thirty. The girls gather their bounty, placing them at the front door.

R-i-n-n-g! R-i-n-n-g!

"Hello . . . Hey, Bryce. Workin' hard or hardly workin?"

"You got it, not if I can help it."

"So who's this blind date that ain't blind?"

"Oh, you mean George?" Bryce chuckles. "That's my cousin."

"Not another one. He's a nice guy, right?"

"I don't know I never dated 'im."

Leora laughs. "He's not married, is he?"

"Divorced four times, seven kids."

"Oh, great, a hobby. Wait a sec." Leora hands the phone to Sydney, shaking her head, laughing. She unlocks the backdoor, settling Wheezer out on the patio with food and unfrozen water. "Wheezer, you be careful. They wanna hurt you." The young feline flops. She hangs coats and sweaters over the scarves stuffed in the hole and opens the other side of his bedroom just slightly so he is not cornered if confronted by the bastards. Wheezer performs an inspection, following Leora into his den. The orange and white purrs, loving the door, walking through to his bed, and squeezing through the other end, coming back around to Leora.

"What da ya think, ah'ight?" His purr is silenced as he sniffs the air; listening, ears back, tail swishing. "That's it. That's the smell. Stay away from 'em." She pets him. "Gaw head. Go play. Do your thing. We'll be back. We won't be long." Leora closes the backdoor, locking it, watching Wheezer's decision for a bit of nourishment.

"Bryce said he'll be here about four-thirty."

"I'm in!" Leora turns around. "Oh, shit! The key!"

The curly duo make a bee line to the front door. Sure enough, upon closer inspection, a piece of jagged metal juts out of the keyhole.

"Wait a sec." Sydney runs to the kitchen for a flashlight.

"Here, Sis, right here. You can feel it."

"That son-of-a-bitch." The jagged piece is almost a point and very sharp. Sydney roots in her Wrangler bag for tweezers in her makeup case. She grasps the pointy end, jiggling it up and down and sideways. The tweezers slip off. She does it again. They slip off again.

"Does it feel like you're movin' it?"

"I don't know. I wanna think I am. That doesn't mean I am."

Leora turns the porch lights on, stepping outside, the warm air condensing on the cold storm door glass. That quick she is back in the warm. "Brrrrr!"

"What's up?" Sydney works diligently on the stuck piece of key.

Leora opens her hand, revealing the other piece. "He dropped it. What a jackass! Didn't even bother ta take it with 'im. What a piece of shit! I hope the lock works after all this."

"We need somethin' a little stronger to grip this. I hope that's all it is. I hope it's not bent too bad."

"Well, if we can't get it out you, gaw head and find Goo Goo. You're gonna get arrested! My car can wait."

"Hey, Momma, strength in numbers. That's plural! And no my mouse in my pocket doesn't count!"

Leora blinks. "Wait a minute. I gave Tink some little tools to go with his erector set. There was a pair of regular pliers, two different screwdrivers, and needle-nose pliers. Let me go look in the tool drawer." Leora searches the drawer to no avail. Now checking the top junk drawer, reaching way in the back and seeing with her hands. She feels the little case, maneuvering it through the maze of life's paraphernalia, grasping it now in two hands, this little vinyl case with 'JUST LIKE DADDY'S'printed on the front. She breathes through her mouth, hustling to her best friend. "Here it is! Here it is! I got it!"

Sydney slides the flap up, unfolding the top, exposing the dark blue handles of a miniature metal tool set, removing the needle-nose pliers. "Oh, my God, these are perfect, Sis." She works her magic with only two fingers and a thumb doing her bidding. The little pliers hold fast as Sydney pulls in all directions, finally dislodging the bent end of the key.

Leora pushes her jacket out of the way on the coatrack, rooting for her keys in her denim bag. She takes the key pieces, dropping them in the little zipper pocket with her homemade roach clip.

Sydney places the needle-nose pliers back in the vinyl pouch. "Where do these go, Sis?"

"Top drawer." Leora locks and unlocks the door with the key, without it, with the door open, with the door closed.

"Is it workin'?" Sydney asks, putting her jacket on.

"Yeah, it's workin'." Leora shoves her keys in her jacket pocket, slipping it on. She grabs a brown bag and the manila envelope before sliding her jeans bag over her shoulder. "Ya ready?"

"Look at you! My worst nightmare has come true! Me lookin' at you totin' a gun! I wanna run!" Sydney piles the two guns on top of each other, carrying them like a set of school books, also slipping her denim bag over her shoulder.

"What about me, Two Guns? I'm lookin' at you totin' ta of 'em! We're are so screwed!"

They lay the brown bags and the envelope on the floor behind the passenger seat then climb into the T- Bird. "Wait a minute! Wait a minute!" Sydney exits the car then leans in, feeling under her seat. Almost immediately, her closed fist touches cold metal. She sucks air.

"It's there, huh?"

"It's right there!" Sydney sits behind the steering wheel, lighting a cigarette, and winding her window down. "It's not in a bag or anything. I guess I'm suppose ta be as stupid as they are and go, 'what's this?' and pick it up."

"Holy shit! Sis! What the hell? We went from zero guns ta five, five, Sis! There's four guns in this car!"

A gray Trainer police car pulls up, facing the front of Sydney's Bird. It is Chief Sill. The best friends scramble out of the car, slamming doors shut.

"Hi," Leora says, walking with Sydney on wobbly legs to meet the chief. She feels anxious, very anxious. Her face is flushed. She feels faint. *I think I'm gonna die!*

Chief Sill exits his car, removing a White Owl, nodding hello. "Ladies."

"We were just on our way ta see you. She wants ta know about her car."

"Well, that's why I'm here. They said they're done with your car in New York, but Chester wants to conduct their own investigation."

"Is that bad?" The brunette gulps air.

"Not really. There's someone, well, ah, there's, ah, some complications and they feel the need to investigate further.

The girls surmise complications because of Rob. They play dumb. Not a problem.

"Okay, they can." Leora nods.

"Oh, they don't need your permission, Sweetie. They wanted me to let you know. The good thing about it is other than the trunk being broke there's nothing else wrong with your car."

"Well, it was found in water, wasn't it?" Leora pulls her jacket closed, shivering.

"Yes, but it was very shallow water, very shallow, not even up to the axle."

"So it's drivable?"

"Oh, yes, but not by them. They'll have to flatbed it. They're not allowed to drive it what with it being involved in an ongoing investigation. That means they'll load it up on a truck and bring it down. You understand? When they're done combing through it for evidence, you get it back. It saves you a trip up there and they pay to transport."

"When are they bringin' it down?"

"Maybe next week. I think you're entitled to a rental." He pops the White Owl in his mouth.

"Oh no, no thanks. I'll wait." Leora looks at Sydney.

"Yeah, we have a car. We ain't takin' a trip. We were, but we don't have ta now, right, Sis?"

Leora nods. "Are they gonna let me know, or should I get a hold of you?"

"I can handle it from my end if you'd like. It's fine with me. Sorta keep 'em on their toes. Cut out some red tape, not that they'd give you the run around."

Or blow smoke." Sydney throws a cheese grin.

"Thank you. So I should call you some time next week. Is that okay?"

"That's fine. Wednesday or Thursday. That should give them enough time to at least get it down here. " Chief Sill climbs into the squad car. "I'm on first shift next week, ladies."

The girls plaster smiles on their faces, waving good-bye, watching him back onto Ninth Street then head to the station. The jittery pistol-packin' mommas are on their way in less than two minutes, afraid the chief might get a call and circle back. The parking lots front and back at Papa's are half full with leftover shuffleboard players—the last game until after the holidays. Goo Goo's Caddy is nowhere to be found. The black van is parked in the back.

"Great! Why can't it be the Cadillac?"

Leora sighs. "Because it would be too easy."

They ride by Goo Goo's looking and looking. No blue Cadillac.

"Yo! Sis! Now what? We can't be ridin' around with four guns . . . and you on the lamb!"

"With Pierre!" Sydney fires it up. They pass back and forth, winding down windows, blasting the heat. Sydney pulls behind the tavern parking lot toward the backdoor.

"I got an idea. Wait here, Sis." Leora fishes through her denim bag, coming up with the bag of dolls. She takes the two pieces of the broken key out of the little inside zipper pocket.

"Quit thinkin, Sis! What are we doin'?"

"You and that mouse again. We, are gonna give these away. I'm gonna stick 'em in the van, call the cops, and tell 'em two guys are dealin' pills out of a black van, wait ten minutes, no, five minutes then walk over ta Heckle 'n' Jeckle and tell 'em they forgot these." She opens her hand, revealing the two pieces of the broken key. "I'll leave and the sorry asses 'ill follow me. If not, the cops'll show and ask who owns the van. Either way, bad-da-boom –"

Sydney smiles, shaking her head. "Bad-da-bing."

"I'm gonna check the van, make sure it's not locked and see if anybody's snorin'."

The redhead hands her best friend a couple dimes. "I'll be here. Hurry up."

"Yeah, after this we'll sleep in front of Goo Goo's." Leora tiptoes down to the van. She opens the passenger door, shoving the plastic bag of pills into the glove compartment. Holding up a wait-a-minute finger, she runs to the back entrance, scaling the four or five steps, opening the back door. The buzz of conversation joins the sounds of the shuffleboard, the registers; the jukebox. She heads for the payphone, slowly tiptoeing around the curved wall to eyeball half a crowd. A guy walking toward the jukebox turns, facing the bar. She knows that walk anywhere. Hector walks as if there is a load in his pants. "I said I'm gettin' my cigarettes outta the van."

"I got a full pack on the floor in the back. Grab mine, too," Jammer yells.

Leora turns, walking quickly toward the rear entrance, opening the office door, slipping inside, and coming face to face with Papa.

Behind Closed Doors

*P*apa stands at the bottom of the spiral staircase. Leora stands against the door, startled, blinking to believe her eyes. Apprehension dissipates. She forces a smile, walking toward Papa's open arms; a sorta cheese smile now morphing into a sneer, a grotesque sneer as the corners of her mouth sink to a grotesque frown, bringing blinding tears, her body wracked with uncontrollable sobbing. "Oh! Papa!" she mutters, burying her face in his chest.

"I'm ah so sorry," the seasoned Italian tells her, embracing her, patting her. "It's ah gonna be good, kabish, Lea-Lea, kabish?"

Leora pulls away sniffling, wiping her wet cheeks. Papa hands her his handkerchief. "No good, Papa, no good. Sydney's gonna get arrested." The frown begins again. The brunette tries to harness the drooping corners of her mouth, signaling the flood gates. "They put a gun in her car! It's never gonna stop!" She sobs in Papa's monogrammed handkerchief.

"Who? Who does this?"

"Who else, Papa? Griff. He didn't do it, but he might as well have. His cronies, gophers, you know, Jammer and Hector. A setup, it's a setup!"

"These ah men, put a gun in ah my Cindy's car? You say this?"

"Yes, Papa, I say this, in the car."

"And ah no questions. You know for sure?"

"Yes, Papa. We watched 'em run from the car. The gun is under her front seat."

Papa rubs his forehead, exhaling, his jaw clenched. "Why would ah they do this?"

Leora blinks. Concern crosses her face. "Because he's never gonna stop! I don't have a car, Papa." She wants to spill her guts; the money, the letter, the guns, Rob, the typewriter, Crow. She feels guilty as if the fault is hers, as if she asked for all of this, as if he will judge her, admonish her; shake his finger at her. "We overheard 'em. They were gonna put it under the sofa cushion! They thought we were upstairs." She sighs, looking around the room, avoiding his eyes.

Papa's face shows anger. "You in ah the house when ah, um, when ah they do this?"

"Yes, Papa."

The old man shakes his head, mumbling in Italian.

"They're here, Papa, sittin' at the bar."

"No Griffonetti, finabla."

"No, Griff is out at the Chateau with his sister, meeting Noodle the slime ball."

"Who's ah this Noodle?"

"Oh, it's a man called Angelo and his buddy, his sidekick, goomba, Tito."

Papa is taken aback. He knows who they are, what they are, what they do. He rubs his cheeks, his mouth, his chin, his torqued jaw. "Who say this to you?" His voice is demanding.

"I say this, Papa. We heard them, Papa, the gophers, they said it. Jammer wanted ta call and ask Griff if it was okay ta stick it in the car 'cause the doors were locked and they couldn't get in the house. That's when Hector told Jammer Griff wasn't around."

You come look ah for me?"

"No, Papa." *You're suppose ta be in Italy.* Leora thinks it but does not say it out loud. "I came ta put 'em in jail, ta set 'em up."

"No, don't use ah the gun. It's ah no good."

"Oh, no, Papa, I'm not usin' the gun. I have the pills that they planted in my car. Remember the night the mayor and everybody was here, when Goo Goo said Griff was gonna get me arrested? They planted pills in my car. They really did. Sydney and I happened ta ride by and saw them at my car. I found 'em that night. Well, I just stashed 'em in their van. I came in ta call the cops, but Hector was on his way ta get cigarettes from the van, so I ducked in here. I don't want 'em ta see me, not yet."

"It's ah gonna be good." Papa begins again, mumbling in Italian.

Leora recognizes the words 'coo yunes' so it must have something ta do with hanging by or slime. She feels better. "They had a key, Papa, hidden under the glider."

Papa looks directly at Leora with eyes of anger. "They have ah the key to the house! The house I sell ah to you?"

"They did, Papa, but we found it and switched it with a different one. They couldn't get in. It didn't work. It broke. They're stupid, and they're goin' ta jail. That's why I'm here."

Papa cusses Italian-style, reaching for Leora, enfolding her in his arms, kissing the top of her head. "I'm ah so sorry for to bring ah the trouble."

Leora's eyes fill. "Papa, you didn't do anything. Who knew?"

Each footstep descending on the spiral staircase pounds in Leora's brain. Her pulse quickens, her eyes widen. She feels faint. Papa rambles on in Italian; his voice raised, accented with abundant hand gestures. Salvatore, Jr. steps to the floor.

I thought you were in Jersey! Leora's eyes dart back and forth to father and son conversing in full blown Italian. She tries catching a word here or there, but they are fluent, too fast for this Irish lass's ears. *You did* not *come down those steps. I did not see nothin'. I did not hear nothin'. You are in Italy! You are in Jersey! Let me outta here!* Jr. nods to her. *I guess that's good. I hope that's good. Please let it be good. I gotta go! Talk to ya a little bit later . . .*

"Hi, Leora. Its' good to see you." Salvatore, Jr.'s voice is soft, almost playful." He finishes listening to his father before turning to Leora, meeting her eyes. "My father says you have a gun."

Leora nods. She and Salvatore, Jr. have a good rapport, don't they? He is fun to work with, isn't he, isn't she?

"And somebody other than you or Sydney, they have a key to your house," Papa's eldest child states while his dark brown eyes ask for an answer.

Leora gives one and more. "No. They did, but they don't anymore. We found it and switched it. They broke it in the door, but we got it out."

"And there's no more. You are sure?" He smiles, sensing her uneasiness.

The brunette nods again.

"My father wants you to find a locksmith and have all the locks changed—" Papa interrupts in Italian – "never mind. He wants to replace your door with a whole new door, a better door, stronger front and back. We will take the gun. In the wrong hands, it becomes a formidable enemy."

"You get ah the door, maybe two. It's ah good." Papa's praying hands bounce with every other syllable.

The conversation with Goo Goo resonates in Leora's head. "I think the gun was wiped clean of prints. We didn't touch it. But I think it's still a dirty gun."

Papa rants in Italian, flailing his hands. His son speaks back softly, striking the palm of his hand with the back of his other, emphasizing every other syllable again and again and again.

He looks at Leora. "Don't worry, we will take care of it."

"Why would they plant a gun in Sydney's car with no finger prints on it?" *Please say somethin' about New York so I can give you everything! Do I wanna give you everything? You bet your sweet ass! Oh! My nerves! Say it! Say it! Say it!*

The two men stand in silence. Sal, Jr. looks at Leora. "Don't worry. We will take care of it."

Aw-w-w! Hurry up! Say it! Leora sighs. "I gotta go. Sydney's waitin'.'"

"No! No! No! Wait! It's gonna be—" Two taps on the door silences the trio. Sal. Jr ushers Leora to the back of the half opened door.

Mario steps in the doorway. "Sophia needs ones."

His father opens the safe, speaking Italian in a three-way conversation. Leora scrunches her face, shaking her head. So much for being a fly on the wall. She might as well be in Italy. Junior stands, holding the door, guarding the secret behind it as Salvatore, Sr. exchanges a pack of fifty-ones for the Grant his younger brother, Mario, produces from his pocket.

"Is it busy?" Junior questions.

"Nah, windin' down." Mario turns to Papa. "Will you be gone before I close?"

Well, there ya go. Finally, somethin' I understand. I guess so it was in English. Papa answers in Italian. *Hey! Was that arrive derci? Maybe Eva got it wrong. Maybe he's not supposed ta be in Italy. Then again maybe he is. I don't know! Only they know, they're family. I'm not! Maybe I'm in deep shit!*

"If Shaun comes around, let me know. I'll be here after our father leaves, in case different circumstances present themselves with last minute details."

"Shaun? He was here already," Mario offers. "He went upstairs." Papa chimes in in Italian. "I heard him tell Marcie and his body guards he'll be right back. They're gonna catch a show."

Did he just say Heckle 'n' Jeckle, the body guards? Leora stifles laughter. *Stop!*

Papa continues what seems to be to Leora a delegation of rules and/or procedures his youngest son is to follow.

"Yeah, Mario," Junior addresses his sibling. "Give them drinks don't let them leave. And if Leora or Sydney come in, give them whatever they want." Papa speaks one last time, locking the safe. Mario walks to him with his European farewell, embracing him, shaking his hand, then turns to his brother, administering a repeat performance.

The three mumble short bursts of foreign dialogue as Junior closes the door behind his youngest brother. He smiles at Leora, not fake or pasted; warm, sincere. "Stay here. I'm going to find Sydney. I'll be right back. Where is she, home?"

Leora shakes her head. "No, she's parked out back, waitin' for me."

"Outside? Oh, good. Let's bring her in here." Junior closes the door behind him.

"You don't think the cops found her, do ya, Papa?"

The old man clears his throat. "Oh no! No, Lea-Lea, my Salvatore Giuseppe will help."

"They bugged the house, Papa. When they had a key. They went inside and bugged the house. I don't think there's a serial number on it, Papa. So how would the owner know it's his gun?"

Sydney bursts through the door. "Yo! Sis!" She bucks her eyes at her boss. "Papa!"

"Where's the what-da-ya-call-it?" Leora blurts.

Sydney looks back and forth at Sydney and Papa. "Shtuff, I mean Sal, Jr. has it. He asked if there was a gun under my seat. I said there certainly is. He took it, shoved it in the back of his pants, and told me ta come in here with you." She throws a cheese smile at Papa. *I thought you were in Italy.* She blinks at her best friend. "What's happ'nin'?"

"Well, Hector was on his way ta the van ta get cigarettes, so I ducked in here. Did you see 'im? Did he see you?"

"Yeah, I saw 'im. Boy, he's as smart as a grape."

"Don't insult the grapes. At least they turn into raisins."

Sydney sighs. "Yepper, I don't care what ya do, ya can't fix stupid. I mean if ya have ta take a leak, wouldn't ya do that first? I don't know, I ain't a guy."

"Makes sense ta me. So I take it he didn't see ya?"

"Hell no, Sis! Ta tell ya the truth, I don't think he can talk and chew gum! Whatever! He came out there with his bottle of booze, keys, and a lighter, unlockin' the already unlocked door, grabbin' his cigarettes off the passenger seat"—Sydney shakes her head—"feelin' around on the seat and the floor then lightin' his lighter and cussin' his ass off, feelin' around the back and yellin' 'Where are they, where are they'!"

"Oh, so you weren't bored?"

"Oh, but wait. Then he decides ta take a leak, and I only know this because he peed all over his hand, holdin' the cigarettes because he dropped his bottle of beer, had ta be almost full 'cause you could tell by the sound it made when it hit the macadam. It broke all over the parkin' lot. He leaned forward, cussin' his brains out, lost his balance, and took a head dive into the side of the van still cussin' up a storm until he caught himself in his zipper." Sydney shakes her head. "Ya didn't hear 'im scream, huh?"

Papa shakes his head along with Leora. "I wonder if stupid is a disability?"

"I don't know." Sydney blinks at her best friend. "I just hope it's not contagious."

Silence reigns.

"Soooo, what's happ'nin'?"

"Papa was just about to give me an answer." Leora turns to him. "How, Papa, how could the owner know it's really his?"

Junior slips into the room. "Really, his what?" he questions.

"Well, how do ya know a gun or anything with a serial number is yours if there isn't a serial number?" Sydney studies Salvatore, Jr.'s profile—his nose, hairline, the shape of his eyes, just like his father. He is far from a hothead just like his father, giving the benefit of the doubt nine times out of ten, just like his father with the rare ability in judging one's character— just like his father. He is a treasure to work with: neat-o, funny, easygoin', beautiful, great (so say the girls), a hard nose but fair, dancing around nothing, just plain straight up. Now, here in this room with Sal

Jr. and his father, the girls feel the ugly; the cold, calculating, unfeeling, deadly, heartless forces. Flaws of his character, the ugly, seeping, rising to the surface of his being uniting to drown his compassion, to flood his reasoning as they quench his anger, seeming to drip from his every movement, his stance, his eyes.

Leora sees it, too, the transformation. Something is afoot, which is fine with her as long as she, too is excluded.

"Well, if it is planted say in your case with no fingerprints and the cops become involved, ballistics could match it to previous crimes. It's possible. Then it doesn't matter if there is a serial number or not. Then, yeah, they could come after you. But that's not gonna happen now. It's taken care of." Junior unbuttons his suit jacket and sits on the edge of the desk.

"What about the other three?" Sydney queries.

The men hold an Italian conversation.

The girls hold a conversation of their own. "Al-say oming-cay own-day airs-stay."

"Oh! My God! E-thay etter-lay? Id-day ou-yay ell-tay em-thay?"

"Ot-nay et-yay."

"E-hay idn't-day o-gay o-tay Ita—" Sydney stops speaking, cutting her eyes at father and son, their faces awash with confusion as they stare at the Nervous Nellies.

Junior gives the girls a little smirk. "What the hell was that, the brogue?" He shakes his head, crossing his arms in front of him.

"Ah'ight." Leora smiles.

Junior smiles back. "You said the other three. Do you have any names?"

"No, what da ya mean name—?"

"Yeah, we do," Sydney interrupts. "Gun, gun, and gun. Not people, guns. Three more guns."

Junior stands at attention, rubbing his thick black hair, catching flies. "You have three more guns?"

He glances back and forth at the partners in crime, blinking wide eyes.

Leora looks at Sydney. "Yes."

Sydney looks at Leora. "Yes."

Italian language flies. Papa sits in the desk chair. He looks weary.

"Where are these three guns?"

"Why?" Sydney asks.

"Did you steal 'em?" Junior straightens his suit jacket. "Did you steal 'em from Shaun?"

Why would he say Shaun? Oh! My God! "Nooo," Leora answers.

"Did somebody give them to you?"

Now it's Sydney's turn. "No."

"We found 'em." Leora clears her throat.

"Where?" Junior pries.

"Well," Leora starts, "they weren't buried."

"Yepper, hey, we know they're important." Sydney exhales. "We have ears."

Papa speaks in his native tongue softly, no flailing of the hands, no yelling.

Junior props himself on the desk with one leg dangling over the end, rocking it back and forth. "They're important?"

"Yeah, they're really important. And bein' in the wrong hands, well, you think that gun you stuffed in your pants was bad . . . ha!"

"Yeah, in the wrong hands, these were formidable enemies," Leora retorts.

"Not anymore." Sydney eyes dart back and forth to Leora, Junior, and Papa.

"No way! Do you know what you're sayin'?"

"Damn straight! No! Way!" Leora blinks back tears. "Are you shittin' me? Do you know the nightmare we've been livin'? Do you know one of the nicest guys in the world is gone? I watched him grow up! He was gonna be a daddy!" She cries, becoming angry with herself for acting like a woman.

Papa folds one hand over the other and taps his fingers on it, shaking his head.

Sydney sniffles.

"This gun I have." Junior thinks a second and begins again. "Look. You say you read the paper. Did you see the picture? Well, guaranteed this is not the gun that was used because that picture is of someone else, Rob. This gun was used before, a while ago."

"So were these," Leora answers.

"I mean years ago. It was used years ago." Junior rubs his mouth and chin.

Sydney nods. "Yepper, and so were these."

"Well, you said there is no serial number, so how can you even make that statement? You've had these all this time and now decide—"

"Oh no, Shtuff, ah, Junior. We just came across 'em today," Leora explains, glancing at Sydney.

"That's right," Sydney says with defiance. "What, you think we've been sittin' on these things? Are you shittin' me, Mister?"

"We were tryin' ta figure out what ta do when we caught Heckle 'n' Jeckle, ah, I mean, Hector and Jammer tryin' to set us up again. So we decided ta set them up then go talk ta Goo Goo."

"You don't wanna talk ta Giuliano. He's bein' watched. You don't wanna involve him." Junior nods to the barmaids. "The picture of the guy in the paper, well, he did work for Giuliano off and on. And for Griffonetti, too. Sorta burnin' the candle at both ends. Caught up to 'im. This gun is a plant because it was used in New York a while back. This is serious."

"So were these." Sydney enunciates a tad bit.

Junior shakes his head. "You don't cabish! You can't say that! There's no serial numbers. You said so yourself."

"Well, they're each in a brown paper bag. We didn't actually touch 'em." Leora crosses her arms. "We didn't really look at 'em. But you can feel the shape of 'em."

"That doesn't mean anything." Junior rubs his face again, thinking. He rubs his lips with two fingers. "Okay." He holds his hands in front of him as if palming a basketball. "Okay, so these guns, you have them, right? You have them in your possession."

"Yepper, them and the letter addressed to the District Attorney's Office."

"Yeah, in New York." Leora's mouth feels full of cotton.

Papa sits up, leaning forward on the desk. Junior is wide-eyed, dumbfounded. "Wait a minute! Wait a minute!" He speaks directly to his father in Italian.

"We gotta go."

"Yeah," Sydney agrees.

"Wait! Wait!" Junior turns to the girls.

"You have ah the letter, Cindy, and ah you have ah some guns?"

"No, Papa." Leora takes a deep breath. She understands they are considered just dames to them, but . . . *Listen, get your head outta your ass. The truth is the truth.* "We have 'the' letter."

"Yepper." Sydney blinks at them. "We have 'the' guns."

"We gotta go make a phone call before those bastards leave."

"What do you want to happen?" Junior looks back and forth at them. "You needed our help. You said you were gonna get arrested. We have taken care of that, have we not?"

"Yes."

"Then tell me. What is it you want?"

Leora stares into Junior's eyes, rolling her tongue in her mouth, chewing on the inside of her cheek. She glances at Papa.

He nods. "Anything ah you want. Tell it to me. I wanna help ah you."

"We . . . they . . . he . . . ah." Leora swallows, glancing at her best friend. She wants Griff gone but thinks better of just blurting it out. She leaves it unsaid, looking at Papa. "Do you know who owns these things?"

Papa studies this young girl's face. He nods.

"You know who owns these things and can get all of these things to him?"

"You mean who wrote ah the letter? No, I'm ah no give it to him."

"Oh no, Papa, not Griff," Sydney states. "It's who Griff was screwin' over. The one with the other two letters. That guy in New York some place!" Sydney and Leora nod back and forth.

"Yeah, you know, Frankie Flowers' friend or brother or whatever." Talk about being tired of pussy footing around. They are. *Pretty face this! Shit or get off the pot! There!*

Junior and senior exchange an Italian dialogue. "You are sure about this?" Junior asks.

"Yes! Yes!" The girls look at the two men, each other, back at the two men giving pronounced nods of approval.

"That's why Griff is such a monster. You can't throw it all out." Leora sighs.

"That's what Griff wants ta do, that or hang on to 'em." Sydney leers at Junior. "We know it's his leverage. Same shit! Different day! Not anymore!"

This will definitely do it. "You're sure you want to do this?"

The girls nod again.

Junior rubs his head, speaking Italian to his father. He spins around to Sydney. "Okay. You said you were gonna be arrested?"

"Yes," Sydney answers, "but you have the gun. You took care of it."

"They don't know that. They can still go to your house and search it. You stay here. Give me your keys. I will go. Where did you put them?"

"Oh, not at the house. Everything's in Sydney's car."

"Outside? You have them, too? In your car, too?" Junior glances at Sydney.

"Yepper, behind the passenger seat. Three brown bags and a manila envelope."

Junior stands in awe, shaking his head, catching flies. "And pills. You mentioned pills."

"Yeah, I stuck 'em in the glove compartment of the van."

"So you still want them arrested, right?"

"With bells on!" Leora answers.

"Yesterday," Sydney adds.

"Good. I called the police from the payphone across the street, informing them I was a concerned parent of a young girl who was given drugs by two men in a black van and such a van is in Papa's parking lot. I told them I hope they get to it before I do. Now go get a drink and watch. My father must leave immediately. I will remain a while here in the office."

Papa kisses both cheeks on both girls. "My Salvatore, he take ah good care. You see." Papa smiles. "That's ah my son keep ah you safe. You see. The problems no more."

Junior bucks his eyes at Leora and Sydney. "Go relax," he tells them, nodding toward the bar before closing the door behind him. The girls stand in the quiet, the silence as the world turns, with father and son descending into night. And the world turns as Junior gathers Griff's fate from the floor of Sydney's car, beginning the purge.

The curly-haired duo walk to the bar where Mario ushers them to Goo Goo's empty seat, serving up pink squirrels and white Russians with smiles and smiles. A celebration. A weight that weighed so heavy on their shoulders now gone, releasing them into tranquility. Finally a feeling of safety, protection. A victory so to speak. The 'dynamic duo' on the opposite side of the bar down past the aperture toward the front door – well, they have cause to celebrate, too, their own victory, yes a strategic placement of incriminating evidence. Although not quite where the boss intended, it is in her possession and she's gonna get nailed! It's not their fault the locks were changed, telling their boss so many times they now believe it to be true. Why, they even spotted her car in the parking lot and called their boss back, telling him to send the police here instead of the house, so all is right as the world turns. They high-five, nudging each other not in the least inconspicuous way, but with loud voices and boisterous laughter, clanging their beer bottles together again and again. And as the world turns, a smug Marcie cuts her eyes toward her hated bartender coworkers trying to contain that oh-so pleasant, self-satisfying smirk tugging the corners of her mouth. But as the world turns, a lone rental car's headlights snake through the night, bringing a means to an end, an end to the mean, an invaluable cargo—deliverance, retribution, finality.

Griff swaggers through the front door and bellies up to the bar next to his sister. Sophia prepares his beverage and informs him it is on the house. Griff nods, blinking at her.

"You're just in time," Marcie announces aloud, licking her swizzle stick, smirking at the bitches sitting at the corner of the bar.

"I'm not too late," Griff says loudly, directing his glare in the same direction.

R-r-ring! R-r-ring! Mario hands the phone to Leora.

With wide eyes, she swallows hard. "Hello."

"It's me," Sal. Jr. states. "How you doin'?"

"I was just thinkin' about, Shtuff." Leora gives a little snicker.

"Well, calm down. It is done. My father is on his way to New York. I am in the office. Don't worry about nothin'. You holler, I'll be right there. All hell should break loose any minute. I'm more worried about my hotheaded brother. You yell my name. I'll hear you."

"Thanks," Leora answers.

"Thank - you. Calm down. This is big. You are safe. They are sending an escort to meet up with my father. When Mario asks if everything is alright tell him; perfect."

"Okay." She lays the phone on the bar repeating the conversation to Sydney.

"Is everything all right?" Mario whispers.

Leora smiles, handing him the phone. "Perfect. Could I have another pink squirrel?"

Sydney drains her white Russian for a refill.

Two officers walk from the rear entrance. Hector and Jammer laugh, elbowing each other back and forth like a couple of school chums.

"Shhh!" Marcie admonishes, stirring her drink, watching the interaction of the two patrolmen and Mario. Griff glares at Leora with a huge self-satisfied sneer plastered across his face. The brunette holds his attention with a glance, shyly meeting his cold stare, licking her lips then scratching her nose with her middle finger.

Griff can hardly contain himself. The bitch is his when her friend gets arrested. He stands, adjusting his hard on his face flushed. He's like a dog—in heat, that is—until the police make their way to the four of them.

"Is that your van out back?" An officer asks Jammer, who is well on his way of being two sheets to the wind.

"No, it's my van," Griff says, leaning back to talk. "It's legal. What's wrong?"

"Were you driving it tonight?"

"Why? What's wrong?"

"Were you driving? We have a complaint."

"A complaint? For what?" Griff's veins begin.

"Dealing, dealing drugs."

"What?"Griff grabs Jammer by the scruff of his jacket. "What's he talkin' about, ya son-of-a-bitch?"

"So you weren't drivin'?"

"Hell, no, they had the van." Griff smacks Hector in his head. "What's he talkin' about?"

"I don't know."

"Sir, sir, there is a complaint of drugs being dealt out of a black van. Can you come with us?"

"What's he talkin' about?" Griff is livid.

"I don't know," Jammer answers. "I don't know anything about drugs. Just the gun."

Griff's eyes about pop out of their sockets. He lunges at Jammer lucky Hector and Marcie are in between them. "Let's go!" He walks toward the back. "Let's go! I said! Gimme the keys!" He rips them from Hector's grasp. "And shut up!"

The whole bar hears Griff go off in the parking lot—eleven, as a matter of fact, if you include the best friends, the barmaid, the manager, oh, and Marcie now scurrying to the rear entrance just in time for the light show from three or four backup units.

Mario orders last call, dismissing his cousin Sophia for the evening outing the lights, locking the front door. It is 1:06 a.m. The phone rings again. Mario hands the receiver to Leora.

Leora takes a deep breath and exhales. "Hello."

"Hope you enjoyed the show. Sorry there was no popcorn. Maybe next time."

"Not if I can help it."

"I'm watchin' here from the office with the lights out. I think they're all in handcuffs. No, wait." Junior laughs. "Jesus! Griff just punched one of 'em in the mouth! Oh, that's funny as shit! Marcie's ridin' the other one piggy back! Hell, I need some popcorn."

Leora gives her best friend a blow by blow. They laugh. Finally come-up-ins.

"When this shit's over, you leave. When they're gone from the parkin' lot." Sal, Jr chuckles. "All four of 'em have a hold of each other on the ground now. All these cops. This is some funny shit! Girl, what in the hell did you start? I'm glad you're on my side. Go get some sleep. You're gettin' new doors tomorrow."

Relatively Speaking

$\mathcal{W}$heezer scoots through the door, stopping at the bottom of the stairs, grooming a bit as he watches Leora place her arm full of presents on the floor, throwing Sydney's keys into her patchwork leather shoulder bag and slipping the bag on the coatrack before hanging her jacket over it. Singing along with The Fifth Dimension coming from the stereo in the den, the brunette removes her shoes in between love rubs from Wheezer. Sydney and Bryce should be coming soon. She stares at the little Christmas tree; its star shining softly above the glow of red, green, blue and white lights reflecting off shiny glass ball ornaments of red, green, blue, silver and gold, sparkling off strands of tinsel, dancing ever so gently in the slightest breeze. Three bubble lights add to the grandeur with their own rhythm of festivity. Candy canes complete the holiday décor. Christmas went well at her parents' as siblings and their families filled their two-story childhood home with fond new memories of crumpling wrapping paper, jovial squeals of excitement, eye-popping surprises, giggles, laughter, and choruses of 'oohs' and 'ahs', especially over her parents brand new RCA nineteen-inch color television set. She leans around the small evergreen glancing out the front window at the drab black and white world. "Give," she yells looking up at the gray sky. "It's cold enough. Ya shoulda done it last night." She drops to her knees, sliding the boxes to her pile of one, placing the night light from the window behind the Nativity out of sight with the can of flea spray. She sticks a finger or two over the top of the skirt into the root ball, deciding to give the live fir tree a drink and at the same time getting herself a glass of ice tea, setting it on the kitchen table. It will be planted out front toward the driveway with room enough to reach whatever circumference and height it so desires, so says Bryce. She empties a soda bottle of water into it, straightens the skirt, then stands, using her foot to push the gifts closer to her one pile. "There."

Perry Como sings "I'll Be Home for Christmas" surrounding Leora, tugging her yesterdays, pulling on memories. Memories of Tink, memories of Christmases—five of them, only five. She fights them no more; sobbing alone, heartsick, closing her eyes, climbing into them.

Wheezer attacks a strand of tinsel, pulling it from the bottom branch. He shakes his head, spitting it on the floor. Nudging it several times, he spies another dangling from the tree, sparkling, teasing. He croutches, wiggling hinny in the air then attacks, swatting it to the floor, pouncing with both feet.

Leora blinks through her tears. "Oh, no! No!" She leans over reaching behind the Nativity for the spray. "No, you're not! Ah-ha!" She lets loose all around the skirt. Wheezer darts into the den. "I told you before you're gonna get sick! Stay away from it!" She removes stray strands of sparkle from the bottom branches. The tree begins to resemble the work of a crocked Santa on eggnog singing "Bingle Jells", rendering him unable to finish his decorating. She cocks her head back and forth, shrugging her shoulders. "Well, if ya don't like it, don't look at it." Her furry friend follows to the kitchen. "We're hungry." She chucks the handful of tinsel in the trash. Dinner at her sister's was around two, over three hours ago. The girl pulls one of the two remaining homemade cheesecakes from the refrigerator. Six 8oz. packages of Philadelphia cream cheese softened at room temperature, ten eggs, two dashes of salt, two and a quarter cups of sugar, three teaspoons of vanilla, sixteen ounces of sour cream, all smoothed together with a mixer then poured into five eight-inch ready-made graham cracker shells, or homemade if you feel the need to crush, grease, then coat cake pans. Bake at three hundred degrees for fifty to sixty minutes. Voila! Leora does ready- made. Six cheesecakes or the five healthy ones Leora chose to make. That was yesterday. It worked out rather well. Bryce's birthday is Saturday. He already claimed one of them, the one Leora places on the counter. The one half gone. She smiles. He wants five more for his birthday, even offering to buy the ingredients. "We're hungry," Leora tells Wheezer again. She cuts the leftover cheesecake in half then cuts one side in half again, placing the wedge on a paper plate, returning the rest to the fridge. She roots for a fork then sits, savoring the cold creamy goodness, dipping a finger tip full for Wheezer. "See, isn't it yummy, Wheeze?" She pulls the ashtray and the shoebox lid out of the oven to finish what she started. *Four apiece. That should be enough.* She counts. *One, two four, eight, let's see, four more.* She slips one between her lips. *Five more.*

Sydney bounds through the intricately carved solid oak front door. "Yo! Sis!"

"Out here!" Leora lays the doobie on the table. "It's showtime." She shoves everything in the oven then sits, fluffing her hair, straightening her teal V-neck Jersey.

The redhead meanders to the kitchen, almost tripping on an orange and white greeting. "Tiger! What are you doin'? I smell flea spray. You better stay away from that tree!"

"How was your famly dinner?"

"Delicious. Both of them." Sydny smiles.

"Where's Bryce?" Leora eats the last bit of cheesecake, licking her fork. "And my blind date named George that ain't blind."

"Well."

"That's a deep subject except when it's shallow." Leora blinks. "What? Oh, he is blind, isn't he?"

Sydney flashes her pearly whites, blinking. "Not exactly."

"What's that suppose ta mean?" Leora stares with furrowed brow, mouth open; eyes blinking.

"Well, he's a little older."

"Well, I'm not gonna marry 'im."

"That's right!" Sydney answers nodding and nodding, looking like the cat that swallowed the canary. "Ah, he's not into herbs anyway."

"So more for us." The brunette cocks her head, scrunching her face. "And . . ."

"He's married." Sydney opens the fridge for a Mick bracing for the scream.

"Whaat?" Leora's eyes pop. "You're kiddin' me!"

"Ya believe it? He got married Christmas Eve, to his third wife."

"Again? That's a sign. Thank you, God!"

"Yeah, seems she's pregnant."

Leora closes her eyes, shaking her head.

"Well, Bryce said he has another cousin that'll go. He called 'im from George's. He went ta go get 'im."

"God! Another one? Busy family! Do they wear name tags? Boy, oh, boy, what we do for love." She smiles.

Sydney smiles back. "Well, this one likes herbs and Seger. It'll be better. George came out to the car and spilled. He never even heard of our Bob." Sydney laughs. "I mean he heard of Old Time Rock n' Roll. He said, 'Oh, he sang that?'"

Leora shakes her head. "Hey, my sister thinks she might be pregnant again."

Sydney sucks air. "What Karen, your oldest? How old is her boy now, seven?"

"He's eight. Not her, Kathy."

The redhead almost chokes on a mouthful of beer. "Wow, how many's that gonna make?"

"Four." Leora takes a drink of tea.

"God, it's an epidemic! How old's her oldest?"

Leora thinks a second. "Gonna be ten." She trashes her paper plate, washing her fork, placing it in the dish drain. "Oh, ya shoulda seen us. I went next door ta visit and look and see what Santa brought the kids. That's when we were talkin' about it. She hasn't said anything to Mom."

"Did she go ta the doctor?"

"Nah-uh, not yet, but she heard about this test. We tried it. You get a spoon and sprinkle some Ajax on it then spit in it. If it fizzles, you're pregnant. I mean this is her fourth one. She was pretty sure. We both did it, she fizzled.You wanna try it?"

"Yepper, I'll get the Comet."

"It only works with Ajax."

"Why?"

"I don't know because it does if it works at all."

"We don't have any."

"Nah-huh. I brought some home in a baggy in my pocketbook."

"Nah-uh! I'm in!"

"It's hangin' under my jacket. Grab your keys, too. They're in there."

Sydney retrieves her keys and the baggy, singing and dancing to "Turn the Beat Around." "Has Eva called?" She sits at the table.

"Might've. I just got home a little while ago." Leora pulls the ashtray and stash from the oven lighting and passing. She swigs her tea then begins again, scooping the stash with the pack of rolling papers, sprinkling it in the tilted box lid to clean it. "She's house simple. She needs a job."

"It was nice of Papa to pay the taxes for you guys ta collect unemployment, even though she's stir crazy." Sydney passes.

Leora nods, hooking an alligator clip on the J. "Yep, all the way from Italy." She blinks profusely taking a hit and passing. "Yeah right."

"I wonder if he really will be back after the holidays. He could just be in New York. Sal, Jr. has power of attorney anyway." Sydney takes a hit, batting her eyes and passing.

"Yeah." Leora bucks her eyes. "All the way from Jersey."

"Yeah right." The girls do a high-five. Sydney rolls a torpedo, twisting the ends. "Whoa, Momma! That's a force'em!" She sits it in line with the others, taking a drink. "Can ya picture it? Mario's sayin' let me call my brother then makes a phone call to Jersey with Sal, Jr. sittin' right there at his kitchen table, right across from him the whole time."

Leora nods, taking another hit. "Yeah, we're not just another pretty face. Their mom was down there. He probably woke her up when he called and told her if anybody calls after we hang up, tell 'em I'm on my way up here then call me and let me know."

Sydney holds her hand out. "Yo! Bogart!"

The brunette, lost in thought, blinks, passing, smiling.

The redhead takes a toke. "Hey, Momma, if we can figure it out, don't ya think the cops can?"

"Yes, I do." Leora inhales. "But figurin' and provin' are two different things. Think about it. Check us out. Griff figured we had the typewriter, but he couldn't prove it." She passes.

Sydney nods. "And Junior just waited a couple hours then drove over to Papa's like he hauled ass up here. And they can't prove it." Sydney takes a toke and passes.

Leora nods. "And how 'bout the fire company wantin' Bopper to go shut the water off 'cause he's a plumber? He told 'em the valve and fuse box were right inside the storage room."

"He asked if the electric was cut. Nobody knew. Are you shittin' me? And when he folded his arms, looked down on 'em and said 'go for it', he looked like a giant Mister Clean with hair."

"I thought the same thing. I wanted ta give 'im a hoop earring. Thank God it happened before Mister Mac got there." Leora takes the last hit on the roach, placing it in the ashtray.

"Yeah, he was afraid somebody was in there."

"That's the night Mario closed early. Go figure."

The best friends nod, looking at each other. They high-five again.

"How 'bout all the water that came gushin' outta there. It was like a waterfall comin' down the steps. That's a big room!"

Sydney rolls another bone, this time smaller, twisting the ends, and setting it in the row, giggling. "Well, it wasn't much of a fire, but they were hosin' it down through the kitchen window when we got there. Between them and the broken pipes, that's a lot a water!"

"Yeah, what'd they say, it was contained? And the smell of gas. The electric company took forever. Even when they set up the wooden horse barricades all the way down at the parking lot entrance, you could still get a whiff of gas every now and then. How stupid are people?"

"How stupid are they?" Sydney mocks Gene Rayburn. "Well, what do we say? No sense in bein' stupid if ya can't act like it. The cops had their hands full tellin' everyone no smokin'. You believe it, grown adults gettin' arrested."

"I thought they were gonna back us up to the trestle past Sixth Street. And then they had ta call an ambulance for the guy who slipped and split his head open on all the water freezin' in the parkin' lot. I saw 'im when you were talkin' ta what's his name, blood all over the place. Ew-w-w!"

"Bryce's sisters were talkin' about it. Oh, Alice pulled me aside and said she gave the papers, the typewriter, the ledger, and the picture of The Beatles to the Feds the day after we gave 'em ta her. I told her we felt bad because of Carl. She didn't blink. She said don't even. He is not the father of her kids, just a lousy stepfather. She told the Feds she finally remembered where she had put everything. She kept her word. We were never mentioned. The mayor's in jail, Carl's in jail. She thanks us so much for such a great Christmas. Oh, by the way, my mom said thanks for the cheesecake. And the one for his mom was a hit, too. I myself had a turkey, stuffing and cranberry sandwich at my second dinner. Alice and Kelly heard it was a fire in the back apartment. A lit cigarette thrown in the trash incinerating aerosol cans in the bathroom. I said, 'Well, if ya ever saw Marcie, you'd understand why there was a shitload of 'em in there'. Two bagger! I told 'em the story about us goin' midnight knockin' after Bryce got home. He said all kinds of fire trucks were passin' 'im headed up Ninth Street. I told Alice Bryce was beat and didn't wanna come with us. He told his sisters he was just about ta doze off when the phone rang. Eva was freakin' out, sayin' she heard on the police radio the bar was on fire, a gas leak, the whole shopping center was evacuated. They called for an ambulance. And then when he said we weren't there," – Sydney mimics Eva – "What da ya mean they're not there? Where the hell are they?"

"She's a piece of work."

"She lit a fire under his ass! His sisters laughed when I told 'em he pulled up leapin' outta the car in his bare feet, skivies, no shirt; what was it twenty-five degrees? I said he got dressed in the parkin' lot! Funny as hell! The broads clappin' and whistlin'.You could see him blushin' from a mile away!"

"And when you walked over to 'im and stuck a dollar in his waistband yellin' Chippendale! Yo! Sis! That was classic!"

"He made eleven dollars, two phone numbers, and an address."

Leora twists the last doobie, laying it at the end of the row on the table then places everything in the lid and out of sight in the oven with the ashtray. "I wonder if it will ever reopen."

"Don't it have ta be dried out first? That's gonna take a while. It's winter time. It's like frozen food in there. All that water damage." Sydney smirks.

Leora nods. "Thank God, it was contained to just Papa's property. It looks, I don't know, it looks weird seein' it all boarded up, pitch-black and frozen. I guess it looks dead, lifeless. It was a great place ta work. I think it's a shame it met such a demise."

"Are ya sad about it, Sis?"

Leora slides four joints to her best friend, looking up at her void of expression. "Only because they didn't find two bodies in the rubble."

"Well, between me, you and the lamppost we know, it's not because they didn't try. It was timed right, you know, ahem, Griff's careless smokin'.

But Griff was an asshole as usual takin' too long down the police station. New York ain't playin'."

"That was really quick, wasn't it?"

"That's because Papa's related. I told ya so. You gotta watch the quiet ones."

"Papa's known everything all along."

The best friends need not know the workings of capos, soldiers, associates. They high-five.

"People were already down here chewin' at the bit. Remember all the prayer meetings and in the mean time, his apartment was trashed, Marcie's apartment was trashed?"

"Yo! Sis! Papa made a phone call before he even left for New York. I know he did. I feel it in my vibes. He told 'em it's the real deal; Get 'em!"

"My vibes were off the wall! I almost swallowed my eyeballs when Junior came down the spiral staircase, but I gotta admit my vibes became delirious when he took charge."

"Yepper, mine got ecstatic findin' out Heckle n' Jeckle were in jail for dealin', which means that son-of-a-bitch and the snake with hair are gonna have to slither under a rock someplace with both sides after 'em."

"Yeah, Sis, the good and the bad chasin' the ugly."

"Tap this, bitch. It's just a matter of time before her and her big mouth leads 'em right to his door. Yo! Sis! Speakin' of doors, how 'bout our spiffy brand new ones?"Sydney belts out "Jet Arliner."

Leora nods, smiling. "Aren't they nice?"

Sydney leans forward, blinking, still kickin' it with Steve Miller Band.

"Oh, ha, ha, you mean, Papa's expert carpenters? Yeah, what was it I said? You look familiar. Don't I know you?"

"Yeah, yeah, and he couldn't look at us! That was funny as hell when you asked 'im where his glasses were, and he said he didn't wear glasses. And then you asked 'im if his last name was Black, and he said no, he always gets mistaken for him!"

"I fell out! But I noticed his hands that night. I know he's a carpenter-slash-hitman."

"Slash detective! He smiled, though, remember? He knew we knew that he knew we knew that he knew that we knew." Sydney blinks, mouth agape, furrowed brow.

"Did you say that right?"

Sydney giggles, slipping the joints inside the cellophane on her cigarette pack, shoving it in her pocketbook. "When are they gonna be done with your car?"

"I don't know. Next week, next year, whatever. Oh, next week is next year. I'm glad I remembered where I stuck the spare key. I didn't know they didn't have the key."

"Poor Carrie."

"I know. My heart aches for her. And I feel so guilty because I don't wanna go near her house any time, let alone today. There's nothin' I can do or say ta lift her up."

"Yeah, not knowin' has got ta be even worse. Hell, it's drivin' us crazy, I can't imagine."

"Just When I Needed You Most" drifts from the den. Leora's eyes overflow. "Crow!" She screams as mournful utterances escape with each sob racking her body. She walks to the counter, grabbing a paper towel, wiping her eyes, and blowing her nose. She sighs. "Overflow." She sniffles.

Sister Syd shakes her head, bursting into tears. The best friends console each other. The redhead grabs a paper towel, drying her cheeks, blowing her nose. "Find this, you bastards."

"I told you Chief Sill said there weren't any leads when I gave him the key, didn't I?"

"Yeah." Sydney sniffles. "But maybe there is, he just can't say anything." She dabs her eyes.

Diminishing shudders interrupt the silence as gloomy scenarios play in their minds.

Enter Wheezer, batting a stolen blue Christmas ball around the kitchen floor, capturing it under the table.

"Oh! My! God! Wheezer, ya little dickens!" The girls go on all fours.

The ornery feline, laying on his side, holds the glass ornament in his mouth by its metal top, clutching it with his front paws, eyes wide, kicking his capture with his hind legs.

"Tiger, have ya lost your mind?"

Realizing they are not in a sharing mood, Wheezer abandons his quarry, bolting to the den. The girls proceed to the little pine, pulling stray strands of tinsel now from the bottom two level of branches and moving Christmas ornaments to higher ground, well, higher branches.

"If Bryce says somethin', we'll tell 'im just hang it from the ceiling."

Leora cocks her head. "Well, it is startin' ta look . . . naked."

"Yeah." Sydney straightens her powder blue sweater, sighing and cocking her head, too. "We can always just hang all the candy canes around the bottom like a skirt."

They laugh, grabbing pocketbooks, placing them on the kitchen table, and throwing their collections of tinsel in the trash. Leora opens her compact mirror, surveying red puffy eyes; red nose. "Great! I look like Rudolph with allergies."

Sydney takes a gander at her reflection. "Yeah, well, I look like your sister."

"Oh! Yo! Sis! The Ajax!"

"Oh, yeah!"

Leora fishes in the silverware drawer for two teaspoons, moving next to Sydney at the sink, handing her one of the utensils.

"So what do we do? Do we wet it?"

"No, no, just get some on your spoon, half or less. It doesn't have ta be a heaping spoonful. Here." Leora dips her spoon into the baggy of cleanser, handing it to Sydney, taking her empty one. She dips that one in then places the bag on the counter. "Ready?" she asks, blinking and smiling.

Sydney licks her lips and swallows. "Isn't it weird? My mouth is as dry as the desert." She rolls her tongue around her mouth.

Leora does the same.

Sydney leans toward the sink and spits. She misses the spoon. "Oh! Shit!"

Leora's turn. She leans toward the sink, hitting her target. The girls stand over the spoon, blinking. Nothing.

The redhead blinks leaning forward, moving the spoon closer to her face. Bullseye. Nothing.

The front door opens. "Whoa! Whoa! Whoa!"

Leora gives an overbite expression to Sydney before they start flying around the kitchen, throwing the baggy under the sink, going out on the patio with Wheezer, replacing his frozen water, replenishing his food supply, wiping the counter, washing spoons, rinsing the sink, locking the back door.

"What the hell happened ta the tree?" Bryce opens the refrigerator, uncovering the cheesecake, choosing the larger piece while checking ta make sure there was still one waiting untouched. He turns around, holding it in both hands. The girls blink at him. "What? I didn't have any down there." They are blinking statues. "What? I didn't! I swear!" He takes a big bite smiling, chewing, savoring, walking to Sydney, wrapping an arm around her and kissing the top of her head.

"Wheezer's tryin' ta eat the tinsel and is pullin' the balls off."

"Owww!" He takes another bite. "What's that smell?"

"Flea spray." Sydney smiles.

"Me and him are gonna have ta have a talk." Bryce takes another bite.

"You can always hang it from the ceiling." Leora slips her doobies into the cellophane on her flip top box of cigarettes, sinking it to the bottom of her bag.

"Mmm, mmm, mmm." He rolls his tongue in his mouth. "Hey, my mom wants ta know if you'll make her some for New Year's. She'll pay ya. I said I didn't care as long as ya make mine first." He gives Leora his widest grin, bucking his eyebrows then frowns. "What? I didn't have any! Swear!"

Leora smiles, shaking her head, pushing the remaining four joints toward Bryce. "Stick 'em in your cigarette pack."

Bryce licks the last of the cheesecake from his fingers, scraping the Js into his hand. "Holy shit!" Look at this one. A turnpike cruiser!"

The girls laugh.

"Oh! Shit! Come on. My cousin's in the car! I almost forgot."

"Ya shoulda brought 'im in!" Sydney swigs the last of her Mick.

Leora places her tea glass in the sink.

"Well, the car's runnin' He ain't freezin' ta death. His family's outta town. He was eatin' a bologna sandwich when I got there."

"He's not married, is he?" Leora turns out the kitchen light. They walk to the front door.

"No."

"You sure, or what?" Sydney stands, letting go of Bryce's hand.

Bryce grins, entwining his fingers with hers. "Yes." He kisses her. "I'm sure." He kisses her again. "Not unless he got married in the car! Maybe he got tired of waitin' and walked home." He laughs, glancing at the little pine. "I'm glad I didn't bring 'im in. Look at the tree! Check it out! From the outside through the window it looks good! But from in here . . ." Bryce shakes his head. "I don't know."

"Awwww, leave it be." Leora opens the front door, locking it.

"Yeah, it's little but it's cute." Sydney smiles.

"Hey, hey, hey." Bryce smiles back.

Leora drops her pocketbook, pulling on black suede boots, then straightens her bell-bottom jeans over them. Bryce holds the three quarter length maroon leather jacket for her. She slips into it, pulling her hair from under her coat over its collar, then pushes her bag on to her shoulder. Sydney turns on the Chritmas candles decoration in the window, unplugging the tree and flicking the outside light on. Condensation frosts the storm door. She steps into black leather boots, straightening her patchwork bell-bottom jeans over top of them. Bryce holds her chocolate full-length leather coat for her. She, too, pulls her hair from under her coat over its collar, grabbing her pocketbook.

"Ready?" Bryce bows, directing the best friends to the door with a wave of his hand.

"Ah'ight," Leora answers, sighing. "Ah 'ight. I'm in."

"Yepper." Sydney opens the storm door. "Oh, my God! It's snowin'!" Sydney turns to a smiling Leora.

"Let it snow, let it snow, let it snow!" The brunette states their breath, condensing with each syllable.

"It's stickin'!" Sydney adds.

Bryce turns off the inside and outside lights, pulling the locked door shut. Three sets of footprints lead to the fogged "Goat".

"Tiger's gonna love this."

"He certainly is. I bet he's busy." Leora stands still in the quiet falling snow. "Circle time!"

Bryce opens the passenger side doors for the girls. An eight track of Bob Seger escapes. "Yo," he calls to his cousin.

Sydney gasps. "What if we get snowed in with Bob Seger?" Her voice is melodious. She settles into the darkness as Bryce closes her door.

"What could be better than that?" Leora answers, still smiling, slipping into darkness, a half-smile on her face for her blind date.

Sydney goosenecks the rear seat to get a good look-see at Bryce's other, other cousin as he closes Leora's door then walks to the driver's side, climbing behind the steering wheel, allowing a flash of light— just a flash—before closing out the cold. The flash blitzes Leora extinguishing her double take leaving a silhouette in the darkness every time she blinks. Her pulse quickens. Bob Seger kicks it. She drops her bag on the floor, turning toward the window, closing her eyes, shaking her head. Second thoughts swirl. She takes a deep breath, exhaling quietly through her open mouth. Apprehention stirs. Maybe she should stay home.

"Ready?" Bryce asks again, revving the engine, throwing it in first. He turns on the windshield wipers and the defroster. Headlights illuminate the falling snow as they pull away from the curb.

"Mada-my-zul!"

Leora turns, blinking at the silhouette leaning toward her.

Leather and aftershave. Intoxicating. His warm hand enfolds hers.

"Kiss me quick."

She complies.

About the Author

$\mathcal{I}$ was born and raised in Delaware County, exactly where this novel takes place. Yes, that is a real recipe for cheesecake! Yes, in the seventies I believe we did what most families did back then; praised God; celebrated life; respected authority; and raised our hands to help, not to hurt our neighbors or fellow man, needing no pat on the back or a plaque to tell us of our good deeds. It was common sense, heartfelt. You earned your way through life.

I remember when I-95 ended at Kerlin Street exit. Progress brought an extension of the interstate highway, over Kerlin Street, over Chester Creek all the way to the Chester Pike Drive-In Movie Theater in Eddystone. I remember it because I rode on it before any car or truck had at it. I ducked under the yellow tape and rode a bicycle all the way up and all the way back. Just me. Later on progress extended beyond the interstate yet again through Philadelphia north to the New England states. The seventies were a time of change, so I thought. I was young. But I learned as the saying goes: "Nothing stays the same but change itself."

I graduated from Chester High School and The Institute of Children's Literature correspondence course.

I like cooking, baking, gambling, crocheting, playing n the dirt (gardening), writing poetry. I have a book of poems entitled "Windswept". I like quiet time or as some people call it patience, like watching a spider spin a web; or if you are lucky enough, watching a child stand and take their first step. How beautiful!

My novel is fiction based on a true story—mine.